DONATION - LOCAL AUTHOR

This book should be returned to any branch of the
Lancashire County Library on or before the date shown

Lancashire County Library
Bowran Street
Preston PR1 2UX

Lancashire
County Council

www.lancashire.gov.uk/libraries

Before The Midnight Hour

TOM GREGORY

authorHOUSE®

AuthorHouse™ UK Ltd.
1663 Liberty Drive
Bloomington, IN 47403 USA
www.authorhouse.co.uk
Phone: 0800.197.4150

Published by AuthorHouse   02/20/2014

ISBN: 978-1-4918-9039-4 (sc)
ISBN: 978-1-4918-9038-7 (hc)
ISBN: 978-1-4918-9040-0 (e)

1

In a very few years Ramuda Textiles, the company started in the South Indian town of Ramuda by the two Brent brothers, Andrew and Arthur, engineers from Aberdeen, had grown into one of the most successful businesses on the whole sub continent. So successful was their first factory that it had been quickly followed by a second built in the same compound as the first and then a few years later by two more in the town of Melur some 220 miles to the North West.

Both brothers were married before they arrived in India but only Andrew, two years older than his brother, had any children, a son George until five years later when Arthur and his wife had a son, Walter.

It was the two founders greatest wish that their sons should follow them into the company and from the outset their education was planned to facilitate this. From the age of about five both George and Walter were taken to the factories by their father and at first enjoyed nothing more than returning the salutes of the blue turbaned factory guards who saluted their fathers as they passed through the factory gate. But the two cousins hardly shared any time together because when Walter was barely five years old and was more interested in playing with the servant's children at the back of the bungalow where he and his closest friend, Pranchis, went 'big game hunting' armed with rifles made from scrap wood, George went to school in England.

All too soon however it was Walter's turn to be taken to school in England and although he went to the same school as his cousin he hardly ever saw him because George had moved on to Technical College and before it was time for Walter to go to the same college George had returned to India. Walter was an excellent student particularly at Technical College but hardly a week went by that he didn't wish he was back in India. During the whole of his stay in England the only contact he had with his parents, apart from letters, which took up to five weeks to arrive were when his Father came to England to buy machinery for the new factories in Melur and again when his parents came on holiday to Britain in the summer of 1904 and even then could not spend a lot of time with them because he had to go to college.

His Father told him what was happening in the factories but neither he nor his mother could tell him what had happened to his friend Pranchis because neither was really aware of what was happening round the servants quarters. All too soon it was time for his parents to return and they had only been back in India for a short time when Walter, for the first time in his life received a cable, never dreaming how the news it contained would dramatically change the course of his life.

He opened the cable with something more than a little anxiety but was completely unprepared for the news that his father had died as a result of being bitten by a krait whilst working in his garden. Walter was horrified. To the Indians the krait is known as 'seven steps' because they claim that if you are bitten you will hardly have time to walk seven steps before you collapse and die. Walter knew this was not true but nevertheless was well aware that the krait was probably the most venomous snake on the continent and that once bitten his father would not have stood much of a chance, Even while he grieved for his father he could not help the ridiculous memory of how when 'big game hunting' with Pranchis every snake they 'killed' was a krait.'

Walter was even more determined to be successful in his studies so that he could return to India as soon as possible and fulfil his father's dream and start working for Ramuda Textiles. So eager was he to do this that even before the results of his final examinations he had booked his return passage to India only receiving the news that he had been successful a week before he set sail on an Anchor line boat out of Liverpool bound for Bombay.

The journey back to India was enjoyable but was made more so because he was delighted to find that James Armitage and his wife Constance were going out to Bombay where James was to set up an office and be the representative for his family's firm which supplied the burgeoning textile industry with ancilliary equipment. He had met James previously when he had visited the Armitage company, first with his father but then on a few different occasions when called upon to do so by either his father or his uncle. It was through these visits that James and he became extremely friendly so much so that James insisted Walter should let him know whenever he intended to visit Bombay so that he could stay with him and Constance. Little did Walter know what an important part James was going to play in his future life.

Back in Ramuda Walter's mother was delighted to see her son again and Uncle Andrew and cousin George were equally welcoming but he had not been back very long before he sensed a change in the relationship between him and them. Instead of the management of the company being in the hands of two brothers it was now father and son

Uncle Andrew was Chairman, the position Walter's father had held and his son was now Managing Director a massive promotion and even though Walter had expected there would be some changes he could not help the feeling that his uncle would not have been unduly concerned if he had not returned. The next year was one of familiarisation, learning the systems and procedures as well as getting to know the staff both Indian and European of both Ramuda and Melur. Neither the visits nor the journey to Melur, which was only slightly less tedious than when he had visited with his father as a little boy, did anything to dispel his memories of the place. It was a lonely town for Europeans because apart from the five men who ran the factories and their wives there were no other Europeans nor were there any reason for any to visit except for people going to the factories.

Since his return he had lived with his mother in the bungalow where he had been brought up often wondering, not if, but when she would return to England so it was no surprise when a couple of weeks after cousin George announced his marriage she told him that instead of returning from Madras where the wedding was to take place she would go on from there to Bombay for the journey home

About a fortnight before Walter and his mother were due to leave for Madras he was in his office checking the previous day's production details when he heard the office door open. Thinking it was the office boy bringing him his usual morning tea he carried on with what he was doing but when he didn't hear the rattle of the tea cup he looked up to see one of the white suited, red turbaned office pewans standing in front of his desk'

'Good Morning Sir' he said 'Mr. Andrew wants to see you in his office.'

"Thank you" Walter nodded "I'll be there right away."

He pulled the last of the books towards him and after a quick look initialled it and put it on the pile he had already checked and a few seconds later entered his uncle's office.

As they exchanged greetings Walter sat down in the chair in front of his uncle's desk. For a few minutes they chatted about things that were not very important whilst Walter wondered why his uncle had sent for him, He was, however not left to wonder for very long.

"I suppose you have heard that Bill Jackson is resigning and going back to England." Walter's heart sank. Now he knew why his uncle had sent for him.

"His wife has been unwell for some time and as she's not getting any better they have decided they want to go back home which means I need someone to take charge at Melur."

He saw the look of disappointment flash across his nephew's face but before Walter could say anything he went on.

"I know it's a lonely place but I need someone I can trust and it will be a great experience for you. Not many men of your age are given the opportunity to manage two factories and of course there will be an increase in salary."

Walter thought "If it's as good as you say why don't you send George because after all who can you trust more than your own son," but he knew it was pointless to try and change his Uncle's decision.

"When I heard about Bill's wife I thought there was a chance this might happen but I can't say I am looking forward to it. It's a damned lonely place for a single man when the only other Europeans in the town are the ones who work at the factories and while I know both you and my father spent some time there it was different because you were both married,"

"Look Walter" Andrew Brent said, "It will probably only be for a couple of years because I plan to send Frank Strickland there but as you know he hasn't been in India very long whereas you've been here all your life."

"When do you want me to go then?" Walter asked.

"Bill has agreed to stay for another three months whilst you settle in so I thought it would be a good idea if instead of just going to Madras to George's wedding you could go with your mother to Bombay, see her off, have a few days holiday, then go direct to Mellur from Bombay. They continued to talk about the factories and about life in Melur until eventually the older man pushed back his chair and putting his hand on his nephew's shoulder, walked to the door with him.

"When you go to Bombay" his uncle said with a smile, "I think the company could pay for a couple of weeks at the Taj so you can have Christmas and New Year in Bombay"

Three days after the wedding of his cousin as Walter was registering in the Taj Mahal hotel he glanced around the reception hall and remarked to himself that even this early in the morning there were more Europeans around than he would see in months, perhaps years in Melur. He confirmed a single room for himself because after lunch he would be taking his mother to the nearby docks to board the ship for her journey back to England,

Taking his room key from the receptionist Walter and his mother followed one of the maroon uniformed hall porters whose bare feet swished across the black and white floor tiles as he led them to the lift. At the fifth floor he led them along the corridor to the sea view room Walter had reserved. The porter placed the suitcases on the luggage stand, took the two annas Walter offered then with a salaam left, pulling the door closed behind him.

Later, after a light breakfast Walter patiently accompanied his mother round the shops to purchase items which she deemed necessary for her voyage home. By the time she had bought all she wanted it was time for lunch which they had in one of Bombay's restaurants after which they returned to the Taj to collect his mother's baggage and leave for the docks.

Walter stayed on board until the last minute then after a tearful farewell from his mother he made his way to the landing stage from where he watched the ship cast off, slowly pull away from the dock and as it gathered speed occasionally waving until he could no longer pick his mother out amongst the crowd of waving passengers.

Back in his room at the Taj Walter stood looking through the open window of his room watching the people as they walked along the promenade which separated the fairly new hotel from the sea and which from the very beginning had become a collecting place for vendors and beggars trying to attract the attention of sightseers or guests of the hotel. A lone policeman seemingly oblivious to the very people he was meant to prevent from gathering there, was idly standing on the pavement just watching the sea as it slowly lapped against the sea wall. Screwing up his eyes against the red glow of the setting sun Walter looked out to sea where there were some small sail boats, most of them fishing but some setting out on journeys to other parts of the country or perhaps even further than that. Looking towards the docks he saw the twin plumes of smoke lazily drifting out to sea which came from the one remaining steamer due to sail later in the evening and realised it was because of these ships and the practice of passengers to spend at least one night at the Taj Mahal hotel either before leaving or after arriving that accounted for the unusually large number of people in the hotel.

After a glance at his watch he left the room and sat at one of the tables where he could watch the entrance to watch for his friend. He ordered a whisky and soda and had hardly tasted it before he saw the tall figure of James Armitage and raised his hand. James spotted him almost immediately and walked across his hand outstretched. The two who had become very friendly during their trip out to India shook hands and as they sat down Walter caught the eye of a waiter and ordered a drink for his friend.

Before he had left for India James' father had impressed upon his son how a little thing like meeting people from the Textile Industry who may be passing through Bombay was good advertising for the Armitage Company and meeting anyone from such a large organisation as Ramuda Textiles was very important but in the case of Walter Brent it was a pleasant duty because the two had become very friendly.

For the next thirty minutes or so they caught up with each others' news which included what was happening in Ramuda and from James what the various textiles firms in the North of the country were doing but eventually the talk about textiles came to an end and turned to the evening ahead,

"I hope you are not doing anything tonight Walter because I thought you being in Bombay was sufficient excuse to have dinner at the Gymkhana Club" James said.

Walter smiled inwardly. He had not arranged anything because he didn't know anyone in Bombay other than James and had been hoping that his friend might invite him for a meal.

"I have nothing arranged" Walter replied "will it just be with Constance and yourself?"

"I have invited two other couples and a school friend of Connie's who is staying with us. Perhaps you may know her she's the wife of William Leather the owner of Oceanic Mill in Bolton.

"Obviously I knew of the company when I was in Bolton but I think it must have been one of the few I didn't visit. I heard people in the industry talk about the factory and I gathered that it was highly regarded but other than that I know nothing about the factory or the family who owned it" he replied. Shortly after they had finished their drinks and James left for home whilst Walter went to his room to change.

It was just after eight when Walter, wearing evening dress, asked the doorman to get him a carriage. By now it was completely dark and as he walked the few strides to his carriage he saw the flashes of lightning out at sea which seemed to happen nearly every night and he wondered why if it rained out at sea why it couldn't rain over the countryside where it was so badly needed. Settling back in his seat he gave the driver his destination and with a slap of the reins the carriage pulled away. It was not a long journey to the club and soon he was striding across the black and white tiles on the floor of the corridor past the various hunting trophies hanging from the white walls which had been presented by members. Entering the lounge he saw James and Constance and their guests seated rounded a glass topped table and he walked across to join them. Constance was wearing a brown off the shoulder dress which complimented her rich auburn hair and looked just as attractive as he remembered her on the ship despite her having given birth to twin boys just over a year earlier. He leaned forward and kissed her lightly on each cheek and after a few words turned so James could introduce him to the other two couples and finally to his wife's friend Margaret Leather. As he sat in the one vacant chair next to Margaret he was pleasantly surprised to discover how young and attractive she was, certainly much younger than he had expected bearing in mind that she was the wife of a factory owner who, in his experience, were never very young. In keeping with the current fashion her blond hair was piled on top of her head and was in sharp contrast to the low cut black silk evening dress. In conversation during dinner he discovered she had come to India on her own because her husband could not afford to leave his business for the time a visit to India would take.

Later in the evening Walter was disappointed when James said that he and Constance couldn't accept his invitation to lunch at the Taj the following day because of previous engagements but was delighted when Constance suggested there was no reason why Margaret shouldn't go and urged her to accept Walter's invitation.

During lunch next day Walter listened as Margaret told him about Oceanic Mill which her husband had inherited from his father. He discovered that his companion was 18 years younger than her husband, been married nine years and didn't have any children. As she talked about her life in Bolton, telling him where she lived he recalled the large houses on the main road to Horwich which he knew was the fashionable area of the town. In return he told her how Ramuda Textiles was started by his father and his uncle and how his father had been killed by a snake.

"How awful" Margaret said, 'so is your mother still in India?"

He explained why he was in Bombay and how, once his holiday was over he had to go to Melur.

Both Walter and Margaret enjoyed each other's company and for the rest of his stay in Bombay they contrived to spend as much time together as possible so much so that when Walter discovered there was to be a dinner dance at the hotel he extended his stay for one day longer than he had planned. He booked a table in a small intimate dining room which had a large window to admit the cool evening breeze and had a fantastic view over the sea but more importantly was semi private but close enough to the main dining room to be able to hear the music and join the dancing whenever they wanted.

That evening Walter was in the foyer early, sitting at a table from where he could watch the entrance so that as soon as Margaret stepped through the door he went to meet her. She was wearing a simple almost severe dark mauve dress with a raised waist line from which the narrow tubular skirt fell to the ground while over her bare shoulders she wore a contrasting light mauve, almost transparent evening stole. Her hair was piled on top of her head but with loose curls hanging down at the back which just touched her shoulders. Walter took her hand and leaned forward to kiss her cheek.

"Good evening Margaret" he said "you look absolutely stunning."

Margaret smiled her thanks at his compliment because this evening she had specially chosen her favourite dress and taken more care than usual over her appearance. As they entered the restaurant the Maitre d'hotel ushered them to the special table Walter had selected and after holding a chair for Margaret, left them to the hovering waiter who handed them their menu's.

The meal was perfect and the music delightful. They dined and danced and flirted with each other laughing at silly jokes that only they would find amusing and later it only seemed natural when Walter led the way to his bedroom. Walter closed the door and put his arms round his partner's slim waist. She leaned back and lifted her face to his. For a moment they just looked at each other then without a word their lips met and Walter felt the rise and fall of her breasts against his chest.

He lifted his mouth from hers and just stood looking down at Margaret who was holding her full bottom lip between her teeth as if she was worried at what had just happened until she reached up and putting one arm round his neck pulled Walter's face down to hers. This time the kiss was more intense and she opened her lips to allow his tongue to meet hers and he felt the shiver of delight when he moved his hands to her waist so that he could caress the bare skin of her back and shoulders and the gentle swell of her breast. Their lips parted and for a few moments Margaret just stood looking up at Walter her breathing short and heavy as if trying to come to a decision. Then still without taking her eyes from his face she started to undo the belt at her waist allowing it to fall to the floor before slowly unfastening her dress which slipped down to her waist from where it fell to join the belt and standing before Walter in her knickers her only remaining garment. Walter reached out and taking her hands held them out to the side.

For a few moments he just looked at her standing in her evening shoes with their diamante buckles, her long legs disappearing into the wide legs of her knickers and above her slim waist and full rounded breasts with their coral tipped nipples.

"Margaret", he whispered "you look beautiful." Quickly he stripped off his jacket, pulled off his shirt and began to undo his belt.

Naked he lay on the bed next to her and as they kissed he caressed her breast the sunburned skin of his hand in sharp contrast to the whiteness of her skin. He slid his hand from her breast and inserting his fingers under the elastic of her knickers started to pull them down over the swell of her hips and despite the heat she could not prevent a slight shiver of anticipation as she raised her body to assist in their removal.

The faint sound of the orchestra in the restaurant mingled with the sounds of taxi horns and the jingle of horse harnesses on the street below coming through the open windows were unheard as Margaret gave herself up to the demands of Walter's lovemaking until they eventually lay side by side their bodies dewy with perspiration.

"Darling that was wonderful" Margaret whispered looking up at Walter from under her long eyelashes as he lay propped up on his elbows before putting her arm round his neck and gently pulling his face down to hers before they rolled apart, and then just lying next to each other holding hands, their feet just touching and occasionally turning their heads in order to kiss, both of them completely satiated.

They lay like this, not talking, looking up at the ceiling as though hypnotised by the slowly revolving fan with the ticking noise it made on every revolution like a metronome providing the beat for the street noises they had not noticed before. From the corner of her eye Margaret watched a lizard silently stalking its prey, an insect in the corner of the wall and ceiling, something which had frightened her when she first arrived from England but to which, even during her short stay, she had become accustomed.

Walter swung his legs to the floor and aware that Margaret was watching padded across the cool floor tiles to the table where a bottle of champagne he had ordered earlier was standing in an ice bucket. Margaret, like her partner, not feeling the slightest bit inhibited about being totally naked sat up and took the two glasses which he held out to her. She watched Walter as he unpeeled the gold foil and the wire from around the cork then carefully started to twist and ease it from the bottle until suddenly, despite his care, the cork shot from the bottle and the liquid gushed out. Quickly he directed the foaming champagne towards the glasses Margaret was holding but at the same time making sure some sprayed onto her naked breasts. Margaret screamed at the shock.

"Oh you beast! You did that deliberately" she laughed.

"Just hold the glasses and stop wriggling" Walter replied as he continued filling the glasses. The couple toasted each other then taking his partner's glass Walter put it on the side table along with his own before turning to lick the spilled champagne from his partner's body. Margaret shuddered with delight at the touch of his tongue and didn't resist as he gently pushed her back and didn't resist as he manoeuvred his body above hers before lowering it until they met in perfect unison.

An hour later they were both dressed and ready to return downstairs but before Walter could open the bedroom door Margaret put her arms round his waist and looked up at him.

"You must think me a dreadful person" she whispered against his lips. "I know you won't believe me but I have never betrayed my husband, in fact you are the only other man I have ever made love to in all my life."

A tear started down her cheek which Walter gently kissed away before holding her close until Margaret lifted her head from his chest.

Walter escorted Margaret to one of the many waiting carriages and for the whole journey they held hands as he reminded her that he had to leave Bombay the next day but suggested that if she wished there would be time for them to lunch together.

Next morning Walter was down for breakfast early, eating his usual breakfast of egg and bacon followed by toast and marmalade then reading the morning paper as he drank a second cup of tea. The rest of the morning he spent shopping for items he knew he would be unable to obtain in Melur but made sure he was at the Ritz hotel in good time where he had arranged to meet Margaret. When she arrived he went to meet her and taking her hand in his he kissed her on both cheeks before leading her into the hotel's circular dining room. She looked beautiful in the fashionable clothes she had brought from England and he could not help the sense of pride he felt when he saw heads turn to watch them as they followed the waiter who led them to their table. As they dined Margaret could not help comparing her husband William, his dour appearance and the way he dressed so unfavourably with the handsome man sitting opposite. Thoughts of her husband were soon dispelled however, when she heard Walter asking what she would like to do for their few remaining hours together. At first she didn't answer.

"I don't know" she whispered.

"Would you like to go back to the Taj?" Walter asked gently.

Margaret blushed slightly because she was well aware what he was really asking. She bowed her head.

"Yes I would like that very much" she murmured.

Walter paid the bill and it was only a matter of a few minutes before the horse drawn gharry was drawing up at the Taj Mahal Hotel. Walter paused just inside the entrance.

"Do you know the story this hotel?" Margaret shook her head.

"The hotel was designed by a Swiss architect who, because he had to return to Switzerland left his plans with the builders and only returned when the building was almost completed. Imagine his horror when he discovered the builders had built the hotel back to front". Walter indicated the doors through which they had just entered. "This entrance should have been on the side facing the sea and the small door on the side where most people now enter should have been the back door." Margaret started to giggle.

"You shouldn't laugh" Walter said mock seriously "because according to the story when the architect saw what had happened to his grand design he was so upset that a few days later he climbed to the top of the hotel jumped off and killed himself". Margaret's hand went to her mouth.

"Is that true?" she asked.

"I've heard the story many times from lots of people" Walter said and many people think it is true but in actual fact the hotel was designed by an English architect and is built the right way round so nobody jumped off the top but the story persists".

About three hours later Walter raised his head from the pillows and leaned over his partner to kiss her full red lips. As he did so she put her arms round his shoulders and gently pulled him down so that she could feel his naked chest against equally naked breasts. Walter raised his mouth from hers and supported by his forearms looked down at her face which was made more beautiful by the tousled hair which framed it. They stayed like that, neither of them speaking for what, to Margaret, seemed an eternity before Walter sat on the edge of the bed.

"Why couldn't I have found you whilst I was in England?" he said, "now I have to leave Bombay and in a few more weeks you will be going back to England and we will never see each other again." Tears welled up in her eyes.

"You know I would love to stay here in India with you but I have to go back. William has always been so kind to me and if I didn't return the shame would be unbearable for him. The scandal may even reach here and destroy us so you do see, I have to go home."

She reached out to him with both arms and he allowed her to pull him down towards her so that her lips could find his. Once again he tasted her sweetness as their tongues caressed until he lifted his mouth from hers to kiss the tip of her nose her eyes and finally both her nipples which seemed to be reaching out to him demanding his attention.

Taking hold of her hands he gently pulled her to her feet and into his arms holding her naked body close he whispered,

"Darling I must get ready. If we don't leave soon I will miss my train and I am already a day late."

An hour later after on last lingering kiss Margaret left the bedroom and made her way to the foyer where she asked the doorman to get her a cab. Up above at the bedroom window Walter watched as she came out of the hotel entrance, climb into an open carriage and, although he had asked her not to, gave a furtive glance towards the window from where Walter was watching.

Walter remained in the bedroom until the light started to fade and the sound of the birds drifted through the open window and then even without looking at his watch he knew it was time to go. At the station a red shirted porter took his luggage and as he was paying the carriage driver Walter told him on which train he was leaving. Immediately the porter set off weaving, his way through the crowd of people which seemed to inhabit railway stations in India as if rail journeys were life changing events to be shared with as many relatives as possible. Walter made his way to the gate and after showing his ticket he passed through and went to the first class coaches and inspected the names of the passengers displayed at every door until he found the one with his name. He looked round and saw, almost like a miracle, the porter with his cases which without any instructions he placed in the compartment.

Three hours later as the train sped through the darkness Walter thought about his stay in Bombay and of Margaret and was surprised that the most vivid picture in his mind was that of watching her dress before she left the room at the Taj. But even as he was recalling this and everything else that had happened he could not help thinking that no memory, no matter how good, would be sufficient compensation for the lonely life he would have to endure for the next few years at Melur.

2

Margaret Leather wakened early and for the fifth day running wasn't feeling very well. The last four days had been terrible not only from constantly feeling sick but also with the effort of trying to conceal how she felt from Constance and her husband. For the first couple of days she had tried to believe it might only be an upset stomach caused by something she had eaten but deep down she knew that was a forlorn hope. She knew what was wrong with her just as she had from the first day of feeling ill. She was pregnant.

It was just over a month since Walter had left Bombay, a month during which her memory had turned from happiness to deep regret and now apprehension and fear as she worried about what her husband would do when he found out. Sitting on the bed with her handkerchief pressed to her mouth she thought of William back home in England. She was sure he loved her but being brutally honest she had to admit that even though she was happy with him and the lifestyle he afforded her she had never experienced the same emotions for him as she had for Walter Brent. But even though she was sure of her husband's feelings for her she knew he would never countenance his wife having a child that wasn't his. Suddenly she jumped to her feet and dashed to the bathroom as she was overcome by yet another wave of nausea so bad it was another hour before she felt well enough to bathe and dress and join Constance and James for breakfast. James always had a typically English breakfast so, since she had started feeling sickly, Margaret always tried to time her appearance for breakfast until she thought that James would have finished but this morning he was a little later than usual and it was all she could do to overcome the nausea which welled up inside her as she caught the normally appetising aroma of eggs and bacon. Exchanging "good mornings" Margaret poured herself a cup of tea in the hope that it would quell the sickly feeling and listened silently as her friends discussed the usual inconsequential things mainly about topics and people she didn't know until James pushed back his chair.

"I have to be off now, darling" he said to his wife who lifed her face for his usual kiss. He patted Margaret on the shoulder as he walked past and then they heard him greet the waiting driver followed by the sound of the horses hooves as the gharry pulled away.

Margaret, as usual had toast with a little marmalade for breakfast something she had nearly every morning but in her present condition it was the only thing she could eat without feeling sickly. Once breakfast was finished she was left to her own devices as her friend busied herself with the servants, particularly the cook who had to be informed of the menus for the day and then issued with the necessary ingredients which were either locked in cupboards or in food boxes to ensure that they were not stolen making sure the legs of the boxes were standing in the ant tins filled with a mixture of water and kerosene to ensure that ants didn't get into the foodstuffs. Finally, she went into the cookhouse to check the large container of water on the stove to make sure it was boiling and then to see it carried into the bungalow, covered with a cloth and allowed to cool when the water would be put through an earthenware filter and stored in empty whiskey or gin bottles to be used for drinking water. ~Constance had carried out this ritual every day after arriving in India when she had been told by an "old India hand" to never trust servants with drinking water.

With daily chores finished Constance and Margaret were sitting on the verandah when the butler appeared and stood silently waiting until Constance looked in his direction.

"Mary Ayah is here madam" he said.

"Mary Ayah. What does she want?" Constance asked.

"I don't know madam" the butler replied.

"Very well". Just ask her to wait I will see her in a minute."

As the butler left Margaret asked who Mary Ayah was.

"Well the word Ayah is a South Indian word meaning a woman who looks after children. In the North including here in Bombay they are called "Amahs" . The meaning is just the same but because Mary is from the South she is always called Mary Ayah. We employed her whilst I was pregnant and until the children went to school and we still do whenever they are here on holiday."

At the mention of children Margaret could contain herself no longer and started to cry.

"Whatever is the matter?" Constance asked as she stretched across to put her hand on her friends arm.

"I have something to tell you and I don't know how."

"Come on Margaret, you know you can tell me anything and anyway it probably isn't as bad as you think" Constance said.

"Oh but it is" Margaret said dabbing her eyes with her handkerchief.

"This is the worst thing that could ever have happened to me I, I'm pregnant" she stammered. Constance sat back speechless.

"Pregnant" she gasped "are you sure?"

"I'm as sure as I can be." I have been sick for a few mornings now".

"I noticed you looked a little off colour but I just thought you had caught a chill or something, it never entered my head you might be pregnant. I suppose its Walter's?" Margaret nodded.

"What are we going to do?" Constance asked "what are you going to tell William."

At the mention of William Margaret cried even more.

"Oh Constance this is such a mess I don't know what to do" she said wiping her eyes. "I can't go back to England in this condition". For a moment Constance didn't know what to say.

"Whatever we may think we won't be able to decide anything until James comes home" Constance said. At the mention of James Margaret started out of her chair.

"Do we have to tell James? Can't we sort it out ourselves?"

"Don't be stupid" Constance replied. "without his help we can't do anything. Try and rest and as soon as he comes home I will tell him what has happened." She got to her feet. "I'll just go and tell Mary I have no work for her" and she left to speak to the waiting Ayah but by the time she reached the back verandah she had changed her mind. Perhaps there was going to be a job for Mary after all. For her part Mary was sure she would be wanted because that was why Ram the butler had sent for her.

At five fifteen, as it did on most days a gharry entered the drive and pulled up at the front door. Ram was waiting as usual and as the gharry came to a halt he opened the carriage door and took his masters brief case. James walked up the steps to where his wife was sitting and as he did every day he bent and gave her a kiss.

Immediately he knew there was something wrong. What had the servants done to upset her this time he wondered but before he could ask Ram was back carrying the tea tray.

"Have you had a busy day dear" his wife asked.

Every day Constance asked the same question and every day James answered in the usual non committal way regardless of whether it had been a hard day or not.

"Not bad" he said looking round "where's Margaret has she gone out?"

"No dear" his wife replied" She's in her room."

"Isn't she well again?" then even as he spoke he guessed what might be wrong, "have you had a row or something?"

"No but there is something I will go and get Margaret" his wife said.

"Tell me what it is before you go for her then I'll be ready" James said as his wife got up from her chair.

"Just wait till I get her" she replied over her shoulder as she carried on walking. She returned a few moments later with Margaret who was holding a handkerchief to her tear stained face. James looked from her to his wife and waited for one of them to speak.

"Isn't either going to tell me what is wrong?" he asked.

Both women started to speak at the same time then both stopped.

"Constance. Just tell me what it is"

"I don't know where to begin" his wife said "I, I . . ."

"Just tell me. It can't be so bad" James said.

"Oh but it is" stammered his wife looking across at her friend who was still dabbing at her eyes. "You see Margaret thinks she is pregnant".

"Pregnant!" he said. "Pregnant, Margaret thinks she's pregnant" his voice getting louder "only thinks. Doesn't she damn well know?"

"Well yes" his wife stammered "she's fairly certain but she hasn't seen a doctor yet. For a few moments no-one said anything the only sound was that of Margaret sobbing in her handkerchief.

"I'm sorry James" she whispered "I don't know what to do."

"You cut short your visit here and go back to Britain and during the trip decide what you are going to tell your husband."

"I can't go home like this. What will William say? The shame will ruin him. I can't go home." Margaret said crying harder than ever.

Constance was just about to say something when James almost exploded.

"You can't go home, well for exactly the same reason as you can't go home you can't stay here either."

He got up from his chair and walked into the lounge and the two women could hear the clink of glass as he poured himself a drink. After a few minutes he came back into the room.

"My God what a mess" he said looking at Margaret, "I know it is stupid of me to ask but I suppose Walter is the father" Margaret just nodded. "Well whatever you decide it had better be done quickly because news in the textile industry travels very quickly and as you said this could destroy your husband's reputation." With one long drink he emptied his glass. "What a bloody stupid thing to do. How bloody stupid" he said angrily.

The rest of the evening was probably the most miserable any of them had ever spent. They dined in almost total silence and when they did speak there was only one topic of conversation during which it was accepted that Margaret could neither return to England nor could she stay in Bombay. James was reiterating this fact for the umpteenth time along with cursing Walter for what had happened when suddenly he stopped in mid sentence,

"Wait a minute" he said "I think I have an idea."

"What is it?" his wife asked anxiously. "If Margaret can't go back to England and she can't have the baby here" then she stopped as a thought came to her "no you can't mean that! Margaret is not going to have an abortion."

When she heard the word abortion Margaret's mouth fell open but before she could say anything James continued.

"No if Margaret can't go back to England and she can't have the baby here she must go somewhere where the baby can be born and then have it adopted."

"I thought of something like that" Constance said "but where can she go so that no-one will know?"

After a few moment James said "there is only one place—Goa."

There was silence for a few moments until Constance said "Goa but no one goes to Goa."

"But that is the very reason why it is the perfect place. If nobody goes there then nobody will know."

James started to pace around the verandah, "That's it Goa." Before either of the two women could say anything he went on "it's fairly easy to get to and hardly any English go there, probably because it belongs to the Portuguese so it possible that no-one will find out about the baby."

"Oh James do you think that would work. How can we arrange it?" Constance asked with relief in her voice.

"I don't know, but I will start making enquiries tomorrow" James said.

Constance was happier perhaps there was a way out of this predicament after all. Even Margaret had stopped crying although she didn't quite understand and certainly had no idea of the full implications of James' plan.

"The first thing that has to be done" James said turning to Margaret,

"is for you to write to William and tell him you won't be returning until" and he started counting on his fingers "next June."

"How can I tell him that he is expecting me home at the end of February" Margaret replied.

"Can we think of something some reason why you would want to extend your visit," Constance asked. For a few minutes nobody spoke until James suddenly said "I have an idea. Why don't you tell him you have had an invitation to go to Kashmir and it would be a pity if you returned without seeing more of India and anyway it would be better to return to England in June rather than February."

Constance smiled across at her husband "What a good idea and what a good liar you are darling" she said. "Not bad is it" he replied with a smile.

Now that they had decided on a plan of action the two women waited anxiously for James' return from the office eager to discover what progress he had made and if they were any nearer putting their plan into action. Almost a week later he was able to tell them that just as he thought, it was fairly easy to visit Goa, and that visitors could stay as long as they liked and reasonable accommodation was available. He said servants were available but thought it would be better if someone went with her as a companion or perhaps a good responsible Ayah.

"Mary Ayah came to see if I had any work for her the same day we found out about Margaret" Constance said "I asked her to come back so when she does I can ask her if she would like to go with Margaret."

"Don't you think she's too old?" James asked "I know she was very good when she worked for us but that was a few years ago."

"You are right she is getting old but we need someone we know who we can trust rather than someone we don't know anything about."

Ram, was summoned from the back verandah and asked to contact Mary Ayah who appeared the next day. She was wearing her usual white sari with its blue border the free end hanging down her back which she used when the sun was at its hottest not only to drape over her head but over any child she had in her arms. Constance introduced Margaret and told Mary that her friend was going to Goa and asked if she would like to work for her whilst she was there. She didn't tell Mary that Margaret was pregnant but she knew that Mary would probably know already just as she had when she was pregnant with her children.

"When will Madam be leaving?" Mary asked.

"As soon as possible and she will be staying there until about next May."

It was all Constance could do not to smile because if Mary didn't know Margaret was pregnant before she certainly did now.

The three women discussed wages and when Mary would start work and although Margaret, like James, thought Mary was old she instantly liked her.

"I'm pleased that Mary is going with you" Constance said after Mary had left, "you'll have no need to worry she is very good and will look after you and the baby but now I, we should start thinking about what you will need to take with you."

During the next couple of weeks even though James had not yet discovered if what he had planned was possible Margaret and Constance started shopping. Constance had her tailor come to the bungalow to make clothes for Margaret who was surprised a tailor could look at her, take very few measurements then make clothes that were invariably right or only needed minor alterations.

James was finding it difficult to find someone to do what they wanted and it was only when he overheard a conversation between two of his friends talking about a Parsee lawyer who had been very helpful in a fairly difficult case that James thought that this might be the person to help them.

A couple of days later he left his office and went to see the lawyer in his office which was situated just of the main road leading to the Gymkhana Club.

Adi Ghosh, a very small man in his mid thirties dressed in European clothes, listened intently only interrupting to ask a question to clear some point as James told him about Margaret and explained the plan he had devised for he to go to Goa. When James had finished the lawyer nodded, "Yes, yes I think your plan might work but what exactly do you want me to do?"

"I need someone who can arrange all the travel, rent some accommodation, find a suitable doctor, register the birth of the child preferably as English and then finally to arrange for the child's adoption."

Three weeks later James received a message from Mr. Ghosh asking him to call and see him the following day.

"I have some good news for you" the lawyer said as they shook hands. "I have looked into the question of Goa as you suggested and I think it is even better then you thought. It is very easy for foreigners to go there and if any children are born then the child takes the nationality of the parent. I have also looked into the matter of adoption and have found a couple, the wife is English, her husband Anglo Indian who want to adopt. He has quite a good job on the railway so they are moderately well off."

"That's brilliant" James said slapping his thigh "It looks as if all our problems are solved.

Very soon the plan was put into action. Margaret had written to her husband telling him about the proposed trip to Kashmir but long before she had received a reply she had moved to Goa with Mary Ayah and was living in a small bungalow overlooking the sea on the outskirts of the small town of Mapuca. Not only had Mr. Ghosh found the bungalow he had also engaged Dr. D'Sousa a local doctor.

One morning almost three months after his trip to Bombay Walter walked into his office followed as usual by the office boy carrying the day's mail which he placed on Walter's desk. On top of the pile was a private letter with a Bombay post mark which he opened immediately but as he read it the pleasure of receiving a letter from his friend turned into a feeling of almost total disbelief at what had happened. As he re read the letter his predominant feeling became one of anger, not because he was going to have to pay for the birth of his child nor at the loss of his friend, although that did upset him, it was a rage directed in part against Margaret but mainly at himself. He opened the bottom drawer of his desk and took out a bottle.

In the short time he had been in Melur Walter had changed. Playing tennis no longer interested him because he was much better than the other players, books bored him and now the only pleasure he had was whisky, the more he drank, the happier he thought he was.

As a result because of his vile temper both Europeans and Indians tried to keep out of his way but of all the staff the one who seemed to be singled out more than anyone was a senior clerk Anil Raghavan. But on this day, the last of the month, Anil Raghavan could afford to relax because tomorrow he would start his annual leave and in three days time he and his wife, Bonesseri, would be in the hill station of Ootecamunde in the Nilgiri Hills.

As usual they took the small rack and pinion train for the final part of the journey to the mountain resort, frequently leaning out of the glassless windows to watch the train's progress always careful to pull in their heads to avoid the small branches of the trees which brushed against the passing carriages. In order to negotiate some of the more acute bends the train would occasionally reverse on to a slip line before, sometimes pushing and sometimes pulling its four carriages it continued up the mountain. As it went along, the train passed both men and women swaddled in blankets against the cold trudging along the side of the track many of them bent almost double under the weight of the load they carried either on their backs or on their heads. The higher the train went the colder it became and for the last part of the journey Anil opened one of their cases and took out a coat for himself and a heavy woollen shawl for his wife until two and half hours after leaving the plains the small train, with a triumphant blast on its whistle, steamed into Ooty station.

Every summer, in order to escape the heat the state legislature in Madras closed down and moved en bloc to work in and enjoy the cooler climate in Ooty where over the years the facilities had improved to accommodate the visitors. There was a golf course, a racecourse which held meetings twice a week, a small theatre where both amateur and touring professional shows were staged and even a hunt which met every Sunday after church. Army officers, members of the government and directors of various companies who had come to escape the heat of the plains rode to a pack of hounds across the hilly countryside followed by spectators both European and Indian alike.

In the evenings, particularly at weekends, the Europeans held dances at the English Club where, while the ladies gossiped, some of the men would repair to the Billiards Room to play the new game called snooker which some of the younger army officers who came to the club had invented.

As well as following the hunt and watching the races Anil and Bonesseri looked at the shops, something Anil never did at home, went boating on the lake and as they did every time they came to Ooty they walked along "Coker's Walk to Devil's leap" to look out over the seemingly blue tinted countryside which gave rise to the name "The Blue Nilgiris'.

Because the hotel where they were staying was situated slightly higher than the town, each morning and evening the air was filled with a combination of wood smoke from the many fires in the town below mixed with the aroma of the surrounding eucalyptus trees. In the evenings it seemed to go darker earlier than it did on the plains and then it was as if someone had thrown a perfumed black cloak over the whole area. There were no street lights or lights from any nearby buildings so if anyone went any distance from the hotel they would have difficulty finding their way back, so like the other visitors, tired because of their activities in the rarefied atmosphere, they usually retired to their room immediately after their evening meal. Their room was lit by oil lamps but even when these were extinguished it was still dimly lit by the fire, its flames casting dancing shadows on the white walls. Each night the couple snuggled under layers of blankets, holding each other tightly for mutual warmth before slowly and tenderly making love, taking care that each satisfied the other before, their desires satiated, falling asleep in each other's arms.

The fortnight's holiday, one of the happiest they had ever spent together, passed very quickly and all too soon it was time to take the little train back to the plains. They passed through Conoor, it's hillsides covered in tea bushes where the different coloured saris worn by the female plantation workers looked like large fluttering butterflies as they picked the tea. Next the train passed through Wellington, where the Indian equivalent of Sandhurst was situated and where the cadets could be seen training, before it's final descent to the plains below.

A few weeks after their return Bonesseri and her mother in law were alone in the house when Mrs. Raghavan who had been sitting very quietly watching Bonesseri suddenly said,

'I think you're pregnant." For a moment Bonesseri didn't know what to say. She thought she might be but she wasn't sure. But how did her Mother in Law know?

"You are pregnant. I know you are" the older woman said with tears of joy running down her face as she reached forward to take Bonesseri's hands in hers. "At last we will have another boy in the family."

Bonesseri started to laugh,

"Wait a minute. Not only do you say I am pregnant now you have decided it is going to be a boy when I am not even certain yet whether I am pregnant."

"I know you are pregnant, I just know you are and I am just as sure it will be a boy" Mrs. Raghavan replied.

"In the evening when they were alone Bonesseri told her husband what his Mother had said. How can she know when even I am not sure yet" she asked.

"I don't know but she is often right when she makes this sort of prediction" Anil said. For the next few minutes the couple talked about their baby and the future he would have but slowly Anil's mood changed.

"You know I have often told you about Mr. Brent" he said, "well the other day I had only been in the office about ten minutes before he was at my desk shouting about something I knew nothing about. I'm sure he is out to get me for some reason or other."

"Oh Anil are you sure?" Bonesseri said "I'm sure you haven't done anything wrong so why would he have it in for you?"

"I don't know. Perhaps it's because he drinks so much he doesn't know what he is doing. Some of the clerks say they have seen him drinking in his office and reckon that he no longer knows what's going on. You know when he first came he wasn't like this so something must have happened."

At the same time that Bonesseri and Anil were talking about him Walter was pouring yet another drink and silently cursing his uncle for sending him to this wretched place.

3

Mary Ayah was resting on the back verandah of the small bungalow to which Margaret had moved when she left Bombay nearly eight months ago. It was a typical Indian bungalow with white walls and a red tiled roof. At the front was a small garden which apart from three small palm trees was open to the road which ran parallel with the sea before turning over a rickety wooden bridge over a dried up river bed and then on to Mapuco about three miles away. At the back of the bungalow there was the usual kitchen and the servant's godowns.

During this time all she and her mistress had done was travel into the little town to buy foodstuffs and with Mary's guidance, necessary items for the baby. Margaret had never shopped in an Indian market before and would have bought things that were either not necessary or totally inappropriate and when certain clothing items were not available it was Mary an excellent seamstress who helped to chose the fabrics and then make them into clothes for the baby.

At first Margaret had been very easy to work for but for the past few weeks, as the temperature had increased and the birth approached she had become increasingly difficult. Nothing seemed to satisfy her, she frequently lost her temper, in most cases over nothing at all, so that Mary and the other servants tried, as far as possible, to keep out of her way hoping that she would sleep and they could relax.

Mary was not looking forward to the birth. Shortly after their arrival in Mapuco they had contacted Dr. D'Souza, the only doctor in the town, an elderly man who was the grandson of early Portuguese settlers and had never lived anywhere else but Goa. After he had examined Margaret he had taken the ayah on one side and told her that in his opinion the birth might be 'difficult' not only because Margaret was older than most women when they gave birth for the first time but because she didn't have 'child bearing hips'.

Sitting with her back to the bedroom wall Mary, although she was mainly dozing, occasionally lifted her head and looked over the verandah rail. The sky was darkening earlier than usual, the temperature was falling due to the sharp breeze which was rustling the tops of the palm trees and there was the welcome earthy smell of rain. Mary knew that the monsoon had already broken in Travancore where she used to live and also in the neighbouring state of Tamil Nad and now it was starting in Goa and particularly in Mapuco. In the distance to her right she could see lightning flashes against the darkening sky and then the first drops of rain splashed in the sand. The drops seemed almost as big as rupee coins and where they had landed the sand became patterned with brown stains which increased as the rain fell harder and faster. Instantly the temperature fell further and Mary pulled the free end of her sari round her shoulders. Suddenly there was a flash of lightning that seemed to come to earth only a couple of hundred yards away followed almost instantly by a vicious crack of thunder which appeared to physically strike the little bungalow and be the instigator of the torrential rain that followed. Mary got to her feet and stood peering through the almost impenetrable curtain of rain the noise of which as it rattled on the roof almost prevented her hearing the call from the bedroom. She turned from watching the rain and rushed to the bedroom, knocked on the door and hurried in as her mistress called again.

The room was quite dark because of the rain and Margaret was frightened by the flashing lightning and the crashing thunder.

Mary helped her from the bed and put a silk dressing gown round her shoulders explaining that the monsoon was always like this. She led her onto the front verandah where they stood watching the ferocity of the monsoon. Peering through the silvery curtain of rain which surrounded the little bungalow Margaret was sure she had never seen a storm as violent as this. Both women stood well back from the rail to avoid the flurries of rain which were being blown in by the wind and was forming puddles on the tiles before running under the rail or down the verandah steps. As the rain swirled about, Margaret could just see out over the garden and the palm trees bending and surging before the fury of the wind, to the sea where only two or three hours earlier there had hardly been a ripple but now had white topped waves foaming up the beach. As they watched, the dark sky was ripped apart by yet another flash of lightning and as the thunder rolled out a large frond was torn from the tallest of the palm trees to be whipped away by the wind and disappear in the torrential rain. Margaret pulled her wrap more tightly around her because the temperature had dropped so much in the past few minutes that she could not prevent a shiver something she had not done since her arrival in India.

The next day dawned brightly with hardly a cloud in the sky. Once again the sea was calm as Margaret and Mary took their usual stroll along the beach but this morning having to be careful to pick their way through the debris left by the storm' The beach was littered with branches torn from palm trees from some distance away, stones had been uncovered as the sand was whipped about and lay where there had never been stones before while other parts where there had been stones were now totally denuded except for jellyfish and star fish which had been thrown up on the beach and left stranded as the sea retreated.

They turned towards the town until they came to the little bridge over which yesterday had been a dried up river bed but was now a small river which had attracted small boys from the town who were jumping into the water or trying to fish. They watched for a while and then started to walk back but hadn't gone very far when they heard the sound of Dr. D'Souza's little car approaching. When he drew abreast he stopped and offered Margaret a lift back to the bungalow which she readily accepted leaving Mary to walk back on her own. At the bungalow they both had a refreshing drink and when Mary returned the Doctor examined his patient.

"You will not have to wait very much longer" he said with a smile "so from now on I will come and see you every day but if you start to have pains send for me and I will come immediately."

Sitting on the verandah after the doctor had left Margaret was very grateful that the rains had made it much cooler even if it was more humid but could not help worrying that apart from Mary she was all alone and whether she had done the right thing in agreeing to come to Goa.

"Is the monsoon finished now?" Margaret asked as she turned to Mary who walked out onto the verandah from the direction of the bedroom.

Mary laughed. "Oh no madam, that was only the first day. The rains will come again tonight and for several more days but it might start a little later than it did yesterday."

Margaret looked out over the calm sea and at the clear blue sky and thought Mary must be wrong. Surely it couldn't rain like it did yesterday.

After lunch she rested as usual and wakened about three o'clock. She went to her usual chair on the verandah from where she could instantly see that the sea wasn't as calm as when she went to the bedroom. The wind was also stronger bringing clouds which were no longer white but a greyish black and soon she could feel the temperature falling and she pulled her wrap more tightly around her shoulders.

"If we are going to walk today we should go now and not go too far" Mary said "it will start to rain very soon."

They had nowhere near reached the wooden bridge when in the distance they heard a peel of thunder so they instantly turned and started back along the beach and had nearly reached the bungalow when Margaret saw some deep blue, shiny pebbles lying on the sand which must have been either washed up or uncovered the previous night. She asked Mary to gather a few and then they walked on arriving at the bungalow just as the first rain drops started to fall.

Even though she had experienced the storm the previous night Margaret could not help flinching at every slash of lightning or at the accompanying roll of thunder. Perhaps it was because she was pregnant that she felt more afraid than she ought to have done and that was probably why she was afraid something untoward was going to happen. As she stood watching the teaming rain make puddles in the garden the servants went round the bungalow lighting the oil lamps and in the corner of her eye she could see the flames of the lamps seeming to dance in rhythm with the storm casting moving shadows on the white walls. Suddenly everything went quiet as if the storm had prematurely ended and then came a vicious flash of lightning followed instantaneously by a tremendous peal of thunder which appeared to come from just behind the bungalow. Instinctively Margaret ducked as if someone had thrown something at her and then she felt the pain.

Mary saw her mistress clutch at her stomach and moved across to her, took her gently by the arm and led her to a chair where Margaret sat holding her stomach gently rocking to and fro. Just as she thought the pain was ended she was seized by another which made her suck in her breath. She had felt slight pains when she was out walking but nothing like the pain she was feeling now. Was the baby starting she wondered but dismissed the thought because hadn't Dr. D'Souza told her it wasn't due for another week at least. She was about to stand up when there was another pain and this time severe enough to make her cry out. Mary, who had been about to go to the back verandah, heard the cry and turned back.

"What is it madam?" she asked.

"A pain"

"Have you had others?" Mary asked fairly certain of what the answer would be. Margaret nodded her head.

"When did they start? Mary enquired.

"Oh I don't know" Margaret replied irritably. "When we were out walking I suppose." Her voice was now almost lost in the noise of the storm and suddenly she felt even more lonely and afraid.

"Is it the baby Mary?" she asked in a plaintive voice'

"We'll wait a little longer but if the pains continue we will send for the Doctor."

The ayah led her mistress to the bedroom and put her on the bed propping her up with pillows but very soon it was obvious the pains were not easing and in fact were occurring with increasing regularity. Margaret was certainly starting to have her baby. Mary hurried out to the back verandah and shouted for the cook who came running from his godown through the torrential rain and the mud of the back garden. Quickly she told him that Madam was having her baby and to go and fetch the doctor. Grumbling about having to go out in the downpour he dashed back to the godown, dragged out his bicycle and holding a large palm leaf above his head to act as an umbrella he cycled off into the storm'

About twenty minutes later Mary, who was trying to comfort her mistress heard a faint voice calling from outside the bedroom door. Surely the doctor couldn't be here so soon. She opened the door and was not surprised when she didn't see the doctor but did not expect to see the saturated figure of the cook.

"What happened? You have been very quick. Is the doctor coming?'

"The cook shook his head. 'I couldn't get into town. The bridge has been washed away. There is no way I can get across the river" he said.

Mary recalled how swollen the river had been that morning and after the storm now it would obviously be much worse. She thanked the cook who ran back to his godown. Mary stood for a couple of minutes just watching the rain and then, as if she had made up her mind about something, she turned to go back to Margaret. Even before Mary could close the bedroom door behind her Margaret was demanding to know where the doctor was.

"Where is Dr. D" Souza. Is he coming?" she asked a note of panic in her voice. Mary just nodded. She had decided not to tell Margaret about the bridge. There was no point in frightening her unnecessarily.

In the next couple of hours the labour pains came more frequently and were much more intense, As yet another pain swept over her Margaret screamed out, "Where's that damned doctor?, Where is he? He said he would be here."

Mary had known for some time she would have to tell Margaret what had happened and as quietly and calmly as she could she told her about the bridge and that there was no way into town. Now Margaret was very frightened.

"It has stopped raining now" she almost screamed, "Go and tell the cook to try again. He must get the doctor"

Mary moved the pillows from behind Margaret's head and gently manoeuvred her into a position where the beby could be born but when she started to lift Margaret's nightdress in order to see if there were any signs of the baby Margaret knocked her hand away.

"Leave me alone. Don't touch me. You don't know what you are doing. Get the doctor" and then screamed as another pain coursed through her body.

"The doctor is not coming. The bridge has been swept away so nobody can cross the river. Just do as I say and the baby will be born."

Margaret felt as if her stomach was collapsing and she grabbed the ayah's hand to help her fight the pain. With each spasm she became more and more frightened. She was having her first baby in a strange land, no doctor and only this old Indian woman to look after her. How she wished she had decided not to stay in India to have her baby rather than go back to England even if she would have had to face the wrath of her husband. How she wished she had never met Walter Brent and blamed him entirely for what was happening but even through all her screaming she could hear the soothing voice of Mary whispering in her ear, and when Mary asked her to open her mouth she just did as she was told.

From the folds of her sari the ayah took a small bundle of green leaves which she had gathered, 'just in case', before the rains started and put them into her patient's open mouth. Mary didn't know what the leaves were called but knew they had the ability to put whoever chewed them into a light trance like state and as a result to reduce pain and were frequently used by village women during childbirth. There was not a lot of taste but as Margaret chewed and swallowed her saliva she felt the pain easing. For the next couple of hours Mary never left Margaret's side, continually mopping her brow and when the pain increased giving her more of the soothing leaves until suddenly Margaret felt as if her insides were tearing apart and she screamed out with a pain which was far more intense than any before.

The storm had long passed and the whole bungalow was quiet the only sounds, the croaking of the frogs in the rain pools and the chirruping of insects when suddenly the silence was broken by a moaning scream followed by the wail of newborn baby. Moments later Mary placed the baby, wrapped in a small sheet, in Margaret's arms.

"You have a lovely boy Madam" she said beaming down at Margaret.

Who was lying, totally exhausted, her hair fanned out on the pillows. All Margaret could see of her baby was the thatch of dark hair on its head which instantly reminded her of Walter but even so soon after the birth she was overwhelmed with sadness at the thought that soon she would be returning toEngland and although she had never wanted this baby would have to leave it behind and never see it again. A few short hours ago she would have given anything if somehow the baby could have been taken from her but now, even so soon after the birth, the memory of the pain she had endured was diminishing. Once again it had started to rain and was lashing against the windows but now she was no longer afraid and just wondered if the accompanying thunder and lightning was a portent of what life was going to be like for this baby lying so peacefully in her arms.

Mary left Margaret and went out to the back verandah where the cook and butler were patiently waiting to hear what had happened and was as delighted as if it had been their own when Mary told them that Madam had given birth to a male child.

Two days later Dr. D'Souza was able to get through to the bungalow and after checking both mother and baby pronounced both were well. Back in town he carried out the instructions of Mr. Ghosh and registered the birth of a male child, Paul, to the parents Herbert and Eunice Williams. He sent off a telegram to Mr. Ghosh so that he could tell both Mr. and Mrs. Williams and James Armitage of the birth of the baby boy and that the birth had been registered as per his instructions, adding that in his opinion the child would be ready to leave Goa in about a month's time.

During this month, despite her initial intentions, Margaret behaved like any new mother. She bathed her son and carried him around the bungalow in her arms. At first she breast fed him and loved the feel of his mouth at her breast and then in order to prepare him for when she had to give him up she spent time feeding him from a bottle. Whenever he cried she was instantly at his side both day and night despite Mary's efforts to stop her aware that the separation, when it occurred, would be all the more harrowing. All too soon that day dawned and two horse drawn gharries arrived at the bungalow.

In the first were Mr. and Mrs. Williams who in looks could well have been the baby's natural parents followed in the other by James Armitage and Dr. D'Sousa. When they had met in Mapuco it had been decided that the Williams' would wait in the gharry while James and the doctor brought the baby out to them but it didn't turn out to be as easy as that. James had to almost fight Margaret to get the baby from her and when he had managed that and given the baby to Mary Ayah to carry out to the waiting couple it was all he could do to stop the sobbing, screaming Margaret from running after the vehicle taking her baby from her.

James paid the doctor his fee which included the rent for the bungalow and money for the servants but when the doctor tried to say goodbye to Margaret she just sat with her back to him holding a crumpled handkerchief to her eyes her body wracked with sobs.

James had decided in order to avoid any trouble on the train to Mapuco it would be better if he and Margaret stayed at the bungalow for another night but the way Margaret was behaving he wondered if that had been the best idea.

Throughout the evening Margaret would suddenly burst into tears and even after she had gone to bed he could still hear her sobbing.

Next morning red eyed with weeping she didn't have breakfast but instead, accompanied by Mary went walking on the beach for the last time. When they returned after an hour or so she was clutching a few more of the blue pebbles like the ones she had gathered before.

"These will remind me of Goa in the years ahead" she said a tear running down her cheek.

After a light lunch James paid Mary double what she was expecting to receive and after thanking her for looking after Margaret so carefully he followed her and Margaret out to the waiting carriage which was already loaded with James' suitcase and all the baggage that Margaret wanted to take back to Bombay. As they approached, the butler with a small half bow put his hands together in the Indian greeting of "namaste". Margaret returned the greeting and then turned to Mary who was standing with a handkerchief to her eyes.

"Thank you Mary. I don't know how I would have managed without you" she said as she put her arms around her and kissed her on the cheek. "I want you to have this" and she put into Mary's hand a small broach consisting of a solitary ruby surrounded by small diamonds that Walter had bought for her.

Margaret only had a fortnight to wait before the sailing date of the ship on which James had booked a passage during which, apart from going to a jeweller and having the blue stones she had collected made into the articles she wanted, she never left the bungalow.

It was a great relief for Constance and James when the day came to take Margaret to the docks where they waited as the porters took charge of her baggage and after all the formalities were completed accompany her on board where a ship's steward showed them to her cabin where yet again she started to cry.

"I don't want to go home. How can I face my husband?" she moaned. "He's sure to find out what's happened."

By this time James' patience was exhausted.

"Look Margaret, Constance and I have gone to a lot of trouble and no little expense to help you we have done all we can to ensure you will be able to return to William but you will have to pull yourself together.

"Don't be so cruel James" Constance said "It is very difficult for Margaret" and she put her arms round her friend in an effort to console. In danger of losing his temper James turned away deciding it would be better if he left the cabin. He went up on deck and had a look round the ship and only returned to the cabin when he heard the stewards calling "all ashore, all visitors ashore."

"It is about time we were leaving my dear" he said gently to his wife. The two friends broke apart and Margaret reached for her handbag and took out a package addressed to Mr. Ghosh.

"Will you please see that Mr. Ghosh receives this?" she said handing the small parcel to James "The instructions are inside."

James assured her he would take it to the lawyer on their way home from the docks and then turning he led his wife and her friend to the gangway where after a kiss on Margaret's cheek he walked down and waited for his wife to join him on quay. The dock workers were waiting to remove the gangway as Constance almost the last one, walked down to join her husband and watched as the gangway was finally removed, the last ropes holding the ship were cast off and the R.M.S. Ophir set out on its journey to England.

James and Constance stood waving until it was no longer possible to pick out Margaret from the other passengers standing at the stern of the ship at which point James gently took hold of his wife's arm and led her along the quay to where their carriage was waiting.

Next day, as instructed Mr.,Ghosh sent the small package from Margaret to Walter Brent. Inside was a letter informing him that he had a son named Paul and that he had been adopted. Along with the letter was a broach made up of little blue stones surrounding a diamond. Why, Walter wondered, would Margaret send him a broach. Unable to come up with an answer he just put it back in the box and threw it into the top drawer of the chest in his bedroom and forgot all about it.

When she reached home Margaret unpacked her belongings amongst which was an identical box to the one she had sent to Walter. Sitting on the bed she opened the package and couldn't believe it. Inside was a pair of cufflinks each made up of blue stones with a diamond in the centre. These were supposed to have gone to Walter obviously she had mixed up the gifts. What did she want with a pair of cufflinks she thought but more to the point what would Walter want with a lady's broach.

4

In order to accommodate religious festivals for the two principal religions, Hindu and Moslem, factories sometimes worked for as long as ten days without a break and then to compensate run for less than the usual six days. If mistakes occurred it was usually towards the end of a ten day run so it was not helpful when auditors from head office arrived at Melur for the annual audit.

It was on the eighth day of a long run when an office messenger came to tell Anil that Mr. Brent wanted him. Wondering what he could possibly want he slid his feet into his chapplies which he always pushed off when he was working so that his bare feet on the cool tiles helped him to keep cool and followed the messenger to the manager's office. He paused for a moment and then knocked on the door and entered. Mr. Brent was sitting at his desk looking at a ledger while in a chair to one side was one of the auditors. Standing in front of the desk Anil waited for what seemed a long time before Walter looked up.

"Mr. Shepherd has been checking the Stores' records and from what he has discovered it seems you have been running a nice little racket" Anil was dumbfounded. He couldn't believe what he had just heard.

"I don't know what you mean Sir" he whispered. He didn't know what the accountant had discovered but it was obvious he was in trouble.

Walter stabbed his finger on the open page of the book in front of him.

"Are you responsible for this ledger?" and even though the book was upside down to him Anil recognized it as one of the Stores' ledgers.

"Yes sir that book is my responsibility."

Walter Brent reached out to the pile of books on the desk and pulled another one towards him and opened it where a bookmark had been placed.

"What about this one?" he asked.

"Yes sir that is also one from my department."

Walter placed the second book next to the first one and pointed to an entry in each of them.

"And these signatures in blue pencil are yours aren't they?"

Anil leaned forward and twisting his head round looked at the two entries and the signatures and he recognized them as his own and still didn't know what was wrong. Walter looked up from the books and stared at Anil without speaking for what, to Anil seemed an age. Eventually he pointed to the first book.

"According to this entry we received and have paid for various items costing over a thousand rupees". He pointed to the second book "but according to this book the spares have never been issued nor are they shown as being in stock and nor are they actually in stock so it appears to me that either we are paying for goods we haven't received or someone has stolen them, either way it is your responsibility."

Anil was speechless. He checked these books meticulously and he was sure they must have been correct when he signed them.

"Can I take the books and check them?" he asked.

Walter nodded and sat back to allow Anil to pick up the two ledgers but as Anil reached the door Walter said,

"I want you back here no later than three o'clock ."

Anil hurried back to his desk where he checked not only the books he had taken from Walter's office but also others he took from the general store but try as he might he could not work out what had happened.

There were only three possibilities.

One. Someone had simply stolen the spares But this was very unlikely

Two. They had never been received or three, someone had altered the books to get him into trouble. Whatever had happened Anil knew he was in very serious trouble. He made a list of all the people who had a reason to use the ledgers starting with the Storekeeper, then the clerks and even the messenger boy who couldn't speak English never mind write it.

One by one he questioned them but at the end he had to admit he was no nearer finding out what had happened. He even went to see some local suppliers from where some goods would have been ordered to check their deliveries but to no avail. He worked through the tiffin break and into the afternoon trying to discover what had happened. The only people he could not approach were the European management but surely one of them wouldn't be responsible for his predicament. He was shocked when a messenger arrived at his desk to tell him that Mr. Brent wanted him. Surely it wasn't three o'clock already. With a heavy heart he picked up the two ledgers and followed the messenger to Walter's office. The scene was just the same. In fact it looked as though the two people in the office had never moved. Silently they watched as Anil placed the books on Walter's desk and stood waiting. "What have you to say" Walter demanded.

Anil tried to speak. He opened his mouth but he couldn't form the words. He tried again and it was as if someone else was speaking.

"I have studied the books sir and they do indicate that something was wrong but I know I would never have signed them when the mistake was so obvious. So I think the only possibility is they must have been altered after I had signed them."

"You're right something is wrong but who altered the books if it wasn't you?" Walter demanded.

"I don't know sir" Anil replied. "I have questioned everyone who has access to the books and all I can say is I'm sure no-one in the Store departments would have stolen anything."

"Well we have paid for the goods and we either haven't received them or someone has stolen them but either way you are responsible."

For the next half hour both Walter and the auditors fired questions at him, other clerks were sent for most of them the same people that Anil had already questioned but the more the investigation went on the more Anil knew he was trapped. Eventually he was sent out of the office while the other European managers were sent for and then after they had left he was re-admitted.

"Well have you anything to say?" Walter asked. "Do you still say you know nothing."

Anil was now very afraid. He was worried about Bonesseri and their unborn baby. They had been so happy when she was pregnant but now if he lost his job because of his so-called dishonesty he would never get another one.

"No sir" he stammered. "All I can say is I haven't done anything. The books must have been altered after I signed them but I don't know who did it or where the missing items are." He looked down at the floor and then at the three Europeans.

"I don't know. I don't know." He said very quietly.

"You don't know and we don't know" Walter said indicating the auditors "but one thing we do know is the firm has lost a lot of money."

"Mr. Brent, I am telling the truth. I haven't done anything" Anil said his voice breaking.

"We don't believe you so I have no other course, you're dismissed. Don't work till the end of the month. Go now, immediately. Get out."

Just for a moment Anil hesitated but he knew that appealing to Walter Brent would not make any difference so he turned and walked out of the office tears springing to his eyes. What would he do? What would happen to his family? He knew he would never get a job like this without references and it was obvious he wouldn't get one from Ramuda.

Looking neither to left or right but aware of all the office staff watching him he walked swiftly to his desk, gathered up his personal possessions and without a word walked out of the office and a few minutes later through the factory gate for the last time.

He didn't go straight home but sat drinking coffee in one of the many coffee shops trying hard to find a solution to his problem. He stayed until it started to go dark so that he arrived home at approximately the same time as usual and although he didn't say anything either to Bonessri or his mother they both suspected that something was radically wrong. When he was out of the room Mrs.Raghaven asked her daughter-in-law what was wrong with him.

"I don't know" his wife said, "but it must be something serious to make him as worried as this." All night Bonessri heard Anil tossing about on his charpoy and mumbling in his sleep but it was only in the morning when he should have left for work that she and his mother discovered what had happened.

"Whatever shall we do?" What about the baby? Your mother can't keep us" Bonessri cried. "Go back and tell them again it wasn't your fault"

"I tried to do that yesterday. They won't listen" he replied. "There is nothing I can do. They won't give me my job back."

"There is only one thing for it then" his mother said as she wiped her eyes, "We'll go to Madras and see if you can get a job there,"

"Mother, you know as well as I that the first thing any firm will do is ask for references. They will want to know where I have been working. No one will employ me."

Next day urged on by Mrs Raghavan, the family left Melur for Madras and to her eldest brother's house. Even though the house was not very large once he had been told what had happened he didn't hesitate to take them and next morning started taking Anil to meet his friends in the hope that one of them might know where Anil might find a job. In the following weeks Anil applied to many different factories and workshops but each time the result was the same. Usually there were no jobs but on the rare occasion there was a vacancy when he could not produce any references the employers were not interested. Soon, despite help from his uncle and the whole household living as frugally as they could, the small savings Anil had brought from Melur were almost exhausted.

Anil became more and more dejected so that it became increasingly difficult for him to go for what inevitably turned out to be fruitless interviews until, just as he thought he was never going to find work, his luck changed. Through the recommendation of one of his uncle's friends he was offered a job in a small textile factory weaving dhoti cloth mainly from yarn spun by Ramuda Textiles. The pay wasn't as good as what he had earned before and wasn't sufficient for a house like the one he rented in Melur, but was enough for one which had neither running water nor electricity.

Now that he was working Anil at last was more like the Anil of old and was so happy in his new job that soon he was thinking it might not be long before they would be able to move into a better house. This dream, however suffered a set back when Bonesseri gave birth to a son they called Prasad Krishnan after the baby's two grandfathers. Unfortunately the birth was extremely difficult and they had been forced to use not only the meagre money Anil was trying to save but had also to seek a loan from a money lender. Now out of his small wage Anil not only had to pay for the upkeep of his wife, their new baby and his mother-in-law but he also had to pay back the money plus interest which he had borrowed from the money lender.

Despite this Anil was happier than he had been for some time and by doing all the odd jobs he could such as writing letters for people, and teaching children to read and write he was well on the way to settling his debts.

Although the baby was nearly a year old it must have been a little unwell because it had cried a lot during the night which meant Anil was still tired when he went to work the following morning only to find the factory manager waiting for him.

"As you know Mr. Brent from Ramuda Textiles came to see us yesterday and he saw you in the office. He told me what had happened at Melur and how surprised he was to see you working here. I told him that I didn't know you had worked at Melur so obviously didn't know what had happened there but now, after what he told me, I don't want you here."

Anil was speechless. He had seen Walter Brent the day before but had tried to make sure his ex boss didn't see him.

"But I haven't done anything wrong" he gasped "and I didn't do anything wrong at Ramuda Textiles either. I have a wife and baby to support. I need the money. You can't discharge me."

Despite all Anil's pleadings less than half an hour after arriving for work Anil was jobless again. Totally defeated and under the watchful eye of the Manager and the office staff he made his way to the door. Anil didn't want to go home because he knew that Bonesseri, worried about their situation, was beginning to blame him for what had happened so for the rest of the day he just wandered aimlessly around the town until it was the time he usually arrived home. As he walked the last few remaining yards to the little house he saw Bonesseri waiting for him with baby Krishnan in her arms. He took the baby from her and as always Krishnan giggled and laughed as Anil tickled him and teased him, lifting him up high and pretending to drop him. This went on for about half an hour while Bonesseri finished preparing their meal and then went inside to eat. He wanted to tell his wife what had happened but refrained from doing so as during his wanderings after leaving the factory he had come up with a plan of action.

It was just past midnight and everything in the little house was quiet. Bonesseri was sleeping soundly and even Krishnan in his little cot by the wall was fast asleep but Anil was staring wide eyed in the darkness contemplating what he was about to do. He had considered this idea once before when he had been forced to leave Melur but now there was no other solution to his problem. When he was working for Ramuda textiles he had taken out an insurance policy the next premium of which was due in a couple of weeks which he knew he could not afford to pay and would therefore lose what he had already paid so if he put his plan into action it had to be now.

Silently he got up from his charpoy pausing only to look down at his sleeping wife and son with tears rolling down his cheeks, he tiptoed from the house.

Half an hour later he was lying between the railway lines his head on one of the cold steel rails through which he could feel the vibration of the approaching train.

Even with the help of the powerful headlight the driver of the night express didn't see the figure of the man lying on the track let alone the tears coursing down his face as he whispered 'Bonesseri. Bonesseri."

When Bonesseri wakened next morning she was surprised to find her husband was not in the house. This was not too unusual as sometimes he had to go to work early but it was strange he hadn't mentioned it the evening before and even more strange that he had left without telling her. She knew he had been rather quiet and obviously worried about something but even so it was unusual so she decided that when she went shopping she would call at the factory to see if there was anything wrong. At the factory gate she was stopped by the guards and when they asked what she wanted told them she wanted to speak to her husband. After a short wait one of the guards took her to the manager's office and she told him why she was here. At first the manager wouldn't meet her gaze, then he looked up.

"He doesn't work here any longer" he said "I sacked him yesterday."

"You sacked him" Bonesseri gasped "Why? What happened? What did he do wrong?"

"Nothing I hope" the manager replied. "Mr. Brent from Ramuda Textiles was here and he told me what your husband did at Melur so I decided it was best to get rid of him before he started his tricks here."

"But he didn't do anything wrong. He was wrongly dismissed" she replied angrily. "Now we have no money. What shall we do?"

"What you do is not my concern. I heard your husband was a thief so I decided not to take any chances. If I had known about this before I took him on he would never have worked here in the first place. I don't know where he is and wherever he is it is nothing to do with me."

As Bonesseri was leaving the factory some railway workers walking along the line to start work saw the mangled, headless corpse which had been thrown several yards away from the track. They reported it and the body was taken away but because the head was never found the torso remained unidentified. A few weeks later Bonesseri received more bad news. The insurance company said that because there was no proof her husband was dead they could only settle the claim if after a waiting period of six years there was still no news of him.

Bonesseri swore then that if and when she did receive the money it would only be used for her son's education. In the meantime, however, she didn't have enough money even to stay in the menial house in Madras so was forced to go back to Ramuda where all her relatives lived and where a cousin and his wife took her and Krishnan into their home.

5

It was getting dark when George Brent brought his car to a halt outside his bungalow at the end of the three hour journey from Ootecamunde where he had been on holiday with his wife and son during the month of May.

A couple of hours later, bathed, changed and feeling reasonably refreshed he climbed the stairs to the upstairs verandah of the bungalow next door to his own where he knew his parents would be waiting to hear news of their daughter-in-law and grandson who he had left behind in Ooty until the cooler weather. They were sitting in their favourite chairs angled in such a position so that they could look out over the garden and where they may get the benefit of any breeze. He gave his mother a kiss and then sat on the vacant chair between them and for the next few minutes answered all their questions about his wife and son and what was happening in Ooty but he could tell that his father wanted to talk about something else. When his mother left them to talk to the cook about dinner his father changed the subject.

"I'm very worried about Melur" he said. "If what I hear about Walter is correct then we have a problem."

George knew what his father was talking about because they had discussed it before they went on holiday.

"The latest rumour is that he doesn't go to the office every day and when he does he is often the worse for wear. His drinking seems to be worse than we thought before you went on holiday."

"Surely it can't be that bad" his wife said who had returned and had overheard her husband. "Only the other day you said the factory seemed to be running well and you know you can't always believe rumours."

"I can't deny that but if the rumours are only half true things are not as they should be." Turning to his son he said "Go down there as soon as you can and see what is going on. I would have gone myself but he is more likely to talk to you."

A week later after his parents had gone to Ooty for their holidays George walked into his cousin's office in Melur hoping to find that things were not as bad as his father had made them out to be but immediately he opened the office door he knew his worst fears were realised. Walter was slumped in his chair and when he looked up it was obvious he had difficulty in focusing who had walked into his office. When he did eventually realise who it was he struggled to his feet at the same time closing one of the desk drawers with his shin in the vein hope that George would not know what was inside. As he stood erect he stumbled slightly and in putting out his hand to steady himself knocked some of the papers that were strewn about his desk to the floor. The cousins shook hands and Walter indicated the chair in front of the desk and then collapsed back into his own.

"Whats going on Walter?" George asked.

"Wha'd 'ya mean?" Walter mumbled.

"Don't be so bloody stupid. Just look at yourself. We've heard about the state you were in so don't ask what I am talking about."

Walter sat at his desk not speaking his mouth hanging open so that when there was no reply even after what seemed an intolerable wait George got to his feet.

"Come on Walter, we can't talk here. Let's go to your bungalow" and he helped his cousin to his feet and led him out of his office and through the empty General Office.

At the bungalow they sat opposite each other at the verandah table and George again asked what had happened to make his cousin start drinking. Yet again Walter didn't answer but just sat looking down at the table as if it was the most interesting object he had ever seen. George tried again.

"Come on tell me. What the hell has happened? Why are you like this?"

"There is nothing going on that's the trouble. Its all finished."

George waited for Walter to tell him what he meant but when he remained silent he had to ask.

"What do you mean. What is finished?"

"I don't have to tell you anything about my private affairs" Walter replied belligerently.

"But I want to know why you aren't doing your job"

"I've told you, it has nothing to do with you, nothing to do with anybody."

Walter struggled to his feet and walked unsteadily towards the lounge and the drinks tray. George hastily followed him and as Walter reached out towards the tray George grabbed his wrist.

"I think you have had enough of that" he said. Walter tried to shake his wrist free.

"Don't be so bloody stupid" he replied. "If I want to drink in my own bungalow I am damned sure you won't stop me."

"You're not having a drink while I am here. I need to talk to you and I can only make sure you understand if you are sober." He pulled Walter back towards the verandah but instead of returning to where they had been sitting he dragged Walter towards his bedroom.

"Look go and have a bath and go to bed and we'll talk in the morning" he said.

In the bedroom George had a quick look round to make sure there were no drinks there and then returned to the verandah where after about fifteen minutes he went back to the bedroom and through to the bathroom where he paused and listened for a few minutes to ensure ⁓Walter was safe before quietly leaving, closing the door behind him.

Next morning George walked out on to the verandah it was only just past six o'clock and the sun had not risen over the horizon. Because this was the coolest part of the day the servants had already rolled up the verandah tatties that covered the space between the verandah rails and the roof to allow the cool morning air to circulate through the bungalow. The compound itself was very quiet the only sound that of the bullock carts rolling past the compound gates taking their wares to market. George leant with hands on the rail looking out across the garden and was startled by a voice from the shadows.

"Good morning" he swung round to see Walter sitting in one of the ratten chairs at the other end of the verandah, a tray of tea things in front of him.

"Would you like some tea?" he asked.

"Good morning Walter" George replied, "Yes a cup of tea woud be very nice. How do you feel this morning?" Walter busied himself with the teapot.

"Damned awful thanks to you but I am sober." Walter replied as he handed a cup to his cousin.

"What's wrong Walter? You never used to drink like this whats happened?" George said as he sat facing his cousin.

Walter just continued looking out across the garden as if he had not heard but just as George was about to repeat the question he spoke.

"Before I came here I went to Bombay to see my mother off to the U.K. and I had a really good time. I like Bombay but then when I arrived here it only made me realise what a damned awful place this is and what I was missing by being here. There is absolutely nothing to do so to help pass the time I started to have the occasional drink."

"But that can't be the only reason for drinking like you do. Something else must have happened" George said.

"There is not much to say George. When I was in Bombay I met a girl who was on holiday from U.K. I dined with her a couple of times and I suppose the memory of that has made me realise even more what a lonely place this is. But as for drinking, well I suppose it has got worse but I can stop if I want."

"Well Walter all I can say is you had better want" George said slowly "Because if you don't you will be on the next boat home."

Despite the fact that everything that had happened was his own fault Walter was angry.

"Are you threatening me George?" he asked.

"No I am not but father is and he isn't pretending either. If you hadn't been one of the family you would have been finished by now."

During the rest of his stay George tried to discover more about Walter's trip to Bombay but couldn't persuade his cousin to give him any further details. One thing he was happy about though was that during his stay he never saw Walter have a single drink and although this was no guarantee he would stop drinking permanently it was perhaps a sign he could control the habit.

Apart from helping Walter, George had also come to check out the two factories and was pleased to find that despite his cousin's drinking they were performing equally as well as the Ramuda factories.

At the end of George's visit the two cousins were sitting on the verandah when the horse drawn gharry which was to take George to the station drew up at the garden gate. Picking up his brief case George, accompanied by his cousin, walked down the path and as they shook hands,

"Remember what I said Walter, no more drinking. There won't be anymore warnings. The next time will be the last and then you'll be gone. You have seen what happens when other people have stepped out of line." He gave a little smile "You know the saying as well as I there's a boat leaves every Tuesday but I don't want you to be on it."

Walter nodded "You're right there won't be a next time I promise."

As the months passed he consoled himself with the thought that some day, please let it be soon, Frank Strickland would be coming to take over the management of the factories so that he could return to Ramuda. Then one day he received a letter which would dramatically change his life.

Like officials at other European companies Walter received invitations to many different functions most of which he declined but this was an invitation from a Mr. Reddy, a very important customer, to attend the wedding of his eldest son and although he didn't really want to go this was one of the few occasions when an invitation could not be ignored.

On the day of the wedding, feeling very uncomfortable in his suit and shirt with its high starched collar and tie, he brought his new company car to a halt and was greeted by Mr. Reddy who led him up the steps of the verandah and to a room where his son and wife-to-be were seated in high backed chairs on the dais. He introduced Walter to his son and then to his bride who was dressed in a red and gold silk sari which when she moved revealed the many gold bangles on her arms. She had a diamond set into one nostril and was wearing gold filigree earings and gold anklets which he could just see under the hem of her sari. Her jet black hair was oiled and combed back from her face and plaited with sweet smelling yellow and white temple blossom.

During the ceremony she never raised her eyes but continued looking down at the floor whilst the groom, a tall thin man, dressed in white trousers of a satinlike material and a silk brocade coat with a high military style collar acknowledged the greetings of the many guests as they arrived.

Walter guessed he would be about 35 years old whilst the bride looked to be about 15 or 16 but then he mused that seemed to be the norm for couples in India.

Walter moved from room to room greeting and being introduced to other guests many of whom had travelled many miles from different parts of South India. He entered a small lounge and was glancing round to see if there was anyone he knew when his eyes were drawn to a young woman wearing a deep blue sari carrying a tray of refreshments and he watched the richly embroidered end of the sari which was draped over her left shoulder, swing in rhythm as she walked round the room and then, he thought, eventually towards him. But all the refreshments had been taken from the tray and she turned and left the room returning a few minutes later her tray full of drinks but this time when there was only one drink left she placed the tray on a table and carrying the drink came across and offered it to him. As he took the glass from her she looked straight into his eyes and as her free hand came up to ensure he had a grip on the glass her fingers gently touched the back of his hand. It was like a mild electric shock but then her hand was gone. He was sure the contact had not been accidental.

"Thank you very much" Walter almost stammered" we haven't been introduced my name is Walter Brent." She looked up at him and smiled.

"I know that Mr. Brent. My name is Nirmala, Mrs Nirmala Rajan, My husband is a cousin of Mr. Reddy. Surprised at how well she spoke English Walter complimented her.

"I studied English at the convent near Madras and I practice whenever I can which is why I came over to speak to you".

"Well you do speak it remarkably well" Walter replied and during the conversation he asked if her husband was present.

Nirmala spun round and pointing she said "Yes he's over there in the corner,

Walter turned and was amazed she was indicating a man almost as fat as he was tall who although it wasn't terribly hot was continually mopping his brow with a big white handkerchief. Walter guessed he must be nearly seventy years old.

Before Walter could say anything he felt her fingers on his hand as she took the empty glass from him. Now any thoughts that he may have had that the first time was accidental were immediately dismissed.

"Can I get you another drink Mr. Brent" she asked smiling up at him from under her lowered eyelashes.

He watched as Nirmala walked away with the swaying walk that all Indian women adopted when they were very young and had to carry pots of water and other things either on their head or their hip, before turning to watch the ceremony.

Within a few minutes she was back and held out a glass to him with a smile. He was about to say something but before he could speak she was mingling with the female guests.

Whilst he chatted with some of the other guests that he knew he was constantly searching the room for Nirmala. Sometimes she wasn't in the room but when she was she appeared to be looking at him also.

After sometime the ceremony was drawing to a close and as many of the guests as possible crowded into the main room where the bride and groom were sitting, cross legged, on cushions on the floor in front of the priest, a little fat man dressed in a reddish brown dhoti, his caste mark finely outlined on his forehead. His hair had been partly shaved so that his hairline started almost on top of his head and then the rest of the straggly greying hair was drawn back into a pigtail. He was chanting prayers to which the couple occasionally responded by slightly bowing towards him. Walter was watching with interest when he smelt perfume and sensed that Nirmala had managed to squeeze into the space next to him.

Because of the ceremony neither could speak and then suddenly it was over and Walter found himself moving with the other guests into the adjoining room where some guests were already preparing to leave. He thanked Mr. & Mrs.Reddy for inviting him then as he walked towards the door he saw Nirmala.

"Would you like to come for tea sometime?" she asked.

"Thank you. That would be very nice" Walter replied.

"I will send you an invitation" Nirmala said and before Walter could say anything else she had turned away and was edging her way through the other departing guests.

Every day for the next few weeks Walter waited for the mail to arrive but as time went by he was beginning to think Nirmala's suggestion of tea had been forgotten when the invitation from Mr. & Mrs. Rajan arrived. On opening it he discovered the invite was not for tea but for lunch in two weeks time at their house situated on the outskirts of a small town about half an hour's journey away on the road to Madras.

Two weeks later Walter was approaching the small town where the Rajan's lived and was looking for the house. He had set out in plenty of time and even though he had not driven particularly quickly it had only taken him just over half an hour. He lifted the invitation off the passenger seat and checked the address again but when he saw a house somewhat larger than the rest he guessed that would be the one. It was an exactly square double storey house it's walls rendered in white cement with verandahs protected by wooden rails on both the ground and upper floors. In front was a well tended garden through which a semi-circular drive led from two gates to the steps leading up to the verandah and the front entrance.

He turned into the drive and drove up to the house and was just getting out of the car as Nirmala appeared on the verandah to welcome him. After they had shaken hands she led him through a curtained doorway into a lounge the windows of which were shaded from the sun with net curtains. She indicated a chair and asked him if he would like a drink.

Thank you" he said "a lime juice or something like that would be very nice."

Nirmala rang a small handbell and when a servant arrived she spoke to him in Tamil and returned in a few minutes with two glasses on a silver tray. After the servant left she raised her glass.

"Thanks for coming" she said.

"Not at all. It is I who should thank you for inviting me" Walter replied. They sipped their drinks and talked about the wedding they had attended and Nirmala asked about the factories but as they talked Walter became increasingly aware that Nirmala's husband had not appeared.

"Is your husband not here?" Walter asked.

"Yes he is upstairs" Nirmala replied "but he is not very well. I suggested to him we should cancel lunch but he didn't want to as he was hoping he would be feeling better today.

"What is wrong with him? Is it serious? "Walter asked.

"I don't know" Nirmala replied. "The doctor doesn't tell me very much because my husband doesn't want him to but today he said it might be malaria, but I think it is more serious than that. Rajan said he wanted to see you but when I checked just before you arrived he was asleep. But now lunch is ready lets eat and then I will take you up to see him."

They ate lunch in the dining room and after coffee Nirmala said "Rajan might be awake now, shall we go and see?"

Walter followed Nirmala up the stairs and into the sparsely furnished room where in the faint light which filtered through the curtained window he could see her husband asleep on a bed under the window. There was a film of perspiration on his forehead and his breathing seemed to be rasping in his throat. Nirmala took a cloth from a bowl of water which she wrung out so she could wipe the perspiration from her husband's forehead. Walter felt a little embarrassed standing in the bedroom whilst Nirmala was tending her husband so he silently left and went back downstairs to the lounge where Nirmala joined him a few minutes later.

"I am sorry my husband is not well but as I said before he so wanted the lunch to go ahead."

For the next few minutes the conversation centred on Nirmala's husband and his illness but then drifted into inconsequential things until Walter decided to ask the question he had wanted to ask from the first moment he had met her.

"Why did you marry a man so much older than yourself?"

At first Nirmala didn't reply but just looked down at her hands as they folded and refolded a small white handkerchief.

"I didn't want to marry him" she said so quietly that Walter could hardly hear her "it was an arranged marriage. My husband owns the land in Ramuda on which my father's house is built and my father wanted to purchase it to avoid paying rent. One day Rajan came to collect the rents and he saw me. He was a widower with two sons older than I and when my father asked again about the land he said that if I became his wife he would give my father the land. It was obvious this was the only way my father would ever get it and also save money on my dowry he would have to pay if I married anyone else which he could then use to make suitable marriages for my two sisters. So he agreed even though he knew I didn't." For a few moments she sat silently looking down at her crumpled handkerchief then she lifted her eyes and looked directly at Walter.

"I never loved my husband and he has never loved me. All he ever wanted was to be able to show off to his friends."

Walter knew the story was most likely a true one. He had frequently heard of marriages like this which had been arranged for some purpose or other, usually financial, and very often between older men and much younger girls.

"I am very sorry" he said quietly, "it must be very difficult for you" and as he looked across at Nirmala he saw a tear run down her cheek.

"Please don't cry. I shouldn't have asked you about your husband like that" he walked across to the settee where she was sitting and sat down beside her taking her small hand in his and when she lifted her tear stained face and looked directly into his eyes, he did what he had wanted to do from the moment he had first seen her at the wedding and slowly lowered his mouth to hers. Immediately she placed her arm around his neck and held him tightly. It seemed as though they were together for hours but after only a few moments he lifted his mouth from hers and looked into her eyes. Now, through the tears, there was a deep smouldering gleam in her eyes which Nirmala tried to hide by lowering her long dark eyelashes. Walter forgot everything as he looked down at her beautiful face. He placed his arm round her waist, his hand coming into contact with her bare midriff above her sari and below her choli as he drew her towards him and kissed her more demandingly than before. Under the pressure from his mouth her lips parted and their tongues met. He had never experienced a kiss like this. Pulling her firm young body closer he could feel the swell of her breasts against his chest and as he stroked her bare arm it caused the folds of her sari to tumble from her shoulder. He raised his lips from her receptive mouth and looking down at her he removed his hand from under the folds of her sari and placed it on her breast. Continuing to kiss her he undid the front of her choli revealing her firm breasts. Almost as if he had previously instructed her Nirmala lent back to assist his searching mouth as he lowered his head to kiss each erect nipple before once again seeking her mouth.

In between each kiss they whispered to each other things which later neither would recall but at the time both welcomed and enjoyed. Walter tried to unpeel Nirmala's sari but without her help he wasn't very successful until she stood, put her hands to her waist and suddenly the sari dropped in folds at her feet and she stood before him wearing only a cotton muslin waist skirt. Walter reached out and putting his hands round her waist undid the string of the skirt and allowed it to fall to the floor. He looked at his companion now completely naked, waiting as if silently seeking his approval. His first reaction as he looked at her young body was the surprise at the lack of pubic hair and then, even through his excitement, he recalled someone had once told him that Indian women removed all their body hair.

He swept her into his arms kissing her repeatedly as he laid her on the long settee then quickly started to undress aware she was watching as he dropped his discarded clothing on the floor with hers. Quickly but gently he lay on top of the waiting Nirmala taking his weight on his forearms. Slowly at first they made love their tongues almost fighting each other as they kissed and then they were moving more frantically until with a moan Walter almost collapsed on his partners trembling body. Nirmala put her legs round his hips to try to prevent him from moving and for a few minutes they remained completely still their bodies covered in a sheen of perspiration their desires temporarily satiated until Walter got to his feet and Nirmala led him to the bathroom where they bathed together.

Over the next few weeks the lovers met whenever they could although it was always difficult and only possible if Mr. Rajan's sons were not at home and as long as he never got any better.

"Surely it is not malaria after all this time" Walter said during their most recent meeting. "There must be something more seriously wrong with him, hasn't the doctor said anything?"

"We have had another doctor here to see him but he didn't tell us anything except he will be back tomorrow with the results of some tests so perhaps we will know something then."

Three days later Walter received terrible news. It was mid morning when the office boy entered his office.

"Sir, there is a messenger outside who insists he must see you."

"What is it about?" Walter enquired.

"He won't tell anyone Sir. All he says is that he must see you and it is very important."

Intrigued, Walter agreed to see him. The office boy left and returned a few seconds later with a youth of about eighteen who walked straight across to the deesk and without speaking handed Walter a sealed envelope. Walter took it from him and turning it over looked at the address. It was certainly addressed to him but he didn't recognise the handwriting. Thinking it was a begging letter or something of the kind he almost handed it back to the messenger unopened but then changing his mind he tore open the envelope, took out a single sheet of paper and the first thing he saw was the signature "Nirmala." His heart leapt with pleasure and anticipation only to sink into despair as he read the letter.

"Walter Rajan died last night. His sons are here and have arranged for his cremation to take place tonight at six o'clock. They are insisting I commit suttee. Please please help me.

Nirmala."

As Walter read the letter again the word suttee seemed to jump off the page at him. He knew about suttee, the age old tradition where a wife, particularly a young wife would choose or be forced to be burned on the same cremation pyre as her dead husband because it was thought that with the death of her husband a wife's life was virtually over. If she lived she would have to wear plain often white saris, probably have to sleep on the floor and perform all the menial tasks in the house and certainly never be allowed to remarry. Besides being a financial drain the family believed the widow would bring bad luck so even though suttee was forbidden by the British authorities it was far more prevalent than they realised so never for a moment did Walter think the note was not genuine.

He stuffed the note into his pocket and looked at his watch. It was already leaving four thirty and before he could leave for Nirmala's house he would have to go to his bungalow to collect things he might need. He hurried from the office and rushed to his car and set off through the compound, out on to the main road whereby constant use of the horn he forced his way through the other road users. At the bungalow he rushed to his bedroom and from a drawer he took out a .38 revolver which he quickly loaded and shoved into the waist band of his trousers. Then from a cupboard he took out a twelve bore, double barrelled shotgun which he also loaded. He stuffed some extra cartridges and bullets into his pockets then ran back to the car and within a few minutes of his arrival was driving out through the compound gate.

At this time of day there was always a lot of traffic on the road. A few lorries but mainly convoys of bullock carts slowly meandering along the road, frequently with their drivers fast asleep making it almost impossible to travel at speed for any length of time. He glanced at his watch yet again. It was going to be touch and go but even if he was in time he didn't have a plan of what he would do.

In the distance he eventually saw the buildings of the town and then the bridge over the river came into view and decided there would not be enough time to get to Nirmala's house. Then he had an idea. The river ahead was the Cauvery one of the religious rivers of India so he knew the the burning ghats would be somewhere nearby so he decided that is where he would go. He crossed the bridge looking to see which side the ghats were on. To his right he couldn't see anything but to his left he saw a track going down to the river which disappeared behind some trees from where he saw a plume of smoke and decided that was where he would go. He turned the car round, made his way back across the bridge and then edged onto the little track. After about a quarter of a mile he rounded the trees he had seen from the road where the track opened out into a space where some people were gathered and where wisps of smoke were still rising from an earlier cremation and an unlit fire awaiting the next . Three of the largest trees were on the side furthest away from the river so that after turning the car for a quick getaway he parked in the shade of their overhanging branches and waited.

He didn't have to wait long. Above the noise of the traffic on the bridge he heard the beating of drums and the wailing of flutes and clarinets which grew louder as the funeral procession turned off the main road and came down the dirt track. The first to appear were the drummers and then the other musicians followed by men carrying a bamboo litter on which the body of a dead man dressed in white was being carried in a sitting position with a young boy standing by his side holding steady the deadman's head. As the procession approached the waiting pyre Walter could not be sure that the deadman was Rajan but then he saw his two sons, either supporting or holding Nirmala walking behind the litter.

Even now despite the desperate situation and the fear of what might happen Walter could not help thinking how beautiful Nirmala looked. As she got closer he could see that her hands and arms were brightly painted with bridal henna in sharp contrast to her plain white sari. Her face had a certain calm, almost a look of spiritual ecstasy because of the drug, probably opium, which must have been forced upon her. Some of the onlookers fell to their knees and tried to touch the hem of her sari in the belief that it would bring them good luck but Nirmala looked neither to the right nor to the left.

The procession came to a halt and two policemen who had accompanied it from the house stood to one side even though what was about to happen was against the law. While two of the men poured ghee onto the wood and the elder of Rajan's sons waited with a torch of twigs which he would light and then thrust into the pyre when the time was right, the dead man was lifted from the litter and placed on the pyre making sure there was sufficient space for Nirmala to sit with her husband's head on her lap.

Whilst these final preparations were going on the musicians were still playing but then suddenly the music changed and the Brahmin Priests began to intone their Sanskrit prayers and one of the brothers assisted by another man led Nirmala towards where her husband was waiting for their final embrace. The other brother lit the torch he was holding ready to light the funeral pyre as soon as Nirmala was in position and it was then as the music stopped that Walter who was now standing at the side of the car reached inside and took out the loaded shotgun and with the revolver in his other hand walked towards the still unlit fire. All eyes were on Nirmala and the men holding her so no-one noticed Walter until he was almost next to the son holding the torch and even if they had they would not have understood what a lone European was doing at the funeral. When Walter placed the revolver against the man's right ear who started to turn but stopped when he saw the weapon out of the corner of his eye. Walter leaned forward so his mouth was near the man's ear.

"Don't move. Do you understand? Don't move" . The man was transfixed "Tell your family to release the woman or I will shoot you." Rajan's son hesitated so Walter pushed the barrel of the revolver harder against his ear and cocked the trigger.

Fortunately for Walter it was just beginning to go dark and most of the crowd were to the left of him which meant in the gloom they could not see the revolver.

"Tell your brother to bring the woman here immediately" he growled.

Now Walter was in a fix. Except for a few words he didn't understand Tamil so was dependent on the man being frightened enough to do as he was told and not shout for help. The priests were silent now waiting to chant the final prayers as soon as the fire was lit, likewise the musicians were waiting for the final act of the ceremony to begin. Walter pushed the gun even harder against the younger brother's ear and suddenly he called out.

Walter thought he heard the words "inge va" which he knew meant come here but he didn't know if he was calling for help or asking for Nirmala to be brought to him so Walter lifted the shotgun so that the man could see that as well as feel the revolver which caused him to call out more urgently than before.

"Secrum, Secrum . Quickly, quickly."

Turning and seeing the plight of his brother being held by Walter the one holding Nirmala, who was just about to put her on the waiting fire, said something to the other man holding her and together half carrying and half dragging her because of the drugs she had been given followed Walter and his prisoner as they backed towards the passenger side of the car.

Suddenly the crowd realised something was wrong and they were not about to see someone commit suttee which meant the good luck which they thought would be manifested on them would now surely turn into bad luck so urged on by two or three of their more vociferous members they started to move forward.

Walter raised the shotgun, rested it on the roof of the car then aiming well above the advancing crowd he squeezed the trigger. The twelve bore shook in his hand but in the enclosed space the noise was tremendous. Instantly the crowd fell back, those in the front trying to get to the rear and none of them moving more quickly than the two policemen who had been moving forward with them. The elder brother who had the revolver in his ear collapsed in a dead faint thinking he had been shot. The crows that had been nesting in the trees shrieked as they took off and the two bullocks in the shafts of a waiting cart bolted creating even more mayhem.

Just before he had fired the shotgun the men holding Nirmala had placed her in the front seat of the car so in the confusion Walter checked the passenger door was shut then raced round to the drivers side, threw the shotgun on the floor near Nirmala's legs climbed in and thankful he had had the presence of mind to keep the engine running slammed the car into gear. The crowd still seemed totally stunned and it was only when he started up the track towards the main road that they started to give chase but they were too late and very soon Walter was turning on to the road leaving them and the stones they had started to throw far behind.

Once up to speed he felt safe enough to put down the unused revolver and to glance across at Nirmala who was slumped in the seat her head on her chest as if she was sleeping. Not yet daring to stop he reached across and tried to pull her into a more comfortable position and it was only when he spoke to her that he realised that even though her eyes were open she had no idea what was happening.

When he pulled up outside his bungalow and reached forward with shaking hands to switch off the engine that he considered the enormity of what he had done. Michael, the butler, heard the car arrive and came running out. When he saw Nirmala slumped in the front seat his mouth dropped open and he was even more dumfounded when Walter lifted her out of the car and carried her up the bungalow steps, straight into his bedroom and put her on the bed. Then whilst retrieving his weapons from the car in case he might need them, he gave Michael a very abridged version of what had happened. As he told his story he walked across to the drinks tray and poured his first drink since meeting Nirmala.

Carrying his glass he walked across to the verandah rails and looked out in the direction of the road beyond and wondered how long it might be before any "visitors" turned up but as it was now completely dark he decided it would most probably only be the following day. His thought were disturbed by Michael returning with a tea tray which he placed on the verandah table. Walter thanked him poured out two cups which he carried to the bedroom.

Nirmala was beginning to recover and asked Walter what had happened. When he had finished explaining to her she expressed great anxiety for both of them. "Its getting dark now" he said "but even so I have not heard anything but I am sure I will be able to take care of anything now that you are safe" he said in a voice which sounded far more confident than he felt.

Next day after lunch they were sitting on the verandah when Walter saw a familiar figure walking up the drive. The tall red turbaned Jemal Singh, the Subhadar in charge of the guards at the factories, came up the garden path and when he saw Walter he came to a halt and saluted.

"Good afternoon Subhadar" Walter said, "Has something happened?"

"There have been two men at the factory demanding to see you Sir."

"Do you know who they are?" Walter asked as he led the tall khaki figure clad on to the verandah. Lowering his voice the guard commander said "They say they are the sons of this lady's husband Sir and they are demanding to see you. I told them you were not in your office and after some argument they left but I think it will not be long before they come here."

"I'll be ready if they do come" Walter said showing Jemal Singh the revolver he was still carrying from the night before. "But thanks for the warning." He reached out for the small handbell on the table used to summon the butler.

"Would you like a coffee or something before you go back to the factory."

"Thank you Sir" the guard commander said "but if it is alright with you I think it might be better if I stayed here for a little while just in case those two do turn up but I will have a coffee thank you very much."

Whilst they were talking, Singh, very much the product of the Indian Army had been standing to attention until Walter invited him to sit down.

Turning to Nirmala he suggested she should go to the bedroom so that if her stepsons did come to the bungalow they wouldn't see her. At first it was as if Nirmala was about to protest but then with a smile of thanks to Jemal Singh she made her way to the bedroom.

Singh sat in a position where he could see anyone entering the compound and even whilst he was drinking he never took his eyes off the main gate. Suddenly Walter saw him stiffen and they both watched as two men walked down the main drive of the compound, stop and talk to a gardener working in one of the gardens who, after a moment, pointed in the direction of Walter's bungalow.

The two men opened the gate and walked up the path unaware, because of the bougainvillaea growing near the verandah that Walter and Singh had been watching them from the moment they entered the compound. When they were only a couple of strides from the steps Walter, his right hand holding the revolver behind his back and Singh walked to the top of the steps.

"What do you want? What are you doing here?" Walter demanded in a loud voice.

One of the two stepped forward and when he did Walter recognized him as the man he had threatened with the revolver the night before.

"You have my father's wife here. She must return with us."

"If I have why should I hand her over to you when all you want is to murder her?"

"We did not try to murder her. It was her wish to commit suttee to become a goddess and help her husband in the afterlife."

"Suttee is illegal. It is forbidden and what you were trying to do was nothing less than murder." Walter replied. "Your father's widow will never agree to return to his house."

The arguments went back and forth with the two brothers arguing that the law against suttee could be disregarded as it was a British Law and didn't matter.

Jemal Singh stepped forward and Walter stopped arguing quite prepared to let the guard commander act on his behalf because it was fairly obvious that the Sikh could probably intimidate the two men far more than he could. Singh looked down at the two for a few seconds and then in his deep bass voice said something in Tamil. The two answered and there followed a conversation lasting about five minutes the three shaking their heads in agreement about some things and obviously disagreeing about others whilst Walter waited impatiently. It always seemed to take ages to discuss things in Tamil but he knew Singh would eventually tell him what it was all about.

Slowly the tone of the conversation changed and the two brothers started to move their heads from side to side something Indians did when they were agreeing or saying yes. Singh turned to Walter.

"I have pointed out to them that their father has already been cremated it is too late for his wife to commit suttee so now we have arrived at what they are really worried about, their inheritance. If their father had died before their real mother there would have been no problem but because he has died leaving a young widow they know their chances of getting anything when she dies are very remote and, in any case, they may die before her. At first they wanted the family wealth to be divided between them but now they agree to it being shared between them and their father's widow providing she gives up all rights to the family home for which in return she can keep all the jewellery her husband gave her."

"It seems a good idea to me" Walter said quietly "I'll go and ask Mrs. Rajan if she is satisfied with that arrangement."

He walked to the bedroom where Nirmala was standing inside the door trying, unsuccessfully to hear what was happening. Taking her hands in his Walter told her what had been discussed.

"Oh Walter that would be marvellous" Nirmala said. "As long as I am left in peace they can have the house but how do I know that at some later date they won't want something else from me and what about yesterday?

They could still go to the police and report you."

"Nirmala, wait. That will not happen. They dare not go to the police because suttee is illegal. I didn't kidnap you I saved your life and if they don't report me who will? Certainly not the two police constables who were prepared to standby and do nothing. No the worst that can happen is that I would be charged for letting off a firearm in a public place and that would only be a small fine. As for Rajan's sons coming back at a later date Singh has told them that any agreement must be drawn up by a solicitor."

A few days later when Walter was at the factory an elderly man arrived at the bungalow asking to see Mrs. Rajan. When Nirmala came out on to the verandah she was confronted by someone she had never seen before. He was very thin and wore wire framed glasses. The end of his dhoti had been pulled between his legs and up to his waist where it was tucked into his belt. Under a dark blue jacket, which at one time must have been part of a suit, he was wearing a shirt and tie and on his feet he was wearing pale blue socks pulled part way up his scrawny calves and brown leather shoes. In order to raise his hands in the usual greeting he had first to hook a furled umbrella he was carrying over one arm and placed his leather brief case on the floor.

"I am Mr. Rajasabhai Pillai I am a lawyer and have been asked by the sons of the late Mr. Rajan to draw up an agreement between them and Mr. Rajan's widow, erm, yourself." With a movement of her arm Nirmala indicated to Mr. Pillai to come up on to the verandah and led the way to the chairs and table where they sat facing each other. Mr. Pillai placed his umbrella on the floor and while Nirmala sat patiently waiting undid the straps of his briefcase and after rummaging inside drew out the papers he wanted.

"This is an agreement I have drawn up in accordance with discussions I have had with the two sons of the late Mr. Rajan and then with Mr. Brent. If you would be so kind as to read it, and if you agree, sign it I can arrange for the transfer of the property to them and the necessary money and jewellery to yourself."

At first Nirmala was afraid that the brothers would have tried someway to alter the terms they had verbally agreed but by the time she had finished reading she was agreeably surprised to discover the agreement was exactly as Walter had explained it to her after he had met the brothers in Mr. Pillai's office.

"If I sign this now when will the agreement be effected?" Nirmala asked.

"As you can see madam the other parties have already signed so it only needs your signature. If you sign now I will go back to town and have it notarised. If I can get this done today then the agreement is effective from today."

"How will I know if it has been authorised?" Nirmala asked.

"I will return tomorrow morning to take you to the bank to obtain your share of your late husband's money and also collect any jewellery that maybe lodged at the bank. Then we will go to the house so you can collect your clothes or anything else that is yours."

"But how do I know that the brothers have not already been to the bank and the house and taken some of the money or even all of it already?" she asked.

"Madam. I would not be party to any agreement if anything like that had happened. I can assure you that the bank accounts have not been touched and I believe all your jewellery is safe but only you can verify that when we go to the house." If after we have been to the house and bank and everything is not to your satisfaction then the police will be involved as per Section 10." He said and leaned forward to show Nirmala the relevant section in the agreement.

After a few more questions Nirmala took the pen that Mr. Pillai offered and signed her name bringing to an end her contact with the Rajan family. The solicitor returned the signed document to his brief case and told her he would let Mr. Brent know as soon as the document had been notorised. He picked up his brief case and umbrella which immediately he was out of the garden gate he opened to protect himself against the heat of the sun and Nirmala watched him walk towards the main road his seemingly large shoes raising little puffs of red dust with every stride.

Next day Mr. Pillai called at Walter's office to tell him he had made an appointment at the bank and suggested that after they had been there they could go to Mrs. Rajan's old house to collect her possessions. At the bank Nirmala and Walter watched as Mr. Pillai made sure that the account of her late husband had been meticulously divided and her share placed in a new account. Once all the formalities had been completed they went to Nirmala's old house where Walter waited whilst she and the lawyer went inside. When they eventually came out Nirmala was carrying a small box containing her jewellery followed by two servants carrying suitcases containing her clothes and other items she wanted which they placed in the car.

They thanked Mr. Pillai for his excellent help and though they offered to take him back to his office he declined saying he had to wait for the brothers to complete their side of the agreement.

On the way back to the bungalow Walter and Nirmala discussed what they thought the future had in store for them. They both appreciated that what they would like to do would not be accepted by either the European or the Indian community particularly if and when the story spread about how Walter had prevented a religious ceremony from taking place despite the fact that the ceremony was an illegal one.

6

The next few months were probably the happiest Walter had ever known despite acknowledging the fact that soon there could be problems. He was well aware that many people, both Indian as well as European, would not be happy with the idea of a European living with an Indian and that before long someone would delight in telling his uncle what his nephew was doing in Melur.

Meantime Walter looked forward to going to work each day but even more importantly the staff at the factories were happier and whether it was because of this or not, even the production of the factories was better. But although he was happy at work he looked forward to returning home, not to an empty lonely bungalow and another bottle of whisky, but to Nirmala and a place of happiness and love where together they talked and laughed, their unhappy pasts almost forgotten. In the evenings, while it was still light, they would walk in the garden where Nirmala tried to teach him the Tamil names of the trees and flowers. In the evenings they sat next to each other on the verandah watching the sun slowly sinking below the horizon turning the sky from blue to pink then dark red, the last rays tinting it all the colours of the rainbow before disappearing into the velvety blackness of the night. This display was always accompanied by the noisy twittering of the birds as they settled in their roosting places for the night and only falling silent when the sun finally disappeared.

Instead of dressing for dinner and sitting in a stuffy dining room as was the custom of many Europeans Walter and Nirmala dined on the verandah by the light of a single lamp placed as far away as possible to attract insects away from where they were sitting.

Occasionally they were invited to dinner by the other Europeans who worked at the factories and just as occasionally they would reciprocate but they were happiest when they were alone just talking and holding hands in the semi darkness with Walter, who now never had more than one drink enjoying a whisky and soda which Nirmala always poured.

They had been together for less than six months when one day Walter, who was in the factory was told by one of the office boys who had been sent to find him that two "Masters" had arrived. Instantly he knew he was in trouble. He had been expecting it and was surprised it had not blown up before now. As he entered his office he expected to see his cousin George and someone else but certainly not George and Uncle Andrew.

"Good morning Uncle Andrew" he said and turning to his cousin "Good morning George".

Only George returned the greeting as Walter sat down at his desk.

"I have heard some very disturbing news" his Uncle snapped "is it true?"

Walter looked at his cousin but there was no help there so he looked back at his uncle.

"I don't know if anything is true until you tell me what you have heard."

Uncle Andrew almost choked trying to regain control of himself.

"You know damn well what I am talking about. This damned Indian girl. A white girl would have been bad enough but a bloody Indian girl."

Walter jumped to his feet.

"This damned girl" he shouted. "this damned girl you don't know anything about her."

"I know you are living with her" Uncle Andrew almost exploded "you can't do that."

"Who says I can't" Walter shouted back. "You? Well I am and I will continue."

"And how do you think you will do that?" his Uncle asked his voice getting even louder. "There will be no job for you here. You know the rules better than anyone. You're father would have told you just the same had he been alive, he would not have allowed it anymore than I." He paused for breath and in a quieter voice he said

"From today, from this moment you no longer work for Ramuda Textiles. We cannot employ someone who goes around shooting at people and then kidnapping Indian girls so that he can live with them. You're finished." From his pocket he took an envelope which he threw on the desk.

"There is some money. You can do what you want with it. Theres also a ticket for the Stratheden leaving Bombay in a months time I suggest you be on it."

Walter tried to speak, to tell his uncle what had really happened but Andrew Brent would not be interrupted.

"I don't want to hear what you have to say. You know the Company Rules. You can't live with a woman without being married and certainly not an Indian or Anglo Indian whether you are married or not so I suggest you had better get back to England and start again because no other company in India will want you after this ".

For a moment he sat looking at his nephew, his anger replaced by a look of sadness and then softly, almost to himself he said "That's the end of it."

Without waiting for any reply Andrew Brent walked out of the office leaving the two cousins just looking at one another.

"I'm sorry" George said eventually "I tried to talk him out of it. I asked him to give you another chance but he wouldn't hear of it. He said your father was more against this sort of thing than he is and would certainly not have let you carry on as you have been doing. And then there are the Indians. You know as well as I, they don't like this sort of thing. They won't even marry out of their own caste never mind a European so what do you think our customers will think?" Walter gave a short laugh.

"So that's it. If we were not in business and dependent on our customers it wouldn't matter. Its not a question of morals it's a question of business.

"Come on Walter you know your father would have reacted just the same whether there were customers or not". George said.

"So what happens now?" Walter said quietly.

"Well father has decided he will go back to Ramuda and I will stay here to make sure that you and your friend leave as soon as possible."

"I can't be ready to leave in less than week but I will clear my desk now so I won't have to come back to the office again."

Whilst he was getting his personal possessions together he thought about the situation he was in. He had no job and he knew his uncle was right, he wouldn't get another job in India as news of what had happened would travel around other British companies very quickly, so the only course of action was to go back to England. But what about Nirmala? He couldn't take her back to England to an uncertain future and most likely the same prejudices as those of his uncle. That wouldn't be fair.

But what will happen to her after he left?

He gathered up all the things he wanted to take and without saying goodbye to anyone, carried them out to his car. Slowly he drove out of the compound for the last time only stopping at the gate when he saw the tall figure of Jemal Singh coming out of the gatehouse.

"I'm leaving today and I will not be coming back" Walter said holding out his hand through the open window.

"I just want to say thank you again for your help." Jemal Singh looked down sadly at Walter from under his blue turban as he took hold of his hand. He had guessed there was going to be trouble when he saw the Chairman and his son arrive earlier.

"Good luck Sir" he said "I am very sorry you are leaving". Then standing back he came to attention and saluted.

With a nod of acknowledgement Walter returned the salutes of the two guards at the gate which also served as his goodbye to Ramuda Textiles.

When he drew up at the bungalow Nirmala appeared at the top of the steps. She knew something must be wrong because Walter never came home at this time of day. The butler, without his turban, also came running round the end of the bungalow. He had been about to have his afternoon nap as he usually did when he heard the car arrive. Walter handed him the two boxes he had brought from the office and followed him as he carried them into the bungalow.

"Whats the matter?" Is something wrong? Nirmala asked.

Walter shook his head and taking her hand he led her across to the two chairs on the verandah. When she was sitting down he told her about the arrival of his uncle and what had happened.

Her eyes, which at first were wide with anxiety, slowly filled and then overflowed with tears. This was something she had been afraid of when she had first moved into the bungalow but which as time passed had become less of a worry but now was a reality. Walter put his arm around her slender shoulders which were shaking with uncontrollable sobbing.

"Why do you have to return to Britain?" she stammered between the sobbing her voice hardly louder than a whisper.

"I have to because nobody will employ me here." He replied. "Wherever I go they will know who I am and if they don't they will ask where I worked before, make enquiries, ask for references and that will be the end of it, no job. But the most important thing is what will you do when I leave. Where will you go?"

"I want to be with you. I want you to stay" Nirmala sobbed.

"I know you do and I want to stay with you. There is nothing in all the world I want more but without work I cannot look after you. Where would we live? How would we manage?"

For the rest of the evening they sat on the verandah discussing many different things they thought they might be able to do but then one by one discarding them because they realised that none of them were practical.

By the time Michael came to light the lamps they both knew, although neither would put it into words, that very soon their life together would soon be coming to an end probably for ever.

Michael served dinner in the dining room but neither felt like eating and in a short time they returned to the verandah where Nirmala poured coffee.

They sat silently holding hands watching the nearly full moon climb through the branches bougainvillaea which was entwined round the roof supports, the silence only broken by the croaking of frogs in the undergrowth. Eventually Walter held out his hand to help Nirmala to her feet and with their arms entwined they walked to the bedroom where a single oil lamp was burning. Walter took Nirmala into his arms and kissed her upturned face, her eyes, the tip of her nose and eventually her ever ready lips their flickering shadows thrown on to the white walls. Eventually he pulled her acquiescent body closer to his and felt the swell of her breasts against his chest and then her hands undoing the buttons of his shirt which he pulled over his head. He kicked off his shoes removed the rest of his clothes and sat on the edge of the bed watching Nirmala as her body emerged from the yards of material of her sari and then when it was removed turned to him removing her choli and her waist skirt which she allowed to fall with the discarded sari before standing naked in front of him. As he looked at her in open admiration she raised her arms out to him offering her body for his pleasure, her tears running down her face dropping from her chin to fall like dew on her upturned breasts. To hide his own tears Walter stood and reached out for her and when she took the two paces towards him he silently took her in his arms, lifted her onto the bed, climbed in beside her before pulling down the mosquito net.

A month later Walter was a lonely figure watching the coastline of India as it slowly disappeared over the horizon. Not only had he lost Nirmala he was also being forced, by his own family, to leave the country of his birth. Even when the coastline had finally disappeared he still stood thinking of the events of the last few weeks. Nirmala had returned to live with her father who now owned a little business in, of all places, Ramuda. She knew that her father knew her husband had died but nothing about what her stepsons had tried to do nor about Walter and as her late husband's family were unlikely to ever contact her she was confident he would never find out.

Walter smiled as he remembered the argument that had occurred on their last night together when he offered Nirmala the money he had received from his uncle. She had become very angry and had started to cry saying she wasn't a prostitute who had to be paid. He felt the pleasure all over again as he recalled how he had taken her in arms and kissed away her tears telling her she was being ridiculous and insisted she keep the money in case of any trouble between her and her father. She had still refused arguing that the jewellery and cash she had received after he had rescued her was enough but in the end he had persuaded her to take it along with a little package which he told her not to open until she was settled in Ramuda.

Strangely another very recent memory came to him. When he was boarding in Bombay there had been a lot of relatives and friends waving goodbye to some of the passengers and his eye had been caught by a woman with a young boy who was waving madly to everyone. Walter, who had no-one to see him off, waved back which made the little boy wave even more enthusiastically.

Walking to his cabin he knew, that although he had promised Nirmala to return to India as soon as possible, he would never see her or India again. But strangely, as he went to bed that night, his memories of Nirmala and India were coupled with that of the little boy waving as the "Stratheden" left the dockside.

7

Corporal 'Wally' Brent handed three unsealed letters to the corporal in the company office. They had to be unsealed so they could be censored to ensure that the people at home did not learn too much from their loved ones about the horrors of the Western Front. As the |Orderly Corporal took the letters he simply glanced at the addresses and then without comment added them to the others waiting for the Adjutant whose job it was to read and censor if necessary. He looked up at Walter and said something but although Walter could see his lips moving he could not make out what he was saying because of the heavy artillery which was banging away as it had been for the last week thankful at least that the noise meant that allied shells were going out and not German shells coming in.

He went out of the heavily sandbagged dugout that served as the office and back down the trenches to where his platoon was positioned. He leant against the wall and propped his Lee Enfield rifle between himself and one of the many short ladders which were spaced out along the length of the trench. On either side of him were men of his platoon, men who had volunteered at the same time as himself and all members of the same 'Pals Battalion'. He lit a cigarette aware that as long as the guns fired and the shells whistled overhead he was safe but when they stopped then he would have to lead his platoon up that damned ladder. Walter glanced at his watch. It was nearly five in the morning and although it was still not fully light it already promised to be a fine, warm day. Walter smiled grimly. It needed to be for what was planned for this first day of July.

The Allied High Command had decided, in their wisdom, that July the first would be the first day of the battle that would end the war with Germany so for the last seven days the artillery had been pounding the German trenches twenty four hours a day.

Every gun possible had been used and more than a million shells of various sizes had been aimed at the enemy trenches so that by the time the British attacked, the Germans would either be dead or too dazed to offer any resistance as the British Army advanced. He looked up and down the trench and wondered just how many of the men, who like himself were nervously waiting for the order to attack, would still be alive in twelve hours time.

As he puffed at his cigarette his thoughts drifted back to what had happened since he left India. On his arrival in England he had made his way to Liverpool to contact a friend who he had met at college and who worked for a firm of Cotton Brokers on the Cotton Exchange. On the day he went to see him the firm had just received some samples of Indian cottons and as none of their staff had much experience of them they asked Walter to look at them. The samples were very similar to the cottons he had been using at Melur and so he was able to give them a very competent appraisal indicating the yarns for which this cotton was suitable along with an idea of their strength and the waste percentage to be expected.

He was also able to advise them of other Indian cottons as well as their expected prices.

The company had been very impressed and offered him a job so that by using his knowledge and experience they would not only be able to offer alternative, cheaper cottons, but also technical advice if there were any production problems.

Walter accepted the job and rented a house in Blundell Sands one of the better residential areas of Liverpool but then his life was about to change again.

In 1914 war broke out, Great Britain and France against Germany a war that was to cost the lives of millions of young men. In late 1915 in response to a massive recruitment campaign some of Walter's friends and colleagues from the Cotton Exchange and the insurance companies responded to the posters of Lord Kitchener pointing his finger at them with the caption "Your Country Needs You" and, in what he could only describe as a fit of madness Walter also volunteered.

After a very basic training the recruits were sent to their companies where they were received by young Company Commanders recruited from the universities and colleges and who had not received much more training than they had. The biggest shortage in the Army, however, was not privates nor officers but non-commissioned officers so that the first task was to find people who had been foremen or some sort of manager and if they liked the look of them promote them to corporal on the spot which was exactly how Private "Wally" Brent became Corporal "Wally" Brent. Lighting another cigarette he thought about the letters he had just handed in for posting, the first one was to a lawyer in Liverpool confirming instructions he had left with him that in the event of his death details of his Will were to be sent to Mr. Ghosh in India which brought on thoughts about his son who he had never seen and probably would never see.

The second letter was addressed to Mr. Ghosh giving him the address of the lawyer in England who he must contact if he had not heard either from the lawyer or himself at the end of the war and finally the third letter to his mother who lived in Harrogate and who, since the happenings in India, had cut him out of her life, trying once again to explain and apologise for what had happened.

His thoughts were interrupted and for a few moments he couldn't understand what had happened until he realised he could hear a bird singing and that apart from that there was complete silence. The guns which had been pounding out their message of death and destruction for the past week were silent. Now it was time for the infantry and he reached out for his rifle.

Up and down the lattice of trenches whistles blew and the men, led by their N.C.Os like Walter climbed up the ladders and out over the parapet of sandbags.

July 1ˢᵗ, 1916, had fulfilled its promise. It was a beautiful Summer's day as the Liverpool Pals, the Accrington Pals and the other volunteer battalions advanced across no-mans land. They didn't run. The High Command had told them there was no need for that because the artillery barrage would have killed off the enemy in their trenches. Just walk out in the sunlight and occupy the enemy trenches. Two or three hundred yards away the German Infantry, who had burrowed deep in their trenches throughout the barrage from the British guns and consequently hadn't suffered many casualties now came out of their shelters and took their places on the firing steps. When they looked out over the sights of their rifles and machine guns they couldn't believe it. The first on the firing steps called out.

"They are coming! Hurry! They are coming". In a mad flurry the others grabbed their weapons and waited for the command "open fire".

The generals who had planned the British attack secretly thought their troops were insufficiently trained to charge and as they thought there would be no, or little resistance insisted they advance at walking pace so on this summer's day the British volunteer battalions slowly advanced across no man's land. As the advancing khaki line neared the German trenches the troops were just beginning to believe their officers when they heard commands being shouted in the German trenches followed by the awful patter of machine guns and the barking sound of hundreds of rifles followed by the sight of their comrades falling around them. There was no cover for the advancing troops and few of them ever reached the 1st line of the barbed wire defences which, according to the plan, should have been destroyed by the artillery barrage but the few that did could not get over the barbed wire and were cut down in the bright morning sunlight.

Walter, his rifle held across his chest was leading his platoon forward. There was nothing to shoot at when he suddenly heard the noise of the German rifles and the men to his left started to fall and he saw the red patches staining their tunics. Gaps started to appear in the lines of advancing men but even as they grew larger the remainder still tried to advance urged on by the few junior officers who were still standing. Walter advanced another few strides and then he felt this hammer blow in his chest followed immediately by another and he fell mid stride, dead before he hit the ground his rifle still unfired by his side.

On this day the first of July out of an attacking force of 160,000 men who set out from the British trenches 60,000 were shot of which 40,000 were killed outright. Even though the Germans held their fire from the stretcher bearers many of the wounded died were they fell, in shell craters or hanging on the barbed wire crying for help which sometimes never came whilst many that the stretcher bears did reach died later in their own trenches.

Even though the infantry suffered such appalling casualties this did not deter the High Command and more and more troops, many from the Empire, were ordered up the ladders of death which meant that when the battle was finally terminated more than 420,000 British and Empire troops had been killed without any tactical advance having been made.

8

Ramuda 1921

George Brent knocked on the door of his Father's office where his Father was checking the previous day's delivery figures the first thing he did every morning. As George walked in he looked up.

"Good morning George" he said and pointing to the book in front of him "The deliveries are not looking too good this month".

"I don't think you have need to worry father" George replied. "We still have some despatches to make to our agents in the South and when they are completed I think you will find our figures for the month will be about the same as usual. I looked at the figures for 1911 yesterday and compared with then our sales are up by about 5%. I think you are comparing them with what it was like during the war and I agree we are not doing as well as then, but like most other firms in India we're doing much better than before the war mainly because imports are much less."

Andrew Brent nodded slowly.

"Yes, I suppose you are right." He paused before he went on. "It must be hell in Lancashire now their exports have been reduced. I was reading in the latest newspapers from home that there had been a lot of short time there now."

George nodded in agreement but having been born in India and lived there all his life he didn't have the same feeling for the English cotton industry as his father.

Andrew sat back in his chair and removed his spectacles placing them on the desk in front of him and then rubbing his eyes with both hands.

"Speaking of Lancashire your mother and I were talking last night and we have come to a decision" he paused. "You know we have been talking about retiring and returning to England well last night we made up our minds. We think it is time for us to go back home."

George looked across at his father. He saw a suntanned face, lined because of his years in the tropics, topped with grizzly salt and peppered coloured hair already white at the temples and although he was still a tall upright man who still played a little tennis George knew his father was not as strong as he had been only a couple of years ago and although he went to the office very day was not as keen about the business as he used to be.

"I wondered when you were going to tell me this" George said and before his father could reply he continued, "I don't mean I think you should retire but I know you have been thinking about it because Mother has been talking to Rose so it's not a huge surprise. Have you decided when you want to go."

"Well we are not going to hang about now we have decided. We want to arrive in England when the winter is over so if we leave here in a couple of month's time not only will it be warmer when we arrive we will also miss the very hot weather here so the next couple of months will give us time for you and I to go round all the factories for the last time."

George was naturally sad that his mother and father were leaving but at the same time he was looking forward to the challenge of being Chairman. But tempering this anticipation was the knowledge that some things would be different. For instance for the first time there would only be one member of the Brent family at the helm of Ramuda Textiles and his thoughts turned to his cousin Walter and the part he would have played. Even though he and Walter had been very different in temperament he had to acknowledge there had been a bond between them and he felt again some of the sadness he had felt when the news came from home that he had been killed on the Somme.

During the next few weeks George and his Father visited every branch of the Company where, without exception the management and staff arranged ceremonies in honour of the retiring Chairman.

The final stop of the tour was at a small ginnery but the ceremony was no different from the ones at the largest factory.

Andrew and George were presented with garlands made of fresh flowers entwined with gold and silver threads followed by long speeches in Tamil eulogising the work of the Brent family and Andrew in particular which then had to be translated into English which seemed to take forever. When this was over the oldest serving Maistry stepped forward and presented Andrew with a farewell gift, this time, a silver tray engraved with images of both the Goddess of Health and the Goddess of Wealth.

Although Andrew had been Chairman for many years he still didn't like making speeches but now because of the occasion he found it very difficult and it was with a slight tremor in his voice that he thanked all the workers and staff for their gift and good wishes and in turn wished them well for the future.

Later, sitting in the back of the large Wolseley tourer, his father gently dozing by his side, George thought about some of the changes the company had made over the years. The biggest had been brought about by the completion of a dam across the river Cauvery upstream of Ramuda, the turbines of which provided electricity for the surrounding area with enough being supplied to Ramuda Textiles to enable New Mill to be converted to electric power and for electricity to be connected to the bungalows of the European staff who as well as lighting now had refrigerators and electric fans.

He looked out at the countryside as the large car sped along. Even transport was different. The company now owned several cars and this, along with the improvement of the roads, although frequently only two strips of tarmacadam, meant staff could move about the organisation more quickly and tours like the one he and his father had just undertaken could be completed in a fraction of the time it used to take.

In the distance he saw a cloud of dust which was quickly coming nearer and George recognised as one belonging to N.V.R. a company which was owned by Verasamy Rajan who used to own a shop outside the factory gates at Ramuda.

A few years ago he had approached Andrew for a loan in order to buy his first lorry which he had quickly repaid and which subsequently become the first of a fleet of lorries which serviced industry all over Southern India but in particular Ramuda. What Andrew and George did not know was that the "N" in the firms name was Nirmala the daughter of Verasamy Rajan that "damned woman" as Andrew once called her and who, in his eyes, was the cause of the death of Walter in France.

Next day Andrew accompanied by his son and their wives as well as all the European and Indian staff and all the workers from the two big factories attended his final presentation. The ceremony was held on a dais which had been specially erected between the two factories he and his brother had built when they first came to India. As the ceremony progressed his mind raced back over the years and he recalled many of the successes and disappointments he and his brother had overcome or enjoyed until as the ceremony drew to a close his memories faded to be replaced with a feeling of sadness as it came home to him that this occasion marked the end of his life in a country he had come to love so very much.

Next morning the servants both past and present as well as all the compound workers were gathered round the company's Wolseley Tourer as the luggage was being loaded. Inside the bungalow Rose and Ethel were crying in each others arms as they said goodbye. Eventually Andrew gently took hold of his wife's shoulders and gently separated her from her daughter-in-law.

"Come along dear, we want to be in Madras before dark". Ethel kissed Rose on the cheek once more and as she picked up her handbag she said with a wan smile "Give my love to Philip tell him we look forward to seeing him when he comes to England to go to school."

"I'll tell him" Rose said through her tears "I know he is going to miss you and his grandfather ."

George picked up his mother's small vanity case which was to go with her into the car and as he did so his father leaned forward to kiss his daughter-in-law goodbye then as he turned to follow his wife out to the car George saw his father wipe away a surreptitious tear from his lined face.

When they appeared the dozen or so waiting people pressed forward all trying to touch the departing couple in order to wish them God's speed. Tears started afresh when Ethel spotted her old ayah who had cared for George from the day he was born until he went away to school and who must have journeyed 10 miles from her native village to see her "Madam" one last time and came forward her hands pressed together in greeting and holding a single flower.

"Namaste Madam" she said through her tears.

Ethel put her arms round the thin shoulders of the sobbing woman and held her close. "Thank you for coming all this way. I'm so pleased to see you."

In the meantime Andrew was saying goodbye to the other servants, one a gardener who had always been a kindly old rogue with whom Andrew had had lots of trouble in the past but nevertheless had come to see his old "Master" one last time. Slowly Ethel made her way to the open door of the car where George had to take a gentle hold of his old ayah and force his mother's arm from her grasp so that his mother could get into the car and at the same time prevent the old woman climbing in with her. Eventually the car was able to move forward very slowly at first until with a blast from its horn it turned out of the garden gate and increasing speed drove down the drive of the compound past the other bungalows whose occupants and servants were stood waving at their garden gates.

Passing the factory compound the car slowed down allowing Andrew to acknowledge, for the last time, the salute of the Jemedar and the factory guards before driving through the crowded streets. Once through the town the driver increased speed only slowing as they passed through the small villages where people still stopped what they were doing to watch the rare sight of a passing motor car. The children waved with excitement but in one of the villages there was one fatherless little boy who didn't.

This little boy's mother Bonesseri told him nearly every day how important it was for him to go to school and although she had to start so early that she could never see him off he never failed to attend. He and his mother had seen this car before and she had told him who it belonged to and although he didn't know everything about his father's death he knew that the family who owned the car were responsible.

Yes, P.K. Ramanathan certainly knew who this car belonged to and he didn't wave.

Two days later after the overnight train journey to Bombay and an overnight stay at the Taj Mahal Hotel Andrew and his wife were standing on the deck of the ship which was to take them back to England. Among the crowd of spectators who came to the port to see the ship sail was Eunice Williams and her son Paul who always insisted his mother bring him whenever a ship was leaving. This was probably because Eunice was always telling him that one day he would go to England to complete his education although she had no idea how she would be able to afford this. But because of the little knowledge she had of Paul's father she was determined Paul was going to England to study textiles and work for Ramuda Textiles which might give him an opportunity to claim what rightfully was his.

"One day you could be on one of those ships" she said totally unaware how soon that opportunity was to arise.

In Ramuda, Nirmala Rajan was busy in the office of the garage owned by her father and herself it was almost eleven years since Walter had left and she had been forced to come and live with her father. At first she had hoped there would be a letter for her but as time past her hopes dwindled until in 1917 she received a letter from a lawyer in Bombay called Mr. Ghosh enclosing a letter from Walter but also giving her the terrible news that he had been killed. At first she had been grief stricken but then mainly through the love and urging of her father she realised she had to get on with the rest of her life.

At first she had helped him in the business he owned just outside the gates of Ramuda Textiles but once she was over the news of Walter's death she set about changing the business. With money her father could give her, the money from Walter and her jewellery as security for a loan she bought a lorry which through her father who was known to the Brent family was contracted to carry raw cotton from the ginneries to their factories. Soon one lorry was not enough so more were purchased and before long the new company was moving all the raw cotton and the yarn it produced for all the factories of Ramuda Textiles.

Following this success it was a natural progression from carrying goods to carrying people so they bought a bus and then another, continually increasing their fleet to serve the needs of the city and the outlying villages which meant that to service this rapidly increasing fleet of vehicles they had to build two large garages, one for the buses and another for the lorries. The latter acted like a magnet for boys who all day and every day hung around in the hope that in return for carrying out some small job for the drivers they might be rewarded with a ride.

One of these was a chubby little boy who probably because he wore glasses, didn't join in the games with the other boys but because the drivers discovered he could read and write and would be useful to them was the one who got the most rides and gave Bonesserie the job of constantly trying to stop him.

When her husband Anil disappeared and she was left penniless with a baby son she had been very lucky to be offered a home with her cousin whose wife was very sick and who in fact died a short time later. Her cousin didn't have a lot of money but with rents from some land that he owned and his farming of other land he was able to provide for Bonesserie and her son in return for her looking after the house and his small children. Like Bonesserie he tried to stop P.K. from going to the garage and tried to help him with his school work always urging him to do well so that he might go to college which would give him a better chance of obtaining a good job at the factories but whenever Bonesserie heard her cousin talking like this it was all she could do to contain herself.

"My son is not going to work for Ramuda Textiles. Look what they did to his father. They murdered him. No, P.K. is not going to work for them. We'll starve before I let him work there."

"But where will he work?" her cousin asked "There is nowhere else around here except the garages and surely that is not what you want him to do and anyway it wasn't Ramuda Textiles that killed Anil it was Walter Brent and he is no longer there so it would be foolish not to allow P.K. to work where they pay the best wages." Eventually the continued arguing by both her son and her cousin wore her down and she had to accept that by the time he was old enough it would be in her son's best interest if he did work for Ramuda Textiles.

April, May and June are always the hottest months in South India but 1921 was particularly hot. The monsoon at the end of 1920 had been a poor one and the countryside was crying out for water. Even supplies from the River Cauvery were limited and the level of water behind the new dam was very low. But nowhere was it hotter than in the city of Hyderabad and particularly in the railway yard of the giant steel foundry where, through the open gates at the end of the yard railway engines pulled flat-bed wagons, screeching and clanging over the points, into position for loading with steel girders for despatch all over the country.

On this particularly hot day the afternoon shift had just reported for work and a gang of about 20 men and two steam operated cranes waited as wagons were shunted into position. Loading them was not an easy job at any time but working in the full glare of the Summer sun with the noise of the steelworks on one side and the noise from passing trains on the main lines just over the boundary wall on the other side made it particularly arduous. The girders to be loaded had already been brought out from the foundry on works wagons and it was the mens' job to transfer them from these to mainline wagons. Clerks with lists indicating how the loads were to be made up accompanied the loaders, sorted out the different items, mark them and stood back as the loaders clambered onto the wagons, hooked the girders to the cranes which swung them through 180 degrees then lowered them onto the waiting wagons were they were finally positioned and secured.

Wagon NoY8312G was proving very difficult to load. The ten girders each weighing over a ton destined for Karachi were proving very difficult to secure because of the irregular shape of the pieces. The loaders scrambled over the consignment threading lengths of chain over and round the individual pieces which were then pulled tight by means of long handled ratchets. As they loaded the wagon nobody noticed that one of the chains which was being pulled tight was, in fact, not tightening because of a link of the chain was hooked on a projecting stud on the wagon. With the chains apparently secured the loaders moved to the other wagons which when they were loaded were hooked up to the small engine which came bustling into the yard to pull them out of the steel works and form them into trains ready for the journey northwards.

One week later Wagon Y8312G was in the Bombay marshalling yards being shunted and manoeuvred into position as part of another train ready for the final haul to Karachi.

Bert Williams was walking alongside one of the tracks in the shunting yard where it was his job to check any new track or repairs to the existing track before it was passed for use. He had checked this section earlier in the day but because he was not satisfied he had told the foreman of the repair gang to re-lay a section. They should have finished by now and although it was almost time to go home he thought if the work was satisfactory he could allow the line to be reopened. He had his solar topee pulled down to shield his eyes from the glare of the sun and because of the overall noise in the yard he didn't hear the approach of the wagons being shunted on the adjacent line. He flinched a little as the first of the wagons, some of which were carrying large loads of steel, passed him, their wheels screeching as the rims of the wheels rubbed against the sides of the rails. He looked up at one with a particularly large load as it came abreast of him exactly at the same time as it came to a juddering halt with a banging and clanking of the buffers. The sudden jolt freed the chain which had been insecurely fastened on Wagon Y8312G and the load started to slip. From the corner of his eye Bert saw the load beginning to move and instinctively threw up his arm as the tons of metal started to slide. His mouth opened to cry out but the scream was stifled as the first piece knocked him to the ground and fell across his legs. For a split second he felt the agony of both his legs being broken and then there was nothing as other pieces followed the first crushing him to death. Some of the workers who were waiting for his decision regarding the repaired track saw what had happened but without mechanical help to lift the girders there was nothing they could do and it wasn't until three hours later the body of Bert Williams was dragged free.

Eunice waited for her husband long after it had gone dark. Surely, she thought, he couldn't be working overtime again but when there was a knock at the door and she opened it and saw Matt Sinclair she immediately feared the worst.

With the funeral over and Paul back at school Eunice slowly recovered from the initial shock of her husband's death and in the evenings sitting alone she thought about her life with Bert. He had been a good husband but if she had married someone else she would probably have had children of her own instead having to adopt. But then there would have been no Paul who she absolutely adored. As the days passed her thoughts turned to more pressing things. Financially she could just about manage thanks to the interest from the compensation she received from the railway company along with interest from an insurance policy Bert had meticulously paid into. This income, although not as much as when Bert was alive, was sufficient for her to live on and pay for Paul's education but was certainly not enough to finance trips to England and it was just as she had become reconciled to the fact that she would not be able to keep her promise to Paul that her fortunes took a turn for the better.

Since coming to live in Bombay it had been her custom that whenever she went into the city she always called at the "The Volga Restaurant" for tea and a chat with Mrs. Booth, who managed the business for the owner, who because of illness had not been near the restaurant for the past two years. On this particular day she was no sooner sitting at her usual table when she was joined by Mrs. Booth who was obviously quite upset.

Eunice waited until the waitress had brought the tea before asking what was wrong. Fighting to hold back her tears Mrs. Booth told her that the owner of the restaurant had decided to sell the business so she was worried in case the new owners, whoever they might be, would not require her services.

When she heard the news Eunice started to think. She had always liked the little restaurant which whenever she called was always busy and she wondered if there was some way she could become the new owner. If, instead of taking the interest and used up the compensation money and perhaps some of the insurance money would she have sufficient to buy the restaurant? Instead of going straight home she called at the office of Mr. Ghosh and told him what she proposed.

Six months later the restaurant was hers, Mrs. Booth retained as Manageress and assured by Mr. Ghosh that the income from the business, was sufficient those wonderful passages to England for her and Paul were booked.

Two months later and almost three weeks after leaving Bombay they were on deck as the s.s. Chusan made its way up the river to Tilbury. It was an autumn morning with the sun trying to clear the early morning mist and although it was only late August, Paul despite his coat, couldn't stop shivering partly because of the early morning cold and also with excitement as he watched the buildings sliding by. Eunice was almost as excited as her son at last she was back in England. Then, from inside the ship they heard the gong summoning the passengers to breakfast and Eunice put her hand on her son's shoulder. "Come along Paul, lets go for breakfast then we will come back and watch the ship dock."

9

Once Eunice had decided she had sufficient money to go to England she had gone to see the headmaster at her son's school told him of her plan for Paul and asked where there would be a good school in England. Without hesitation he told her of his old school in Sherborne in Dorset and also volunteered to support her application for a place for Paul. She never knew whether it was because of this support or not but was delighted when Paul was offered a place for the Autumn Term due to commence in September.

For the rest of the time before their departure Eunice had set about finding all she could about the South West of England and Sherborne in particular and only a few hours after landing at Tilbury she and Paul were leaving the train at Sherborne .

Eunice arranged with a porter for their luggage to be kept at the station until they found somewhere to stay and on the suggestion of the porter they set off on the short walk to the Half Moon Hotel where Eunice enquired if there was any available accommodation.

"We have two single rooms on the first floor on the side furthest from the Abbey" the receptionist said, "it's the best side because you will not be disturbed by the Abbey clock which rings all night I am afraid."

Eunice signed the register and as she did so asked the receptionist if she could arrange for their luggage to be collected from the station and for directions to the bank to which she had already sent funds.

"Doesn't this look a delightful town?" Eunice said as they made their way to the bank.

"It's a lot different from India" Paul replied looking up the narrow street, "there is hardly anyone about and it is so clean and quiet."

After they had been to the bank they crossed the road to a small paved square where they passed an old circular building which they learned later was called "The Conduit" the place where the monks from the Abbey used to come to wash their clothes or just sit and talk and behind which, Eunice had spotted an estate agents. They entered the office where sitting at desks were two men very obviously father and son and who looked as they entered.

"I'm looking for a small place to rent" Eunice said explaining she had just arrived with her son from abroad.

"We don't get many properties to rent and I don't think we have anything at the moment" the older man said turning to his son for confirmation.

"You're right father" the young man replied "but what about that place Mr. Barker mentioned to us a few weeks ago."

"I had quite forgotten about that, but do you think he was serious?" his father said. "It was only a passing conversation." "Do you really think he wants to sell his flat?"

"I don't know" his son replied "but we could give him a ring."

While the young man was on the 'phone his father explained that Mr. Barker was the General Manager of a factory on the outskirts of Yeovil who had purchased the property to house some engineers who were installing machinery at the factory, work that was now finished.

The young estate agent put down the 'phone and said that Mr. Barker would like to meet Eunice to discuss the possible sale or rent of the flat. and before the day was out an agreement had been drawn up and a week later Eunice and her son moved into the flat in Long Street.

Almost six years to the day after they had first arrived in Sherborne Paul and his mother were on the train from London to Bolton, a trip they had made a number of times to visit Paul's Uncle Jack and Auntie Edith Glover. Edith was the sister of Eunice's late husband and she and her husband had promised that Paul could stay with them while he was studying at the local technical college.

Paul had never understood why his mother had always been so determined that he should go into the textile industry. Even after coming to England he still wasn't sure what he wanted to do and it was only because of Norman Barker, their landlord in Sherborne, who when he heard Eunice's plans for Paul had taken him on many occasions to the factory and got him interested that had made him decide it might be a good idea and his mother might be right when she argued that, what was probably the largest industry in India, would offer him the greatest opportunities.

Uncle Jack must have been watching from behind the curtains because immediately the taxi came to a halt he came down the garden path calling out to his wife who hurried behind him wiping her hands on her apron.

As they got out of the cab Uncle Jack boomed, "Hello Eunice, Paul, had a good trip?"

"Very good" Eunice replied giving her sister-in-law a peck on the cheek. Paul smiled his greetings and started to help the taxi driver with their suitcases. Uncle Jack dressed in his usual thick flannel shirt with no collar and dark trousers held up by both braces and a wide leather belt, picked up a couple of the heaviest cases as if they were empty, which caused Paul to marvel at the size of his Uncle's forearms. Paul followed the adults down the path passed the small but well tended front garden and into the front room of the council house, a room furnished with a dining table, four dining chairs and two easy chairs complete with cushions placed at an angle infront of the open fireplace. In the hearth a brown earthenware teapot was warming while on a hob on the edge of the open fire stood a kettle with steam spiralling from the spout. The lid and a little of the edging round it were brightly polished reflecting the flames of the coal fire but the rest was coated with soot from constant use.

Aunt Edith took a brightly coloured kettle holder from it's hook at the side of the fireplace and lifting the kettle from the hob poured water into the teapot which she covered with a tea cosy. Leaving the tea to brew she bustled into the kitchen, the only other room on the ground floor to reappear moments later with a freshly baked fruit cake. She cut four large wedges and placed one on each of four plates which she handed round along with cups of tea. Paul sat eating his cake not really listening to what the adults were talking about when suddenly his Uncle was talking to him.

"Neaw lad what dost reckon. I've getten thee a job int' mill like we talked about last time tha were 'ere ." Before Paul could answer Eunice said,

"That's marvellous isn't it Paul? What will he be doing?"

"Well ah say I've getten 'im a job I've getten 'im an interview but ah know Mr. Leather will gi'it him. E says e can be a trainee which means e as to work in every department and learn all about different processes."

"That's wonderful" Eunice answered.

Uncle Jack went on "Mr. Leather wants to see thee on Monday morning at eleven o'clock."

"This is working out better than I hoped" Eunice said. "It means I can see Paul start his first job and start college before I go back to India."

Uncle Jack held up one of his large tattooed arms, "Owd on a bit Eunice. He's not getten job yet tha' knows."

"He will. He will" Eunice said leaning back in her chair with a smile of satisfaction on her face "and anyway he is going to college job or no job."

On Saturday morning Paul took the tram into town and walked across the Town Hall Square which was dominated by the Town Hall itself with its steps leading up to the entrance which was guarded by the two stone lions which looked out across the square towards the white cenotaph, a memorial to the men of Bolton who had died in the war. He walked through Ship Gates where the Grapes public house formed an arch over his head leading to Bradshawgate where he paused to look at the statue of Samuel Crompton, the inventor of the spinning mule, a Bolton man and one of the principle architects of the industrial revolution. A few minutes later he turned right into Churchgate where the Earl of Derby was beheaded in the Civil War. He carried on down Churchgate as far as the Grand Theatre and, after reading the posters advertising the current variety show he glanced up at the clock on Trinity Church and decided he had better have something to eat before meeting his Uncle who was taking him to watch Bolton Wanderers play the Arsenal. He crossed the road, his nose leading him towards a shop selling hot meat and potato pasties where he bought his lunch which he ate on his way back to the tram terminus where he was to meet his Uncle. Trams arrived every few minutes and even before they had come to a complete halt men wearing their blue and white favours, some carrying wooden rattles with which to cheer on their favourites, were jumping off to meet their friends or nip into the pub for a last drink before going to the match.

Paul watched the trams unloading and, at last, saw his Uncle descending the two steps from the tram and went to meet him.

For the past few days he had been appraised of the merits of the local team and now was a co-opted supporter of the Wanderers. They were joined by some friends of his Uncle who had also been waiting for him and they set off for Burnden Park. Everyone who went to the match had their favourite place inside the ground and Uncle Jack was no exception.

He led his small party passed the main stand to the turnstiles at the corner where after shuffling along in the queue they paid their shilling and sixpence and took up their position leaning against a tubular steel crush barrier just to the left of the goal at the Great Lever End.

Paul looked round the rapidly filling ground which by the time the match started would probably contain a crowd of about 30,000, mainly Bolton supporters interspersed by the few Arsenal supporters wearing their red and white scarves and hats who had made the journey from London.

"It's a large crowd" Paul commented.

"Aye it's noan so bad but tha' wants t'see it when likes o' Man City are 'ere, then it's a crowd aw'reet."

As they waited for three o'clock and the kick off they were entertained by the best efforts of the Bolton Silver Prize Brass Band and cheered as a one legged man, dressed in running shorts and vest, a casualty of the war, hopped round the pitch his two assistants carrying a stretched out blanket behind him with which they caught the coins that the spectators threw as a reward for his efforts. Surely this wasn't a part of the land fit for heroes which the Government had promised.

The clock on the top of the stand was approaching five to three when the ground erupted with whistles and jeering as the red and white shirted Arsenal team ran out followed by cheers as the Wanderers emerged accompanied by the band playing "The Great Little Army".

After the match Paul was as pleased as his Uncle, his cronies and the rest of the crowd that their cheering, shouting and swinging of rattles had urged Bolton to victory. On the way home they bought the "Green Final" not only to find Bolton's position in the league but more importantly to see if the opinion of the paper's reporter coincided with theirs.

Later that evening contented after a meal of Aunt Edith's stew and dumplings but tired after their efforts to overcome Arsenal, Paul and his Uncle rested in the two easy chairs on opposite sides of the blazing coal fire. Paul alternately dozed and thought about his forthcoming interview while Uncle Jack sat opposite contentedly sucking on his dirty old pipe and occasionally drinking from the pint glass standing on the corner of the table. The curtains were drawn and the whole house was quiet as if resting from the exertions of the week just ending before preparing for the demands of the week to come.

The following Monday Paul battled his way through the wind and rain as he walked towards the Oceanic Mill. The good weather of Saturday and Sunday had disappeared, driven away by the wind of the North West, the direction that always brought rain to Lancashire. He saw the door to the gate house his Uncle had told him about and after forcing it open against the wind he had to strain to stop it banging behind him. A sliding window to his right was opened by a large lady with a formidable bosom who enquired what he wanted.

"I have an appointment with Mr. Leather" he said.

"Wait theer" the large lady said eyeing him up and down before closing the window then turning to disappear through a door on the other side of the room. Paul looked at her domain. On two sides of the room were wooden benches which had been scrubbed almost snow white on which stood wooden racks of leather covered rollers. Fastened on the wall above one of the benches was a large white cupboard with a red cross on the door. He subsequently discovered that Mrs. Barton had many different duties one of them being to revarnish a number of rollers every day which were brought from the factory and another to administer first aid in the case of accidents but as Paul had already discovered her main task was to ensure no-one entered the factory until they had been vetted by her. His eye carried on round the spotlessly clean room to the large fireplace with its roaring fire and the shiny black leaded oven which was heated by the fire when necessary and as usual with this sort of fireplace there was a hob on which stood a black kettle even larger than his auntie's. He was just contemplating if it could be possible that Mrs. Barton actually lived in the gate house when the door opposite opened and she beckoned him to come inside. He pushed open the door making sure he wiped his feet before stepping on to the spotless black and white tiled floor and followed her up a flight of stairs then waiting as she knocked on a highly polished mahogany door. \when a voice called out Mrs. Barton pushed open the door and stood back allowing him to enter.

Mr. Leather was older than Paul expected. He was very tall with a shock of white hair and dressed in blue trousers and a fawn coloured jacket.

"Good morning Paul" Mr. Leather said. "You're Uncle has told me about you" He indicated a chair for Paul to sit down.

For the next hour or so he questioned Paul about his education and his life in India. He asked about his parents and said he was sorry when Paul told him how his father had died. He asked about his ambitions and Paul gave him all the answers he thought the older man wanted to hear making sure he did not mention that he intended to return to India once his technical education was completed just in case he was not offered a job.

Mr. Leather explained what Paul would have to do and then said he would take Paul round the factory so that he would have some idea what it would be like to work there. He led the way down stairs and opened a door leading out into the mill yard. It was still pouring with rain and large puddles had formed in the cobbled yard. Holding the door open he pointed to the large green door in the side of the mill some twenty yards away.

"You run ahead your faster than me" Paul took one look at the pouring rain and set off dodging the puddles towards the green door followed as quickly as he could by the owner holding an umbrella.

Paul pushed the heavy door open and held it for Mr. Leather as he hurried in. They were standing on a landing with steps to their left, one flight leading down to the cellar and the other to the floors above.

Mr. Leather pushed open a green painted sliding door opposite to the one through which they had just entered and if Paul thought the noise was loud when he was just standing on the landing when this door was opened his ears were assailed by a racket the likes of which he had never heard before. Mr. Leather allowed the door to slide shut behind them and led the way past the machines to a door at the other end of the department and up some stairs to a much quieter department where the bales of raw cotton were opened and fed into the first machines of the cotton spinning process.

For the next hour Paul followed Mr. Leather through the various departments as he explained the different processes, Carding, Spinning, Winding and finally the cellar where the yarn was packed and stored ready for despatch. Because of the noise of the machinery nearly all the tour was explained by Mr. Leather pointing and exaggerated mouthing of words so that Paul could lip read.

Back in his office Mr. Leather discussed with Paul what he had seen and from the questions Paul asked it was obvious to the owner that Paul was interested in, and understood to a certain extent what he had seen and then Mr. Leather finally told him he was prepared to offer him a job as a Management Trainee.

"Start next Monday. You will work the same hours as everyone else, start at seven finish at five and on Saturdays from seven to twelve. Your pay will start at seventeen shillings a week which we will review each year depending on how you perform. You will, of course have to go to the Technical College where each year you must pass examinations to proceed. Do you understand?"

Paul nodded and they shook hands.

After lunch Paul went to the Technical College to enrol in the cotton spinning course which, provided he was successful in the yearly exams it would take six years to become an Associate of the Textile Institute.

10

The next six years passed relatively quickly. His mother had returned to India just after he started work but he was happy staying with Aunt Edith and Uncle Jack. He was successful both at college and in the factory where he learned how to operate the different machines and then, working with the overlookers and mechanics, how to service and repair them. In Winter, rain or shine he went to watch Bolton Wanderers and in Summer he went, again with his uncle to watch cricket.

From the beginning Mr. Leather had taken a great interest in him, so much so that for the past few months, not only had he been showing him the office routine but he had also been taking him to the Cotton Exchange in Liverpool whenever he went to buy cotton where he showed him how to appraise the cotton samples, knowledge which would serve him well in the future.

He had enjoyed his stay in England and was waiting for the results of his final examinations. He could not have had a better practical education than the one he had received at Oceanic Mill. The operatives had taught him how to operate the various machines, the overlookers had shown him how to maintain them but as he had grown he had received another sort of education. For this his teachers were the girls in the factory, both married and single to who he was young, good looking and very different from the men in their lives.

One of the first encounters occurred when he was about 18. One day, just before five o'clock when most of the machines were stopped for cleaning he was using a lift usually used for transporting material between floors and was just closing the lift doors, when Mary, a married woman with two children slipped inside. As soon as the slow moving lift was between floors Mary threw herself at him, her arms round him so that he could hardly move, her pelvis grinding against his and her lips seeking his mouth. "Oh Paul" she panted "I have wanted to do this for a long time." He didn't know what to make of it. He had been warned about some of the girls but he had never thought of Mary like this. He could hardly move and truth to say he was a little scared.

"Can't we meet sometime?" she pleaded just before the lift reached the next floor. Paul couldn't speak afraid that when the lift stopped someone would open the doors and see them and tell Mary's husband who worked two floors up moving 400lb. bales of cotton as if they were bags of sugar. Just then the lift stopped and someone started to open the doors. Quickly Mary twisted away and without so much as a backward glance his would-be lover walked out.

Another embarrassing occasion occurred a few months later. One lunchtime when the factory was stopped he was heading towards the exit when he heard someone calling his name. He turned into the narrow alleys which separated the machines and following the sound of the voices came round one of the machines and couldn't believe what he had seen. Her workmates had grabbed hold of a young girl about 15 years old who had not been working at the factory very long, stripped her completely naked and were now holding her with her legs and arms stretched out wide.

"Take her out Paul~" they cried, "look how lovely she is." He stopped undecided what he should do and then turning on his heel he walked away in the stupid hope that the girl might think he had not seen her, a hope that was completely dashed when she went home at the end of the day and never returned.

When he worked in the Winding Department he was attracted to one of the winders, a girl called Audrey who from time to time agreed to go to the cinema with him. To Paul this was never going to be the start of a great love affair but a hope that, if he went about it in the right way, Audrey might be the one to initiate him into the mysteries of sex. Unfortunately he had chosen someone who thought she saw a way to marry into a better way of life if only she played her cards right.

Fortunately for Paul his technical education was proving far more successful than his affair with Audrey and in June his final examination results arrived informing him that as a result of his successful years at the college he was now an Associate of the Textile Institute. Now all he had to do was to find a suitable position with an organisation in India.

His delight at successfully completing his studies was tempered by the worry for his Uncle Jack who, before he became an overlooker, had been a mule spinner and like so many others he had contracted Spinners' Cancer caused by the abodomen coming into connect with the mineral oil used on the machines as he leaned over to piece any broken threads. Unfortunately the discovery that the mineral oil was to blame and the later change to vegetable oil came too late and for the past two years Paul could only watch as his uncle's health deteriorated until he was confined to the house and could no longer go to watch his beloved Wanderers and so was dependant on Paul to tell him about the match when he came home.

During his time in Bolton Paul had seen frequent adverts which appeared in the Bolton Evening News and the Manchester Guardian, usually under Box numbers for factory managers to work in many different countries such as Peru, China, and last and most importantly for Paul, India so that when one appeared for a manager in India shortly after he had received his A.T.I. he applied for it.

He had already decided that when he answered any of these adverts he wouldn't divulge that he was born in and had lived all his life in India. Another reason he didn't want to tell them about India was because most contracts were usually for three years and which at the end of that time there was a free passage back to England and six months paid leave something you obviously would not receive if you lived in India.

In response to his application he was called for interview at a textile machinery manufacturers where he was interviewed by the sales manager who told him that the firm was Ramuda Textiles.

After some time he told Paul he would recommend him and if Ramuda were interested he would have to have a further interview with the Chairman of the Company, Mr. Brent, who was due to arrive in England shortly.

A few weeks later Paul was called for an interview with Mr. Brent and within minutes he felt confident he would be successful and so it was no surprise when he was told the job was his and asked when he could be ready to leave for India. Paul suggested he would be ready in a months time so George Brent said the company would arrange a passage for him around the end of August. Just then the office door opened and a young man walked in. He was almost as tall as Paul and probably about two or three years older but whereas Paul was fair he was quite dark. George Brent looked up and smiled when he saw his son Philip.

"I've just recruited Mr. Williams and he will be coming to Ramuda sometime in September." The two young men shook hands and as they talked Paul discovered Philip had studied textiles in Oldham.

"I don't know why, but I feel I know that young fellow from somewhere" George Brent said after Paul had left.

Philip laughed, "You are always saying something like that. You have been in India longer than he's been alive. You can't possibly know him."

"I suppose you're right but I still think he looks familiar. But it isn't important. I think we have a good fellow there."

The following Monday morning Mr. Leather with Paul driving set off for the Cotton exchange in Liverpool and just as he always did he explained yet again the importance of these visits. Paul listened quietly to the speech he had heard so many times which, as usual, lasted until they were on the outskirts of Bolton. Once he had finished there was no further conversation and Paul glanced across to see if his employer had fallen asleep. Usually the older man was quite talkative but this morning he looked worried.

"Is something the matter" Paul enquired. For a moment or two there was no response then Mr. Leather said, quietly," I may as well tell you, I have decided to sell the factory."

Paul glanced across and if he didn't believe what he had just heard when he saw Mr. Leather's face he did.

"Sell the factory. Why are you thinking of doing that?"

"There are a number of reasons but principally it is because I am nearly seventy five and I don't think I want to struggle with the factory during a war." Paul interrupted, "Through a war! What do you mean? There is no war."

"No. But there will be in the next few years. It is unavoidable." Mr. Leather said. "This fellow Hitler will cause trouble. Some time he will have to be stopped and like last time it will have to be this country that does it and we will not be ready. Business will become very difficult and I will be too old. I have had a few approaches in the past from the large combines and I think it is now time to listen to what they have to say."

Paul was surprised at what he had just heard but realised it gave him the perfect opportunity to tell his employer about the job he had been offered in India.

Mr. Leather didn't say anything and Paul wondered if he had understood what he had just said. Mr. Leather turned from looking out the window.

"I think you are doing the right thing" his employer muttered almost to himself, "go to India. Get away from Europe . Get out before the balloon goes up."

About half an hour later he and Paul were in their agent's office where samples of various cottons were laid out for their inspection.

Paul took some of the cotton from the first sample to appraise its suitability and then while Mr. Leather discussed prices with the agent and confirmed his purchases he went across to another table where there were some Indian samples to see if he could get some idea of the types of cotton he would be using in India.

Later as they were talking out of the Cotton Exchange Mr. Leather paused. Perhaps it was the conversation in the car which made him look at the plaque which had been erected in memory of the Cotton Exchange staff who had been killed in the Great War.

"My brother's name is there" he said. Paul looked through the names Adams, Andrews and other names starting with "A" and the "B's" and one name caught his eye. "Brent Walter and he wondered if this had been some relative of the Brent's from Ramuda Textiles. Probably not, he thought. Most likely it was some other poor chap with the same name and he continued reading down the list.

"Most of these were killed with my brother at the Battle of the Somme" Mr. Leather said.

On the way back Mr. Leather decided not to go back to the factory and directed Paul to drive him to his house. Although Paul knew he lived somewhere on Chorley New Road where the better off people lived he didn't know which was the house until his passenger pointed to one standing in its own grounds. Paul swung the car through the ornamental gate posts, up the circular drive and came to a halt at the front door.

As they got out of the car the door opened and a uniformed parlour maid stood to one side to allow Mr. Leather to enter.

"Good afternoon Alice is Madam in the sitting room?" and not waiting for a reply led the way across the hall to a door on the left.

"Come in Paul" he said as he opened the door to the sitting room and walked across to his wife who was sitting on a comfortable looking settee and gave her a kiss on the cheek.

"Hello William. Have you had a good day?" Mrs. Leather asked

"Quite good" he replied and half turning to Paul "This is Paul Williams, my dear, the young man I have mentioned to you before. You remember he has been working at the factory for the past few years but now has surprised me by telling me he was born in India and is shortly going back there." Paul stepped forward and shook hands.

"How do you do Mrs. Leather I am pleased to meet you" and as they shook hands neither Paul nor Mr. Leather noticed the look that momentarily flashed across Margaret Leather's eyes.

"Good afternoon Paul. My husband has told me about you."

Mr. Leather told his wife about the trip to Liverpool and about how the cotton prices were fluctuating and had just about finished when there was a knock at the door and Alice entered pushing a trolley on which there was tea, sandwiches and cakes.

As they ate Margaret watched Paul whenever she thought the other two were not looking at her, wondering if what she was thinking could possibly be true. Was there something that reminded her of Walter Brent or was it just because he would be about the same age as the son she had left in India that sparked the idea that was coursing through her brain. She tried to dismiss the idea as being totally impossible and yet, there was something.

"Where do you live in India?" she asked.

"My mother lives in Bombay" Paul replied. "But when I go back I shall be working in Ramuda." The mention of Ramuda really shook her but again she didn't let it show.

"You said your mother lived in Bombay does your father not live there as well?"

"No I am afraid not. He worked on the railway but was killed in an accident and then shortly afterwards my mother bought a restaurant in Bombay."

Now Margaret was really shocked because she was sure that Mr. Ghosh had told her the husband of the couple who adopted her son worked on the railway.

As they continued eating Margaret enquired about his schooling and other aspects of his life in India until her husband interrupted,

"you will have to excuse my wife" he laughed "she went to India on holiday a number of years ago and still talks about it."

"Really when were you there?"

"Oh it was a long time ago now, before the war" she replied.

"It was in 1912 when she went and stayed over until 1913" Mr. Leather said.

Paul laughed "That's a coincidence it's the year I was born."

This was too much. This is more than a coincidence Margaret thought but even if she knew for sure that this young man sitting in her lounge was her son what could she do? She would have to let him walk out of her life just as she had been forced all those years ago.

Even after they had finished eating Margaret and Paul continued talking about India a conversation only interrupted when the clock standing in the corner chimed the hour.

"I didn't realise it was so late" Paul said "I should be leaving." As she continued to watch him she was now convinced that she and her son had been together for the only time since he had been taken from her arms and she wondered if she would ever see him again. As her husband led Paul to the door she hurried upstairs so that they would not see the tears she could hold back no longer.

Friday morning came at last. Paul's final day at Oceanic Mill. Next week he would be on his way to India. He turned into the mill yard pleased that he was nearly inside because it was an unusually cold morning with a strong wind blowing from the East. He hurried up the few steps to the main door and pushed it open pleased to be out of the cold then climbed the stairs to the third floor spinning room which, including his office was only illuminated by the early morning light coming through the large windows. He changed into his overalls, the last time in his working life he would ever wear them and then sitting in the old spindle backed chair he spread the Manchester Guardian on the desk and tried to read it in the dim light. He was just glancing at the sports pages when the line shafts started to turn and the lights, which only worked when the engine was running, slowly increased in brightness allowing the operatives, who were paid according to the weight of the yarn they produced, to start the machines to take advantage of every turn of the huge steam engine.

Paul folded the newspaper and left the office to check attendance. There probably wouldn't be any absences today because it was pay day. All the spinners in this department were women most of them married and often working on machines next to those of their mother or daughter. It was not unusual to have three generations of a family working side by side and their menfolk in other departments.

Because of the heat in the factory which was necessary for cotton spinning the women wore as little as possible usually just a thin overall and in most cases bare foot as well. As he passed Mary she looked up at him and smiled as she always did and Paul smiled back and nodded, both of them aware of the episode in the lift. A few aisles further on he saw

Mona who he disliked intensely and then Henry a young man of about twenty three who was slightly mentally handicapped and was employed to transport material from one department to another. He recalled the time when one day just as the lunch break started Henry was pushing a truck of yarn past some girls, including Mona, who were sitting on the polished wooden floor eating their lunch. Mona had put her coat next to her on the floor when one of the metal wheels of the truck that Henry was pushing ran over, not only her coat, but the cigarettes which were in a pocket. She had jumped up swearing at the bemused and frightened lad and grabbed him then urged on by Mona the other girls held him whilst she undid his overalls pulled them down bent him o ver his truck and was about to beat him with a large empty wooden bobbin when he had come along and stopped them.

After checking there was a complete staff he returned to his office to collect the books in which was entered the previous days production to take them to Mr. Leather. At the factory door he hesitated, not only was it cold but it had started to rain. He tucked the books under his arm and set off at a run towards the gatehouse where he pushed open the door closing only to wipe his feet before entering just as he had been instructed the very first time he had come to the factory. Mrs. Barton was sitting in front of the open fireplace, the heat from the fire making her face redder than usual. After exchanging a few words Paul asked her if Mr. Leather was in.

"Aye'ave taken 'is cup o' tay up to 'im". Paul smiled and walked through the inner door to the office above.

He sat down and put the production books on the desk so that Mr. Leather could look at them at his leisure. As usual the owner poured a cup of tea for Paul and as they drank they chatted about the factory and as Paul got up to leave Mr. Leather asked him to come and see him at four thirty.

Later that day Paul sat in his office looking through the window at the busy spinning room he was a little sad at the thought of leaving but his passage was booked on the "Warwickshire" a Bibby Line ship leaving Liverpool next Wednesday. He had already purchased all the things he thought he would need for the journey so he was ready to go. His thoughts turned to Uncle Jack who was now desperately ill with the disease that was eating away at his insides. The doctor frequently came to see him but had told the family there was little he could do except to increase the doses of morphine. At first his uncle had tried to manage without the drug but was now absolutely dependent upon it. Paul recalled the first time he met his uncle and how he had been amazed at the size of his forearms with the brilliant tattoos. Now those arms were shrivelled and even the tattoos seemed to have dulled even as his life ebbed away. Paul hoped the end would be quick but even though his uncle was in constant pain he waited every day for Paul to come home and give him news of the factory. When he had first stopped work his workmates came to see him but as the months passed fewer people called and now as he deteriorated further it appeared as if "Big Jack" was only holding on until Paul left for India. The rest of the day passed slowly with nothing happening to upset the daily routine. He had been upstairs to the Winding Department and confirmed his date for the following night with Audrey, one of the winders who he had been dating, which although she didn't know, it would be his last Saturday in England but then at last it was nearly four thirty and time to go and see Mr. Leather.

When he entered the owner's office Mr. Leather was standing in front of the highly polished cupboard which Paul had never seen opened before but which, as Mr. Leather turned to greet him, he saw cut glass decanters and glasses.

"What would you like to drink?" he enquired. At first Paul didn't know what to ask for because he didn't normally drink spirits but then finally asked for a whiskey.

Mr. Leather handed Paul his drink and sat down at the table at the other side of the office. As they sipped their drinks they reminisced about the past seven years, about people who either still worked at the factory or, in some cases, had left and, in particular, Mr. Leather asked about Uncle Jack.

As the afternoon light started to give way to Autumnal darkness Mr. Leather got out of his chair, switched on the light and then walked across to his desk and from the top drawer took out a small black leatherette case.

"I want you to have this" he said handing it over to Paul who pressed the button on the side of the case which allowed the lid to spring open revealing a matching gold pen and pencil set.

Paul looked up at Mr. Leather and held out his hand.

"Thank you very much" he said "I never expected anything like this they are marvellous, thank you very much."

"I wanted to give you something to remember your time at the mill and to thank you because you have probably done more for me than I have for you. You see Margaret and I were never blessed with children and you gave me the opportunity to pass on the skills and knowledge I would have passed on to my own son if we had been fortunate enough to have one."

Paul thanked him again for the gift and for all the help he had given him during his stay at Oceanic Mill.

"Oh there is one other thing" the mill owner said as he fished in his jacket pocket and pulled out a small package, "Margaret wants you to have this. She told me to tell you that you are not to open it until you are entering Bombay harbour. I don't know why or what it is but she thought you might like it."

Paul took the package and turned it over in his hands trying to imagine what it might contain.

"That is very kind of Mrs. Leather" he said putting it in his pocket. "Will you please thank her for me".

After chatting for a little longer the two shook hands and Paul walked down the stairs and out of Oceanic Mill for the last time. Once in the street he looked up at the office window where he could just see the top of the owners head as he sat at his desk.

Next evening his last Saturday night in England, Paul was among the crowd walking along Great moor Street just as the tram from Farnworth came to a halt at the terminus. He arrived just as Audrey stepped down and with her arm in his they walked round the corner into Bradshawgate.

"Where would you like to go" Paul asked.

"There is supposed to be a very good film on at The Capitol" Audrey replied. "Shall we go there?"

Paul led the way across the road and round the corner to the brightly lit entrance of the cinema. The first film was a trailer for next week's film which gave the audience time to settle down before the newsreel and then the main film which people in the circle watched through wreaths of blue tobacco smoke which spiralled up from the audience below. Once they were seated Paul put his arm under hers and she readily put her hand in his. After a short time he pulled her hand on to his lap and held it with his other hand which enabled him to put his free arm round her shoulders and gently pull her nearer to him and for Audrey to put her head on his shoulder. Paul slightly turned his head in Audrey's direction and disengaging his hand from hers reached up and gently lifted her face to his so that he could kiss her.

As they kissed Paul was already planning what he would do next. He didn't have any feelings of love towards Audrey, to him this was just a sexual adventure which he was hoping he could bring to a satisfactory conclusion this evening.

He lowered his lips to hers yet again gently stroking her cheek as he did so. Now neither of them were watching the film. He looked down at Audrey who was sitting with her eyes closed and her mouth slightly open. He kissed her again and as he did so slowly moved his hand inside her coat and on to her firm breast. Through the thin material of her blouse he could feel the nipple proudly erect and he gently squeezed and teased it even more. They stayed like this as the film ground on, neither of them watching or aware of what it was about.

Paul whispered "Do you want to see anymore of this or shall we go?" Audrey smiled back at him and said softly

"I don't know what the film is about let's go" she replied. After they had left the cinema they walked along looking at the shop window displays and during their conversation it was soon obvious to Paul that Audrey didn't know he had left the factory.

Because the weather was warmer than it had been for the past few days they just continued walking in the direction of Farnworth where Audrey lived. Holding hands they laughed and joked and it wasn't long before the town was behind them and they were walking up the slight hill just before the football ground. Occasionally a tram rattled by and an occasional car but there was nobody else about. Paul had it all planned and by now Audrey had a good idea where they were heading long before they reached the turning into Raikes Clough a well known spot for courting couples. Paul turned into the lane surprised that Audrey allowed herself to be led so easily but he would have been even more surprised if he had known what was in her mind.

She had decided she was going to become Mrs. Paul Williams and was prepared to use any means to make this happen. After all, as her mother regularly pointed out he was certainly a better catch than anyone else she knew so she had made up her mind not to let him go.

Walking down the darkening lane he put his arm around his waist and held her close, occasionally stopping to kiss her ready lips. Eventually he turned off the main path along the smaller track until, on the right, he saw a grassy bank partially hidden by some bushes. He led Audrey off the path behind the bushes and lying down on the grass pulled her down beside him. Propped up on one arm he looked down at her and as he stroked her cheek with his free hand he whispered what he thought she wanted to hear.

"You know we have wasted precious time. When I first saw you I wanted to ask you to come out with me but I thought someone as attractive as you must already have a boyfriend." Though it was dark Audrey could see his eyes glistening a few inches from her face.

"I had been seeing someone else but that finished before I ever saw you" she lied.

Paul lowered his face to hers and started to kiss her and in response Audrey slid one arm around his neck so that when he wanted to end the kiss she encouraged him by holding his mouth on hers for just a little longer. Silently they lay in each others arms as Paul teased his partner, kissing her eyes, the tip of her nose, her ears before at last her mouth gently opening her lips to tease her tongue with his.

Encouraged by her response he started to undo the buttons of her blouse which he pushed to one side revealing a pink brassiere. With little difficulty and with no resistance from Audrey, he pushed the shoulder strap to one side and eased the cup of the garment down and put his hand on her naked breast. Audrey was holding him tightly trying to draw him closer seeking his mouth with hers as he removed his hand from her naked breast and slid it down to the hem of her skirt which was now above her knees. He started to stroke her thigh at the same time lifting her skirt higher until he felt the bare flesh above her stocking. At this Audrey withdrew her lips from his and turned her head to one side at the same time wriggling her hand down between their two bodies and taking hold of his hand on her leg.

"No Paul" she gasped "Don't do that!"

Without a word Paul continued kissing her and disengaging his hand from hers wriggled his fingers inside the leg of her panties causing Audrey to abandon all resistance and thrust her lower body to meet his searching fingers. Paul eased his body away and started to pull her panties down and became even more encouraged when she responded by arching her back to enable him to pull them over her hips,

"Do it. Please, Please do it. Do it now" she panted.

Paul undid the front of his trousers and lowered his body down on hers as, almost like a sacrifice she lay waiting for him. With an inbuilt knowledge which belied his experience he brought the softly mewling Audrey near to the climax she was seeking then deliberately teased her by slowing before almost bringing her to completion again.

"Oh Paul don't stop. Don't stop. Please do it this time I can't wait any longer" and as she desperately arched her pelvis to meet his they climaxed simultaneously. To stifle her screams of pleasure he pressed his lips to hers their bodies fused together trembling in rhytham to their individual delights.

As their spasm eased Paul raised himself on his elbows and looked down at his partner until Audrey put her arms round his neck and pulled his face down to hers.

"I love you" she whispered. "When you first came to t'mill I wanted you but I never thought you would ask me to go out with you what with me only being a winder and you a manager."

Paul stopped her talking by kissing her and then with his lips close to her ear,

"I never thought like that. To me you were a very beautiful girl and I wanted to take you out."

When they were both fully dressed Audrey placed her arm through his and with her head on his shoulder Paul led the way back to the main road. As they walked Audrey never stopped talking and from what she said Paul was pleased she had no idea he would never be at the factory again.

As they approached the main road Audrey said she didn't want anyone from the mill to see them near Raikes Clough or even together until she had told her parents about him.

"You know what gossips are like at the factory" she said.

This suited Paul. Even though he had left the factory he didn't want anyone to see them together either. For him, tonight had just been a very successful initiation into sex and nothing more.

After walking about half a mile so that they were nowhere near Raikes Clough and people might guess what a young couple had been doing, they came to a tram stop just as a tram approached. Before it came to a halt Paul gave Audrey a kiss and as the tram moved off crossed the road and without a backward glance started back towards the town centre.

11

December 1941

Paul was sitting in the bar of the Taj Mahal hotel in Bombay. It was three years since he started work in India and according to his contract he should have been on leave in England but because of the war he could not go. Although the country was on a war footing and detachments of the Indian army had been sent abroad, mainly to the Middle East, the country had not been affected too much. One of the more obvious changes was the proliferation of street rallies mainly in the larger cities caused by a section of the Congress party under the leadership of its former president Subhas Chandra Bhose seeking the chance to demand independence while Britain was preoccupied by the war in Europe. These meetings although disruptive were usually well controlled by the police but occasionally would break out into fighting which often ended with the arrest of some of the leaders but not before the mob set a car or a bus alight or in Calcutta, their usual target, a tramcar.

So like other Europeans Paul had to take his leave in India so he had come to Bombay not only for its attractions but also to see his mother. Unfortunately he had only been able to arrange his leave at the last minute only to find that it coincided for a couple of days with a visit by his mother to friends in Poona.

He emptied his glass and nodded to the barman who poured him another whisky. As he reached for the soda siphon he noticed the cuff links he was wearing which had been the contents of the package given to him by Mrs Leather. He looked again at the gold monogram 'WMP' obviously the initials of William and Margaret Leather along with his own on a blue background which he had thought was enamel but had been told by Rose Brent, the wife of the Chairman, that it was in fact made from stones found mainly on the West Coast.

As he sipped his drink he recalled the faces of people who worked at the factory and smiled as he remembered Audrey. She must have had a bit of a shock when she discovered not only did he no longer work at the factory but had gone to India. Anyway she was probably married by now with a couple of children. After signing his bill he slid off the stool and headed for the door. On the square in front of the Gateway to India he saw a crowd of people. He knew what was happening and with nothing better to do he walked across and stood at the edge of the crowd who were watching the snake and the mongoose exhibition a regular pavement attraction which never failed to attract tourists.

An old man squatted on the pavement with a cobra in front of him which appeared to dance as he played a flute which he waved about in front of the snake. When he had decided he had gathered a sufficiently large audience he continued playing the flute with one hand whilst with the other pulling out a mongoose from a sack lying at his feet. Holding it firmly he started to tease the snake pushing the struggling mongoose near the reptiles head then snatching it away before the snake could strike. Only when his assistant, a young boy, had collected enough money from the spectators did the old man stop playing the flute and released the mongoose which hopped around dodging the lightening strike of the enraged snake waiting for the opening which would allow it to attack.

Paul had seen this display many times before and wondered if the snake ever won this continual battle because he had never seen the snake win which was probably fortunate for the old man because it would be far easier and cheaper to replace the snake rather than the mongoose. When the little drama was over the crowd drifted away and Paul crossed the road to the tram terminus where he boarded one of the vehicles and climbed the stairs to the top deck. Among the passengers were other Europeans both male and female who were there to see the sights because this was the tram which went along the notorious Grants Road.

Grants Road was as bright and active as the previous streets had been dark and dismal because it was the centre of prostitution where every sort of sexual activity was available and from where they were sitting, the passengers on the tram could look down at the procession of people engaged in the world's oldest profession. By just watching it was almost impossible to tell if these garishly dressed cavorting creatures were male or female because along with the ordinary prostitutes there were homosexuals and transvestites as well as the castrati, young men who had been castrated when they were young especially for this life who danced around the pedestrians, touching them and pulling at the sleeves of their shirts or jackets to embarrass them in an attempt to obtain money.

But all this was not what made Grants Road infamous. What made it notorious was the row of dingy cages and their inhabitants which could easily be seen from the top deck of the slow moving tram. Each of the cages held one girl fastened to the wall by a chain long enough so that if she had a customer she could take him behind the curtain which divided the cage. The girls in these cages, some of them Europeans, their breasts uncovered because of the skimpy saris they had to wear thrust their hands through the bars of the cages in an attempt to attract potential customers. All of them were nearing the end of their lives as prostitutes and though they may have started their working lives in the ornate establishments at the top of the road, over the years they had been traded downwards until they had arrived in these cages where only a few annas were required to buy their services.

On the crowded road cycle rickshaws and gharries, their drivers sounding their bells and shouting, all added to the noise and seemingly impossible confusion as they jostled for position dodging pedestrians, wandering cows and stray dogs alike all of them trying to go faster than the crowd would allow while through it all, the tram, with the driver clanging his warning bell inched its way along the track. Once it had passed the last of the cages and market stalls, however, there was no longer such a dense crowd and although the bright lights had given way to comparative darkness the tramcar was able to increase speed so that before very long it was approaching the end of the road where the passengers could make out some of the houses, now brothels, standing in their own grounds which a few years ago had probably been owned by the wealthier members of society, people who were perhaps in the State Government or in commerce but who had quickly left as soon as the road turned to its own type of commerce.

On its journey back to the terminus the tram didn't return down Grants Road so its progress was much quicker which meant that less than an hour after leaving Paul was back at the Taj.

As he entered the bar he heard someone calling his name and he saw James Armitage sitting with two other men sitting at a corner table. Although he had met James on a number of occasions both here in Bombay and in Ramuda when James made his annual visit to the mills neither were aware of the part they had already played in each others life.

James introduced Paul to his two friends and ordered drinks.

"How long are you planning to stay in Bombay?" James enquired.

"Paul couldn't tell him about his mother so he trotted out the story he had already invented to cover up the fact that he would be staying with her.

105

"Well I only arrived yesterday but I have to leave on Monday because I want to see some friends in Delhi. I don't know how long I will be there but I might come back for a few days before I go back to Ramuda."

"Ramuda. That's a terrible place. Who would want to live there?" one of the men said. James smiled.

"I know what you think about anywhere that isn't Bombay or Delhi, George but it just happens there are some very big textile mills in the South and the ones in Ramuda are probably the biggest. I agree not everyone would choose to live there but it isn't so bad is it Paul?"

"Oh yes it is" Paul replied with a smile "it certainly isn't like Bombay. In fact if you couldn't get away once in a while you could go crazy."

As they sipped their drinks their conversation turned as conversations always did, to the war and the lack of success for the allies.

"On thing the war has done is to help the textile industry" Paul said "Because Lancashire has not been exporting as much, the factories here have been forced to produce more."

"Well you had better make hay while the sun shines" one of James' friends said "because that will change when the war is over."

"I don't think it will" Paul replied "once something becomes established it is not always easily reversed."

"Paul is right" James said. "The war has helped the cotton industry but it hasn't helped me much. Its now almost impossible to get spares from England and America so engineering shops are setting up to make many of the spares required not only for the textile industry but other industries as well so even when the war is over they will probably carry on."

During dinner they continued to discuss the war and the effect it was having on India little knowing the dramatic event that was about to take place which would change the status and policy of India and countries all over the Far East forever.

12

Today, Sunday, December the 7th was going to be the day that Colonel Jenkins of the Fourteenth Horse and Officer commanding the Army Garrison in Poona had thought would never happen. All through his army career he had played polo and since coming to India it had been his ambition to play in the team that won the Inter Regimental Polo Cup. As a player he had never managed it having twice been defeated in the final but as he lay in bed waiting for the dawn he rehearsed the speech he would have to make at the celebratory lunch when the team from his regiment was successful in the final to be played here in Poona later this morning. The possibility that the team might lose never entered his head. He was convinced that later today his wife would be presenting the cup to Major "Dicky" Dickson the team captain. He was just beginning to doze when he was disturbed by someone knocking at the door of the bungalow. Quickly he threw back the single sheet that covered him, slipped from under the mosquito net then without even bothering to put on a robe and his glasses padded out of the bedroom, opened the front door to reveal Lieutenant Francis the duty officer.

"I'm sorry to disturb you Sir" the young officer said "but there's been a call from H.Q. They want you to call them back immediately."

"What time is it Francis?" he asked and was told it was almost five o'clock. "Damn and blast it" he muttered under his breath I'll put some clothes on and be with you in five minuts. You can start to call them back" and as the duty officer set off back to the garrison office Jenkins went back inside to get dressed.

"What is it David? Is something wrong? His wife asked sleepily.

"I don't know dear" he replied as he dressed "There's been a call from H.Q. so it must be something important.

He strode off towards the office as fast as he could, his limp, the result of a polo accident, more pronounced when he was hurrying wondering what the call could be about. He just managed to get to his office when the 'phone rang.

"Jenkins here" he growled and then after a pause "Good morning Sir" then he stood in complete silence with only the occasional "yes Sir" until eventually he said "I will see to it immediately Sir" and replaced the receiver. He stood for a few seconds just looking at the telephone and glancing at his watch he called for the Duty Officer.

"Tell the clerk to go to the Guard Room and get the Guard Commander and tell the R.S.M. I want him and while he is doing that you go and get the Adjutant and the Company Commanders, I want them here immediately." Within minutes the clerk had given the Guard Commander the message and as he turned to leave the Guard Room the men not on guard asked him what was going on.

"How the bloody hell do I know" he said "but I will tell you one thing whatever it is it is bloody important."

The first to answer the C.O's summons was the R.S.M. complete with his pace stick and just as smart as he always was closely followed by the Adjutant and the Company Commanders. When everyone was present Colonel Jenkins told them what had happened a few hours ago at Pearl Harbour and explained because Germany had allied itself to Japan the U.S.A. had declared war on Germany as well as Japan and the U.K. had declared war on Japan.

Instructions had also been received that the whole garrison except for a skeleton staff had been ordered to leave by 1330 hrs. for Bombay where they would camp until sea transport could be arranged.

As the officers departed to carry out his instructions Jenkins set off to his bungalow where his wife was anxiously waiting for him.

"Whats happening David?" she asked as soon as he entered. He guided his wife to a chair and sitting facing her told her what had happened at Pearl Harbour and that he had received orders for the whole garrison to leave for Bombay

"Why do you need sea transport, where are you going" she asked. "I dont know" he replied "I suppose I will only find out our final destination when we arrive in Bombay but I suppose it could be somewhere in Burma." "What about me and all the other wives and children" his wife asked "what will happen what will we do?"

"I don't know" he said taking hold of his wife's hands "But you know as well as I that sooner or later the army will come along and tell you what you have to do. For the time being you will all have to stay here in Poona and you might not move at all but perhaps you could go to Simla but I am afraid I just do not know."

"I think it's probably more likely that this place will eventually be put on a war footing which means, of course that wives and children won't be able to stay but decisions about wives and family will not have been made just yet.

L/Cpl "Dusty" Miller was sleeping off the effects of the night before he had been to the Blue Parrot with his mates where the attraction of music and girls had just about compensated for the hangover the cheap booze had given him. He wasn't on duty today and was fast asleep when suddenly the Barrack Room door was flung open and Sgt. Calvert, a small peppery man with a red face and black moustache bellowed ~"~Get on Parade" and just in case the likes of Dusty hadn't heard he marched between the two lines of beds and wherever there was a stationary body on a bed took hold of a bottom corner lifted it, and then let it crash back to the floor screaming at the occupant to "get on parade You have five minutes."

The shouting went through the sleepers brains like the scream from some banshee from hell and even though the men leapt out of bed protesting that they were not on duty they still rushed to get ready. They washed and dressed, all the time cursing the fucking Army and the bastard sergeants but all the while still trying to be on parade in the five minutes Sgt. Calvert had demanded.

"Is this some bloody stupid exercise? What the bloody hell is going on?" "I'm not on duty." "Which stupid idiot had this daft idea?" But despite their cursing the men were soon on parade where the C.O. was waiting to address them.

For the rest of the morning all hell broke loose as the various sections not only packed their personal equipment but that of their particular sections into the lorries which were hurriedly being fuelled by their drivers and mechanics.

Five hours later Dusty was at the wheel of "Bessy" the three ton Morris Commercial Truck, steering it towards the barrack gate at the start of the journey to Bombay. Beside him sat his friend Pte. Bill Brown who along with Dusty was responsible for ensuring that "Bessy" reached her destination. "Bessy" was an important part of the convoy because unlike the other lorries she didn't carry troops or their equipment but spares such as engine parts, wheels, tyres and a large container of petrol. It was because of the petrol that Dusty and Billy, both non-smokers had been chosen to drive "Bessy."

"Why are we going to Bombay?" shouted Billy above the noise of the engine.

"I'm buggered if I know" Dusty replied as he changed gear "you 'eard the C.O. he said we 'ad to go to Bombay and if 'e sez we go to Bombay then that's what we bloody well do."

"This would 'appen on a stop day" moaned Billy.

"D'you think the bloody Japs were worried about that when they were bombing the Yanks at Pearl Harbour this morning?" Dusty said.

"'ow d'you think I feel? I was with Alice last night and I was supposed to be seeing her again tonight."

Alice was one of the many Anglo-Indian girls who frequented the nightclub in the hope they might find a soldier they could eventually persuade to marry them and then take them back to Britain the land of their dreams. Billy knew his pal had been seeing Alice for about the last three weeks.

"Well 'ow did you get on did you get it?" Dusty glanced across at him.

"No, but I am getting bloody nearer. I reckon another couple of weeks will see me with my leg over" he said with a smile. He took his hands from the wheel and rubbed them in anticipation of the event and to dry the perspiration on his hands to enable him to grip the wheel more firmly.

They approached the barrack gates where a red capped military policeman waved them out and directed them on to the main road to Bombay many hours away. Once on the main road the convoy started to increase speed and the two in the cab of "bessy" where able to renew their conversation.

"Well she's a good looking lass" Billy nodded "and she's got a great figure but now we have moved out it looks as though you won't get another couple of weeks with her." As he changed into top gear Dusty glanced across at his companion.

"I reckon we'll be back in a few days time. You know what this lots like they don't know their arse from their elbow. This flap will die down and then we will all come rolling back, you'll see."

Almost the last vehicle to pass the barracks before the convoy started to leave was Eunice Williams in her Austin car.

She didn't drive herself so she employed a driver and always insisted he never drove too fast and although they were a couple of miles in front of the convoy the distance between them didn't increase.

Soon the small car entered the ghat section, a twisting turning descent down the mountains leading to the plains below. Some of the bends were easy to negotiate but others were hairpin bends which even in a small car had to be negotiated carefully in order to allow for the traffic labouring up the steep incline. The driver eased through one of the sharper bends and was beginning to turn for another when there was a lurch and a bumping noise from the back of the car. The driver guessed they had a puncture and turned the car to the side of the road. As soon as they came to a halt both Eunice and the driver got out to discover the back near side tyre had punctured. After a quick check the driver started to unload the luggage from the boot in order to get to the spare wheel. Near the back of the convoy Dusty started down the twisting road automatically hauling on the steering wheel to guide Bessy through yet another hairpin bend when suddenly there was no resistence from the pedal under his right foot.

"The brakes 'ave gone" he shouted. Instantly Billy grabbed the handbrake situated between him and Dusty and heaved on it as hard as he could while Dusty unsuccessfully fought to engage a lower gear but now the lorry was in neutral and the handbrake under these circumstances was not sufficient to hold the lorry which started to go faster and faster so all Dusty could do was to try and steer the runaway vehicle.

~With the contents of the lorry crashing and banging behind him and almost standing upright with his right foot pumping the useless brake pedal he heaved on the steering wheel to negotiate yet another bend.

"Please God don't let anything be coming up" he prayed then yelled at his companion to jump out but Billy took no notice seemingly unable to take his hands off the handbrake which he was still pulling with all his might. They saw the lorry in front on which they were quickly gaining disappear round a tight curve to the left and even though they were now travelling far too fast Dusty somehow coaxed Bessy round the curve but then couldn't straighten the lorry out of the turn. To his horror the lorry in front pulled away to the right and Dusty saw then the stationary car at the side of the road. With the camber of the road and the speed they were now travelling he knew he could not pass the car so in one last despairing effort he pulled the steering wheel as hard as he could to the left in an attempt to run into the cliff and hopefully stop before he hit the car. But even as he did he knew it was too late and then he saw the woman standing near the car and a man with a red turban crouched at the back wheel. As they heard the noise of the approaching lorry they both looked up and the man in a despairing attempt to escape flung himself into the rain ditch. With tortuous screams of ripping, scraping metal Bessy slid into the stationary car and the stores including the petrol came hurtling through the canvas side which burst open as they struck the rockface. Momentarily there was a deathly silence and then with a tremendous "whoosh" the petrol ignited. The lorry behind the stricken wagon braked to a halt as did all the following wagons the occupants of some of them carrying fire extinguishers fought the blaze but the fire was too fierce to even think of trying to save the four victims.

Next morning as Paul walked up the path to the door of his mother's bungalow he was met by his mother's butler with the information that his mother had not returned as she was supposed to the night before. Paul was surprised at this because his mother was most punctilious about meetings and being on time and he could not remember an occasion when she had been late let alone not turn up at all.

Worried, he walked across to the teak table where she kept her address book and looked up the telephone number of her friend in Poona.

They were surprised to hear it was Paul who was ringing but even more surprised when he asked if his mother was still with them At first there was silence then,

"We heard earlier that there had been a terrible accident on the road to Bombay between some Army lorries and a civilian car but we didn't worry because your mother left before the Army convoy" Mr. Campbell said "but now you have told us that your mother has not arrived I don't know what to say." Paul thanked Mr. Campbell and replaced the receiver

He was about to rush off to the Police Station when he remembered that he and his mother had an appointment with a solicitor called Ghosh so he looked once more in the address book and a short time later he was telling the solicitor about the accident and his worry that it was his mother's car that was involved. The solicitor suggested that they cancel the appointment so that Paul could go to the Police Station and a short time later he was in the office of Inspector Mills.

"I don't know about your mother Mr. Williams but yesterday there was an accident involving an Army truck and a stationary car. We think the car must have had a puncture and the driver was changing the wheel when an Army truck carrying petrol went out of control and crashed into the stationary car. Unfortunately four people, two of them soldiers in the truck, a Sikh who we think must have been the driver of the car and a woman who was probably the passenger were all killed."

"Was the woman my mother?" Paul asked.

"I am afraid we don't know because all four bodies were so badly burnt that identification is impossible. The Army authorities know who the two soldiers were and we know the driver of the car was a Sikh because other members of the convoy saw him as they passed but we don't know who he and the woman were. Do you by any chance know the registration number of your mother's car."

Paul reached into his coat pocket where he had put some of his mother's documents just in case the Police wanted them. He watched as the inspector compared them with the report of the accident and when he saw the policeman's jaw line stiffen he feared the worst.

"I'm very sorry to have to tell you this Mr. Williams but your mother's car is the one involved in the accident so it is more than likely that she was the passenger who was killed.

"But you don't know for certain that it is her. It just might not be my mother, so why don't you let me see the body?"

Inspector Mills looked at the man opposite.

"It's amazing how people cling to the most impossible ideas" he thought then he said, "I don't think that would be a good idea, Mr. Williams. All four bodies were so badly burned that identification is totally impossible and we recommend that no-one sees them" he paused, "however we do have a few items that survived the fire, just wait a few minutes and I will fetch them." He got up from his desk and left the office. "How many more times must I do this sort of thing" he grumbled to himself. "I should retire in three months time but now I bet this bloody war will change everything." After a few minutes he returned carrying a badly burned suitcase which he placed on the desk.

"This was found inside the car. Do you recognize it?"

Paul shook his head as the policeman opened the case and started to remove the badly burned contents. There were only remnants of clothes but one of them was the same colour as one of his mother's favourite dresses and one she would have surely taken with her to visit friends. Inspector Mills moved the remains of the clothing to one side and took out a small leather box but even though it was badly burnt, Paul recognized it.

"This jewellery box maybe our best hope" the inspector said as he flipped open the lid and put the little box on the desk. A look of anguish came across Paul's face as he reached over and took out some of the pieces. Here were some earings his father bought for one of his wife's birthdays, a broach bought one Christmas he couldn't remember how many years ago and in one corner a ring he had bought for his mother's birthday when they were in England. With great sadness he remembered how he had thought the ring contained real diamonds and rubies and how he had saved his spending money in order to buy it and now here it lay, proof that it really was his mother who had been killed in this dreadful accident.

Neither man spoke until Inspector Mills said very gently,

"I am very sorry Mr. Williams" and he held out his hands, "I am afraid I must ask for the jewellery. We have to hold on to everything until our enquiries are completed."

Just then there was a knock on the door and a policeman entered to tell the inspector a solicitor called Ghosh who claims to represent Mrs. Williams had arrived and wants to know if he can be of any assistance. Inspector Mills looked across at Paul.

"Yes, he is my mother's lawyer. She and I should have had an appointment with him this morning".

Even though he had never met the lawyer before, he very quickly felt, just as his mother had, that he could trust the little man and very soon with his help he was able to satisfy the policeman that the body was indeed that of his mother. He sat back, completely devastated as Mr. Ghosh filled out all the necessary forms the police required and then when all the formalities were completed he accompanied him back to his office.

"I don't know what to say" Mr. Ghosh said "I can hardly believe what has happened. Its only just over a week ago that I last saw her and she was telling me how much she was looking forward to seeing you." Because this was their first meeting and because of the tragic circumstances it was a little awkward for both of them but nevertheless Paul was only too ready to agree when Mr. Ghosh asked if he would like to leave the arrangements for the funeral to him because he didn't want anyone at Ramuda Textiles to know that he had been born and brought up in India.

After the funeral which took place three days later and one day before he had to return to Ramuda, Paul and Mr. Ghosh returned to the lawyer's office and after they were seated Paul handed him a list he had compiled indicating which of his mother's effects he wanted to keep. The lawyer glanced at it and put it to one side of his desk and then opening a drawer took out a manila file tied with pink ribbon which he placed on the desk in front of him.

Still not speaking he slowly untied the ribbon and then said to Paul "This is your mother's Will which I have to read to you".

Mr. Ghosh took out an envelope addressed to Paul from the folder.

"I helped your mother write this letter so I know it's contents and in my opinion I think it might be better if I go through it with you".

Disregarding Mr. Ghosh's suggestion Paul decided he would read it himself and he took the letter from him. Inside were two sheets of paper which he straightened out before he started to read while Mr. Ghosh sat watching the different emotions crossing his face. When Paul had finished reading the letter he looked up at the solicitor with tears running down his face.

"What does this mean?" he asked "Did you know about this?" Mr. Ghosh nodded.

"Yes, I told you before you opened it that I knew what it contained."

Paul picked up the letter and started to read it once more.

Dear Paul,

Writing this letter is the most difficult thing I have ever had to do in my entire life. Let me begin by telling you once more how much I love youand how much I have always loved you. I have also been so proud of you and I am sure that no mother had a better son. But that really is the very problem and why this letter is so hard to write because no matter how I try to say what I have to say I will not get it right so the only way is the simple way. I am sorry, Paul, I am not your birth mother. You are not my natural son. The manyou knew as your father was not your real father either. He was my husband but we could not have any children and when an English lady, who was on holiday in India, had a child which she could not take back to England she and your real father decided the only thing to do was to have the baby adopted. You, my dear Paul, were that baby.

But I want you to know that both my husband and I thought of you as our child and we could not have looked after you any better than if you had been our very own.

We were both so proud of you and loved you so very much. Please forgive me for being a coward and not telling you sooner but I wanted you as my son for as long as possible.

Goodbye, all my fondest love,
Mother

As the lawyer sat quietly waiting Paul read the letter over and over until after about the fourth time he looked up,

"But she doesn't tell me who my real mother and father are. Do you know?"

Mr. Ghosh looked down at the papers in front of him and selected an envelope. He checked the writing on the front then handed it to Paul, who for a second time that day opened a mysterious envelope. With a feeling of apprehension he withdrew the sheet of paper inside and started to read whilst Mr. Ghosh sat back in his chair quietly waiting for the questions he was sure would follow as soon as Paul had taken in the contents.

France 1916

Dear Paul,

You are reading this letter because of a combination of quite disparate circumstances. The first of these is because I am dead. If that were not so you would not have this letter in your hand. The second is that your adopted mother has died, or the third the happiest of all reasons, is that you are now thirty years old.

When I agreed to your adoption I stipulated you should be urged to persue a career in textiles. My family, the Brents, have large interests in textiles in India . . . .

Paul looked up at Mr. Ghosh with a look of incredulity while Mr. Ghosh, with a slight movement of his hand, urged Paul to finish reading the rest of the letter.

. . . . My father, Arthur Brent being one of the founders of Ramuda Textiles. I was expected to take over from him when he retired but instead

I decided to leave the company and return to Britain. No, that is not true. I didn't just leave the company I was dismissed, not because of you, but for something else, even so I often hoped I would return to India but unfortunately it was not to be. But now perhaps you will understand why I wanted you to make textiles your career and, perhaps, if possible, join Ramuda Textiles.

The last question you will want answering is "who is your mother?" Unfortunately I am not empowered to tell you. I had to agree that it would be up to her to make herself known to you. If this has not happened then I can only say that for some reason this is what she wants. For my part I am only sorry I cannot tell you all this in person but I want you to know I never stopped thinking about you.

May good luck and future happiness be yours forever.

Your loving father,
Walter Brent.

Paul came to the end of the letter with a feeling of great sadness and also surprise. He looked up at the silent lawyer then read the letter over again before putting it down on the desk. Mr. Ghosh then handed Paul another envelope which he ripped open and took out the contents. There were a number of sheets of paper clipped together the top one being a letter from a firm of solicitors in Liverpool, England, which stated they had been instructed byMr. Walter Brent to draw up his Will and forward a copy to Mr. Ghosh of Bombay along with any relevant correspondence.

The next page was a letter from the British War Office informing the next of kin that Corporal Walter Brent had been in killed in action on July the first 1916. The Government expressed their sympathy.

He then read the next page which turned out to be the last Will and Testament of his father but after all he had read and been told he just could not absorb all the detail.

"Have you seen this?" he enquired, stupidly ignoring the fact that Mr. Ghosh had put all the papers in the envelope.

"Yes I know what is there" the lawyer said.

"Does it mean what I think it means?" Paul asked.

"Yes it does. Your father inherited his father's shares in Ramuda Textiles so all the shares are yours. The value plus cash left in England

comes to nearly ninety thousand pounds but that is not all we have
to attend to there is the matter of your Mother's or should I say Mrs.
Williams estate. Paul held up his hand.

You corrected yourself then Mr. Ghosh. Please remember in future if
you refer to my mother then that person is Mrs. Williams but having said
that, there is one thing I have to ask, One last question, Do you know the
identity of my Natural mother?"

"Yes I do."

"Well who is it?"

"I'm afraid I cannot tell you. Part of the agreement when you were
adopted was that I had to keep secret the name of the woman who was
your natural mother and, as a lawyer, I cannot break that promise but if
you wish I will write to her and ask if, after all these years, I can reveal her
name to you particularly in view of the fact that Mr. and Mrs. Williams
and your natural father are now all dead." Paul sat deep in thought trying
to take in all that he had heard in the past few minutes.

"No. Perhaps I should wait. If my mother wants to contact me then
she will," He paused and then continued,

"You know when I heard the name Brent a few minutes ago I didn't
think of Ramuda Textiles I don't know why. I suppose I should have
because it isn't a very common name but for some reason I didn't. Do you
know anything else about my father?"

"Not really" the lawyer replied. "I know that after you had been
adopted he went back to Melur for a couple of years or so then apart from
an exchange of letters the next contact I had with him was when he called
to see me before he left for England.

Paul tried to recall that he had heard about Walter Brent but all
he could remember was the story he had been dismissed because of a
drinking problem. But a drink problem in India was not uncommon.
Many people who went to India drank a lot but they didn't lose their jobs.
Suddenly a thought came into his head, a thought which over the next
few years would grow until it dominated his entire life. What if George
Brent and his father wanted him out so that George, who was younger
than Walter would become chairman of the company. In the years ahead
the more he thought about it the more he convinced himself they made
his drinking an excuse to get rid of him. There was no doubt the Brents
had sacked him, he went back to England to join the army and was killed.

If he had not been dismissed he would have been chairman instead of George. Although he had never known his father in these few minutes in this office in Bombay the seeds were sown for what would eventually grow into a burning hatred for the Brents. His thoughts were interrupted by Mr. Ghosh.

"Can we now talk about your mother's estate" he said. "I don't suppose you will want to keep the restaurant or the bungalow so if you wish I could put them up for sale, pay off any outstanding debts, in fact settle all your mother's affairs."

"You are right. I would be very pleased if you would see to things for me." Mr. Ghosh slid a paper across the desk.

"I prepared this Power of Attorney. It means I can act without continually having to refer to you."

"When everything is settled how much do you think I will receive" Paul asked.

"I have done a rough calculation" Mr Ghosh replied "and I think it should be in excess of two lakhs of rupees.

Paul could hardly believe it with the money from his father and now his mother he was probably worth in excess of £200,000.

13

Because the war prevented many of the usual imports from Britain the Indian textile industry was busier than ever as it tried not only to make up the shortfall but also to meet the demands of the war effort and none more so than the mills in Ramuda whose staff were particularly hard pressed because of George Brent's "war work". Early in 1940 he had been asked if he would take charge of recruitment for the armed forces in the Ramuda District so had opened an office in part of the Rex Cinema in the centre of the town, which he staffed on a part time basis with clerks from the factory. At first, when the war was confined to Europe it had not been very busy but now with the war against the Japanese coming ever nearer to India there were many more volunteers so that he had to spend a lot more time at the recruiting office. Not only did he spend more time there but he also recruited many of his staff, both European and Indian, which meant that the remainder and in particular his son, Philip, had to work longer and harder than before.

It was already dark as, Paul, who had just returned from the factory after the last of a tiring 10 day run, sat on the verandah with his usual glass of beer contemplating the events of yet another busy day and, as almost every night, his thoughts turned to the one subject that not only dominated his entire life but was changing his whole character.

The initial anger that Paul had felt when he had been told about his father and his own birth and adoption had festered and grown so that now he was blind to the failings of his father and spent hours plotting and discarding ideas of how he could make George and Philip pay for what they had done. He was now totally convinced that when they took away his father's job they became responsible not only for his death but also the loss of his son's heritage. The fact that they never knew Walter had a son just didn't matter.

One option was to do nothing until after the war. George Brent would retire and that would only leave Philip to deal with but then what sort of revenge would that be after all George Brent had done? No he must not be allowed to get off scot-free.

Despite his almost pathological desire for revenge Paul knew he could not act precipitously and so until a chance occurred he decided that the best thing that he could do was to make himself as indispensable to the company as possible so that when he did strike suspicion would be diverted from him. As a result he was often called upon to act in Philip's place when a visit to Melur was necessary and it was during one such visit that he learned more about his father.

As Paul got out of the car in Melur he couldn't help but think how the compound and factories were a replica of those in Ramuda but then, of course, they would be because the Brents had used the same plans for both.

He walked through the large office acknowledging the salaams of the clerks as he passed and entered the corridor where the senior managers had their offices and after knocking on the door of the last one, walked in.

Jack Howarth, the General Manager, looked up and seeing who it was got to his feet his hand outstretched. A few minutes later the two men were drinking tea and from then until well into the afternoon they discussed matters concerning the Textile Industry and the mills at Melur in particular. Paul had been waiting for this opportunity to come to Melur on his own because he wanted to find someone who might remember his father and what happened to cause his dismissal. Obviously it would be no use talking to the Europeans because they were not in Melur when Walter Brent was dismissed and could only tell him whatever they had been told by the Indian staff. Evan asking some of the older Indian staff might be risky so he knew he had to be very careful but he thought he knew someone who might be able to help him. From his previous visits he remembered that in the compound where the Europeans lived there was a tennis court with a pavilion in which there was a billiards table looked after by an elderly man who was helped by three small boys or "chokras" to maintain the tennis court and the pavilion. Whenever tennis was played the old man was the umpire and scorer while the three boys acted as ball boys. Even if the old man must have been nearing seventy he would play if there was a player short and often would play with the first player to arrive until the others turned up which is what Paul intended tonight. Leaving Jack to finish off his daily routine he hurried to the bungalow reserved for visitors and foregoing tea, changed and rushed out to the tennis court where, as usual, the marker and three chokra were waiting.

As soon as Paul appeared the marker led the others on to the court and they took up their positions, one at each of the base lines and the oldest at the net deputising for the marker. Paul made a pretence of tying his shoe laces while engaging the old man in conversation which he directed to memories of Europeans who had worked at Melur. He told Paul he had started to work at the tennis club as a chokra and could remember Mr. George, Philip's father as ayoung man before Philip was born and he could also remember seeing Mr, George's father and uncle the two men who had started the company.

"Didn't Mr. George have a brother who also worked here?" Paul asked knowing full well he was wrong. The marker took off his glasses and cleaned the lens on his shirt.

"No Sir. Mr. George didn't have a brother he had a cousin but he didn't stay long he went back to England."

"What was his name then?" Paul asked looking away as if he was only mildly interested. "What happened to him?" He hoped the other tennis players wouldn't arrive just yet because this old man might be the only person who could tell him about his father.

The marker shuffled his feet and looked down at the ground, obviously a little unsure about how much to say to Mr. Williams. Paul was just about to urge him to carry on when he cleared his throat and looked up.

"The man you are thinking about was Mr. Walter Brent" he said. Paul could hardly contain himself. This man knew his father and had probably played tennis with him. He wanted to know more before the others arrived.

"Mr. Walter came here about 1909 or 1910 I can't remember just when but I know he left in 1912. There was a lot of trouble. Mr. Walter liked to drink and he drank too much." He waited hoping he had not said too much then he went on.

"But he was a good tennis player Sir. We often used to play together and sometimes we would play billiards."

"Was it because of the drinking Mr. Walter had to leave?"

"I don't know why he left but there was something else." Paul waited.

"There was some trouble with an Indian lady. We heard she was being forced to commit suttee and Mr. Walter rescued her and brought her back to his bungalow. How Mr. Walter knew her or why he rescued her nobody ever knew but I remember she was very beautiful. She stayed in his bungalow with him until Mr. George's father found out and then he went home."

"What happened to the lady when Mr. Walter was sent back to England. Did she go as well?"

"I don't think so Sir. All I know is she left here the same day as he did.

I don't think anyone knows where she went," and as the other players started to arrive Paul turned to join them.

Not long after his visit to Melur Paul was in his office and reached out for the pile of mail which had just been put on his desk. On top of the pile was a square envelope which he knew would be an invitation to some damned wedding or christening and in his mind he was ready to throw it into the waste paper basket. But this one was different. Opening the envelope he took out a gold embossed invitation from the Chairman of N.V.R. Transport the company which transported all the raw cotton from the ginneries. The Chairman of N.V.R. was holding a reception for Mr. Rajagopalachariar, one of the leading figures in the Congress Party and so Paul knew that this would not be a run of the mill invitation but one that he would have to attend.

Although he obviously knew the Company Paul had never met Mr. Rajan so in the next few days he set about finding out as much as he could about him. Mainly through talking to other Europeans and some of the Indian staff he discovered Mr. Rajan had once owned a shop opposite the factory gate. There had been four children but the eldest son had died when he was in his teens then much later his eldest daughter returned to live with him after her husband died and it was shortly after that the transport company was started. It was rumoured that she was the driving force in the company and had badgered her father into approaching Ramuda Textiles for a loan which he obtained because George Brent not only thought a transport company would be successful and useful but because he knew and trusted Mr. Rajan.

On the day of the reception Paul drove up the winding road which led to the large house on the top of the hill and after parking walked across the sandy parking area and up two steps to the immaculately polished marble floored verandah where he was met by the Sales Manager of the company who he had met many times who introduced him to Mr. Rajan.

Paul remembered that he had seen the old man at the factory but had never spoken to him. They chatted for a few minutes before Mr. Rajan led him across the room to where Mr. Rajagopalachariar was sitting next to a very attractive lady dressed in an ivory coloured sari who was listening very attentively to what he was saying. Her hair was brushed severely from her face and hung down in a plait intertwined with temple blossom. Her jewellery consisted of obviously expensive earings and a large diamond ring on one of the fingers of her right hand.

After introducing Paul to the main guest he said "May I introduce you to my daughter". Paul was a little surprised that instead of putting her hands together in the normal Indian greeting she held out her hand. Her handshake was firm and she looked directly at him. Even though he guessed she was old enough to be his mother she was still very attractive with a smooth complexion, lipstick on her full lips and her eyes made up in the fashion of Indian women. Much to his surprise Paul found he could converse with her unlike most Indian women he had met who would usually only mumble a reply to a question or answer through their husband even though they could, very often, speak better English than he could and was very disappointed when her father took her away to introduce her to other guests.

Paul joined some of the other guests and on more than one occasion when he glanced across the room he was surprised to see Mrs. Rajan very obviously looking in his direction before she turned to give her attention to the person sitting next to her. As the guests stood talking occasionally moving from one group to the other, waiters carrying trays of different drinks moved among them but just as Paul was about to join a group containing Mrs. Rajan he was thwarted by her father clapping his hands together and announcing that lunch was ready whereupon Mrs. Rajan excused herself to join the principal guest and lead the way into the large dining room next door where a buffet style meal was waiting. Paul was handed a plate by one of the waiters which he filled with a selection of samoosas, bahjas, chutneys and pickles promising himself he would return later to sample the varied selection of cakes, fruits etc. He carried his plate across the room to a vacant chair and as he ate he could not help but smile to himself when he thought how well the chairman of the company had done to permutate a small shop and a loan of the few thousand rupees into a business that afforded a lifestyle like this.

Wilst he was considering this he bcame aware of someone standing near him and when he looked up he saw the ivory coloured sari of Mrs. Rajan.

"May I join you?" she smiled down at him. Paul his mouth full of samoosa, tried to balance the plate whilst struggling to get to his feet and at the same time swallow what was in his mouth.

"Don't get up" she said with a smile sitting on the chair next to him "How are you enjoying your life in Ramuda?" she asked. She was only carrying a wine glass from which she took a sip. Paul put down his fork

"Very much he said. I always wanted to come to India and when a position with Ramuda Textiles was advertised in the local paper I applied and was lucky enough to be accepted so here I am. But just at this time I should not be here because if it hadn't been for the war I would be on leave in England".

"And if you had gone back to England on leave would you be planning to return or have you had enough of India?" she asked.

"No, er I mean yes" and he laughed. "Yes I would be coming back and no I haven't had enough of India." How could he explain that India was really his home. They talked while Paul finished eating and Mrs. Rajan pointed to his cuff links.

"Where did you get such lovely cuff links?" she asked. Paul glanced at the blue cuff links and then turned his wrist so Mrs. Rajan could see them more closely. She examined the monogram while Paul explained that Mrs. Leather the wife of the owner of the factory where he worked in England had given them to him just before he left for India.

"What does the monogram stand for?" she asked.

"She never told me but I suppose the W is for Mr. Leather whose first name was William and the M must be for Margaret his wife and I suppose the 'P' must be for me.

"They are certainly very nice." Just then a servant came across and whispered something to her.

"I am afraid you will have to excuse me. My father wants me." Mrs. Rajan said.

Three days later Paul was sitting in his office when one of the office messengers entered carrying a plain white envelope and he was very surprised when he read the short note it contained. It was from Mrs. Rajan asking him if he could come to the house around 11'o'clock the following morning. He read the note for a second time. What on earth could Mrs. Rajan want with him. He couldn't begin to guess but whatever it was he knew he would be there.

It was exactly 11'o'clock when Paul walked on to the verandah and was surprised to see Mrs. Rajan and not the butler waiting to greet him.

She led him to some cane chairs at the back of the verandah away from the direct sunlight and no sooner were they seated when the same butler he had seen at the reception appeared with a tray containing glasses and a jug of fresh lime juice which he placed on the table and after filling two glasses disappeared through the same curtained door through which he had appeared.

Mrs. Rajan sipped her drink and then put it down on a silver coaster.

"I suppose you are wondering why I asked you to come here today" she said. Without waiting for a reply she reached inside her handbag and took out a small jewellery box which she placed on the table in front of Paul and indicated for him to open it. Paul lifted the box from the table and pressed the catch at the side of the box. His mouth fell open when he saw what was inside. He could not believe it. Lying on a bed of white silk was a replica of one of his cufflinks. Except for being larger it was identical. He knew it was a ladies broach made out of the same material as his cufflinks but when he looked at it more closely he just could not believe it. It had the same monogram. Eventually he looked up.

"Where did you get this?" "What is it?" There were so many questions he wanted to ask and so many answers he needed.

Mrs. Rajan held up her hand her long fingers appearing to bend slightly backwards in a typical gesture he had seen used by Indian dancers.

"I will try to explain as best I can" she said, "I will start with the brooch. I received it from your father before he returned to England." Paul gasped . "you received it from my father? You knew my father, Walter Brent."

It was now Mrs. Rajan's turn to be surprised when Paul told her about his mother's death and about her will. Mr. Ghosh her lawyer gave me a letter from my father but he didn't tell me about my real moth . . . ." And he stopped. If his father had given this brooch to Mrs. Rajan then she must have been the girl he had been living with. It was because of Mrs. Rajan he had been sent back to England. Could it be that Mrs. Rajan was his mother?

Without thinking how impossible this was he gasped,

"Then you are my mother. That is how you come to have this brooch."

Mrs. Rajan was almost speechless this was not the reaction she expected.

"No. Paul I am not your mother but I could have been. I certainly loved your father and I lived with him but I am not your mother." She told him how his father had saved her life after her husband had died and her relatives were trying to make her commit suttee and then how he had looked after her even though he knew it would probably mean the loss of his job with Ramuda Textiles. Paul listened and was horrified at the thought of Mrs. Rajan being made to commit suttee. He could not contain himself.

"But then who is my mother do you know?". Mrs. Rajan shook her head.

"I think it would be best if I told you about this" she said picking up the brooch. "This was made at the same time as your cuff links here in India. A young and as far as I know very attractive young English woman came to India on holiday. She met and fell in love with Walter Brent, not a very difficult thing to do because, believe me, your father was a very handsome man. Eventually she discovered she was pregnant and as she was already married it was obvious she could not return to her husband so she, along with the friend she was staying with and her husband and with the help of a lawyer in Bombay hatched a scheme for her to have the baby in Goa. She wrote to her husband in England telling him she had a chance to go to Kashmir and would he mind if she stayed longer in India than she had planned.

He agreed but instead of Kashmir she went to Goa where she had her baby, you!

While she was in Goa Mr. Ghosh the lawyer looked for a suitable couple to adopt you and arrange for the adoption as soon as you were born."

As Paul listened he realised the important part Mr. Ghosh had played in his life and how lucky he had been that the lawyer had found the Williams who had been willing to adopt him.

"Before your mother left India" Mrs. Rajan continued "she had some jewellery made from some stones she had found on the beach in Goa, cuff links for your father and a brooch for herself.

Paul immediately realised that something was wrong.

"If she had the brooch made for herself and cuff links for my father how do you come to have the brooch?" Mrs. Rajan smiled.

"Well I think this is where the story becomes a little ridiculous. "I think when she had the jewellery made she probably put the cuff links and the brooch into identical boxes and then sent your father the wrong box."

"But how did you get the brooch?" Paul enquired

"When your father left he wanted to give me something that was precious to him and what could be more precious than this brooch so that if I ever met you I would be able to show it to you and tell you what I have just told you."

"But what about my mother . . . ." and then he stopped.

"Margaret Leather had the cuff links so the initials of the monogram were not for who he had thought. The "M" obviously is for Margaret, the "P" for Paul but the "W" is not for William but for Walter."

Paul was silent, his head bowed as he tried to come to terms with what he had just heard and the realisation that although he didn't know it at the time, he had met his real mother. He looked up at Mrs Rajan and smiled.

"Thank you very much Mrs. Rajan for all you have told me." He said.

"Paul I want to be your friend. Please call me Nirmala and remember if ever there is anything I can help you with then don't hesitate to ask me. After all I owe your father my life."

Driving back to the factory Paul was still trying to come to terms with what he had just heard and how his life should have been so different.

But one irrational but recurring thought was how badly he thought his father had been treated and that if his uncle had not dismissed him he would probably still be alive. To Paul it was almost as if his father had been murdered and it was then he decided that no matter what he had to do nor how long it took he would avenge his father's death.

14

Ramuda 1942

Every evening when Paul was alone in his bungalow his thoughts invariably turned to his father and what had happened to him until, ignoring any thoughts that his father had been the architect of his own dismissal he became completely obsessed with the idea that he had been cheated. He convinced himself he had been unjustly victimised and it was his duty to seek revenge. Every night he conjured up ways by which he could right the wrong but every plan always foundered on one important item. Even if he removed George Brent and his son there was no way he would assume control of the company a position he now believed should be his. After all he had only been with the company for just over six years so until he could sort out this problem there was nothing he could do and was no nearer to solving his problem until one day he was invited for a game of tennis and lunch at the home of Mark Hood and his wife.

The Hoods were not very good tennis players. Mark had a slightly deformed leg which slowed him down and Vera only played because her short skirt and tight blouse showed off her figure. Vera with her long blonde hair and petite figure liked the attentions of the opposite sex and Paul in particular and took every opportunity to touch him or put her arm round him whenever they played tennis together or if she could get near him in the swimming pool. He was prepared to put up with Vera, however, for the convenience of going to their bungalow which was not on the compound with the other bungalows but stood in its own grounds near the factories and was the only bungalow in the company which had its own tennis court and swimming pool.

Later in the day Paul remembered Mark had not said what time he wanted to play tennis so when he was passing Mark's office he went in. He didn't bother sitting down but as they talked he noticed the heading on one of the files on Mark's desk. B & M Textiles. Immediately he wondered why Mark would have a file on a small textile factory not very far from the temple and then he recalled a discussion he had overheard a few weeks ago between Philip and his father about having to refuse orders or how could they increase production. Could this be their answer, where they thinking of buying a factory? It would make sense. He tried to see more of the file but trying to read it upside down without attracting Mark's attention was impossible but from the little he could see it appeared that Mark was preparing a report on the company.

"I suppose about ten thirty will be early enough" Mark replied, "that should give us three or four sets before it really gets hot." They chatted for a few minutes before Paul returned to his desk where he sat thinking about what he had seen and what he thought it meant and a plan began to form.

It was just after ten thirty on the stop day when Paul turned his car into the drive of the Hood's compound and pulled up in the shade of some trees behind two other cars which he recognized as belonging to the Ashtons and the Johnstons. As he got out of his car a servant arrived to take his case and tennis racket and then led him along a path through some bushes to the side of the bungalow where Mark was sitting in a reclining chair watching Bill Ashton and his wife Grace playing Ray and Peggy Johnston. He turned his head as he heard Paul approaching

"Good morning Paul. Thanks for coming". But before Paul could reply Vera coming from the direction of the house called out,

"I'm so pleased you could come. What about a drink?" she said pointing to the various bottles on a drinks trolley." Paul waited while Vera poured the orange juice he had asked for and with glass in hand he sat down next to her husband.

"Are Philip and Alice not coming?" he said.

"No, Philip rang to say that Alice was not feeling very well" Vera said. As they talked they watched the court where the Johnstons were on the point of winding up a very one sided game.

"I suppose you want to change?" Mark said getting out of his chair, "I'll show you where to go" and he led Paul towards the house.

For the next two hours or so the group played tennis and Paul could not help wondering if the others noticed how Vera arranged it that he was her partner and how often she touched him and praised him whenever he won a point regardless of how easy or difficult it had been. Usually he found this a nuisance but today it was essential for what he had planned.

Eventually Mark declared it was too hot for anymore tennis and that a swim would be a better idea and in no time at all they had all changed and were cooling off in the pool. As he swam around Paul could not help wondering how Mark and Vera had ever got together. He was a gentle person, portly with a pale unhealthy looking complexion and despite playing tennis was not very athletic whilst Vera was slim to the point of thinness, tanned and very animated. Paul was enjoying the coolness of the water when he saw Vera pouring herself a drink so he swam across near to where she was standing, hauled himself out of the water and on the pretence of reaching for a glass rested his hand on her shoulder. This was the first time he had ever touched her like this but he left his hand where it was until she had filled his glass and handed it back to him. Never taking his eyes off her he took a deep drink and then held out his half empty glass.

"May I have a little more?" he asked with a smile. Putting one hand on Paul's as if to steady the glass Vera refilled it and then as if by common consent they both sat on the edge of the pool with their feet dangling in the water drinking and watching the others. Then almost nonchalantly and not appearing to worry if any of the others were watching, Vera traced her long fingernail along the outline of his shoulder blade. Paul quickly looked round to see if anyone, particularly Grace Ashton, who never seemed to miss anything amiss, had noticed but even she didn't appear to have seen what had happened. He turned his head slightly to find Vera looking at him. As their eyes met her pink tongue slowly licked her full bottom lip. Without a word Paul finished his drink and slid into the pool to join the others who were throwing a beach ball around. A few moments later he was just coming to the surface when he felt a hand on the front of his trunks. He shook the water from his eyes and looking round saw Vera swimming away.

Paul submerged again and swam across to the other side of the pool where he turned and stood with his knees bent so that he was almost totally under the water as Vera approached. He took a deep breath and sank down and with a push from the side of the pool he glided under the water towards her with his arms outstretched. As he passed under Vera he slid his hand under the top of her swimsuit and took her breast with its enlarged nipple, because of the cold water, in his hand and at the same time held her arm with his other hand so that she could not swim away. Vera had to stop swimming but almost before she realised what had happened Paul, still under water released her and with a strong kick turned and resurfaced at the other side of the pool where he again stood with the water up to his chin looking to see if anyone had seen what he had just done. Vera was swimming towards him but before she could reach him he again ducked under the water and pushing away from the wall swam underneath her allowing his hand to slide along her body from her breast, across her stomach and between her legs. She tried to catch hold of him but she was too late and before she could turn he was at the other end of the pool where he hoisted himself out of the water and without looking back walked over to the drinks table.

He stood chatting to Grace Ashton and Mark Hood at the same time watching the pool where Bill Ashton was floating on his back, occasionally moving his hands to keep him steady and the Johnsons were standing with the water just covering their shoulders, talking and occasionally swimming a few yards while Vera was slowly swimming across the pool totally ignoring him. Mark picked up his towel and began wiping the last remaining drops of water off his body that the sun had not already dried.

"I think I have had enough?" he said.

"I'll just have another few minutes then that will be it" Paul replied and taking a couple of strides dived in only surfacing when he had completed a full length of the pool underwater. He touched the end wall and taking a quick breath turned and started back. He was about halfway across the pool when he felt a pain like stabbing needles on his back. He stopped swimming and tried to look at his back to see what had happened.

"Did I catch you with my nails?" Vera called out. "I'm very sorry I didn't see you." Her eyes were glittering with excitement a she drew the tip of her tongue across her small white teeth.

"It's not much" Paul said as he sank back into the water and continued swimming. He completed ten lengths of the pool and at the end of the last one, without seeming to slow down, put his hands on the edge and in one movement sprang out and walked across to the chair where he had left his towel and started to dry his hair.

"I hope you feel better after that" Mark said "would you like another drink?" Paul nodded and pointed to the table where he had left his empty glass. As Mark reached out for it he saw the scratches on Paul's back.

"Is that what Vera did?" he asked "I thought I saw her catch you as she was flailing about. Her nails are like daggers" but before Paul could reply Vera called out from the shade of the verandah that lunch was ready. Mark led his guests, still only wearing their swim suits, across the spiky grass of the lawn to where tables had been set out for a buffet lunch. As

Paul was leaning over to spoon some food onto his plate Mark again saw the scratches on Paul's back.

"Have you seen what you did when you were swimming across the pool?" he said to his wife. "Those nails of yours are too long." Vera looked at the damage more closely taking the opportunity to slide her fingers along Paul's back.

"Did I do that" she enquired innocently.

"Oh it's nothing really" Paul said "It was probably my fault anyway. I should look where I am going."

"I think you should have something on those scratches, come inside and I will see to them for you" Vera said.

"No, no they will be alright. I'll attend to them when I get home". Mark Hood had filled his plate and was just about to sit down.

"I think it would be better if you let Vera put something on them old chap" he said.

Paul shrugged his shoulders and followed Vera as she led the way into the bungalow where as soon as they were out of sight of the others she grabbed hold of his hand pulled him towards her and pushed her body up against his. Standing on tiptoe she put her arm round his neck and pulled his head down, his mouth to hers. Paul was surprised but throwing caution to the winds he put his hands round her waist and held her close as with his tongue he opened her lips and caressed her tongue with his and at the same time sliding one arm from her waist so that he could hold her close. Despite this Vera managed to ease her pelvis away from his to allow her to stroke the bulge at the front of his swimming trunks. Responding to what she was doing Paul moved slightly and slid his hand into the top of her swimsuit to caress her breast and tease her hardened nipple. They remained like that for what seemed like ages but in fact was no more than a few seconds until Paul, frightened that the others might notice if they were away too long took his mouth from hers and stood back leaving Vera open mouthed and breathing heavily.

"The cream" Paul whispered, "go and get the cream".

Vera looked up at him for a moment as if he was speaking in a foreign language before reluctantly walking into one of the bedrooms from where she soon reappeared with a tube of ointment.

As she approached, Paul turned so she could squeeze some of the ointment on to his back and rub it into the scratches she had made.

"When can we meet?" she asked her lips against his back.

"I don't know but we will have to be very careful" Paul whispered.

"Mark is going somewhere with Philip tomorrow and I have to go to the opticians for an eye test", Vera said, "so couldn't we meet when I come out of the opticians?"

"I don't know but I will try. I tell you what. If Mark does go somewhere I will ring you" Paul said.

He leant forward and gave her a kiss before turning and walking out to join the others who were already eating lunch.

Back in his own bungalow he had to admit that although Vera would not be his choice of a girlfriend he had enjoyed his encounter with her at the pool but more importantly he had discovered during lunch that she did a lot of typing for her husband and so might be a source of information. Just what information he wasn't quite sure but he would like to discover more about any purchase of B. & M. Textiles or, in fact, anything else that her husband was currently working on and that he didn't know about.

Later mulling over what had happened at the Hoods he wondered if what had happened could possibly be the start of his revenge against the Brent family for the treatment of his father.

Next morning, as Vera had said, Mark and Philip left early to visit one of the cotton ginneries about 80 miles south of Ramuda and so, as he had promised, Paul rang her and couldn't help but smile when the 'phone was picked up almost as soon as it rang. In case any of the Indian telephone operators were listening to the conversation he told her that her husband had asked him to meet her from the opticians and that he would be waiting for her at eleven o'clock.

Exactly at eleven Paul arrived outside the opticians and Vera, who had been watching for him came out and climbed into the seat next to him.

"I don't think anyone saw us" she said looking round anxiously, "I was watching the street before I came out but I didn't see anyone."

Even as she was speaking Paul had the car moving away down the crowded road. "I didn't see anyone either" he replied "and even if there had been anyone around I am only giving you a lift."

Paul drove quickly, expertly weaving the car through the throng of other road users until after a few minutes he turned on to the bridge across the river and then onto the road which led out of the city in the opposite direction to the factory. Taking one hand from the steering wheel he put it on his companions thigh and Vera placed her hand on his.

"Where are we going?" she asked.

"I don't know. I thought we could head in the direction of the old temple and see if we can find somewhere quiet." Paul replied. He glanced at Vera who smiled and gave his hand a little squeeze. The car sped along leaving a plume of red dust in its wake as they quickly left the town behind until about twenty minutes later the ruins of the old temple appeared. As they approached Paul spotted a little track and turned into it immediately having to slow down to a walking pace in order to avoid the deep ruts. Carefully he drove into the shade of a group of tamarind trees and switched off the engine unaware of the two little boys who had been playing and had hidden at the approach of the car. He turned to Vera and putting his arm round her shoulders gently pulled her towards him. Vera did not resist and lifted her face and open lips to his. He flicked his tongue between her teeth at the same time stroking her arm placing his hand on her breast. She was already aroused and was finding it difficult to control her breathing as he caressed her breast and teased her swollen nipple. He removed his mouth from hers and gently kissed her eyes and the tip of her nose. Vera looked up at him.

"I could not sleep last night thinking about today~" she whispered huskily "I would have been so disappointed if we hadn't been able to meet."

Paul stroked her thigh allowing his hand to creep beneath her skirt which by this time had ridden high above her knees.

"I told you I would meet you if I could. I have been looking forward to this just as much as you."

His stroking fingers moved from flesh to the smooth silk of her French knickers, when she had chosen them this morning she knew it would make it easier for him to do what she wanted him to. As he gently stroked her pubic hair she shuddered slightly and a moan escaped her lips. As they kissed Vera placed her hand on the front of his trousers and stroked him in time with the movement of Paul's hand on her. She lay back looking into his eyes her nipples standing out beneath her thin cotton dress, her pink tongue moistening her bottom lip.

"Make love to me please, I want you" she said reaching forward struggling to undo the buttons of his trousers at the same time as Paul reached higher underneath her dress and started to pull at the waistband of her knickers.

Vera lifted her body off the car seat to allow Paul to pull her only piece of underwear down to her ankles which she kicked off and left lying on the floor of the car. Paul now as aroused as his partner lifted his head and looked around. Unable to see anyone he opened the car door.

"Come on. Lets get out we can't do it in here" he said. They scrambled out of the car and Paul led Vera further into the shade of the trees before pulling her into his arms at the same time undoing the remaining buttons of her dress revealing all of her body. She wrapped her arms around his neck and her legs around his waist and as she clung to him Paul entered her waiting body.

"Oh. Oh. Please. More. Faster please, faster Oh Paul its happening" and she threw both her head and the upper part of her body backwards so violently that Paul almost overbalanced as she ground her pelvis against his in an effort to increase the thrust of his body against hers. It was all Paul could do to hold her such was the force of her arching body and the sensation of its own fulfilment'

Vera hung in his arms, quivering and moaning, fighting to regain her breath until Paul gently kissed her swollen lips and then eased their bodies apart before starting to laugh.

"What are you laughing at?" she demanded angrily.

"Well just look at us" he replied "me with my pants round my ankles and you, no knickers and your dress hanging off." Still laughing he bent down, pulled up his tousers and fastened his belt. "I don't care what I look like" Vera said and taking hold of both sides of her dress she pulled it wide open revealing all of her body not only to her lover but to the two boys who had been quietly watching all that had happened.

"Let's do it again she said, but Paul only reached forward and pulled her dress together.

"No, we should be going back" he said "I have to get back to the office. If we are careful there will be many other times like this,

Reluctantly, Vera fastened her dress and after one last kiss they got back into the car and while Vera was retrieving her knickers from the floor Paul started the car and only then as it went towards the main road did the two little boys stand up to watch it leave.

During the drive back Paul directed the conversation to Mark and the work he was doing at the factory. He told her how Mark had told him how grateful he was that she helped him when confidential things needed typing. "This latest project he is working on is very important" he said "I know I wouldn't like the responsibility of recommending the company to spend 200,000 rupees to buy a factory." He waited to see if Vera would take the bait fairly certain that if the company were thinking of buying B. & M. Textiles the price would be more than 200,000 rupees.

"200,000 rupees" she spluttered–"it will cost much more than that" "It can't" Paul exclaimed with the right amount of astonishment in his voice.

"It certainly is" Vera replied. "In fact the precise figure is 520,000 rupees." Paul almost laughed out loud. The morning had turned out better than he hoped. Not only had the sex been good he now had the information he wanted.

After dropping Vera he was back in his office and reaching for the telephone. After a few second he was speaking to Nirmala Rajan who had always told him not to hesitate if he thought she could be of any help to him and who he thought just might be the person to help with the plan he had in mind. She was pleased to hear from him and delighted when he asked if he could come to see her.

"Paul you know I always look forward to seeing you so why don't you come round about seven o'clock."

It was just after seven when Paul climbed the stairs to the upstairs of the Rao house. Even though the day had been hot the house felt cool because of the breeze which was just strong enough to ruffle the long curtains hanging at the various doorways and he realised why Nirmala's father had built the house where he had. There was never a breeze like this in his bungalow.

Once the butler had served drinks Nirmala listened whilst Paul told her about B. & M. Textiles and the reason why Ramuda Textiles wanted to buy it.

"What price are they asking?" she asked.

"I don't know what they asked but I know that Mark Hood has pencilled a price of 520,000 rupees."

"What is it you want me to do then?" Nirmala asked.

"Well if you could find out what price they originally asked and then, if possible, the lowest price they would accept, I could tell the Brents and arrange a better deal which obviously would do me a lot of good."

"I don't really know a lot about this company" she said "but I think I might be able to find out what you want." "How soon do you need this information?"

"I don't know. I don't know if the accountant is going to try and get any further reduction in the price or even when he will hand his recommendations to the Brents but I am sure it will be fairly soon."

Nirmala promised she would do her best and suggested she might have some news for him before the end of the week. The conversation drifted to more general things and then as it always did, whenever they met privately, to the subject of Paul's father. The time passed quickly and Paul was surprised when he glanced at his watch to find it was almost eleven o'clock.

"I had better be going" he said as he stood up, "I didn't realise it was so late.

As Nirmala walked with him to the top of the stairs she coud not help but smile to herself when she saw, just as it had been with his father, that she barely came up to his shoulders and when he turned to say goodnight she saw the resemblance that perhaps no one else would notice. She watched until the car disappeared round a bend in the road before she turned away wiping a tear from her eye. Was it really all those years since she had said goodbye to Walter Brent?

Paul decided not to go straight home but drove through the bazaar area which was still busy and then eventually passed the gates of B. & M. Textiles through which he was able to see the front of the factory. Like Ramuda Textiles it was built of stone but compared to their giant factories this one was just a baby.

Days passed and he still hadn't heard anything from Nirmala when he overheard part of a conversation between Philip and his father which was enough for him to know that Mark had presented his report so soon it would be too late for what he was trying to do. Twice he reached for the telephone to call Nirmala but each time changed his mind. He knew she would contact him if she was able to help him.

The next day was Sunday, a stop day, and he was on his verandah reading the newspaper when something caused him to look up. An Indian youth was propping his bicycle up against the garden wall and as Paul watched he pushed open the gate and walked up the path. Paul got to his feet to meet him at the bungalow steps with a feeling he had seen him somewhere before.

"Good morning Sir" the messenger said pulling a brown manilla envelope from inside his shirt and handing it to Paul, "Mrs. Rajan asked me to deliver this". Only then did Paul remember the messenger was one of Nirmala's servants.

"Mrs. Rajan said there would be no reply" the messenger said and with a salaam he walked back down the path to his bicycle. Before the messenger had mounted the bike Paul had the envelope open and was taking out the letter. He read it quickly and then read it again only this time more carefully, very happy with what Nirmala had discovered.

He did not know how she had done it but she had discovered that the man who owned the factory had died and left it to his son who was a doctor in Delhi. The doctor was building a hospital there and needed money urgently to complete the project so had decided to sell the factory he had inherited for which he was prepared to accept 385,000 rupees for a quick sale.

Paul put the letter back in the envelope and locked it in a drawer in his bedroom and then set about planning how best to use the information. One idea, among many, was to buy the factory himself in which case he could either sell it on to the Brents or run it himself. He soon discarded this idea and all the others because none of them would satisfy his craving for revenge whereas if he helped the Brents now it might benefit him later on.

That night, lying under his mosquito net he was still thinking about what he should do until the normal sounds of humming mosquitos and the whirring of the ceiling fan punctuated by the occasional skuffle of the squirrels in the roof lulled him to sleep but not before he had decided what he would do.

The following morning Paul saw Philip and his father arrive at the factory but waited about an hour until he was sure Philip would be alone in his office before going to see him. The Managing Director indicated the chair in front of his desk and Paul sat down.

"I believe you are negotiating to buy B. & M Textiles" Paul said after a few minutes of discussion about various items appertaining to their own factories. Philip smiled.

"How do you know that?" he asked. And before Paul could reply he said, "we thought it was a secret. Who told you about it?" . Now it was Paul's turn to smile.

"You know by now there are not many things you can keep secret in this organisation. I overheard a conversation and I started to make some enquiries."

"Well there is no reason to try and deny what you say, in fact our acceptance of their price will be going to them tomorrow."

"The deal is completed then is it?" Paul enquired as innocently as he could.

"Well yes it is. Why do you ask?" Paul ignored the question and looked up at Philip from under his eyebrows.

"385,000 rupees seems a good price to pay for a factory like that" he said. Philip looked up with a surprised look on his face.

"385,000 rupees. Where did you get that figure from?" he asked.

"Well that's the price you are paying isn't it?" Paul replied as innocently as he could.

"I don't know what you have heard or where you heard it but the price is much higher than that" Philip said.

"I must be wrong then" Paul said starting to get out of his chair "but I heard that the owner had died and left the factory to his son who is a doctor in Delhi and is not interested in the business. I understand he is building a hospital there and needs some money so he has decided to put the factory up for sale and providing a deal can be done quickly he is prepared to sell for 385,000 rupees.

"I don't know how you know about this Paul but you seem to know far more about B. & M. than I do" and he indicated for Paul to sit down again.

During the next few minutes they discussed the purchase of the small textile factory and the part it could play in the organisation during which time, without divulging the source of his information, Paul convinced his cousin that the factory could be purchased for much less than he and his father had been prepared to pay.

A few minutes after Paul left his office Philip went to see his father and told him what he had just heard.

15

The overnight train from Delhi rushed Southwards past the outlying villages of Madras the roaring maw of the firebox lighting up the faces of the two firemen as they shovelled yet more coal causing the cloud of black smoke which streamed back along the long line of coaches.

In a first class compartment Paul was awake and reading the newspapers he had bought before leaving Delhi where he had been with Philip and Mark Hood for the meeting between the firm's lawyers and those of B&M Textiles to complete the purchase of the factory in Ramuda but while the others had stayed in Delhi to attend to some other company business he was travelling back alone. He had slept for most of the journey but now, washed and shaved, he was impatient for the train to arrive. Thinking about the new factory he could not help smiling as he recalled how George Brent had called him into the office and thanked him for his help in the purchase of the new factory and had given him a bonus of 1500 rupees and wondered what the old man would have thought if he had known that he was giving it to his nephew and more importantly what his nephew's plans were. Putting his hand in his pocket he took out a jewel box and opening it took out a pale blue sapphire ring. He held it up to examine it yet again and even in the comparatively dim light of the compartment he could see the five points of light which shone out of the stone which he had heard indicated a stone of great quality. Carefully he replaced the ring and as he returned it to his pocket he silently thanked Nirmala for the help she had given him and anticipated the moment when he would give this present to his most favourite lady.

It was just before eleven o'clock when the small villages gave way to the urban sprawl of Madras and only a few minutes more before the train crawled into the station and with a final judder came to a halt.

Paul picked his way through the throng of people ignoring the outstretched hands of the beggars and the porters who offered to carry his single suitcase and took a taxi to the Connemara hotel.

He walked through the busy foyer and looking past the other patrons he saw her sitting in the corner.

Vera Hood, aware that her husband was not planning to return immediately had booked room seventeen as she and Paul had agreed and as soon as she saw Paul she got up and made her way to her bedroom followed by Paul a few minutes later.

This meeting was typical Vera behaviour. Since they had first made love she was now demanding they meet even when it was not safe and threatening to tell Philip and his father about their affair if he did not agree. Philip knew that if they carried on as Vera demanded it would only be a matter of time before they were discovered and then just like his father before him his life at Ramuda Textiles would be over and this was certainly not a price he was prepared to pay.

Gently he knocked on the bedroom door and immediately it was opened. He stepped inside and only just had time to push the door closed before Vera flung herself into his arms her mouth reaching for his. As they kissed she scrabbled with the buttons of his shirt in order to slide her hands onto his bare back.

"I thought you had not arrived" she gasped "I seem to have been waiting ages not daring to leave the foyer in case I missed you",

"I was hoping you would be here as well" he lied "when I walked into the foyer I couldn't see you at first and I thought you had not come." As he was speaking Vera stepped back out of his arms and started to unfasten the buttons on her dress which she allowed to fall to the floor and stood in front of him wearing only her brassiere, panties and shoes. Paul held her at arms length and even though he had decided he must end the affair, when she was with him and behaving like this, he found it almost impossible to resist her. Slowly he released her hands and then putting one arm round her shoulders and the other under her legs he lifted her and carried her easily to the bed where, with her eyes never leaving his she removed her last remaining garments.

An hour or so later the two lovers were lying side by side completely naked their bodies glistening with a film of perspiration. They lay silently holding hands with only the sound of the distant traffic to disturb them. Vera was happy. Sex, to her, was almost as important as breathing and sex with Paul was the very best.

Paul was not as happy as his partner. Being with Vera was exciting and he enjoyed making love to her but was becoming more and more worried that she might get careless and Mark discover just what was going on. During the trip to Delhi and the return journey to Madras Paul had been wrestling with the problem of Vera. While his body wanted to continue their liaison in his head he knew that the longer it went on the more dangerous it would become because of Vera's recklessness and that one day, perhaps sooner rather than later, their affair would be discovered Pushing his fears temporarily to the back of his mind he gave her a gentle kiss on the cheek.

"We should be getting up" he said "we can't go down to the restaurant together and it would be better if we did not meet until dinner time". Vera put her leg across his body to hold him on the bed but he easily removed it and stood up holding out his hand as she scrambled off the bed and came to him. Hand in hand he led her across the warm tiles to the bathroom. Under the shower they washed and they kissed, caressing and holding each other close with their wet, slippery hands and arms until eventually Paul broke away and they dried each other with the large white towels.

"I will have to be leaving soon" Paul said as he started to get dressed.

"What do you mean you will have to be leaving? We are going to spend the night together." Vera said. Unaware that Paul had not booked a room at the hotel she continued,

"You go to your room now and then we will meet in the dining room in a couple of hours so we can dine together because if we don't and we have been seen by someone who knew us they would think it very strange to see us sitting at separate tables and then afterwards we come back here or go to your room."

"We can't do that, I have to catch the train back to Melur" Paul said

"To hell with the train. Go tomorrow, it won't make any difference whether you arrive tomorrow or the day after.

"You know I can't do that. I have to get back" Paul replied.

"Oh no you don't" Vera replied her voice getting louder. "I know what it is. Now you have had what you want you just want to get away. You don't give a damn about how I feel. I thought you wanted to spend the night together just as much as I do".

No matter how he protested and tried to quieten her, Vera's voice brcame louder and louder. Eventually in an effort to stop the screaming and shouting he grabbed hold of her and threw her onto the bed where she still continued her tirade of abuse.

Jumping on to the bed beside her he grabbed a pillow and held it across her face but even then he could still hear her and despite her hands clawing at his wrists he pressed the pillow down even harder Suddenly he realised the screaming had stopped and Vera was lying completely still. Was this some trick he wondered as he slowly removed the pillow and then he saw her lying with her mouth wide open a dribble of saliva on her chin. He put his hand on her breast to feel for a heartbeat but there was none. He took hold of her wrist and tried to find a pulse but again there was no sign of life. Vera was dead. He had killed her. He sat on the edge of the bed with his head in his hands as he tried to think what to do. But he couldn't think. His whole life, never mind his career, was in jeopardy. Ideas of what to do flashed through his brain some more stupid than others then slowly he calmed down and he realised that what Vera and he had done to prevent them being seen together and the fact that he had not booked a room could work in his favour. All he had to do was walk out of the hotel without anyone seeing him near the bedrooms and he would be away scot-free.

Covering Vera's lifeless body with a sheet he took a towel from the bathroom and wiped every surface and every article he may have touched and on which he may have left a fingerprint. Next he emptied the drawers containing Vera's possessions and scattered them on the bed putting anything valuable in his pocket along with her wedding ring and other jewellery which he took from Vera's body to make it look as if there had been a robbery. With one last look round he carefully opened the bedroom door and hung the 'do not disturb' sign on the door knob and closed the door and locked it. He then crossed the room to the window and opening the curtain looked out. Not seeing anyone he opened the door leading on to the verandah and stepped outside leaving the door open behind him.

He walked swiftly across the garden towards the entrance to the hotel pausing only to drop one of the earrings he had taken from Vera's body before again pausing to make sure he would not be seen and then stepping over the low wall on to the paved surface and casually walking to the door as if out for an evening stroll. Then as if making up his mind he walked across to one of the waiting taxis telling the driver to take him to the Ritz hotel. Once there he entered and then after a few minutes took another taxi to the railway station, retrieved his suitcase from the left luggage office where he had deposited it on his arrival and then went to the first class waiting room to await the departure of his train to Ramuda.

Even after all he had done to cover his tracks would the police soon be walking into the waiting room to arrest him he wondered and although he appeared outwardly calm he was actually in turmoil. Every person who entered the waiting room caused his heart to beat faster until they sat down and only when, at last, he was on the train did he begin to feel safe.

It was nearly ten o'clock in the morning when Paul walked out of Ramuda station. As he ate breakfast back in his bungalow he wondered if anyone had found Vera's body yet. He went over the events of the day and then the turmoil of the night becoming more and more confident that he would not be associated with her murder and at the same time feeling less and less remorse for what had happened. Breakfast finished, he decided that before going to the office he would go to see Nirmala not only to tell her of the success of his visit to Delhi but also to give her the ring he had purchased. It was only when he was turning into the drive of her house that he wondered if she would be in and that he should have called before he set out. But his fears were allayed when Nirmala's head appeared above the upstairs verandah rail.

"Hello" he said with a smile as he got to the top of the stairs "I should have called but I wanted to see you".

"It's lovely to see you. I hope everything went satisfactorily".

"Everything was perfect. Because of your efforts we were able to buy B. & M. for far less than the company first thought".

Nirmala smiled, pleased that she had been able to help this young man who, to her, was so obviously Walter's son. Each time she saw him she was able to recognise little mannerisms, the way he moved his head for instance, that reminded her of his father and couldn't understand why other people like George Brent who after all was Walter's cousin and had grown up with him, did not associate Paul with Walter. Paul finished telling his friend about what had happened in Delhi and then took the small package from his pocket and held it out to her.

"What is this?" she enquired turning the unopened package over and over in her hand.

"Just a small gift to say thank you" he replied.

"I don't want anything from you Paul. I am just happy I was able to help you" she said.

Paul watched as Nirmala unwrapped her gift and was pleased when he heard a quick intake of breath. She took the ring from the box and turned it round and round.

"Do you like it?" Paul asked.

"Oh it's so beautiful" she whispered

"Well try it on then" Paul laughed. He watched as Nirmala slid the ring onto her finger and then held out her hand so she could see it.

"It's lovely" she said her eyes shining with pleasure. "You shouldn't have bought me this, you didn't need to".

"I didn't need to but I wanted to. You are a very good friend and you have helped me a lot." He could tell from the way Nirmala still turned the ring on her finger to look at it that he had made a good choice. He glanced at his watch and got to his feet,

"As much as I would like to stay and talk I'm afraid I must get back to the office." He gave a little smile "I haven't been there yet because I wanted to see you first to tell you what had happened".

It did not take long after leaving Nirmala before he was at the factory

The first thing he had to do was to inform George Brent of the success of their purchase of B. & M. but as he went along the corridor to the chairman's office he wondered if he would be in or if he would be at the cinema where he had set up the recruitment office which the Madras Government had asked for and where, for two or three days a week, he worked as the recruitment officer .

Paul knocked on the chairman's door and was a little surprised to hear George Brent's call to come in.

"Good Afternoon Mr. Brent, I didn't know if you would be here or if you would be at the recruiting office" Paul said.

"I'm giving it a miss today Paul. It's not very busy just now because everyone is busy planting their crops." The Chairman couldn't contain himself.

"But enough of that, how did you go on in Delhi?"

Paul told him at length about the meeting and then he smiled,

"I'm sure all the formalities will have been completed by now so I suppose Ramuda Textiles are the new owners of B. & M."

"That's splendid" George Brent said "this factory is going to help us enormously. You know Paul you did very well for us. You saved us a lot of money. Before Philip left for Delhi he and I had a talk about the management of our new acquisition and we decided that if we were successful then you should be the person to run it so I am pleased to tell you that you will be the General Manager of our new acquisition."

Paul was delighted. He had hoped this would happen but he was still a little surprised George had told him so soon. He stammered his thanks and took Mr. Brent's hand in the proffered handshake.

"Don't thank me Paul" George Brent said "You deserve the promotion. I expect Philip will be back tomorrow so if everything went as smoothly as you suggest and the factory is ours then I want you and he to go to the factory to get it reorganised and running properly just as soon as you can."

Just as he finished speaking the telephone rang and the Chairman picked up the receiver. He didn't say anything but Paul watched as his facial expression changed from one of pleasure to one of deep concern.

"Dead did you say? Murdered?

He listened a little longer occasionally asking a question before saying "Thanks for letting me know. Please keep me informed of anything that happens and he replaced the receiver.

"That was terrible news" he said to Paul, "Vera's been murdered apparently by a burglar.

"That's dreadful" Paul said "Have they caught him?" "Apparently not" said the Chairman so I suppose we will just have to wait."

"What about Mark" Has he been told yet do we know?"

In the following week after Mark and Philip had returned police officers from Madras arrived at the factory to interview friends and Marks staff but the investigators were already convinced it was a burglary gone wrong so the investigations in Ramuda were soon completed.

Mark was terribly upset by what had happened and when the Chairman suggested he might prefer to stay for some time in Ooty where his children were in school, he gladly took up the offer.

Four months later Paul was sitting in his office looking out through the French windows across the red shale path through green lawns that led to his bungalow which was just out of sight round a curve in the path. On the other side and through the main office was the factory from where he could just hear the incessant drone of the machinery.

Although he was looking out he was not really seeing anything as in his mind he reviewed what had happened since he first came here. All the improvements that he and Philip had discussed and many more besides had either been completed or were near to completion. This rapid progress was due to the fact that the Brents had decided that Bill Ashton would move to the factory with him to manage the technical side leaving Paul free to handle the commercial side of the business and to integrate the new factory fully into the Ramuda Textiles organisation. Already down time on the machines had been greatly reduced and efficiency increased simply because Bill had introduced a crash maintenance programme on machinery where maintenance had been seriously neglected. At the same time Paul had been able to reorganise the office so that they followed the same methods as the parent company. But the most important change was the fact that the employees, both in the factory and the office were happier than they had been under the previous owners.

He smiled as he recalled the first time he had walked into this office followed by a young office boy wearing a dhoti and a long sleeved shirt which was far too big for him. On the desk was the usual pile of books that seemed to be imperative in organisations in India

What the devil are these?" Paul said. The office boy paused momentarily, "Books" he replied.

Paul couldn't help but laugh not so much at the obvious answer but at the stupid question.

"What am I supposed to do with them" he asked trying to contain his amusement at the serious look on the boy's face while at the same time standing on tip toe in an effort to read what the top book was about.

He realised he would be all day and beyond trying to find out what all the books were about so he signed without really looking at them and decided that each day he would set aside a dozen books which he would peruse in detail and assess the value of the information they contained and eliminate the ones that were not necessary. Following this policy he came across a book made up of yellow paper, the pages of which were merely stapled together with each page ruled off into columns. The first column was just a list of dates going back many years, the second was initialled by different people, obviously supervisors and in the third column was the signature of the manager and, turning to earlier pages, managers before him. There was no other information, the dates were not regular so Paul had no idea what it was about or why the book should come to him. He sent for the supervisor who had initialled the last entry and asked him what the book was for.

"I'm sorry Sir, but I don't know" the supervisor replied.

"You don't know, but you and the other supervisors have been signing this book for at least the last five or six years"

"I know who has been making the book out Sir" the supervisor said hurriedly "it is Ramaswamy the cotton writer".

"You had better get him then and we will see if we can find out what this is all about". The supervisor hurried from the office and it seemed as if the door had hardly closed before he was back followed by an old white haired man Paul recognised from his tours round the factory.

Ramaswamy's job was to record the numbers of the cotton bales as they arrived in the compound and when they were used.

Paul had spoken to the old man during his daily inspections of the factory and knew he could speak English so was surprised when he turned and left the office before the supervisor translated what he had said. Paul looked enquiringly at the supervisor.

"This book tells us every time we have oil delivered for the boilers Sir" he said.

"But I don't need to know when we have oil delivered so long as the engineer knows and it certainly has nothing to do with Ramaswamy".

"Yes Sir", the supervisor replied "but the factory used to be coal fired and this book told us when coal was delivered".

"But this would still have had nothing to do with the cotton writer and it would not have been necessary for the manager to know".

"Yes Sir, but the coal arrived in railway wagons which were shunted into the mill yard and had to be emptied immediately or the factory would have to pay demurrage and as the factory did not have spare labour for this job we had to employ a contractor who brought his own labour".

"But I still don't understand why the manager had to know" Paul said.

"As you know Ramaswamy's desk is at the back of the factory overlooking where the coal was offloaded so when the contractor arrived with his labour he could see all that was happening. The contractor always used female labour because this was the cheapest available and as the unloading was done by hand the women always removed their saris so they would not get them dirty and either worked in the nude or with just a loin cloth. The manager at the time knew this and liked to watch so he started this book so that he would know when the coal arrived and therefore when the girls would be working and although the factory no longer uses coal the book now tells us when oil is delivered because no one has given any instructions for the book to be discontinued."

Paul still smiled whenever he thought of the coal book but at the same time recalled this was only one of the many small things he had done to improve the efficiency of the office staff while in the factory itself he had been successful in introducing increased workloads, in return for better pay which had improved the efficiency and of course the profitability of the factory.

Philip, occasionally accompanied by his father, came to the factory almost every week and though they always expressed their satisfaction at the way the factory was improving it only served to reinforce Paul's determination to avenge the death of his father. The fact that his father had died in France was of no importance, to him it was the dismissal by the Brents which had led to him joining the army. Paul knew it was unlikely he would ever be any higher in the company whilst George and his son were there so the only way he could get the revenge he wanted was to remove them. But to get them both to leave the company which the family had started from scratch was a problem to which he could not find a solution until what had happened to Vera, after all if he could get away with one murder how easy would it be to get away with more?

His thoughts were interrupted when he realized there was an unusual quietness. He hurried from his office so that he could look across the yard and saw workers streaming from the factory and then sitting down closely together in the yard so that it would be impossible to walk between them without touching them particularly with their shoes something which anyone, especially Europeans who wear leather shoes, should be careful not to do because leather comes from cows, animals which are considered Holy by all Hindus. He had heard of this form of protest before but had never witnessed it and wondered what had happened to cause this demonstration. Out of the corner of his eye Paul saw a supervisor approaching who had obviously managed to cross the yard before the crowd had been large enough to stop him.

"What's going on?" Paul enquired.

"Sir there has been a terrible accident in the card room" he said. "One of the card setters was setting a card and inserted his gauge before the machine was absolutely stopped and his hand and then his arm were dragged into the machine.

"Bloody Hell" gasped Paul. "The setting between the flats and the cylinder is only 'ten thou' and it took his arm in" he said in almost total disbelief. He felt sick and his buttocks twitched involuntarily as he thought of the pain the man must have suffered as his arm was dragged into the small space between the two surfaces which were covered with small needles which combed waste out of the cotton.

"Where is the man now?" he enquired.

"He is on his way to hospital but the severed arm is still in the machine which is why the workers are sitting down. They will not go back into the factory until the arm has been removed. Paul glanced at his watch. It was nearly half past one and in half an hour the second shift would be arriving for work so if nothing was done soon there would be twice as many workers crowding into the yard and then God only knows what might happen. This could not have happened at a worse time. Something had to be done.

He looked at the workers who were sitting quietly, some of them crying and he made up his mind. He stepped off the verandah and then slowly and carefully he started to walk between them assuming that while he didn't want to touch them they also didn't want to be touched by his leather shoes. Choosing his route carefully he walked where he could see the largest spaces and, as he hoped would happen, the workers swayed away so as not to be touched. Quicker than he had anticipated he was through the crowd and into the silent factory. The mill engineer had stopped the large steam engine which meant that not only all the machinery was stopped but there were no lights either so that the further one went from the entrance the darker it became and because the machines were stopped the hotter it became. In the gloom he made his way along the rows of machinery until he came to the machine which had been partially dismantled in order to free the injured man whose tools were still lying on the floor in a pool of blood. He hoped that what he had heard had been greatly exaggerated but now he knew this was not the case and there was a distinct possibility that remains of the severed arm were still in the machine and would have to be removed before the workers would come back into the factory.

During his training in England he had taken this type of machine apart many times but never in circumstances like this. Done properly it would normally take an experienced mechanic a good couple of hours to take a carding machine apart but driven on by the thought that the second shift would soon be arriving, Paul worked harder and faster than he had ever worked before. Turning the machine by hand he removed the necessary parts hoping against hope that he would not find a severed arm. Eventually what he did find were pieces of flesh, bone and sinew ground into little pieces and embedded in the sharp needle points of the wire which meant that the only way to clean them out was to treat them like impurities from the cotton and brush them out with a revolving brush. He walked across to the rack where the brushes were kept and with difficulty manhandled one down to the floor and drag it to the damaged machine and even though it was usually a two man job he somehow managed to lift it into position but now he needed the mill engine to drive the machine. He made his way to the nearest office where he was able to use the internal telephone and instruct the engineer to run the engine for five minutes. As he hurried back to the dismantled machine he was surprised to hear footsteps approaching and as the engine started and the lights started to glow he saw in the increasing light the department mechanic, the man who had probably freed the injured worker in the first place. Without a word he followed Paul and as the engine gathered speed they put the necessary driving belts on the machine and the cylinder and cleaning brush started to rotate throwing out the remains of the severed arm. After precisely five minutes the engine began to slow down and in the fading light they removed the cleaning brush and with handfuls of raw cotton wiped down all the surfaces of the machine so that hardly any evidence of the accident remained. In the last of the light Paul turned to the mechanic to thank him and saw tears rolling down his brown cheeks. Paul didn't speak but just nodded his thanks while the other man put his hands together in the 'Namaste' greeting which was his way of saying thank you to Paul. It was only as they walked out into the bright sunlight that Paul noticed how the mechanic's shirt and dhoti were stained with blood and looking down how his own usually pristine white shirt and trousers were just as bad. Walking back to the office was easy as the protesting workers were already standing and making room for him to cross the yard and climb the steps to the office verandah where he stood watching the overlookers marshalling the outgoing shift through the factory gates and allowing the next shift to enter. He stood watching until he saw the lights coming on in the factory followed by the noise of the machines starting up before making his way to his office where the office boy was waiting with the ubiquitous pot of tea.

At the end of the week he was invited to dinner with Philip and Rose where on his arrival he discovered that along with Philip's mother and father Ray and Peggy Johnson had also been invited. Drinks were served and as usual the men discussed the week's happenings at the factories and of course the accident at Paul's factory and his reaction to the workers sitting in the yard, an incident which George said he could only recollect ever happening once before. The ladies who were not very interested in what happened at the factories discussed, what to them, were very much more important matters such as the difficulties with servants, the unavailability of certain foods or, more importantly, what foodstuffs Spencer's had.

Overhearing the two conversations, the men discussing work and the ladies their domestic troubles which were the main topics of conversation at any gathering, only highlighted for Paul the disadvantages of working in a one company town like Ramuda. Unless there were visitors to introduce other topics or bring news which was not reported in the newspapers then there was nothing else for the few Europeans to talk about.

The butler came round all the guests asking if they wanted another drink and after ordering a whisky and soda Paul tried to turn the conversation to the only other topic, the state of the war. He turned to Philip and in a voice loud enough for the others to hear he said,

"The war news seems to be improving a little now that the desert campaign is going a little better." Philip nodded.

"Yes things do seem to be looking up. We received a letter from home the other day which said the air raids were not as frequent now that the American air force and the R.A.F. were bombing Germany more."

"That's as maybe but we will still have to invade Germany" his father said, "the war won't be over until we do."

"But surely the invasion will happen soon so if we are lucky the war might be over by next year" Rose said.

"I can't see it being over as soon as that, Mother" Philip said "and even if the war in Europe was to end this year, which of course it won't, we will still have to defeat the Japanese and after that we will have to be prepared for big changes in this country. Already militants are talking about Independence and how they will fight for it if necessary and if the rumours about food shortages and riots in Calcutta are true it might happen sooner than we think."

"You're right" Paul said. "I think there will certainly be trouble over Independence. I was only reading in the 'Statesman' the other day that the Muslims are talking about having their own State but I don't think there will be any real trouble regarding this until after the war."

"I read the same article" George Brent said "but I don't think the Muslims will be allowed to have their own country because if that happened then the Sikhs, for example, would want their own country then who knows perhaps the Tamils would want the same so I don't think it will be allowed to happen. India will remain as one big country."

Just then the butler entered and whispered something to Rose who interrupted the discussion to announce dinner was ready.

As they ate the conversation continued with George and his son still discussing the war situation and the future of India while Paul was dragged into the conversation about shopping between the ladies sitting on either side of him until he became aware that George Brent was talking to him.

"I know what the 'Statesman' said the other day but what do you think, will there be independence after the war?"

"In my opinion there is no doubt that India will gain its independence and I think, although I hope I am wrong, there might be a separate Muslim state but I also hope, whether it happens or not, that there will be no bloodshed. As for the textile industry there are sure to be changes particularly to the trade with Britain. Once the war ends they will want to start trading with India as they did before but, I'm sure, India will resist because our industry is now too big to allow as many imports as before the war. But Lancashire will not be the only problem. I'm afraid there will be greater problems for the textile industry. Even before the war rayon was eating into the traditional cotton markets but now these new yarns like nylon are supposedly more versatile than rayon or cotton and if this is so then their increased use must affect cotton spinners like ourselves so I think we may be facing new and greater challenges once the war is ended."

Whilst he was speaking all other conversation seemed to stop as everyone listened to what he had said.

"I hear what you say Paul but I just can't believe that the new yarns you talk about will replace cotton" George said.

"Well for what it's worth I think Paul could right" Ray said "I am not saying the new yarns will replace cotton completely but I do think they will certainly have an effect on the cotton trade. For instance the United States are already producing nylon in large quantities for many different things not least for women's stockings and in the short time these have been on the market American women won't wear anything else so imagine what that has done to the hosiery manufacturers in America already".

"I knew you would start talking about women's stockings" his wife said with a laugh "but seriously I have read about them and I can't wait to try them".

They all laughed but no matter how they tried to persuade him George Brent would not be moved.

"I agree with Paul" his son said, "but I think the most important thing will be the changes that will have to be made in the trade between Britain and India".

"There won't be any change in that direction" George said emphatically "Lancashire will not give up it's trade with the Empire".

Philip put down his knife and fork and looked directly at his father.

"But that is the whole point, father. After the war Lancashire and the rest of Britain will have no option because so far as India is concerned there will not be an Empire".

At the end of the meal the three ladies left the table whilst the men remained, smoking, and drinking port at the same time still discussing the textile industry and the effect of the war and eventually got round to George Brent's work at the recruiting centre.

"Is recruitment for the armed forces still good even with the riots and Ghandi's civil disobedience meetings?" Paul asked.

"Fortunately Mr. Gandhi doesn't get down to the South so what he has to say doesn't effect us as much as if we were further North. I suppose we register about eighty to a hundred names each week but of course after registering a lot of them just disappear but I suppose about twenty or thirty enlist which is not too bad".

"Eventually George Brent pushed back his chair and led the other two out to the verandah where the ladies were already sitting. After many years in India Rose Brent was still very badly bitten by mosquitoes so in the evenings the lights were kept purposely dim and the ceiling fans were always switched on in an attempt to keep the insects at bay and even with these precautions, in the evenings she always sat with her legs in a pillowcase

For the next few minutes the butler was busy serving drinks after which he said goodnight and with a salaam turned and disappeared through the curtains to the stairs at the back of the bungalow.

"I had a visit from the police at the recruiting centre this morning" George Brent said, "It was an Inspector called Massey from Madras who is investigating the death of Vera". Immediately all conversation stopped as his wife asked what he had wanted but no one seated at the table was as anxious as Paul to hear what the policeman had said.

"He confirmed that Vera had been murdered in her bedroom at the Connemara, most likely by a burglar who suffocated her with a pillow. He said it looked as if she had been killed to stop her raising the alarm when he entered her room, probably thinking the occupants would have gone down to the dining room for dinner.

"Why do they think it might have been a burglar?" his wife asked.

"Well, apparently the room had been ransacked with all her clothing and things scattered about but there was nothing of any value which made them think there must have been a burglary Although the bedroom door was locked from the inside the verandah door was open. They searched the grounds for footprints but although they didn't find any they did find a solitary earring which they believe the burglar must have dropped in his haste to get away. They interviewed the staff of course but apart from one of the bedroom cleaners who thought there had been a youngish white man in the corridor, none of them could help and as the policeman said, this was not much help as there were many youngish forces personnel passing through Madras every day so unless something else turned up there was not much more the police could do."

"Where is the policeman now?" Paul asked.

"Well he's on his way back to Madras but first he has to go to Ooty and tell Mark how Vera died and confirm that the earring they found did belong to Vera.

Because he didn't work in the main compound Paul had not known about the visit of the policeman and had been quite shocked when George Brent started telling them about the Inspector's visit but now his continual nagging fear that one day he would be found out could be put to one side and after dinner he returned to his own bungalow feeling much happier than he had for some time.

16

Submarine 217 of the Imperial Japanese Navy was cruising on the surface of the Andeman Sea in a North Westerly direction. It had left Port Weld in Malaya where its captain Kazuo Nishimura had been given his instructions, and some time later after passing the Northern tip of Sumatra had changed to their present heading which would take them to their destination on the East coast of India about a hundred miles North of Madras. Standing on the conning tower were the captain and his second in command and one of the ratings who was scanning the flat sea through a pair of large binoculars. The two officers were talking about home and the war when the lookout suddenly interrupted and pointed out acoss the sea. Instantly the two officers raised their binoculars and looked in the direction of the lookouts pointing finger. At first neither of them saw anything and then almost at the same time they both saw a shape of something on the Western horizon. Just in case, Nishimura ordered his second in command and the lookout below while he stayed to identify what they had spotted. Through the lookout's more powerful glasses he was soon able to see it was a ship, certainly not a merchantman so he decided to dive before it got any closer. Giving the command down the voice tube he climbed down the ladder closing the two hatch doors behind him. As he stepped off the ladder the warning klaxons stopped their clatter, the last of the well drilled crew were settling in their action stations and the submarine's deck was already tilting. Just as the crew was beginning to think they had not been spotted the submarine was violently rocked by three explosions close to the starboard side. Even though the crew was very experienced there were some cries of alarm instantly suppressed by the officers but the most frightened man, too scared to even cry out, was the one passenger, the reason for the submarine's journey.

Standing behind those controlling the vessel was an Indian, Ramad Wari a naik or corporal in the Indian army before he was taken prisoner. He had always been a supporter of those politicians who wanted independence from Britain and hearing the rumour that the Japanese were forming an Indian battalion to fight against the British decided that he would defect. So one night when he was on patrol in the jungle he waited until he couldn't hear anyone moving and slid away from his position as lookout and made his way in the direction of the enemy.

Despite his best efforts the Japanese soon picked up the noise he was making and if it hadn't been for one of their soldiers, less experienced than the rest, Wari would never have been on the submarine. In fact he wouldn't have been anywhere again. This young Japanese soldier couldn't wait to shoot his first enemy and as Wari approached he raised his rifle and fired a couple of shots even though he had only heard a noise but hadn't seen anything. Both shots narrowly missed the sweating Indian who threw himself down behind a fallen tree trunk and started calling out, not in Japanese which he couldn't speak but in English the only foreign language he knew. Fortunately for him the same young soldier who had fired at him had studied English at school and was able to tell his sergeant what the Indian was saying. The sergeant was very suspicious but told the soldier to call out and tell whoever was out there to show himself with his hands in the air and warn him if he did anything wrong the Japanese would not hesitate to shoot him and there was also the danger that his ex comrades might have a go at him as well. For what seemed an eternity he waited for the next order and then he was told to walk the short distance to where the Japanese were waiting. He only seemed to have walked a few strides when he suddenly felt something prodding him in the back urging him forward. He had not seen or even heard the man who had circled behind him and was now urging him forward with the muzzle of his rifle.

He was taken from the front line and questioned by Japanese intelligence officers who amongst other things asked him why he had surrendered, where he came from in India and why and where he had joined the army. He told them why he had surrendered and that he came from a small village South of Madras and had joined the army at the recruiting office in Ramuda. After the interrogation was over and Wari had been put with the few other captives in a barbed wire compound one of the officers who had questioned Wari went to see his commanding officer and told him what had happened.

"The most interesting bit of information was that he was recruited at Ramuda by a man called Brent."

"So what is important about that" his superior asked.

"I'm not sure but we have had quite a few prisoners just recently and all of them were recruited in Ramuda. All of the others were captured but this one surrendered to us so that he could join the Indian battalion because he says he hates the British and wants them out of India. If that is the case then I wondered if it might be a good idea not to send him to the Indian lot but to send him back to India as a spy and if he gets the chance to get rid of this recruitment chap who recruited him. I know in the overall scheme of things this would only be a miniscule part but the effect on the South Indian population that someone could come and kill a prominent European might deter other volunteers and anyway think of the propaganda, the newspaper headlines, "Japanese strike in Ramuda."

His superior officer burst out laughing.

"You know it might not be a bad idea even if the Indian papers are forbidden to tell the story I suppose we could certainly broadcast it. We could give him a bit of training and probably send him back in a submarine. Yes, I'll put it up to H.Q. and we'll see what they think of the idea."

Ramad Wari, for all that he was fanatically opposed to the British in India was not a brave man but when the idea of going back to India to kill George Brent was put to him he quickly realised that it might be better than fighting in the jungle with the Indian Brigade for God only knows how long so he had agreed.

To Wari the attack on the submarine seemed never ending. After the first three depth charges there had been a period of quiet until the hydrophone operator signalled to the captain that the enemy ship was returning. The whole crew stood, not speaking, holding on to anything they could as the ship was rocked again by three more depth charges the first some distance away but the last rocking the boat so severely that small leaks appeared in the submarines hull which were quickly staunched by the well trained crew. Even though Wari was quite brown he was so frightened his face looked as if it had been covered in chalk. He stood mumbling to himself more afraid than he had ever been in his life.

After the dripping water had been stopped the crew didn't move, all eyes and ears on the hydrophone operator who quietly announced that the enemy were returning yet again. This time the sound of depth charges were heard in the distance followed by total silence which was eventually broken by the sound of the ships telegraph as the captain ordered half speed ahead.

The rest of the night and all of the next day the submarine continued on it's course towards India sometimes submerged but frequently on the surface as the ships batteries were charged. It was almost ten in the evening when the Captain and his second in command were standing on the conning tower. The captain who had been scanning the ocean let his binoculars hang from the strap around his neck and glanced at his luminous wrist watch.

"Although I can't see any lights anywhere I think we should wait until after midnight to reduce any possibility of being seen when we put our brave spy ashore." he said and the two officers chuckled at the thought of Raman Wari being particularly brave after the way he had behaved during the depth charge attack. The Captain gave an order through the voice tube and almost immediately the engine revolutions dropped until the submarine was barely moving forward.

For a couple of hours they waited until at last the Captain with a last look at his watch, gave the order for more speed and the submarine started on the last few miles of it's journey.

When it was only about half a mile from the shore the submarine came to a halt and the second in command went down from the conning tower to reappear a few moments later through a hatch on the foredeck followed by three members of the crew dragging a small rubber dinghy which they inflated and placed in the sea. One of the sailors called out to someone below and eventually Wari appeared dressed only in a white shirt and dhoti with sandals on his feet. Concealed in the folds of the dhoti was a loaded pistol and 500 Rupees, more money than Wari had ever held in his life. One of the sailors helped him into the dinghy then followed him and started to row towards the shore only a few hundred yards away. Soon the rubber craft was scraping the shingle and Wari stepped into the gently lapping water carrying his sandals and holding up his dhoti to keep it dry. He pushed the small craft off the shingle with his foot and helped the oarsman to turn it round before heading up the beach where he stood looking back for a few seconds a little surprised that he could no longer see the dinghy and could only just make out the submarine which gave him confidence because if he could only just make it out knowing that it was there it would be very unlikely that anyone on shore had seen it.

He continued walking up the beach towards a clump of gently swaying palm trees and discovered a track leading away from the beach to a road where he put on his sandals and turned to his left in the direction of Madras. The road whilst it led southwards also led away from the coast until it eventually joined a main road and again he turned left and after about an hour of steady walking came to some bushes which concealed a small clearing where he decided to rest until daylight.

Next morning he was wakened by the sound of traffic and the dim light from the rays of the morning sun showing over the horizon. He put on his sandals and set off walking until he came to a small collection of huts where although it was still only about six o'clock women were already sweeping the dust away from their doors. Fires which had probably been smouldering during the night were now burning brightly heating up the contents of the small brass pots which were placed upon them for the family breakfast. Near the well other women and children were talking as they waited their turn to fill up their brass or earthenware pots. There were very few young men around probably because they had gone to tend to their bullocks in readiness for their work in the fields. As he approached, the activity round the well ceased and the people fell silent. It was not often that someone appeared, walking at this time of the day. One old man got to his feet as he approached.

"Good morning stranger. Where have you come from?" Ramin Wari had his story all prepared.

"I come from Madras but I have been to Calcutta for the funeral of my cousin. Yesterday I was on my way to the railway station when I was attacked by a gang of thieves who stole my money, my watch and my railway ticket. I knew it was no good going to the police so I went to a transport garage I knew of and asked the drivers if any of them were going to Madras and if they could give me a lift. Unfortunately none of them were going to Madras but one was going to Mysore and offered me a lift until the junction a few miles back where I got down and started walking but no lorry stopped for me so when it was late I slept in some bushes."

The small crowd that had gathered while he told his story were all concerned at what had happened to him. One woman asked if he had eaten and when Wari shook his head she immediately led him to her hut where she made him sit outside the door whilst she went inside to prepare tea and cut him thick slices of bread. The old man who had first spoken to him came and sat by his side.

"My son drives a lorry and later he will be calling on his regular journey South so I'm sure he will give you a lift."

Although it didn't really matter, in order to stick to his story that he had to get back to Madras as soon as possible he asked what time the man's son usually arrived.

""I don't know. There is no fixed time but I don't think you will reach Madras before nightfall." For the rest of the day Wari waited hoping that each lorry that approached the village would be the one but they all rushed passed raising a cloud of duct. At last just as the light was fading a lorry approached and pulled into the side of the road coming to a halt outside the hut where the old man and Wari were sitting. The old man went forward and greeted the driver as he jumped from his cab while at the same time a couple of men who had been sitting nearby went to the back of the lorry where they were joined by the drivers mate who lowered the tailboard. The three men began unloading various packages which they carried into the old man's hut. Watching all this and the speed at which the packages were unloaded made Wari think what was happening was not legal but then it had nothing to do with him. When the last box had been unloaded the tailboard was refastened the driver and his mate were given refreshments after which they were ready to resume their journey South. Wari edged his way forward unaware if the driver had been asked about a lift but determined not to miss the opportunity.

"This man has to get back to Madras" the old man said to his son, "can you give him a lift?"

"Certainly, but he will have to ride in the back" his son replied. Wari smiled

"Thank you very much" he said "I would rather ride in the back of a lorry than walk much further,"

The driver and his mate climbed up into the cab and with Wari wedged between two large packing cases in the back, the lorry, with a large puff of diesel smoke from it's exhaust, burst into life and after a tortuous grating of gears, pulled away from the village and onto the road for it's journey to Madras.

As he settled down Wari checked that the revolver he had been given on the submarine was still securely fastened to his waist beneath his shirt and dhoti and wondered what the villagers and the two men in the cab would have thought if they had known about it. He smiled to himself. Certainly they would not have given him a lift.

As the lorry trundled on Wari intermittently dozed or watched the road unfurling behind him occasionally wakened by the sound of lorries going in the opposite direction or the slowing down of the vehicle as it passed through the various sleeping villages. It was just past midnight when the lorry finally slowed as it made it's way through the Northern outskirts of South India's largest city and eventually down Mount Road until they reached Spencer's store where the driver pulled up and called out to his passenger who, very stiffly got to his feet, his body aching from sitting on the wooden floor of the lorry and jumped down. He walked round to the passenger door of the cab and put his head over the windowless door.

"Thanks for the lift. You have been a great help to me. I didn't think I would reach Madras tonight" he said.

The two men waved away his thanks and as they shouted their goodbyes the driver let out the clutch and the lorry moved away leaving Wari standing on the side of the road wreathed in a cloud of diesel fumes. He watched as the lorry drove away, still heading South, before turning to start on the last leg of his journey which he knew would certainly be more comfortable than the journey so far.

He knew Madras very well and soon he was at the entrance to the railway station where he looked at the information board to find out the time of the next train to Ramuda. To his surprise he discovered that the evening train which should have left at 10-30 had been delayed for some reason and was now only due to leave at 02-30. He had expected that he would have had to wait until the following evening but now he could travel in an hour's time, surely a good omen. He walked over to the ticket window and even though he could afford to travel first class because of the money h e had been given on the submarine he nevertheless bought a third class return to Ramuda. Holding the small piece of pasteboard in his hand he walked across to where the food sellers were still gathered because of the late departure of the train and bought some poppadoms, vegetable curry and coffee which he ate crouched with his back against the wall of one of the closed offices. He finished the coffee which had been supplied in a brass cup and returned the empty cup to the coffee man who had been watching him to make sure that he did just that. He then made his final purchase, some betel nut and some beedies the small cigarettes, hand rolled in thin brown paper and tied with fine cotton thread. He lit one of the small cigarettes and drew the smoke hungrily into his lungs. At last he was home but then his thoughts turned to what he was here to do.

Subconciously he ran his hand round his waist and his fingers first felt the remainder of the money he had been given and then the only other article he had brought from the submarine, the gun, the barrel of which was warmed by its contact with his skin

Later today he was going to shoot a man. Not just any man but according to the Japanese an important Englishman. He knew it didn't really matter whether he did it today or some other day just as long as he did it but he had made up his mind that it would be better to do it as soon as possible so that he could be away from Ramuda with less chance of being seen by someone who could identify him. All through the journey on the submarine and the lorry Wari had tried to work out if what he had to do would be easier because he didn't know the victim but know him or not he had to do it. All that he knew was that it was the recruiting officer, probably the one who had recruited him although try as he might he could not remember what he looked like or even who it was. All that mattered was the Japanese wanted him killed.

About nine o'clock Paul Williams was on his way to the cinema to see the Chairman to discuss the future purchase of cotton for the new factory. As he approached the level crossing the damned gates were closed. This annoyed him because whenever he had to cross the railway lines the gates always seemed to be closed against him and now again this morning. As he sat waiting he wondered why they were closed when there wasn't usually a train at this time and wondered if it was the train from Madras and why

It was late. There was nothing he could do except sit and wait as the pedestrian traffic, bullock carts and the odd lorry and car all congregated waiting for the train to pass. Eventually in a cloud of smoke and steam the train slowly made its way into the station and Paul leant forward and started the engine. As soon as the gates opened there was the usual rush of pedestrians, cycle rickshaws, bullock carts and finally cars and lorries all jostling with each other to carry on with their interrupted journeys. After crossing the railway tracks Paul turned to his left to make his way to the cinema where George Brent would be supervising recruitment as he did most mornings. As he approached the cinema the passengers from the train which had held him up were leaving the station among them Ramin Wari who had decided that before going to the recruitment centre he would first go to pray at the large temple a few streets away.

On his way he bought puffed rice, fruit including the ubiquitous coconut and a garland made up of roses and marigolds held together by silver thread. Just inside the temple he smeared his forehead with white ash and renewed the caste mark removed his sandals and gave them to a young boy in charge of a stall, for safe keeping until he returned.

Inside, the temple was a warren of passages and alcoves many with idols of different gods all of them with a collection of devotees praying and offering gifts like the ones he had bought.

Sadhus or holy men, some of them completely naked, some with hair which had never been cut and yet others with their hair and body caked in dung from the religious cows, walked among the throng which included priests who were recognisable by their shaved heads except for a 'topknot' which they believed would be necessary for God to pull them up to heaven when they died, and who officiated at ceremonies throughout the building.

In the distance Wari saw a patch of light and made his way towards it and came out into a large open space in the centre of which was a tank of water about twelve yards square where some of the temple elephants were being ritually washed. He watched as they were first scrubbed with stones, rinsed and when they were dry had intricate religious tracings drawn on their heads and trunks. They were then clothed in richly embroidered gold and silver headdresses and back cloths then finally when these were in place a chain with a bell at each end was draped across their shoulders so that the bells rang as they walked.

Wari turned away and still carrying his gifts walked back to the annexe where there was an idol of his own personal god. He spread the newspaper containing the fruit and the puffed rice at the feet of the idol putting the fruit on top of the rice then with a couple of blows cracked the coconut on the floor. It was important that the coconut should break into two equal halves if his 'poojah' was to be successful. He checked the two halves. They were not exactly equal, but well, he had seen worse. He placed them on the newspaper and sank to his knees before the idol. First he placed the garland he had purchased at it's feet then taking the newspaper with all his offerings he moved it in a circle three times all the while praying and then with his head almost touching the floor he reached out and placed the newspaper next to the garland.

He remained on his knees, his hands together in supplication, as he continued to pray for success and forgiveness for what he was about to do, occasionally ringing the bell which hung on a rope supported from somewhere above before reaching forward to gently touch the idol's feet. His poojah finished he got to his feet, made his way to the entrance where he collected his sandals and set off towards the recruitment office.

For about the past three months George Brent had been deeply worried. Not so much about the business, after all it could not have been more successful.

It was one day when he was sitting in his office at the factory. He didn't know when his eyes closed but the heat and the hypnotic beat of the overhead fan lulled him into a gentle doze. As he had become older he had found the fierce heat, particularly in April and May, increasingly difficult to endure and though she never complained he knew that Rose was finding life in India harder as every year went by. Dozing but not really asleep, his mind ranged over all manner of things and juxtaposed differing events into different time frames. Faces long forgotten came back into his mind as his thoughts drifted and one that seemed to come more frequently was that of his cousin Walter who he used to play with as a child but who had been sent home in disgrace and then killed in the last war. Suddenly his eyes opened and he sat upright in his chair.

"But I have seen Walter recently" He tried to clear his brain and reassemble his thoughts. "This is rubbish. How could I possibly have seen my dead cousin?" He tried to focus his thoughts but only succeeded in becoming more confused until he decided it was all only a dream but even so he still hadn't totally dismissed it from his mind when he went to see Philip before leaving for his bungalow. As he approached the office door opened and Paul came out who seeing George held the door open for him. As they passed George saw Paul in profile and as he had often done before he could not help but think he had seen him somewhere before and then he realised it was not his cousin's face he had seen in his dream but that of Paul—wasn't that strange?

All the way back to the factory Paul was worried. He had seen the look flash across George Brent's face when they had passed and he wondered if George had realised he might not be who he said he was.

Ever since the death of Vera and even more so since the recent additions to the company, Paul had been thinking out ways of furthering his ambitions and gaining total control of Ramuda Textiles. For some time he had realised it would be necessary to remove George Brent and now he had seen the way the Chairman had looked at him he was aware that time may not be on his side. But how? That was a problem he had not solved but little did he know that fate would shortly intervene and that with only a little assistance from himself the problem of George Brent might be no more.

As the queue of volunteers were processed no one was aware there was a potential murderer slowly moving forward waiting his turn to face George Brent. Paul, as always was standing just behind the Chairman in order to assist if necessary, with the interviews as George, with the help of one of the mill clerks acting as interpreter questioned each possible recruit. One by one the volunteers stood in front of the table and one by one they were either accepted or rejected until it was the turn of a dark upright young man who stood with one hand in the folds of his dhoti. George asked his name and the man replied Wari, Ramin Wari." As he replied George turned to his clerk,

"I need some more consent forms. Can you get some please."

Paul moved to the same side of the desk as Wari so that the clerk could pass through the door at the back of the office leading to the store room.

Seeing his chance and quite prepared to shoot two English men instead of just one Wari took the revolver from inside his dhoti and levelled it at George's head. What happened next saved Paul's life and ultimately offered him the chance he had been looking for. As if in slow motion he saw the revolver and Wari jerk at the trigger and realised that in his haste Wari had not allowed for the recoil of the weapon with the result that the shot went wide burying itself in the wall behind his target. Already Paul was reacting but he was too late to stop Wari firing again the bullet smashing into the old man's chest. Blood spurted everywhere and just for another vital moment Wari seemed paralysed with horror at what he had just done before turning to level the revolver at Paul. But Paul was already moving. The little time between the two shots just sufficient for Paul to grab the gunmans's wrist and turn the gun away from himself. As they struggled the gun went off again and Paul felt a searing, burning at the side of his chest. As they continued to struggle the gun went off again and slowly Wari's grip on the revolver slackened and he slid to the floor leaving the revolver in Paul's hand. Paul looked at George Brent who was sprawled in his chair with blood oozing from his chest and running down his starched white shirt. Taking all this in at a glance Paul realised what an opportunity had been presented to him. Without a second thought about what he was about to do he raised the gun and leaning across the desk fired at the injured man killing him instantly. He dropped the revolver on the floor and was just bending to see if Wari was still a threat when the duty policeman, who was always in the vicinity of the recruiting office, cautiously entered the office. Paul straightened now trembling with shock at what had happened but more at what he had just done but still had the presence of mind to call out to the duty clerk, who had remained in the other office when he heard the first shot, to telephone for the mill doctor and then the police. Only then did he realise how much the side of his body was hurting and looked down to see the blood on his shirt. Slowly he pulled the shirt from his trousers and, afraid at what he would find, looked down at his injury. Whatever had happened the bleeding did not appear to be as bad as he first thought and when he wiped the blood away he discovered how lucky he had been. A fraction of an inch closer and he would have been seriously injured but as it was the bullet had obviously nearly missed him altogether but had scraped the flesh covering his ribs on the left side of his body leaving a wound about three inches long. He sat down with his back toward the two dead men and waited for the arrival of a senior policeman.

17

P.K. Ramanathan had finished his breakfast and although the radio was switched on he was only half listening as he thought about the changes that had taken place at Ramuda Textiles since the deaths of Mrs Hood and the Chairman George Brent. As expected George's son Philip had been made Chairman of the company and probably, because there was no one else, Paul Williams had taken his place as Managing Director. P.K. had to admit that since they had taken over the reins of the company there had been a lot of necessary changes. P.K. did not like Paul Williams. There was something about him, and he didn't know what, that didn't ring true. Of course there were always rumours circulating round the offices about the European staff but why did there always seem to be more concerning Paul Williams than any of the others? One thing that puzzled him was his reputed friendship with Mrs. Rajan who since the death of her father was now the sole owner of a transport company which not only owned a large fleet of lorries, many of which worked for Ramuda Textiles, but also many of the buses which operated in S. India. It was rumoured she had helped in the acquisition of B and M textiles a purchase, which again, according to rumour, Paul Williams had been very involved with. If this was so P.K. wondered why she should only have elected to help the company after the arrival of the new managing director? He didn't know the answer but he was determined to find out.

His thoughts were interrupted by an announcement on the radio. The American air force had dropped a bomb of unbelievable power on the mainland of Japan at a place called Hiroshima. It was a place he had never heard of but the news broadcast and the newspapers the following day were united in the opinion that now the war would soon be ended and indeed three days later when a similar bomb, now called an atom bomb, was dropped on a place called Nagasaki, the war with Japan was over and for the first time in many years the world was at peace.

Like most of the other works and factories, Ramuda Textiles closed down for two days so that their workers could join in celebrating the end of the most tragic war in the history of the world. But did the end of the war bring Independence any nearer? Surely after the assistance given by India to Great Britain including the death of many of their troops in Europe, the desert and the Far East, they would not be denied their independence any longer. Mr. Churchill one of the leading objectors was no longer the Prime Minister in Britain so when would it happen?

One day about six months after the end of the war Paul arrived at the office followed, as usual, by one of the office messengers carrying the morning newspapers. He settled into his chair and spread the papers on the desk. The headlines about the war had been replaced with others speculating about independence. All the papers said it would happen

But none of them knew when or in what form. Ali Jinnah leader of the Muslims had now decided that they should have their own state, Pakistan and would not listen to any other suggestion whilst Nehru, the leader of the mainly Hindu Congress party and most of the British Government wanted to retain India as a multi cultural and multi religious entity.

Ever since the end of the war the differences between the aspirations of the Hindus and Muslims caused trouble in the larger cities like Calcutta and Bombay resulting in skirmishes at meetings which had to be broken up by the police and which at first had been mainly stone throwing but was now growing into pitched battles with more lethal weapons being employed.

There was not too much trouble in the smaller cities like Ramuda but what there was, was usually aimed at the factories, which because they were British owned, served as good targets for the political leaders to show their followers how strong they were with the result that hardly a week went by at Ramuda textiles without a minor 'sit in' or a strike in one of the departments which caused other sections to stop as well.

Paul folded his newspaper and was looking at some reports when there was a knock at the door and Mark Hood entered. After Vera's death he had lived in Ooty but shortly after the death of the chairman the doctor treating him had decided he was fit enough to return to Ramuda and his old job at the factory. Until Mark returned Paul had hardly ever thought about Vera, it was almost as if she had never existed, but now, her husband was back he was a constant reminder of what had happened. At first Paul had tried to avoid him as much as possible but soon realised that if he carried on like that people might notice and begin to wonder so instead he had gone out of his way to spend time with Mark and as the relationship became easier, so once again the memories of Vera began to fade.

After a brief discussion about production in New Mill, Mark returned to his office and Paul followed him out to go on his usual morning tour of the factories for which he had to go through the large, main office where even though he had seen this scene many time he never ceased to wonder at the massive amount of paperwork produced by the vast army of clerks. The various sections, stores, personnel, sales and finance all had a European manager who in turn had at least one Indian assistant who almost without exception was a Brahmin. From the very beginning the various departments had been arranged so that no section was totally British or Indian in the belief that this, along with all the checks and balances that were used, would reduce the chance of anything dishonest occurring. But there were drawbacks. It took a long time to get anything done because everyone wanted evidence of what they had done or not done which meant that instead of verbal communication letters were sent between departments which were only a few yards apart and then books had to be signed and countersigned to prove that the various letters had been sent and received and so from department manager to the lowest clerk hundreds of books or letters were signed or countersigned every day. One advantage of these systems however was that if something had to be done at a certain time on a specific day then it would be done or if it wasn't then it must surely be because the world had come to an end.

Stationery, yet again, all the paper and books that the office consumed Paul again silently thanked Nirmala for telling him about the small printing company which had been for sale and which he had persuaded the company to buy so that now the company could print its own stationery.

As he walked through the accounts department one of the assistant managers, a tubby light skinned Brahmin dressed in a snow white shirt and dhoti wearing thick lensed glasses which Paul always thought made him look like an owl stepped forward and greeted him with a salaam.

"Good morning Sir" he said. "Can I remind you that it is Ayuda Poojahh today and the accounts department would like you to attend their ceremony which we will be holding at half past three this afternoon?"

Paul didn't like Ramanathan and would probably have been surprised to learn that the Brahmin liked him even less and yet even more if he had known the reason why. He always felt the chubby Indian was forever watching him and would be happy to see him in trouble but despite this feeling he accepted the invitation and putting his hand in his pocket took out a few rupees.

"Thank you P.K." he said.

With a smile P.K. took the money and returned to his desk. As Paul continued through the office he was stopped two or three times and invited to similar Poojahs by the other departments and each time handed over a few rupees. Although he considered many of the festivals to be a nuisance he actually enjoyed "Ayuda Poojah" because not only did he understand what it was about but in its own way it benefitted the company.

It was always a two day holiday when the workers were allowed to bring their relatives into the factories to show them where they worked and the machinery they operated. However on the day before the holiday each section carried out their own little ceremony or "Poojah" for which they needed the money which Paul and the other Europeans gave so they could buy the things needed for the ceremony such as fruit, puffed rice, sweets, joss sticks, garlands and powdered dye for making the red caste marks on their foreheads. When it was time everything was laid out in front of an idol or picture of whichever God the workers of that particular section worshipped.

Once the Europeans were seated the small ceremony began. Some of the tools used in the particular section were laid out in front of the idol or picture which was draped with a garland. In the offices the tools would be pens, ledgers and typewriters whilst in the joinery section there would be saws and hammers etc. One of the men considered to be the most religious would, while incanting a prayer or mantra hold up a tray to the God on which was a small pile of white ash and a small amount of red dye along with the stub of a burning camphor candle. After offering it to the God it was then offered in turn to everyone present starting with the most senior European or Indian, who, followed by everyone else would first hold his hands to the flame of the candle take a pinch of the ash which he smeared on his forehead followed by a pinch of the red dye to make a cast mark or tika. The person conducting the ceremony would thank God for ensuring that the tools worked well for them during the previous year and asked that they would continue in the coming year.

When the prayers were completed the senior person was garlanded and the coconut cracked open. This always brought the ceremony to a close and the managers would move on to the next section where exactly the same ceremony would be repeated. When they went home however, there were always small parcels wrapped in newspaper from each of the ceremonies which they had attended, containing some of the fruit and puffed rice that their money had helped to purchase and which were invariably snapped up by the bungalow servants.

The Ayudah Poojah ceremony in the finance section was conducted by P.K. Ramanathan just as Paul knew it would be and as he went through the ceremony Paul could not help but think what a good priest the man would have made. He was bare footed and wearing only a dhoti, his bare chest smeared with white ash which made his skin seem old. His glossy, lightly oiled hair was pulled back into a pony tail and he wore his usual brown, horn rimmed glasses. He performed the ceremony with great dignity and when he cracked the coconut it broke as near to the middle as made no difference.

Later that evening Paul was sipping his usual whisky thinking about the Poojah ceremonies he had attended until his mind wandered as it often did to Philip and the last part of his plan. Suddenly he stopped drinking, the glass half way to his lips as he recalled the Poojah in the garages where he had seen Philip's car over the inspection pit and a plan started to form as how he could finish off what he had started in such a way that nobody would even begin to suspect what he had done. Next month Philip and Alice were going on leave to the U.K. accompanied by Philip's mother who because of the war had been unable to return to England something she had wanted to do after the death of her husband. As soon as the war was over she had wanted to leave India immediately but had been persuaded to wait until a little later when the weather might be warmer in U.K. This meant that, because he could not go on leave at the same time as Philip, Paul's trip to England would be delayed but he was prepared to put up with this because if his plan was successful he would not be in the country when his cousin died.

During the following week Paul decided that instead of just checking the two factories as he usually did he would walk round the whole complex. He visited the large general store which, apart from the thousands of spare parts, had six coffins in stock ever since thirty years earlier a European had died and the company could not provide a coffin for him. When he thought about this story he could not help thinking that if his plan worked the stock would be down to five. After visiting the garages he passed the milk shed a concreted area covered by a roof supported by pillars at each corner but with no sides very similar to an English open barn. As always there were women sitting cross legged on the concrete all of them with babies, but some with older children as well, all of whom needed feeding but instead of the women staying at home or going home to feed their children the company allowed a member of the family to bring the children to the factory and the mothers a short time from their workplace to go to the 'milk shed' to feed them. As he passed Paul glanced at the women all of them looking older than they probably were nearly all of them wearing bangles on their arms which partially hid their religious tattoos. Some, perhaps a little richer than the others, wore a jewel pierced into their nostril and almost without exception they wore heavy jewellery in their pierced ear lobes which, depending on how long they had been wearing it, had stretched the ear lobes so much that in some cases the hole in their ears had stretched to well over an inch wide. In fact it was not uncommon for these women when walking alone at night to be robbed by a thief lying in wait, who, with his knife slashed the thin ear lobe and took the jewellery

Passing the end of the milk shed he stopped for a moment to watch the cotton labourers unloading and stacking cotton bales from either lorries or railway wagons that had been shunted into the yard. The stacks were built by arranging the bales into steps up the side of the stack so that with two men on each step, wearing only loin cloths because of the unremitting heat lifted the 400lb. bales to the step above until the stack was completed.

Shortly after one of these tours he was working at his desk when the telephone rang. He reached across and lifted the receiver and recognised the voice of Govinder one of Nirmala's relatives.

"I have some bad news" Govinder said. "Nirmala is very sick. I asked her if I should call you and even though she told me not to disturb you I thought you would want to know."

Paul could not believe what he was hearing although it was a few weeks since he had last seen her she had not said anything then about being unwell.

"What is the matter with her?" he asked. "Has the doctor been to see her?"

"Yes that is why I have called. He says she is very ill. You know she has been going to Madras fairly frequently telling us she was visiting friends well the doctor has just told me she was really going to see a specialist who when she saw him on her last visit a few weeks ago told her there was nothing more he could do. The specialist told the doctor here in Ramuda but Nirmala made the doctor promise not to tell anyone but now because she has become much worse he has broken his promise and told me what is wrong with her."

"Look Govinder, I have a couple of things I have to do here but it will not take me very long. I will come as quickly as I can".

Less than an hour later Paul was shaking hands with Govinder on the verandah of Nirmala's bungalow and following him up the stairs. He led him to a bedroom just off the verandah and knocked on the door which was opened by an Indian nurse dressed in a blue edged white sari who when she saw Govinder stepped to one side allowing him to lead Paul across to the bed where Nirmala lay covered to the chin with a pure white cotton sheet. Her eyes were closed and her face which was usually a light brown colour appeared darker but with a ghostly look as if someone had dusted it with powdered chalk. There were lines of pain near her lips and she was breathing very shallowly. The two men stood looking down, neither of them speaking when suddenly, as if she knew someone was there, she opened er eyes and a smile came to her lips.

"Hello Paul" she said almost in a whisper. "I told Govinder not to call you but now I am pleased that he did". With an effort she took her arm from under the sheet and held out her hand. Paul took it in both of his amazed at how thin her arm was and how bony her hand felt when usually it was so soft and delicate.

"I wanted to see you" Paul replied. "I have called a few times but each time you seemed to be in Madras".

"I had to go to see the doctors there because I haven't been feeling well for some time".

"But why didn't you tell me?"

"I didn't want to bother you Paul, you have other things to think about without me causing you further worry".

"You know that no matter how busy I am I always have time for you" Paul said giving her hand a gentle squeeze. "You should have told me what was happening but now I am here tell me what the doctors say. When are you going to be up and about again?" he asked aware of the answer even as he spoke.

Nirmala's eyes flickered from Paul's face to Govinder's and then back again as tears filled her eyes.

"I am afraid I will not be getting up and about as you put it Paul. The doctors have told me there is nothing they can do for me."

Her voice gave way and tears rolled down her cheeks which Paul wiped away with his handkerchief.

"Nirmala, what are you saying?" Paul said real consternation in his voice "surely there must be something that can be done, someone you can see."

"You musn't talk like that" Govinder said "very soon you will be feeling better." Nirmala took Paul's handkerchief from him and held it to her eyes.

"No I'm afraid not. I am not going to get better."

Both Paul and Govinder, the European and the Indian from vastly different cultures but joined in their concern for her looked down at the woman on the bed.

Both had benefited from her, one from the wealth she had brought the family with her entrepreneurial skills the other with the help and advice she had given him over the years. Both of them would have done anything to help her but they were both totally helpless.

"No, I won't get better" she whispered "I have cancer" and before either of the two men could say anything she continued, "I have only about a month left".

Paul felt the tears pricking his eyes and momentarily turned his head so Nirmala would not see as he struggled with his feelings. Nirmala had almost been like a mother to him and given different circumstances she might indeed have been his mother.

Govindar had tears rolling down his face and although he tried he could not entirely stifle the low moan that escaped from between his trembling lips. Paul was aware how much Govindar and the rest of the family relied upon Nirmala. She had started the company with her father and since his death had ensured it continued to grow, buying more companies and turning them all into the successful business empire the Rajan family now controlled. Paul put his arm round Govindars shoulders and for a few moments the only sound in the room was that of the large ceiling fan.

"Govindar, will you let me have a few minutes alone with Paul" Nirmala asked. "There are a few things I have to discuss with him".

Govindar nodded and with tears still rolling down his cheeks, turned and walked out of the room.

"How long have you known about this Nirmala?" Paul asked gently as he moved closer to the bed.

"With a quiver in her voice Nirmala told him that she had first seen the doctors in Ramuda over a year ago and then about eight months later had started going to Madras to see specialists who after further treatment which had not been successful had come to the same conclusion as the doctors in Ramuda. She wiped the tears from her cheeks and looked up at Paul.

"I didn't tell Govinder to call you today, I was going to leave it till later but now that you are here there are things I have to tell you."

"Not now" Paul interrupted "wait until you are feeling a little stronger."

Nirmala reached up and put one finger to his lips.

"I won't get any stronger Paul so I may as well tell you now." She patted the edge of the bed and Paul carefully sat down. "I wanted to see you by yourself Paul because I want to tell you about your father. None of my family know anything about him or what happened. I loved him and he loved me and if it had not been for his bravery and kindness I would have been dead long ago. You have probably heard and believe that your father was dismissed because of his drinking but the real reason he was dismissed was because he rescued a young woman who was being forced to commit suttee and then went on to protect her from her dead husband's family, at the same time ensuring she received her share of the money from her husband's estate." She paused for a few seconds but before Paul could say anything she went on,

"I was that woman. He rescued me from the funeral fire and took me to his bungalow where we lived together until his Uncle and Nephew found out about our liaison. As a result he was dismissed and without a job had to leave the country and I returned to Ramuda to live with my father. Eventually with the money from my dead husband's estate and a loan my father obtained from your uncle, who was unaware of who I was, my father and I were able to start our transport company". She paused for breath and to gather her thoughts, holding up her hand as Paul tried to interrupt.

"No, no wait until I have finished" she said quietly. My family and I owe Walter Brent a lot and it is a debt we obviously can never repay". She raised her slender arms to her neck and unfastened the thin chain she always wore and held it and the small key which was fastened to it in her hand.

"There's a box over there" she said, raising her hand slightly off the bed and pointing to a chest of drawers, "Will you bring it to me please?"

Paul brought the intricately carved, sandlewood box and held it so Nirmalla could open it. With difficulty she inserted the key and opened the lid. Inside amongst some pieces of jewellery there was a bank book which she silently handed to Paul. Puzzled he took it from her and when she didn't speak opened the cover and saw his name. He turned to the next page and saw that from just before the start of the war money had regularly been deposited. He turned over the pages all of which showed similar deposits the only difference being that as the years passed the amounts increased. He looked at the last page. The total was almost 200,000 Rupees. He glanced through the pages again.

"What is this" he asked "what does it mean"

Nirmala smiled at Paul's surprise and her face lit up for a few moments like it used to. For a few brief moments she wasn't sick, she wasn't dying.

"It's your account" Paul. I started it for you when I realised who you were shortly after you arrived in Ramuda". Paul held out the bank book but Nirmala refused to take it back.

"I can see it is my account but why?" "Why have you done this?"

"I did it because your father was unable to provide for you as he would have wanted. He saved my life, protected me, took me into his house even though he knew what would happen when his uncle found out. He knew he would probably be sent back to England which is what happened and as a result was killed in the war Perhaps later he might have come back to me but either way he would certainly have provided for you so you see because we loved each other so much I feel I owe it to his memory to help you". A smile crossed her face. "And given different circumstances you know, you might have been my own son".

Paul listened without interrupting to all she had to say and when she had finished, tired from speaking, he reached out and took her hand in his. He argued that he did not need the money and that the help she had already given him over the years was more than sufficient to repay any debt she thought she owed but she was adamant the money was for him and no amount of arguing would make her change her mind until finally she started to cry.

"Please Paul, I want you to have it. For your father's memory please take it. The thought of one day giving you this has been such a great help to me since I heard I was going to die so please don't disappoint me now".

With tears now running down his face as well. he bent forward and gently kissed Nirmala on her cheek as exhausted just by talking, she closed her eyes.

During the next two weeks Paul visited his friend as frequently as he could, sometimes every day but each time it was obvious his friend was rapidly deteriorating. Now there was an ashen tinge to her normally healthy brown skin, her once rich blue black hair was sparse and lifeless and in her drug enduced sleep it looked as if her body had already died and was only waiting for her heart to stop.

Two days later sitting in his office the telephone rang and after listening to the caller he said, "I'll come straight away. Is the doctor still with her?" He realised the question didn't matter and did not wait to hear the reply as he almost threw the handset back into its cradle and dashed to his car. With a plume of red dust trailing behind him he sped out of the compound and out onto the main road, sounding his horn almost continuously as he carved his way through the maelstrom of carts, pedestrians and animals. The faster he tried to go the more he seemed to be held up and as he drew near he prayed that the level crossing would be open. The crowd parted as he approached and for once he was just in time to cross before the gatekeeper closed the gates to clear the line for an approaching train. Afterwards he could hardly recall his dash through the town but eventually he braked to a halt and was out of his car before the engine died. Without closing the door he ran up the verandah steps and up the stairs where Govindar, who had heard his arrival was standing at the open bedroom door with tears rolling down his cheeks.

I'm sorry Paul, you are just too late" he sobbed Paul's shoulders drooped, he felt shattered as he followed Govindar into the darkened bedroom to join members of the family who were standing round the bed. Because of his height he could look over their heads to see the body of his dear friend, his surrogate mother, her usually flashing dark eyes closed, lying covered to the chin with a white sheet. The lines of pain seemed to have magically disappeared from her face and it looked as if she was sleeping. As he looked down he was filled with a mixture of sadness and anger. Deeply saddened by the death of this wonderful woman and at same time angry because he had been to late to see her before she died.

He turned and went out on to the verandah followed by Govindar where the two men silently shook hands. They stayed together quietly talking, remembering Nirmala during which time Paul realised he probably knew more about the dead woman's life than anyone in the family.

Two days later Paul and Mark Hood representing the company, along with Nirmala's relations and friends waited at the burning ghats on the bank of the river Cauvery. In the distance they could hear the sounds of reedy flutes and clarinets

Accompanied by the frenzied beat of the drummers leading the funeral procession. As was customary the dead woman was dressed in a pure white sari and decorated with garlands. They came down the slope to the river's edge were Nirmala and the bamboo charpoy on which she was lying was placed in the centre of the funeral pyre. Wood was then placed around the body including generous amounts of sandalwood which is always present in every funeral and finally ghee and oils which were poured onto the wood to accelerate the fire

Nirmala had no children to light her funeral pyre so the duty fell to Govindar who stood holding a burning torch while the elderly priest dressed only in a loin cloth, his bare chest and forehead smeared with white ash, recited the necessary prayers. When these were finished members of the family stepped forward with flower garlands which they draped as near to Nirmala as they could reach. As the last relative moved back Paul stepped forward carrying a single red rose which, because of his height he was able to place on his dead friend's clasped hands. Then with tears coursing down his face Govindar stepped forward and put the flaming torch to the ghee soaked kindling placed at various points round the funeral pyre and then as the fire took hold tossed the burning torch into the flames. Both Paul and Philip watched as the fire started to burn furiously but both turned away when they saw the flames, whipped up by the breeze from the river, reach the charpoy where Nirmala lay.

It was not a long drive back to the factory, but then it was not a long drive to anywhere in the city of Ramuda and soon Paul was back in his office where he sat, silently staring at the opposite wall, the faint smell of sandalwood clinging to his clothes, thinking of his friend who he had lost for ever. Not only that but apart from Philip's mother Rose there was nobody left who knew Walter Brent and there was no reason why she should ever think about the man her father in law and husband had sent back to England and subsequently to an early death.

From the moment Paul had heard about his father he had never blamed him for what had happened or even considered that he was the architect of his own dismissal. All he believed was that if the Brents had not dismissed him he would still be alive.

He reached out for some papers on his desk but stopped half way as his eyes fell upon the cufflinks he was wearing and he recalled the story

Nirmala had told him and it dawned on him there might still be one other person left in the world who remembered his father and he wondered if his real mother could still be alive. As he thought about this he remembered again the story of the cuff links and the person who had given them to him and he wondered if it was possible that he had already met his real mother?

18

Ramuda November 1946

Paul had been home for lunch and from the back seat of the car he was looking past the driver's head and through the windscreen at the road ahead. Even though the rest of the world was rapidly changing since the end of the war this part of India and this road in particular was just the same as when he had first seen it except that as they approached the factories the congestion was worse than ever. This was because the two great factories owned by Ramuda Textiles were on strike. A strike brought about because the management wanted to increase workloads an opportunity George Brent had declined when, during the war the other companies had asked him to join with them when they were improving their productivity and were suffering similar strikes. The government then had ensured the strikes ended quickly but now, although they knew they would not receive much help from that direction Philip and Paul knew it was essential to introduce the revised workloads in order that the company could remain competitive. They decided the best time to do this assuming there would be resistance, would be when orders could be fulfilled from stock. Unfortunately this meant that the best time to introduce the changes would be about two weeks before Philip and his wife returned from the U.K. When discussions failed the expected strike was called but what was not anticipated was that the workers would decide on a 'sit in' strike, something that had never happened before.

From the beginning of the strike the personnel department had met with the workers representatives but no progress had been made principally because the management, acting under instructions from the police, insisted that the workers must leave the compound before any negotiations could take place.

The police had been present at the factory from the outset but because of the general unrest in the city due to the disturbances and marches regarding the possible partition of India after independence they had only been able to send a token force of a few constables so in a meeting with Paul the police chief had said that he would formally request the help of the Malibar Police, a force Paul had never heard of.

He was told that this force which operated in Madras State had only been in action since the war and was made up of special police recruited in Malabar, so they would not be afraid of acting within Madras safe in the knowledge that unlike the families of the Madras police their families in Malabar would be safe from any reprisals.

Paul got out of his car outside the main office and looked across at New Mill, strangely silent but with groups of workers looking out of the open windows or gathered on the fire escapes and knew without going to look that it would be the same in Old Mill. Another car drew up and Mark Hood got out.

"So when are these Malabars supposed to be coming" he said as he looked across at New Mill "have we any idea when they will be here?"

"I was told it would be sometime today but I hope they arrive before this lot take it into their heads to start wrecking the place" Paul said nodding his head in the direction of the factory.

He had hardly finished speaking when a blue three ton lorry, with the word "Police" on the side came swinging round the corner of the factory and pulled to a halt in a cloud of red shale dust. The tailgate dropped and a khaki clad figure carrying a Bren gun fell into a prone position on the ground the muzzle of the gun supported on a tripod pointing at no-one in particular and yet everyone in general. As soon as he was in position more figures dressed in similar uniforms dropped out and a sergeant deployed them in an arc round the vehicle. The front passenger door opened and a young Indian officer climbed down, looked round at his men, and satisfied he walked across to Paul and Mark.

"Good afternoon" he said, "I am Captain Pillai of the Malabar Police. I have orders to report to the Managing Director. Mr. Williams."

"Good afternoon" said Paul stepping forward, "I'm Paul Williams, thanks for coming." Then with a smile he indicated the prone gunner.

"Is that necessary" he said. Captain Pillai turned to look and a slight smile crossed his face.

"This is our usual method of deployment. In our business we never know what we might be facing when we arrive so this is our routine and in any case it usually has a good effect."

"I'm not complaining" said Paul. "I didn't know quite what to expect when you arrived but it was certainly impressive. Shall we go to my office and I will tell you what is happening."

Capt. Pillai spoke to his sergeant in what Paul thought was Malayalam a language not to unlike Tamil, and then followed Paul to his office where for the next half hour or so Paul told him about the strike and why it had happened. He explained not only why it was necessary to get the workers out of the factories before discussions with the Unions could begin but also to make sure there was no damage to the machinery. Capt. Pillai nodded his head in agreement, "that will be our first job."

"But can you do that with such a small force?" Paul asked.

"Oh I think we will be able to manage that for you" Pillai replied with a smile "we have had reasonable success in the past when we have had to move large numbers of people."

Pillai then asked to look at any plans of the factories so Paul opened a cupboard, took out some plans which Pillai studied, occasionally asking questions until satisfied, he pushed back his chair.

"I'll go and have a look round the compound and decide on the best way to move the strikers out." He said in a matter of fact voice.

"Do you want anyone to go with you?" Paul asked.

"I don't think so. I have an idea of the layout and I think it would be better if the management keep out of the way for the time being and anyway Inspector Martin from the local Police should be here soon so he will be able to tell my anything I want to know." He started for the door and Paul followed him as far as the main office where Mark was standing with Martin, who had just arrived.

"Well what do you think. Can they sort this out.?" Paul asked nodding at Pillai and Martin as they walked out of the office.

"I don't know" Paul answered, "But I think I would rather have this lot on my side than against me."

About an hour later Pillai and Martin returned to Paul's office.

"We have decided what we are going to do. We will wait until about 4-30 when it is a little cooler and then I will call for the leaders of the strike and persuade them to leave the factory so that peaceful negotiations can begin. Paul's mouth dropped in astonishment.

"What. Just like that. You are going to talk to them then they are going to leave the factory?" They won't come to talks never mind leave the compound" Mark said with a short laugh of disbelief.

"I think they will talk to me" the Malabar officer said quietly and suddenly both Paul and Mark began to think he might be right.

About 4 o'clock Inspector Martin moved his local police to different positions mainly around the perimeter of the compound with two or three, augmented by Ramuda Textiles own guards, just inside the workers gate. Pillai explained he wanted both the local Police and the factory guards away from the main action so that at a later date they could not be blamed by the strikers for anything that might happen. Nothing else happened until 4.30 when, watched by the strikers in the factory windows, the office staff and all the Europeans from the main office windows, Captain Pillai and his sergeant accompanied by a clerk from the Personnel Department to act as interpreter, walked across to New Mill.

Asked to remember anything about the strike long after it was over the first thing that came to Paul's mind was the crunch of the gravel under the boots of the two Malabar Specials as they walked in otherwise total silence towards the factory. They stopped at the doorway and the Sergeant called out for the leaders to come and talk with Capt. Pillai but as everyone expected there was no reply nor did anyone come out. The Sergeant turned to the clerk who handed him a paper on which were already printed the names of the leaders of the strike.

Again in his best parade ground manner the Sergeant called for the leaders to come out and talk but this time, referring to the paper, he called for them by name but again there was no response. Capt. Pillai and his Sergeant had a short discussion which ended when the N.C.O. turned and shouted out an order to some of his men who were standing near the main office door. Immediately two of them sprang to attention and then quick marched across the compound to join him, passing the Captain as he returned to the office. There was the a short pause in the proceedings while the Sergeant instructed his men and then without any fuss they disappeared inside the factory leaving the Sergeant and the clerk standing at the door.

Only the soldiers and a few of the strikers knew what happened next but after a few minutes the three strike leaders emerged rather quickly followed by the two Malabar Specials. The sergeant spoke to the clerk who shook his head from side to side confirming that the three men were the strike leaders and not imposters. With his job done the clerk hurried away followed by the three leaders and their escort who were taken to a small office where Paul and Mark were waiting.

At first the discussions made no progress until Mark showed the leaders some alterations which the management were prepared to concede providing the Unions also gave way on some of their demands. Now the talks seemed to go round and round as was the case in most discussions of this kind with none of the Union leaders wanting to be the one to condemn the new conditions outright in case they were blamed by the management for prolonging the strike, nor would they be the one to agree afraid they would be blamed by the workers for accepting without having all their demands met. Eventually after about two hours of fruitless discussions the Union leaders decided they wanted to go back to the workers and tell them what had been discussed. As they stood up to leave Capt. Pillai, who had not said anything during the discussions moved to the door so that they could not pass.

"Do not forget, whatever happens, whatever your decision, the workers must leave the factory after the next meeting and you must be back within the next half hour" he said.

The three shook their heads as if in agreement but they all had a look on their face as if to say there was no chance of that happening. Pillai looked intently at each one in turn and then moved away from the door.

As they went out the Sergeant who had been sitting outside sprang to his feet barring their way until he received a nod from Pillai then he and the two constables who had brought the leaders from the factory, led them back.

Paul, Mark and Pillai were drinking tea in Paul's office when just before the allotted half hour was up a clerk knocked on the door and informed Paul that the leaders had returned. The three entered led by Shastri, the leader of the Communist Party, a young, very dark skinned man sporting a "Joe Stalin" type moustache and with a sneering supercilious look on his face indicating how very pleased he was with his own importance. He was wearing only a dhoti which allowed him to show off his not insignificant physique which, allied to his bullying and that of his henchmen had not only gained him leadership of the Communist Union but also the strike which he had ordered would be a "sit in". As he swaggered into the office the Sergeant signalled he wanted to speak with Capt. Pillai who slipped out of the office before the door closed.

Paul and Mark listened to what Shastri had to say, trying to hide their disappointment that the earlier discussions had not been successful. They tried to argue but it was soon obvious Shastri did not want an agreement and was working to his own agenda. It was also obvious that but for him the other leaders would probably have agreed to the company's proposals. As they argued there was a knock at the door and a clerk came in and gave Paul a note, he read it through then left the office where Capt. Pillai was waiting.

"My Sergeant and I want to have a few words with Mr. Shastri before he goes back to the factory" Pillai said. "We want to go somewhere quiet and I think we have found a suitable place."

He led Paul down the corridor to where there was a large walk-in safe, inside which three men were stacking coins on shelves. It was here the trays of coins were prepared for the wage clerks who, every shift went to give every worker the few coins which made up the production bonus they had earned the previous day and which was probably the only money their families had to live on because most of their monthly wage was needed to pay off landlords and money lenders.

Paul and the Captain went back to the room where Shastri was still arguing and quickly brought the meeting to an end. Pillai opened the door and the three Union men filed out into the corridor where the Captain "accidentally" stood in front of Shastri allowing the two others to be led away by one of the Malabar Specials while he and the Sergeant took Shastri in the other direction. Whether Shastri was being afraid of being singled out he certainly didn't show it as he swaggered along, sticking out his chest, nodding and winking at the clerks quite unprepared for what was about happen as he was led in the direction of the large safe.

As they approached the Sergeant suddenly grabbed the Union leader, pushed him into the large safe and a constable who had been standing behind the open door pushed it shut. Paul turned to Pillai with an inquisitive look on his face.

"When my Sergeant took Shastri back to the factory earlier on Shastri did a very silly thing" Pillai explained. "In an act of absolute stupidity he walked in front of the Sergeant, turned and lifted his dhoti to show his supporters what he thought of the Malabar Specials and that he was not afraid of them."

Paul was surprised at what was happening but he knew that what Shastri had done was the biggest insult one Indian could give to another and even though officially he could not support what was happening he could not help but be very pleased at what was happening.

About ten minutes later, during which there had been no sound from inside the safe the door swung open and one of the constables who must have been in the safe from the beginning walked out. At first glance Paul could only see the Sergeant but as the door opened wider Shastri slowly emerged not walking but crawling his arms and legs hardly able to support him his head barely raised from the concrete floor. Paul had no idea what the two policemen had done to the strike leader because there were no obvious marks on his face or body but whatever had happened inside the safe he was obviously in great pain.

The sergeant apparently totally unconcerned by whatever had happened waited until Shastri was clear of the door and then stepping round the crawling man spoke to his superior officer who listened then nodded as the Sergeant turned and marched away.

"The Sergeant has gone to bring the other strike leaders so that Shastri can tell them to leave the factory" he said simply.

Shortly afterwards the strikers started to leave the premises except for about 50 or so of the more vociferous of Shastri's supporters who gathered in front of the offices shouting abuse at the management and the police. As soon as he saw what was happening Captain Pillai issued orders to his men who, unnoticed by the shouting strikers, formed a distant circle around them before beginning to move inwards herding the mob into an ever decreasing space.

Each of the soldiers had a lathi, a brass tipped cane about a yard in length and usually carried in their belt, which they withdrew and started to bang the brass tip on their steel helmets which were slung on their packs at their hip. At first the noise was barely audible above the noise of the strikers but slowly as the noise of the rabble subsided the rat tat tat sounded even louder and more ominous. Now the strikers were nervous and wanted to leave the compound as urgently as before they were determined to stay but the circle of troops prevented this and there was no escape from them as the soldiers relentlessly still banging their lathis squeezed them into an even smaller space.

Eventually when all that could be heard was the noise of the canes the Sergeant blew two sharp blasts on his whistle. Immediately the banging stopped as the Malabars reversed their hold on the canes and swinging them furiously attacked the herded men. The swishing of the canes through the air and the thud as they landed on target was quickly drowned by the cries and screams of the strikers as they fought to get away from the flailing canes driving them towards the gate.

Paul was horrified by this display of force. As he watched the canes rise and fall he felt pity for the men who were being so savagely beaten and was so engrossed that at first he didn't realise Mark was speaking to him.

"I'm sorry Mark, I didn't hear what you said."

"I was saying that I didn't expect anything like this" Mark said.

"I have never seen this lot in action before but they are certainly bloody efficient." Paul said. "There is no doubt that if ever we have a sit in strike again then we call this lot in as soon as we can."

The detachment of special police stayed in the mill compound for the next three days during which time talks were held between the Personnel Department and the strike leaders with Captain Pillai "looking on" which eventually ended with an agreement more or less on the same terms that Shastri and the others had refused earlier simply because Shastri had lost all heart for the struggle.

On the third day the Malabars watched as the workers came back to work, totally impervious to the surly looks and whispered comments until at mid-day when it was obvious there would be no further trouble, they were ordered into their waiting vehicles by Capt. Paillai who after shaking hands with Paul climbed into the seat next to his driver.

Two days later when all the mess had been created during the strike was cleared up, the factories were running as if nothing had happened and Paul was sitting at his desk having completed his daily inspection of the two factories. This inspection had taken longer than usual because instead of just visiting one or two departments as he normally did he had visited every part of the compound to satisfy himself that everything was back to normal ready for Philip's return from England and his own departure shortly after.

During the last week not only had he been worrying about the strike but he had been trying to come up with a plan to remove Philip, the last obstacle in his dream of becoming chairman of the company. In the past he had thought of different schemes but one by one they had been discarded until now he had what he thought was the perfect plan one so simple that if it worked he would never be suspected because he would not even be in the country. For the past three weeks he had been using Philip's car whilst his own was being serviced and resprayed but tomorrow it would be ready. His thoughts were interrupted by a knock on the door and Mark Hood walked in and placed some ledgers on the desk.

"These are the insurance details you were asking about" he said as he sat down. "Oh good" Paul said, "I'll have a look at them later."

"I had a letter from Vera's younger sister this morning" Mark said conversationally, "I wrote to her a couple of weeks ago asking if she would like to come down for a couple of weeks. You remember her? She came to stay with me for a few weeks when I was up in Ooty."

"I do remember your sister-in-law came to stay with you but I never got up to Ooty whilst she was there so I never met her. In fact until you just mentioned it I didn't realise Vera had a younger sister. When she was in Ooty and people talked about your sister-in-law I somehow thought they were referring to your brother's wife because I thought Vera was an only child.

"Oh no. Elizabeth is a year younger than Vera. She married an army officer and came out to India shortly after Vera and I. Unfortunately he was captured at Singapore and it was only when the war ended that Elizabeth was told he had died in Changi Jail."

"That's bad luck. What has she been doing since he was captured?" Paul asked.

"Well obviously she couldn't go home immediately so she went to Delhi where she landed a job in some Government Office or other. Something to do with transport I think, so she did quite well what with her salary and her husband's Army pay but after Independence there will no longer be any work for her so she has decided to return to the U.K. but before she does she is spending a few weeks going round India."

"When is she arriving" Paul asked.

"Well that's it, she should be here on Thursday morning the day after Philip and Alice get back, the same day you invited me to dinner so I'm wondering if I could bring her along."

"Of course you can, no problem." "How long is she planning on staying?" Paul asked.

Paul stayed in the office long after the other Europeans had left and it was beginning to go dark when he walked out to Philip's car. What he had decided to do could not be done either at the factory or his bungalow so he planned to drive out somewhere remote and quiet. In the boot of the car he had the necessary tools he required and also some old clothes. Once out of the factory compound he was soon threading his way through the narrow streets of the town heading for the main road to Madras. Once on this road he was able to increase speed and he settled down for the rest of the journey going over and over in his mind what he had to do aware that after that success or failure would not be in his hands.

After about fifteen minutes his destination, a large rock formation, was in sight and after checking there were no other road users around he turned off onto the red shale track he remembered so well. Unable to use the lights and because he didn't want to raise a dust cloud he travelled very slowly into the shadow of the rocks and through a narrow cleft, turned the car round ready for leaving before switching off the engine. He got out of the car and stood listening for the sound of any other vehicle but other than the ticking from the engine of his own car as it cooled there was nothing. He walked back the way he had come until he could see the road and stood absolutely motionless for another ten minutes until satisfied there was no-one about he walked back to the car, lifted a small case from the boot from which he took out the old clothes and a hacksaw he stripped off his shirt and trousers then dressed in the old shirt and khaki shorts and still carrying the hacksaw and a torch he slid on his back under the front of the car.

He knew exactly what he had to do. With the hacksaw, in which he had fitted a new blade, he started to saw the track rod of the left front wheel. He was very careful to make sure he only made one cut and there were no other scratches and by the light of the torch he frequently stopped sawing to check and make sure the track rod was not weakened too much because he had to drive back to the bungalow with the weakened track rod and although it was he who had weakened it he had no idea how long it would last or when it would break.

When he was finally satisfied that the cut was deep enough he wiped the surface of the rod to reveal the shiny surface where he had cut. But he was prepared for that. He reached into the pocket of his shorts and took out a tin which contained a mixture of brown shoe polish, mud and oil which he had prepared in his bungalow and which he smeared into the cut. With a cloth he wiped away the excess and examined what he had done. Three times he applied this paste until at last he was satisfied that what he had done would not be notice ed unless there was a thorough inspection.

He slid out from under the car, quickly changed into his normal clothes then drove to the entrance in the rocks where he waited until a couple of vehicles moving in the direction of Ramuda had disappeared and the dust plume they raised had settled, then after another quick look round he set off back to Ramuda. His only worry that he had not damaged the track rod too much which would cause it to break before he got back to his bungalow.

Two nights later Philip was sitting on his verandah drinking a very "thin" whiskey and soda as he waited for Alice to get ready to go to Paul's. The weather was very hot for the time of the year and both he and his wife felt very uncomfortable after the comparatively cold weather of England. He heard a car and looking out saw Mark Hood and his sister-in-law arriving at Paul's house next door. He called out to Alice and they both went downstairs where their butler was waiting with a torch and to say goodnight. Philip took the torch and they set off to walk the few yards to Paul's bungalow flashing the torch from side to side in case there were any snakes or more likely scorpions on the road. Less than five minutes later they were walking up the stairs of Paul's bungalow where Paul was waiting to greet them and although he had obviously seen Philip he had not seen Alice since her return from England. He gave her a kiss and with a laugh told her how he was doubly pleased to see her, not only because she and Philip were back but because he could now go on his long awaited leave. He led them across the verandah towards Mark who welcomed Alice with a kiss on the cheek and then introduced Philip and Alice to his dead wife's sister.

After she had been introduced to Philip and Alice, Elizabeth Young smiled and in a low husky voice said "Please don't call me Elizabeth only my Mother ever called me that. Everyone calls me Beth."

Throughout dinner Paul could not get over how much Beth was like her sister it was not the physical likeness but more the way she talked, the movement of her hands and how she turned her head to look directly at the person who was addressing her. He listened as Beth explained how close she and Vera had been right up until Vera had married and left for India with Mark and how, just over a year later, she had married an Army officer and had been able to come to India when he was posted to Poona.

After the meal they returned to the verandah where the two women sat together while the men stood drinking and discussing the factories. This was one of the disadvantages of living in a one company town. Of necessity working collegues were also social friends and because it was rare that anyone had any news the only common topics of conversation was about work for the men and about children and shopping for the ladies. Everyone always promised they would not split into groups like this but it always seemed to happen. Paul was telling Philip about the strike and how the Malabars had dealt with it when Alice interrupted them

"Do you realise you have been talking "shop" for over an hour? Don't you think the rest of it can wait until you are in the office?"

Philip looked at his watch. "Goodness I didn't think we had been talking all that long." He smiled at Beth.

"We don't usually talk business as long as this but Paul was telling me about the strike that occurred whilst Alice and I were in England."

"I understand" Beth said. "It is interesting to hear about factories. I have never seen factories like these, in fact come to think about it I don't think I have ever seen a factory before. Where we lived in Somerset there was nothing like this." She turned to Paul.

"How do you like living in Ramuda" she asked, "Didn't you find it a bit strange when you first arrived from England?"

Paul couldn't tell her that he been born in India and that coming to India for him was in fact a case of returning home.

"Well when you work in a factory it doesn't really matter where you are." He said. "The factories are the same whether they are in Ramuda or Rochdale. Its when you are not at work that Ramuda does not compare favourably to, say Bombay, where there is much more to do and you can have friends from outside the company. Here arguments between men at the mill can sometimes spill over into arguments between the wives and vice versa." As he finished speaking Beth smiled.

"But that is not your problem is it? You are not married." Paul nodded and was about to speak when Beth continued.

"I knew before I met you that you were not married because Vera often mentioned you in her letters". His heart missed a beat.

"I hope it was always something good." he smiled, hoping he his the anxiety he felt.

"Oh it was always something good don't worry. She wrote so much about everyone here that I felt I knew you all before I arrived but she often mentioned how good you were at tennis and how she liked to play with you." Paul immediately thought of the double meaning but before he could say anything Mark interrupted.

"Yes Paul is a good player and he and Vera made a good team."

Paul looked directly across at Beth but he didn't think she was teasing him or that she knew what had gone on between him and her sister.

The rest of the evening was spent talking about many different things but as with nearly all the Europeans in India the main subject was Independence. Beth remained fairly quiet as the others gave their views on what they thought might happen but silently agreed with Philip who thought that independence would make very little difference.

"The Indians can't run the country themselves" he said "they will always need someone like us to help them." Paul shook his head.

"I don't think so. This country will manage far better than we think. They might want us to stay a few years but after that they will not be dependant on anyone." The conversation about independence carried on for sometime until Philip glanced at his watch and looked across at his wife.

"I think it is time we were going Alice" he said "its almost half past eleven and Paul will have lots of things to do before he leaves tomorrow."

"You don't have to worry about me" Paul said with a laugh "I have almost done all my packing. Half an hour tomorrow and I will be ready for off so why don't we have another drink?"

"No, I think we ought to be going" Alice said as she walked across and gave him a kiss on the cheek. "Thanks for a lovely evening and I hope you have a good time in England. Don't forget it will be cold when you get there" she said with a laugh. As they were saying goodnight Paul asked Beth if she would still be in Ramuda in June when he returned.

"I don't really know" she replied "I'm planning no making a tour round the South. I want to go back to Ooty for a little while and then perhaps go to Kodai and across to Cochin so I might be here when you return but I don't really know."

As they drove home Mark asked Beth "What do you think of the Brents?"

"I liked them. Alice was very sweet and said she hoped I had enjoyed my stay and that I should return before leaving India for good. Philip also seemed very nice and from what I could tell he seemed to be pleased that you had got over your problems and were back at work. But if you had asked me what I thought about Paul" she hesitated before she went on "I think there is something" and again she paused "I nearly said sinister about him. I know that sounds dramatic but I don't know if I would entirely trust him".

"Why do you say that?" Mark asked glancing across at her.

"I don't know, I really don't. He is a good looking chap, in fact he is very handsome but there is just something that says to me, be very wary of him".

"I don't know why you say that. He has been very helpful since I came back to work and he is very good at his job."

I would imagine that he is. He is probably one of those people who are good at anything they do, but didn't he get the job you were hoping for?'

"I suppose he did but that was my fault. If I had not gone to pieces and started drinking after Vera died I would have been promoted but that is hardly Paul's fault" Mark said, never taking his eyes off the road.

"Don't get me wrong I think he is very attractive and this little something I have mentioned, this hint of danger or whatever it is, perhaps only adds to his attraction" Beth said with a little laugh as Mark turned the car into the drive, lighting up the front of the house with the headlights.

He brought the car to a halt under the porch and as he reached forward to switch off the ignition he said with a laugh,

"I think I am going have to keep a brotherly eye on you."

Next day Beth was sitting on the verandah sipping a glass of fresh lime juice, the morning paper which had occupied her for all of ten minutes lay crumpled at her feet. As she sipped her drink she watched the gardener at work swinging the curved metal grass cutter as he slowly moved from one end of the lawn to the other. She watched, but her thoughts were elsewhere. One of the reasons she had come to Ramuda was to see if she could get any idea why her sister had died. Knowing how her sister had been as a young girl, never satisfied with just one boy friend but always seeming to think it was necessary to have two or three at the same time and then taking great delight in keeping them apart, she could not help but wonder if Vera had been unfaithful to her husband and that had led to her death.

She always knew that Vera was not madly in love with Mark and had only married him for the security he offered so Beth wondered if there had been anyone else. But who?

After only a few days she realised there were not many European candidates the only unmarried one being Paul Williams but then she knew whoever it was need not have been single nor come to think of it would he have to be European but Paul Williams was the sort of man Vera would have been attracted to.

In the main office at the factory someone else was thinking about Paul Williams but then for P.K. Ramanathan Paul Williams and the Brent family were an obsession. From the moment he could first remember, his mother had drummed it into him that Walter Brent had driven his father to suicide and even though he knew Walter Brent had been killed in the first world war he still hated the Brents. He knew also that Paul Williams was very friendly with Nirmala Rajan who, it was rumoured in the Indian community, had been saved from the funeral pyre of her dead husband by Walter Brent but what was the connection between that and her friendship with Paul Williams? P.K. didn't know but perhaps in the next few months during the turmoil in India during independence and as now seemed likely, partition, something might happen which would provide him with the opportunity to find out the reason for the friendship between Paul Williams and Mrs. Rajan.

19

Bolton Febuary 1947.

It was no wonder Paul felt so cold. The weather was the coldest in living memory Even the train from Manchester to Bolton, which was heated, had only seemed marginally warmer than it was outside. He had sat, huddled in his overcoat, looking out through the steamed up carriage window at the never ending white, frozen landscape which was occasionally obscured by snow showers, often waiting impatiently as the train slowed or sometimes even stopped in order to negotiate frozen points. But then, at last, after what seemed like ages but was in fact only seven hours after he had left the ship at Tilbury, he was signing the register at the Swan Hotel in Bolton. On the desk he noticed a copy of the Bolton Evening News and his attention was caught by the word India, the only part of the headline he could see. He opened the paper and started to read.

"Lord Louis Mountbatten appointed Viceroy of India."

Paul read the rest of the article, the gist of which was that Lord Mountbatten who would be the last Viceroy of India was to take up his appointment on the 20th of March. He replaced the newspaper and wondered how this news would be received in India. Most likely it would be seen as one of the most important steps towards independence that had been taken despite the fact that the present Viceroy, Field Marshal Wavell had been working hard to broker a settlement between Mr. Nehru who wanted a united India and Mr. Jinnah who wanted a separate Moslem state, Pakistan.

The receptionist handed him his key along with some envelopes.

"These messages came for you Sir" she said.

Paul followed the porter who led him upstairs to a room which had a window looking out on to Churchgate. To his right he could see, in the middle of the road, the commemorative cross to the Earl of Derby who had been executed on that spot during the civil war and then, past the cross, to the Capital cinema on the other side of the road and a smile crossed his face as he recalled the last time he had been there. He looked to his left where the majority of the traffic streaming out of Bradshawgate turned left into Deansgate and although he knew there was something different couldn't at first, think what it could be and then he realised, there were no trams. The old clanking monsters on which he used to freeze going to work before he went to India had given way to buses.

Turning from the window he sat on the edge of the bed and read his messages, all of them from textile machinery companies confirming visits. The first of these was not for a few days so he decided that the following day he would set out on a private visit of his own, one he had never stopped thinking about ever since Nirmala died.

He woke early just as he did in India and went down for breakfast only to find that he was too early. The newspapers had not yet arrived so he decided he would go for a walk. As he headed to the door the man behind the receptionist said,

"If you are going out Sir, you had better put your overcoat on it is still freezing out there."

Paul cautiously opened the door and immediately felt a gust of wind that felt as if it had arrived non-stop from Siberia.

He closed the door and turned to the Night Porter.

"Hell that's cold. The wind is like a knife."

Five minutes later he walked out of the hotel into Bradshawgate and set off in the direction of the railway station. He had only walked a few strides before he nearly fell full length on the frozen pavement which made him slow down to a speed he knew would not keep him warm. Nevertheless he struggled on but after only half the distance he wanted to walk he decided to return to the warmth of the hotel and stay there until it was warmer. During breakfast the weather worsened. It started to drizzle with occasional flurries of snow which were whipped up by the wind so, disappointed that he could not do what he wanted, he decided to stay in the hotel for the rest of the morning and read the morning papers.

After lunch dressed in his thick overcoat, scarf and gloves he set off. He had read in the morning paper that this winter was probably the coldest for over a hundred years and he wasn't surprised as he shivered inside his heavy coat as the wind whipped round the corner of the hotel. On his brief walk before breakfast he had noted which bus he needed and where the bus stop was situated and so he crossed the road and joined the two other people who were waiting, muffled in heavy clothes, their backs to the wind, for the number 33 bus to Horwich.

As he was not exactly sure where the house he wanted was situated he bought a ticket to Horwich although he was certain he would not be going that far. All he had to do was watch out for the house and when he saw it get off the bus at the next stop. As the bus swung to the right at the end of Deansgate Paul was amazed to see a queue, mainly of women, waiting outside the gas works. All of them had either, prams, soap boxes on wheels or bicycles as they stood huddled against the biting wind. "What are all those people doing in this weather?" he asked the bus conductor who glanced to where Paul was pointing.

"Where as tha bin? Yon lot are waitin for a bit o'coke. It's bin like this a' Winter. There's no coal nor owt." Paul was amazed. Although he had read in the papers this morning about the fuel shortage and because of the frozen points, the inability of the railways to distribute what there was, he had not realised the situation was as bad as this.

The bus turned onto Chorley New Road and before long was passing a building Paul remembered, Bolton School. As the bus continued Paul saw that many of the houses had piles of snow on the gardens piled there when their owners had cleared their paths and drives and which would probably still be there even into late spring. As he looked out, occasionally wiping the condensation from the window, he noticed that the houses were now bigger and the grounds in which they stood more expansive and then suddenly he saw the house he was seeking. He remembered the gateposts he had driven through on his one and only visit and he leapt from his seat. The conductor hesitated.

"We'r nor at terminus yet tha knows" he said. Paul nodded.

"No I know but I have just seen where I want to go".

"When he was outside the house he was seeking he stood looking across the garden which, when he had visited before, had been immaculate but now bore the ravages of winter. He looked at the house. Was it because of the garden that it too looked tired and in need of some attention? He hesitated for a second or two before he walked up the curved drive to the front door where again he paused before reaching out to ring the doorbell. He didn't hear it ring but after a few moments he heard someone approaching. The lock turned and the door opened to reveal an elderly lady in a grey dress, wearing spectacles and with an enquiring look on her face

"Excuse me but does Mrs. Leather still live here?" Paul asked and wondered if the woman in grey was going to answer.

"Er, yes Mrs. Leather does live here." Again there was a pause.

"Well would it be possible for me to see her?" Paul asked.

"Mrs. Leather is not very well. Who are you?? I have not seen you before."

"My name is Williams, Paul Williams. Before I went to India I used to work for Mr. Leather. At the mention of his name the grey lady's face seemed to soften and she stood back from the door.

"Mrs. Leather used to talk about you a lot before she was ill" she said "you had better come in".

Paul stepped into the hall and the grey lady closed the door behind him and led him into a room at the back of the house which despite the best efforts of an electric fire was not very warm.

"I'm Mrs. Knowles" she said "Mrs. Leather's housekeeper. You do know that Mr. Leather is dead?" Paul nodded. "Yes" he replied. "He wasn't too well when I went to India and I heard that he had died. When I worked at the factory I used to go with him to the Cotton

Exchange in Liverpool and it was on one of those visits when I brought him home that I met Mrs Leather." Paul pulled up the sleeve of his coat and showed Mrs. Knowles his cuff link.

"In fact when she knew I was leaving for India Mrs. Leather gave me these. There is a monogram on them and I wondered if she might know what it means." Mrs. Knowles leaned forward to look.

"let me take it into her and if she is awake I'll ask her if she remembers it but I am not sure if she will be able to help."

"What is the matter with her?" Paul asked in a worried voice hoping that his journey had not been in vain.

"Her health started to decline shortly after her husband died. She had a stroke about two years ago and then just over three months ago she had another one which affected her speech and now she can't speak very well and neither are we sure how well she can see or hear." Paul unfastened one of his cuff links and handed it over to the housekeeper.

"When I decided to come to Bolton I didn't know if Mrs. Leather was still alive even but now I am here and she is as ill as you say, would it matter if you allowed me to come into her room with you?"

Mrs. Knowles stood with her hand on the door turning the cuff link over and over in her hand considering what Paul had said .

"Very well Mr. Williams come with me" and she led the way down the hall and halted at a door which Paul remembered was the sitting room where he had first met Mrs. Williams.

"Wait here and I will see if she is awake" the housekeeper said. She entered the sitting room closing the door behind her but then almost before the door was closed it was opened again and she was beckoning him inside. Immediately he was struck by how warm the room was and then he saw the huge coal fire burning in the large Victorian fireplace. In front of the large sash window was a bed which dominated the whole room, placed so that the occupant could see the garden and the main road. Mrs. Knowles beckoned Paul closer to the bed and for the first time he saw Mrs. Leather. Her skin was yellowed like old parchment and although her eyes were closed a single tear had run onto her lined cheek. Her lips, held in a tight line because of the pain, were much thinner than he remembered and wisps of straggly grey hair peeped out from under a white cotton night cap trimmed with narrow pink ribbon. A lump came to his throat when he saw how cruel the years and illness had been to her. Mrs Knowles leaned forward.

"You have a visitor" she said in a loud voice but for all the response she got it was if she had never spoken.

"Mr. Williams from India is here to see you" Mrs Knowles said. This time there was a movement as Margaret Leather tried to move her head. The housekeeper moved nearer.

"Do you want to see Mr. Williams, Margaret? She asked. This time Margaret Leather tried to withdraw her hand from under the white coverlet. Seeing these movements of her head and her hand Paul moved to the side of the bed and leaned forward just as her head turned to look at him. Mrs. Knowles took hold of the sick woman's hand and placed Paul's cuff link into it closing her fingers over it. Paul watched as the fingers slowly started to move to examine the object and a frown creased her forehead. Her eyes opened and she turned her head until she was looking at Paul and Mrs Knowles and her eyes focussing first on her housekeeper and then slowly turning to look at him. For a second or two he was sure she didn't know him but then her lips started to quiver and tears ran down her lined face. Mrs. Knowles bent forward and wiped her cheeks with a small lace handkerchief and Paul reached forward to touch her hand. As he did so he saw her lips move to form one word, "Paul". Although there was no sound Paul knew she could see a little. He put his face nearer to hers and ridiculously whispered the only word he could think of, "Hello" but then he was quickly reassured that it was not ridiculous when the sick woman's lips formed the word "Hello".

For the next half an hour Paul sat on a chair at the side of the bed talking to the woman he thought might be his mother knowing she could see him, perhaps only faintly, but more importantly that she could understand what he was saying even though she could not reply. He told her about his life in India, about growing up there, about his parents and what had happened to them and was surprised how easy it was to talk to her even though the conversation was totally one sided but he knew she was listening as she absently turned his cuff link over and over in her hand. He reminded her of his visit to the house before he had left for India and as he talked he wondered how he could ask what he so desperately wanted to know.

Mrs. Knowles interrupted and Paul nodded his acceptance when she asked if he would like a cup of tea, aware that when the housekeeper left the room it would give him the chance to ask Margaret Leather about the monogram on the cufflink. Gently Paul reached out and took hold of her hand and took the cuff link from her but still held it where she could see it.

"W.M.P. what does that mean? What do the letters stand for?" he asked looking down at the stricken woman in the bed but she just lay as if he had never spoken. He repeated the question and waited the silence only broken by the deep ticking of the ormolu clock on the mantelpiece. Again he asked the question.

"Please Margaret tell me what the letters mean, What does 'W' mean". Slowly her eyes focussed on his.

"Walter" she mouthed silently. He breathed a sigh of relief. She was telling him the thing he wanted to hear more than anything else.

"M" he asked "What does 'M' mean?" His eyes never left her lips and just when he thought she was not going to answer they started to move. "Margaret. Me" she mouthed and her mouth broke into a little smile.

Paul then asked her about the last letter, the important letter, hardly daring to breathe, afraid that Mrs. Knowles might return before Margaret replied. He was about to ask her again just as she moved her hand and rested it on his where it lay on the white sheet. He put his head nearer to hers so that he would be sure to catch whatever she might say.

"Paul. Paul. Son" she whispered and her eyes closed as tears coursed down her face. Paul was unable to speak. At last he knew for certain, although he had never really doubted that what Nirmala had told him before she died, was the truth. MargaretLeather and Walter Brent were his mother and father.

His thoughts were disturbed by the entry of Mrs Knowles carrying a tray. He stood up in order to clear a space on a nearby table but also so that he could surreptitiously wipe the tears from his eyes with the back of his hand. For the next half an hour or so, despite his excitement at what he had discovered, he drank tea and made small talk with the housekeeper whilst his mother, now totally exhausted slept.

"I think she has done too much for today" Mrs. Knowles said, "Why don't you come back tomorrow?"

Paul nodded and then remembered.

"I can't come back tomorrow I have appointments all day right up to the evening and the same the following day. I don't know what I may be doing on Saturday and Sunday but I will certainly come on Monday afternoon".

"Come whenever you can Mr. Brent" Mrs. Knowles said as she turned to look at Margaret sleeping peacefully. "She seemed very pleased to see you". Paul placed the empty cup and saucer on the tray and got to his feet.

"What about your cufflink?" the housekeeper asked. Paul smiled and rolled back his sleeve of his jacket.

"I already have it, thank you. Mrs Leather let me take it back whilst you were making tea".

The housekeeper led the way back to the room where he had left his overcoat and as he put it on confirmed that he would come again on Monday but if she wanted him for anything she could contact him at the Swan Hotel.

He set off down the drive shivering in the cold of the early evening after the warmth of his mother's bedroom. It was already going dark but in an effort to save power because of the fuel crisis none of the street lamps would be lit until later. On the pavement he paused before setting off for the nearest bus stop and as he looked back at the house he had just left he could not help but compare it with the last and only visit he had made when it had appeared to be such a welcoming and happy place.

During the next three weeks he was busy visiting different machinery makers but as often as he could, usually every other day he visited his mother and Mrs. Knowles who looked forward to his visits nearly as much as his mother did. On one occasion it dawned on him that this frail old lady he was coming to see along with his cousin Philip were his only living relations because even his adopted Uncle and Aunt with whom he had lived when he was studying and working in Bolton had died.

His visits to the house on Chorley New Road consisted in the main of sitting at his mother's bedside waiting for her to open her eyes then telling her about India and what he knew about his real father. Because she could not speak he was never sure that she understood all that he was saying but on occasion she would smile or nod her head.

With only two Saturdays of his visit to England left Paul decided to brave the cold and go to the football match as he used to do with his uncle Jack and in the evening revisit one of his old haunts the Grand Theatre.

After lunch he left the hotel and purchased his theatre ticket then leaning against the biting wind he set off to catch the bus to the football ground. When he arrived at the terminus he was surprised that apart from a bus inspector studying a timetable there was nobody else around. As Paul approached he looked up.

"Art gooin' t'match?" he enquired and as Paul nodded the Inspector shook his head,

"It's bin cancelled. Pitch is frozzen" and he carried on examining his schedule so with nothing else he wanted to do on such a cold day Paul turned and hurried back to the warmth of the hotel.

The second performance at the Grand Theatre started at 8.15 so about eight o'clock he left the hotel for the short walk along Churchgate to the theatre where five minutes later he was climbing the red carpeted stairs with their shiny brass stair rods to the circle and taking his seat in the back row next to the centre aisle. The Grand was just as he remembered it from his visits before the war. The seats were the same deep red as the carpets and almost the same colour as the stage curtains which before the show and during the interval, in accordance with the fire regulations were hidden by the safety curtain which was painted to resemble an advertising hoarding containing adverts for Bolton firms of which the most prominent was for the local brewers.

There were very few seats still vacant when members of the orchestra emerged from under the stage to take their seats in the orchestra pit and started to tune their instruments. The house lights dimmed and then as he did every evening, both at the start of the show and after the interval, the last member of the orchestra appeared from the direction of the bar. Because of his equipment the drummer could not get to his position any other way so he strode over the orchestra pit rail always settling on his stool just in time to respond to the descending baton of the conductor.

The show was typical music hall with it's assortment of 'acts'. The first was two girls in brief costumes who sang and tap danced and played saxophones and then after the usual line up of comedians speciality acts the show ended with a well known radio star who sang accompanying himself at the piano. Second rate the show certainly was but Paul always enjoyed his evenings at the Grand. As the final curtain came down he stood with the rest of the audience for the national anthem and then joined the people shuffling down the stairs towards the exit until eventually clear of the doorway he was able to skirt round the crowd and hurry to the hotel where unknown to him the night porter was waiting for his return.

"Good evening Mr. Williams. I have a telephone message for you" he said picking up a piece of paper from the desk and handing it to Paul who thanked him but didn't read it immediately thinking it was probably from someone who wanted to change the arrangements for a meeting and it wasn't until he reached the bottom of the stairs that he glanced at it and what he read, one foot on the bottom step, and read the message properly.

Message for Mr. Williams.

Mrs. Leather is seriously ill and asking for you.

Please come as soon as possible. H. Knowles.

Message received at 8.30

Paul glanced at his watch and saw it was already turned half past ten. He thrust the note in his pocket and went back to the desk.

"Get me a taxi please as quickly as you can" he demanded.

To Paul sitting on the edge of the back seat, every traffic light seemed to be against them and it was not until they turned into Chorley New Road that the taxi was able to go as fast as Paul wanted and even though the journey seemed to take a long time, only less than twenty minutes had elapsed since asking for a taxi in the hotel and arriving outside his mother's house. He quickly walked up the drive towards the house which, except for a faint glow around the edge of the curtains of the front room where his mother lay, was in total darkness. He pressed the bell push and although he didn't hear the doorbell ring inside the house within seconds he heard the bolts on the door being drawn back.

"Thank goodness you have come" Mrs. Knowles said standing to one side to allow Paul to enter before closing the door behind him then leading the way into the front room. He walked across to the bed where Margaret Leather lay with the white sheet pulled up to her chin. Except for her head and one arm which lay on top of the bed covers Paul would not have believed there was a body in the bed because the bed clothes seemed absolutely flat. His mother had looked very ill on his last visit but now he could hardly believe she was still alive. A wisp of lifeless grey hair had escaped the confines of her bedcap and her eyes were closed. Her bottom lip drooped slightly as she sucked air into her lungs with a slight hissing sound and the skin on her arm, which lay motionless on the top of the sheet, was a wrinkled yellowish white relieved only by the tracery of blue veins.

"It was obvious she was very ill" Mrs. Knowles said, "so I sent for the doctor but he didn't arrive until just after eight o'clock and then he didn't stay very long because he said there was nothing he could do. I thought I had better send for you and since then I have been sitting with her telling her that you were coming. I think that telling her that is the only thing that has kept her alive".

As she was speaking Paul removed his top coat and placed it on a chair near the window and then sat down next to the bed and with one finger gently stroked his mother's emaciated arm. Mrs. Knowles indicated that she was going to make some tea and then almost silently left. He let his eyes wander round the room taking in the elegant furniture and the ornaments and when his eyes returned to his mother's face he was surpised to see her eyes wide open looking up at him.

He knew from his last visit that his mother could hardly speak and had barely recognized him and so it was most likely she was not looking at him but was staring into space. He leaned forward and gently spoke, his voice sounding unnaturally loud in the silence of the room. "hello Mother, he said "it's Paul, can you speak to me?" He didn't know what to say and didn't know if his mother could hear him. He continued to repeat what he had said emphasising his name and all the time continuing to gently stroke the still arm which lay under his hand. He looked up as the door opened and Mrs. Knowles entered carrying a tray.

"I think she is awake" he said "but I don't think she knows who I am or even if anyone is here." Mrs. Knowles put the tray down.

"If her eyes are open then she can probably hear you so just keep talking and perhaps she will respond." As he continued to look at his mother he saw a tear rolling down her cheek. He took a cloth from the bedside table and gently wiped it away talking to her as he did so. Then he realised that although there was no sound her lips were moving. He leaned closer but still he could not tell what his mother was trying to say.

"Don't try to speak Mother, just rest" he whispered but still her lips continued to move. Mrs Knowles came over to the side of the bed and looked down, both of them totally silent, straining to make out what Paul's mother was trying to say but the only sounds to be heard were the ticking of the clock and the gentle sighing sound of the dying woman's breathing. Paul watched his mother's lips and although he couldn't hear her he suddenly knew what she was trying to say.

"I think she is saying top drawer, top drawer over and over again. I think she wants us to get something from a top drawer' and as he spoke they both saw an almost imperceptible nod from the frail lady.

The housekeeper walked over to the chest of drawers at the other side of the room and opened the top drawer. She could not understand what her employer might want because she, Mrs Knowles, knew everything there was in that drawer. She slid it open and looked inside

But as she expected there was nothing but clothing. Paul never took his eyes away from his mother. He watched as she seemed to know where Mrs. Knowles was searching and he realised she was trying to move her head from side to side.

"She doesn't mean those drawers he said "are there any others she could be talking about?" His eyes alighted on a highly polished mahogany smokers cabinet standing on a shelf. It had two glass doors and through the glass he could see, on one side a blue wedgewood pot for holding tobacco and on the other side a rack for holding pipes, no doubt used by the late Mr. Leather, but then, more importantly below the rack and the china pot he saw two drawers. Paul walked across to the cabinet and although the doors had a lock, when he tried them they opened to his touch and he was then able to slide open the top drawer. Inside were some documents which he drew out and carried across to the bed where he placed them next to his mother's hand. She nodded slightly and the semblance of a smile crossed her lips. Her fingers were playing with the red seal which secured a small envelope. Mrs Knowles leaned forward.

"Do you want us to open it?" she asked and Mrs Leather slowly nodded her head. Paul took the envelope, broke open the seal and lifted the lightly gummed flap. Inside was a short letter, only a few lines, to inform the reader of the name and address of the solicitors where her will was deposited.

He looked up and saw the tears rolling down his mother's wrinkled cheeks as she tried desperately to speak. He too had tears in his eyes as he placed his ear close to her lips. Now he could hear her faint whisper.

"I'm so sorry Paul, very sorry' she whispered, "I love you". The last word was hardly more than a sigh as her eyes fluttered and closed and the sound of her breathing ceased. Paul sat unmoving with Mrs Knowles standing by his side holding a small lace handkerchief to her eyes with one hand her other hand resting on his shoulder the room totally silent except for the clock and the coals burning in the fire. Eventually he looked up at the housekeeper.

"My mother's dead" was all he could say over and over, "My mother is dead" as he brushed the tears from his eyes with the back of his hand.

On Monday morning Paul and Mrs Knowles walked into the offices of his mother's solicitors and asked to see Mr. Grey the solicitor named in the letter. After a short wait Paul was shaking hands with a man about his own age who expressed his condolences but added that he had not known Mrs Leather as she had been one of his father's clients before he retired.

Paul explained how essential it was that the necessary formalities be completed as soon as possible in order for the funeral to take place because he had a passage booked for India in ten days time.

"We have already contacted an undertaker who will arrange the funeral for Thursday afternoon providing he receives the death certificate today" he said.

"That should not present a problem" Mr. Grey said as he took the envelope bearing his father's name which Paul handed to him which he opened and read before placing it on his desk.

"I will have to read your mother's file and look at her will but if you give me the name of the undertaker I will get the death certificate and have it delivered to him".

Even without his previous appointments Paul would not have been able to make all the arrangements for the funeral so it mostly fell to Mrs Knowles who knew where to contact friends and relatives and to Mr. Grey who completed all the legal formalities.

Just after half past one on Thursday afternoon, the day of the funeral, Paul paid off the taxi outside his mother's house and as he walked up the drive he shivered under his heavy overcoat. All morning there had been flurries of snow which, unable to stick to the frozen ground had been blown by the brisk North West wind into small drifts at the kerbside and corners of buildings. As he approached the front door it was opened by Mrs. Knowles who, dressed all in black, must have been watching for him.

He followed her into the kitchen where there was a large fire burning in the old fashioned grate with a large copper kettle steaming gently on a trivet its base just touching the burning coals. Without asking, Mrs. Knowles made tea and as they sat drinking, the housekeeper tried to answer the many questions Paul had about his mother.

"Did she ever talk about me?" he enquired.

"No. Not really. I knew there was some great sadness in her life but she never told me what it was although the way she talked about her trip to India I guessed it had something to do with the time she spent there." She leant forward in her chair and from behind her took a copy of the Bolton Evening News.

"I don't know if you saw this on Monday night" she said "but I kept it just in case". The paper was folded so that he could read an article with a photograph near the bottom of the front page under the headline,

Late Factory Owner's Wife Dies.

The photograph was of Mr. Leather and his wife which had been taken by the paper's photographer at some civic occasion and under the photograph a few lines about the late Mr. Leather's career in business and Mrs. Leather's work for various charitable organisations. Finally it mentioned that Mr. Paul Williams, who before the war had worked for Mr. Leather at his factory in Farnworth before leaving to work in India, was now in England on holiday and would be among the mourners. It then gave the date and time of the funeral which was to be held at Heaton Cemetery and the name of Mrs. Leather's solicitors, Grey and Markham.

Paul read the article through, angry and surprised that the newspaper had been able to discover so much about him and hoped that none of it would reach India.

"Have the reporters been here?" he asked.

"They came but I refused to speak to them as I did not think it was any of their business" Mrs. Knowles replied in a tone which suggested Paul should never have thought that she might do such a thing. He glanced once more at the photograph before handing the newspaper back to Mrs Knowles and got to his feet.

"The undertakers will be here shortly" he said "so I will look at my mother for the last time".

Paul stood just inside the room breathing in the perfume from the flowers and wreaths surrounding the coffin which was resting on two trestles in the space where the bed had been. The only light came from the partially drawn curtains which provided just sufficient light for him to look round. On a dresser were two photographs the nearest one being of William Leather who looked exactly as Paul remembered him. The other was of his mother. He picked it up and holding it up to the meagre light studied it more closely. There was no doubt she had been very good looking and he could see why, even though she had been married, his father had been attracted to her. Still holding the photograph he walked across to the coffin. His mother seemed to have changed. Was it because there was now no pain that she didn't look as old as the night she had died? As he looked down he suddenly found himself thinking about his other mother, the one who had looked after him and made him study, planned his life and who, because she had brought him to England had unknowingly made it possible for him to find his birth mother. He stood a few seconds more before leaning forward and kissing his mother's cheek for the first and only time.

The funeral where Margaret Leather was laid to rest in the same grave as her husband was very sparsely attended. Apart from Mrs. Knowles and Mr. Grey, the only two people Paul knew, there were a cousin of his mother and his wife, some relatives of Mr. Leather and Representatives from charities his mother had supported. Standing at the graveside Paul glanced round at his fellow mourners and it was then that he saw, sheltering against the wind and the rain against the trunk of a tree, a young woman, her arm through that of a boy nearly as tall as herself who Paul guessed to be about twelve years old. At the end of the short service Paul led the weeping Mrs. Knowles in the direction of a waiting car both of them sheltering from the rain under the one umbrella. At the car Mr. Grey caught up with them,

"I wonder if you could both come back to the office so that I can read the will to you and explain it's contents" he said. Paul turned to Mrs Knowles who was holding a white handkerchief to her face.

"You get in the car I won't be a moment" he said and leaving her and the solicitor he walked across to the stranger and the boy still sheltering against the tree. As he approached them he didn't recognise her although the boy looked strangely familiar. The woman wore a dark coloured coat with the collar turned up which with a flimsy scarf knotted under her chin provided the only protection against the wind and rain. The boy was wearing a blue raincoat, a schoolboy cap, grey knee length stockings, ankle high black boots and as the wind blew his coat Paul could see his red knees between the edge of his short trousers and the tops of his stockings.

Hello Paul" the woman said. Because of the turned up collar of her coat he still didn't recognise her but when he looked down at the upturned face of the little boy he realised he might be looking at himself.

"You don't know who I am do you?" the young woman said and Paul raised his eyes from the lad to look more closely at her.

"Audrey . . . ." but he couldn't remember her last name.

"That's right Audrey. Audrey Hobson and my, our son, Ian".

"What are you doing here? Why have you come to the funeral?"

"I can tell from your face you recognised our son so you should know why I came to see you". At first he didn't know what to say.

"Well we can't talk here". He paused, "Look I'm staying at the Swan so why don't you come round this evening. We can talk then?" It did not take her long to decide.

"Right. I'll be there about half past six but it had better not be like the last time you said you would meet me only for me to discover you had gone to India. This time you had better be there because now I know where and how to find you" and without waiting for a reply she tugged at the little boy's hand and tramped off towards the gates of the cemetery. Paul stood for a moment watching her walk away pulling the boy along before he turned and hurried to the waiting car.

Mr Grey led Paul and Mrs Knowles into his office and almost as soon as they were seated a young girl came in carrying a tray with tea cups and tea pot etc. He waited whilst she poured the tea and then taking a folder from his desk drawer he untied the pink ribbon which held it.

"This is a very simple will" he said. "There are only two main beneficiaries' and he looked from one to the other. First you Mrs Knowles. In recognition of your devoted service to both herself and her late husband Mrs. Leather has made you a bequest of twenty thousand pounds". Mrs. Knowles gasped and then tears started to fall which she hastily tried to halt with her screwed up handkerchief.

"Oh thank you, thank you" she stammered as if it were Mr. Grey who was giving her the money and no matter how they tried to console her, both he and Paul were only able to reduce her crying to a gentle sobbing behind her handkerchief. Eventually Mr. Grey said,

"Unless you have any questions or there is anything else I can help you with, Mrs. Knowles, there is no need to detain you any longer. If you wish I can arrange to have you taken back to the house. Still dabbing at her eyes Mrs Knowles said,

"Thank you I think that would be best". Paul stood and took the housekeeper's hand and as he and Mr. Grey led her to the door he thanked her again for all the help she had given him during the past few days and told her he would come and see her before he left. He went back to his chair and waited for the solicitor to return.

Back at his desk Mr. Grey continued with the will.

"There are a few minor bequests to people like the gardener and the woman who helps with the cleaning and a couple of charities your mother supported and of course some household bills which I will not receive until after you have left all of which should not come to more than five thousand pounds. The residue along with the house and contents is left to yourself. In order to try and ascertain a reasonably correct estimate of your inheritance I asked an Estate Agent to value your mother's house which they valued at not less than ten thousand pounds which of course will be exceeded if you include the contents. You will also inherit stocks and shares and cash to a value of two hundred and ten thousand making a total of not less than two hundred and twenty thousand pounds.

In the few days since his mother's death Paul had given some thought to what he would do if the house was left to him. At first he had thought about keeping it but then he had decided against this. He was amazed at the amount of money his mother had left him and realised that there was no need for him to go back to India but he instantly dismissed this idea There had been no news from India regarding Philip so he presumed his plan to kill his cousin had been unsuccessful. He looked up and forced a faint smile.

"I'm sorry I was trying to come to terms with what you have just told me. I have already given the matter some thought and I have decided to sell both the house and the contents".

For the next half hour the solicitor advised Paul regarding probate for the will, the sale of the house and possible investments. After some discussion the eventually agreed what should be done and Paul signed a plan of action along with a letter of authority so that Mr. Grey could act for him in his absence. Once these formalities were completed they shook hands and after thanking him for his help Paul walked the short distance back to the hotel.

It was exactly half past six when Paul walked down the stairs and saw Audrey talking to the receptionist. Her dark coat was the same one she had worn at the cemetery earlier in the day and the headscarf which she carried along with her handbag also seemed to be the one she had worn earlier. If he had not recognised her before as the girl he knew a few years ago he certainly recognised her now. She still had long light brown hair which fell to her shoulders and she still looked directly at whoever she was talking to. She was older but still had the trim figure he remembered. All this he took in as she stood unsmiling, waiting for him to cover the distance to where she was standing. He contemplated shaking hands but that seemed too formal but before he could decide she said,

"Hello Paul. It has been a long time".

For almost the first time in his life Paul didn't know what to say.

"Shall we sit down' he said lamely indicating some chairs. When they were seated Paul asked her if she would like a drink.

"No thank you" Audrey replied, "I didn't come to drink with you. I want to know why you left me and what you intend to do about my son".

"I, I didn't know you had a son" Paul stammered.

"No wonder you didn't know. You were off to India. Gone. You had no intention of ever seeing me again and you couldn't tell me. I have had to struggle all these years to bring up Ian."

"But I didn't know about the baby" he answered lamely.

"Haven't you got married?"

"Don't be cruel as well as stupid" Audrey said contemptuously, "How could I get married with another man's child? Who would have had me? I am here tonight to find out what you are going to do to help me and your son". She looked directly at him her dark eyes holding his, "or tomorrow I go to a solicitor".

Audrey sat back in her chair never taking her eyes from Paul's face but by now Paul had recovered some of his old composure. Ever since he had agreed to this meeting he had been worried about what might happen but just as he thought, the problem could be sorted out quite easily. All he had to do was dig in his pocket. But how deep? That was the question he had been wrestling with all day. He reached into his inside pocket and took out an envelope which he held out to her.

He watched as she took out the cheque he had written earlier and turned it round so that she could read it and saw her eyes open wide.

She could not believe it, fifteen thousand pounds. During her journey to the hotel she had been trying to work out what she might get from Paul but never in her wildest dreams had she thought it would be anything like this. Paul could see from the look on Audrey's face that he had surprised her and immediately knew he could have settled for much less had he known, without a doubt, that the boy was his and had decided to try and make his son's childhood as good as the one provided for him by Bert and Eunice Williams. His thoughts were interrupted by Audrey.

"Thank you Paul" she said "I don't know what to say. I never expected anything like this. I came here ready for an argument and now I just don't know what to say. Thank you very, very much".

"When we last saw each another it never entered my head that you might become pregnant. My only thoughts were about going back home to India but I have thought about you often" he lied. "I never thought that you, we, would have a son but when I saw him looking up at me I knew he was mine and that I had to help. I know I can't make any conditions but I would be happy to think that with the money you will make sure he has the best education possible and, who knows, perhaps go to Bolton school and then onto University".

"The teachers are always saying he is a clever little lad and should go to Grammar school but I was always worried, until now, that I might not be able to afford it" Audrey said excitedly. "But now I will be able to buy us a better house, perhaps a semi with a bathroom, furnish it and still have enough left to make sure Ian has a good education".

Paul ordered some drinks and for the rest of the evening they talked about the future and the old times during which Paul asked about people he had known at the factory. He told her he was leaving for India again at the end of the week and Audrey suggested that after she had bought the new house she would write to him to give him her new address so that whenever he came to England in the future he could come to see his son. She also promised to write and tell him how Ian was getting on at school.

They had dinner in the hotel and it wasn't until just turned ten o'clock that Paul ordered a taxi. At the door of the cab Audrey turned and standing on tip toe kissed him and then with tears in her eyes whispered,

"Thank you Paul. I wish you were staying in England". Paul closed the door after her as she settled in the back seat and then, despite the cold, stood at the edge of the pavement until the taxi turned into Bradshawgate and disappeared from view.

20

India. February 1947.

Philip Brent was dozing in the back seat of his car and didn't see the oncoming lorry which for some reason swerved towards them. Nathan, Philip's driver reacted almost instantaneously and swerved to his left but as the front left wheel sank into a large pothole, he could do nothing to prevent the car rolling over onto its side and finishing upside down in the roadside ditch. It was only discovered later that the front left side track rod had broken or perhaps Nathan might have retained control.

Philip had no idea how long he was unconscious, probably only a few minutes, but when he came to he felt a tremendous pain in his left arm which he knew immediately must be broken. When he tried to move to ease the pain in his arm he was almost overcome by pains in his chest and realised he must also have at least one broken rib as well. For a few moments he lay motionless fighting the waves of pain and when he opened his eyes again he realised blood had run down his face from a cut somewhere on his forehead. Brushing the blood from his eyes he turned his head to look for his driver. Nathan was on his back with the steering wheel seemingly pinning him to his seat and did not reply when Philip called his name Slowly and carefully Philip using his good arm eased his broken arm on to his chest where it lay without much pain. He rested for a while but then gingerly started to free himself from the stricken car fighting to overcome the pain from his broken ribs. Mainly by pushing with his feet on the opposite side of the car and then against the two front seats he was able to ease his body through the open window until, at last, he was free of the car and could allow his tortured body to rest. The lorry which had caused the accident had not stopped nor was there anyone else who might be able to help so for the time being it was up to him. He heard a moan and realised Nathan was not dead as he had first thought but was recovering consciousness. Still nursing his broken arm he struggled to his knees and looked through the open window. Nathan was lying motionless under the steering wheel with blood bubbling from his nose and with one leg twisted at an almost impossible angle because the foot was trapped under the foot pedals.

Philip instantly decided it would be better to try and free Nathan whilst he was still unconscious because if his leg was broken it would be more than he could do with only one good arm to free it without causing his driver a lot of pain. To support his injured arm Philip opened his shirt and carefully placed it inside next to his body then reaching inside the car he unceremoniously twisted Nathan's foot free. He knew he couldn't drag him from the stricken vehicle until suddenly Nathan gave a loud snort, spraying blood everywhere, and after a few blinks opened his eyes. Philip talked to him to reassure him telling him to wait before trying to move and was rewarded when after a few seconds the drivers eyes started to focus and he knew who was talking to him.

"Your leg was trapped Nathan" Philip said "Can you tell if it is broken?" He watched as Nathan squeezed his thigh then felt his knee before finally wriggling his toes.

"It hurts, Sir, but I don't think it is broken he said as he reached up to wipe the blood from his face and wincing as he did so, "but I think my nose is broken".

"You are probably right Nathan but what about anything else? Can you get out of the car?"

The driver started to wriggle himself free and with the help of Philip's one arm squeezed out of the window and into the ditch where Philip told him to flex his arms and legs to check if there was any damage to them. A few seconds later it seemed that apart from what looked like a broken nose the only other damage Nathan had was a bruise on his forehead.

"Can you reach into the back of the car Nathan?" Philip asked, "There should be a towel somewhere?"

They both wiped the blood from their faces and then Philip asked Nathan to tear the towel in half to make a sling for his arm saving a small piece to use as a pad for the cut on his head. There was now nothing else they could do except sit in the shade of the upturned car and wait for a passing vehicle.

The journey back to Ramuda seemed interminable. The lorry which had picked them up could only travel slowly and although the road had seemed relatively good when travelling in the comfort of his own car Philip was made painfully aware that it was a different matter for larger vehicles. The lorry seemed to hit every pothole and each time he felt as if he was being lifted bodily off the lorry and then dropped back. The red shale dust thrown up by the vehicle plumed out behind them but occasionally flurries of wind blew it and the exhaust fumes over the two passengers so that by the time the lorry pulled up at the hospital in Ramuda their clothes smelt of petrol and were covered in a film of red dust which clung to their perspiring bodies leaving Philip feeling as if he had been at the bottom of a rugby scrum for the past few hours.

Three days later with his arm in plaster, his ribs taped and two stitches in the cut on his forehead Philip was back at his desk when the phone rang. He lifted the receiver and heard the gravelly voice of Jim Taggart telling him that the wrecked car had just arrived in the workshop'

Less than ten minutes later they and a few of the passing Indian workers were looking at the wrecked car.

"Well it's a bloody mess no mistake" the Chief Engineer said "how fast were you going?"

"I don't know" Philip replied. "I had been looking at some reports and I think I was dozing when I think I heard Nathan sounding the horn. When I looked up there was this damned great lorry coming straight at us. Nathan swerved, I heard this big thud and then we were on our side and sliding into the ditch where we finished upside down."

"You were damned lucky. You're sure it wasn't Nathan's fault?"

"Absolutely certain" Philip replied, "if it hadn't been for him the lorry might have crashed into us. I suppose it was only because the road was uneven and we hit a pothole or something that the car turned over and went into the ditch. It was certainly not Nathan's fault, he's a damned good driver. Is there anything wrong with the car that might have made it turn over like it did?"

I've only glanced at it so I don't know but I'll get one of the garage men to have a look at it but from the state of the car you were damn lucky to escape with just the injuries you have. Which reminds me I haven't asked how you are this morning?" Without realising he was doing it Philip eased the position of his arm.

"It's not too bad now" he said. "There is very little pain as long as I am not tempted to move it but it damn well itches inside the plaster and as long as I don't laugh the ribs don't hurt either." Taggart gave a short laugh.

"Changing the subject" the engineer said, "While you are here I could get the drawings for the new bale store and then we could go to the site where we intend to build it in case you want to change anything. They walked out of the garage and Philip waited while the engineer went into his office for the plans. When he returned they set off to where cotton bales were being unloaded from railway wagons which had been shunted down a spur off the main railway line which ran on the other side of the factory wall. .

"As you know most of the bales for New Mill are stacked here until they are called for by the factory. When it is raining this is difficult for the workers, the cotton has to be covered with tarpaulins which cost a fortune so an open sided bale store with an overhanging canopy over the railway track for the trucks to run under for unloading will be much better for the cotton and the workers who have to unload it."

"What is the exact position of the building?" Philip asked .

Taggart walked a few yards down the railway track looking for a mark on the back wall of the of New Mill then marking the point with his foot he said,

"It will start here" and raising his arm to point "and will stretch for 50 yards down there to where those empty wagons are standing.

"That is a hell of a building Jim, are the plans finished?"

"Yes, that's why I thought it would be a good idea to look at them here so that if you agree with what we are planning to do we can get started".

P.K. Ramanathan was returning to the main office after visiting the General Store and was passing the entrance to New Mill when his thoughts were interrupted by a muffled bang from somewhere inside the noisy mill followed by the sight of workers running from the doorway. P.K. tried to stop one of the men.

"What's happened?" he shouted but the man just carried on running. P.K. put out his hand and grabbed another of the men and asked the question again.

"I don't know. I was in the card room when I heard this loud bang and the sound of machines breaking up and screeching to a halt. There was a lot of dust and smoke and people came screaming as if they had been hurt. Some workers came running out of the Blowing Room shouting there had been a bomb and as the engine slowed down the lights went out". P.K. let the man go and struggling against the tide of people coming out tried to enter the factory. Eventually he made his way to the Blowing Room just as Philip and Jim Taggart, who had also heard the explosion entered through a door at the back of the factory.

The Blowing Room, where the bales of cotton are opened and hand fed into machines which clean out the heavier impurities, was a shambles. Of necessity these machines are big and extremely strong, usually made out of cast iron and yet Philip and Jim could see through the smoke that one of them had been almost split in two as if by some immense drop hammer. The large rotating beaters, some of which were covered in spikes designed to beat the dirt and dust from out of the cotton, had burst apart causing sections and the covers that usually covered them to be thrown in all directions. The leather belts which drove the beaters and conveyor lattices had snapped and were either wrapped around the twisted drive shafts in the ceiling or hanging like streamers. Someone opened a door at the back of the room and in the better light Philip saw the large figure of George Smith one of the two Spinning Masters who managed the factory checking the condition of the other machines. There was the sound of hurrying feet as the other Spinning Master, Joe Harvey came rushing in then stopped dead as he saw the scene of devastation.

"What a bloody mess" he said "what the devil's happened."

Before Philip or the engineer could reply there was a shout from George Smith at the other side of the room,

"Someone's injured here, get the doctor.

"I'll do it" Harvey said turning and hurrying out of the door through which he had just entered.

Philip moved quickly to the back of the devastated machine where George Smith was crouching over a figure on the floor. At a glance he could see that the victim had suffered massive injuries. Crouching down he saw one of the man's legs was lying at an unnatural angle and blood was seeping out from behind a wad of raw cotton which George was holding to the man's chest. Distraught, he sat back on his heels and in the faint light looked at the face of the injured man who, despite his dreadful injuries was still conscious and mumbling something through his betel stained lips. Philip leaned forward to hear what the man was saying and was surprised to find he was speaking English.

"Down with the Raj. Down with the British" he said and then with what proved to be his last breath he sucked in air and spat into Philip's face.

Philip recoiled with shock, the mixture of spittle, blood and betel juice dripping onto his pristine white shirt. He grabbed some cotton and scrubbed ferociously at his face and his shirt just as Joe Harvey returned with Doctor Ramiah. The doctor squatted down and putting his fingers to the side of the man's neck confirmed that he was indeed dead. Under instruction from the doctor, two men who had followed him from the dispensary with a stretcher placed the dead man on it and carried him away.

George Smith pointed at Philip's stained shirt.

"What was all that about?" Subconciously Philip again wiped at his shirt with more cotton.

"I don't know but I think he was probably the one who put the bomb in the machine which went off before he had time to get clear. Why he should do it now when independence is near beats me but perhaps he felt he had some score to settle and while there is all this unrest thought now was a good time to do it." He shrugged and threw away the stained cotton.

"We will probably never know the real reason."

Joe Harvey had been looking round the rest of the machines in the department.

"I don't think it's as bad as it looks you know" He pointed to the stricken machine. "apart from this one I don't think the others are badly damaged.

Still running his hand over his face Philip walked round the bombed machine to where 'Mac' Taggart was looking up at the line shafting.

"This is a bloody mess" the engineer intoned in his Scottish accent as he looked around "but it's nae as bad as it might have been. If we cut that belting down over there" he said pointing to some belts wrapped round the shafting, "then undo that coupling over there you can have four machines running almost immediately and by the weekend we will have the shafting relined and then all of them will be running" he pointed to the shattered machine "except that one. There's nothing I can do with that." He turned to Joe Harvey, "so if you can get your lot to strip it down and get it out everything else should be running by Monday."

"That's great, thanks Mac" Philip said "but apart from the people we need to clean up I think we should stop both mills until Monday and get everyone out of the compound.

Hardly waiting to hear what Philip was saying Taggart strode off to organise what had to be done while Philip and the others turned with the intention of organising some labour to start clearing up and to do what Philip had suggested and met Keith Hood coming in.

"What's happened' he enquired as he turned to walk back with them towards the door Philip explained about the bomb and what he had decided to do.

"I thought it must be something serious because all the workers from here are in the yard and now the workers from Old Mill are coming out to join them."

The four Europeans stepped out into the bright sunlight where the workers, just as Mark had said, were standing or sitting in groups waiting to be told what to do. Without hesitation Philip led the others through the crowd and had just reached the office verandah when suddenly there was a disturbance at the back of the crowd. Workers were starting to fight whilst others, mainly the older ones, were trying to calm the situation. Neither Philip nor the others could understand what the fighting was about until an elderly Maistry who was sitting near the verandah informed Joe Harvey that the fighting was between some of the Muslims and Hindus. Each faction was accusing the other of causing the explosion in New Mill. Luckily the older workers were able to persuade the fighters to stop but Philip knew that if the workers could not be persuaded to leave the compound it would not be long before something happened to start them fighting again. He hurried through to the telephone room shouting to the operators to contact the Police and when the operator indicated a telephone he snatched up the receiver and still watching the compound through the window was telling the officer at the other end of the line about the bomb when he saw the first rollers from the ring frames on the second floor come hurtling out of the open windows. Until then he had not realised that the workers on the second floor had not left the factory and had now taken it upon themselves to start hurling the metal rollers, some of which weighed about a pound, on to the crowd below.

"You had better get here bloody quick or we will have no factories left" he shouted down the phone before slamming it back on its cradle.

At first it looked as if the throwing of the rollers might be a godsend as a lot of the workers, in order to dodge the missiles started to run towards the gates and out into the street but a few tried to pick up the rollers and throw them back while some of the more compassionate tried to help the eight or nine men who had been hit by the missiles and were lying on the ground. Suddenly there was a lull in the shouting and the missile throwing followed by a terrible screaming as a body hurtled out of a window and crashed on the concrete below.

"Please God. Let there be no more' Philip whispered to himself as he hurried towards the verandah which he reached just in time to see a second unfortunate come flying through the window, struggling in an attempt to try and land feet first. Above the noise of the fighting and shouting he heard the wail of approaching sirens and hoped that those in the mill would also hear them and stop the fighting but before the police vans swung into the yard two more bodies were thrown out to lie with the others among the hundreds of ring frame rollers which lay in the compound like large unmelted hail stones.

Almost before the lorries stopped the police, wearing tin hats and armed with rifles, were leaping out of the vehicles. The first constable over the tail board dropped to ground with a bren gun something they had learned from the Malabar specials. Out of the leading lorry jumped a young British Police Inspector Philip had never seen before who, at a glance, took in the scene, the bodies and the occasional roller still coming through the open windows. He said something to his sergeant who barked out an order. Four of the constables lined up and at a further command raised their rifles to their shoulders. The sergeant hesitated and then came the command "Fire". The rifles barked almost as one and instantly there was silence in the compound. The four soldiers stood like statues their rifles to their shoulders awaiting the next order whilst the others at a command from the Inspector stationed themselves along the length of the office verandah. As soon as they were in position the sergeant instructed the four who had fired the warning shots to lower their weapons and join their comrades.

The Police Inspector watched the deployment of his meagre force and then blew three long blasts on his whistle and the thin blue line began to advance towards the silent factory where the workers standing at the windows suddenly disappeared.

Philip made his way over to the parked lorries and made himself known to the Inspector.

"Have you enough men to handle this?" he enquired. The Inspector looked down from the running board from where he was watching his men advance towards the factory.

"In a word no, but they don't seem to know that" he said with a grim smile indicating the workers coming out of the mill and making their way to the gate.

Just then Philip heard the sound of more vehicles approaching

Then two more police lorries swung round the corner of the factory which, before anyone got out, the Inspector directed round to Old Mill.

Although a lot of the workers had already left Old Mill there were still some throwing rollers from the upper windows who when they saw the police, foolishly switched their aim to them. Just as Philip arrived he saw one roller land on the tin hat of one of them which caused a cheer from the throwers in the windows. Although Philip didn't hear it this must have made the sergeant to give a command to his men to move back a few yards which brought even louder cheers from those inside the factory. Their joy was short lived, however, when the policemen after another command, raised their rifles and each independently fired one shot at the windows. Philip saw two of the workers who were about to throw further missiles suddenly collapse, their white shirts stained red. Instantly the noise level dropped and the fusillade of missiles stopped whilst those coming out of the factory ran even faster towards the gate.

Four policemen where ordered to enter the factory and make their way up the stairs and within minutes the flow of workers coming down the wide fire escapes increased. At first it was a few but before long they were falling over each other in their haste to get out of the factory and make their way to the main gate. As Philip watched the crowd coming from the factory getting smaller he was joined by the company doctor who had been attending the injured in New Mill and hurried across to examine two bodies lying on the ground beneath two adjoining windows.

After a cursory examination he looked across at Philip.

"There is nothing I can do for these two. I am afraid they are both dead."

"How many casualties were there in New Mill?" asked Philip.

"It wasn't as bad as I expected" the doctor replied, "four were thrown out of the windows but fortunately only one was killed so up to now the total is three dead and three injured."

Philip then told him of the two men he had seen who were shot and would probably still be in the factory so accompanied by one of the policemen the doctor hurried up the fire escape and disappeared into the silent factory. Within a few minutes he reappeared at the door.

"There's nobody up here either dead or alive but I can see somebody was injured because there's blood on the wall, but I suppose they must have been helped away by the others.

Philip looked down at the dead men, both of them Muslims, probably set upon like the ones in New Mill by the Hindu majority, not because of any personal trouble but because of the fear and hatred that was gripping the nation due to the policy of partition. Which faction had placed the bomb in New Mill didn't matter because it served as the catalyst for the Hindu majority, led by a few hotheads, to terrorize the comparatively few Muslims in the same way their counterparts were doing all over India and in the same way the Muslims were terrorizing Hindus in what would later become Pakistan. Even though Hindus and Muslims had lived peacefully with each other for many years these gangs would not heed the men of reason of both religions who were striving desperately to ensure the transition from British rule to Home rule was managed as peacefully as possible.

Philip stood holding his aching arm, surveying the scene with a heavy heart finding it hard to believe that these two factories, probably the largest in India and far away from the troubles in the North had been brought to a halt by a bomb and rioting.

He was suddenly aware of someone standing to one side and not quite in his line of vision and turned to see the portly bespectacled figure of P.K. Ramanathan who gave his usual salaam.

"This is a bad business P,K," Philip said and the Brahim shook his head from side to side in agreement.

"Yes Sir. This is a bad day. I never thought I would see anything like it. I am wondering who would do such a thing, putting a bomb in the factory."

Shaking his head Philip accompanied by P.K. turned to follow the last of the casualties being carried to the dispensary.

"Is there anything I can do Sir?" P.K. asked.

"Yes, send out some of the messengers from the office to find all the Europeans and tell them to come to the Tiffin Room."

The Brahmin nodded and walked away holding the hem of his dhoti in one hand so that he could walk more quickly.

At the dispensary Philip walked into the treatment room where Dr. Ramiah was attending the victims. Glancing at one of them lying on a stretcher he recognised one of the Maistries from the spinning department, an old man who usually wore a large ochre coloured turban which he had most likely lost in the fall. He squatted down by his side.

"What happened?" he asked gently. "Who threw you from the window". The injured man looked up at Philip and then haltingly told him what had happened. He said that news of the explosion in New Mill had soon come to Old Mill and then they heard that as well as some of the workers being injured some had been killed. Immediately after this news some of the workers in Old Mill started shouting the Muslims had done it and began to chase the few Muslims who worked in the factory. Some of the younger ones managed to escape but the old ones were caught and thrown from the windows. He managed a grim smile.

"I'm too old to run Sir, so they soon caught me. I didn't struggle. What was the use? They took me to the window where I tried to jump rather than be thrown." His face creased with pain and he closed his eyes.

"Do you know who did it? he asked. "Do you know who threw you from the window?" The man's mouth tightened for an instant against the pain and then he opened his eyes and looked directly at Philip.

"I don't know who it was there were so many", and then he closed his eyes.

Philip stood up aware that the answer he had been given would be the only answer to any enquiries either he or the police might make but he also knew that revenge would be exacted somewhere, sometime.

As he left the dispensary the unusual silence in the compound was broken by the sound of the soldiers clattering down the fire escape of New mill and then marching across to the sergeant who told Philip the factory was now empty. Philip then set off to New Mill where he was met by the police inspector who told him the mill was empty and his men were looking round the compound to make sure there were no stragglers left. Philip thanked him and then made his way to the Tiffin Room.

Philip ordered tea and sat in his usual chair at the head of the oval table. He was just finishing his first cup when George Smith walked in closely followed by the other department heads, the engineers and the Europeans from the office led by Keith Hood. Philip waited until David had scurried round serving them with whatever they wanted, mainly tea, before he started to speak.

"I think it might be a good idea if I go over what has happened" he said. He then quickly summarised all that had happened from the moment the bomb went off in New Mill ending with the deaths in Old Mill . When he had finished he asked if any of them knew more than what he had outlined. There was a short pause and then Keith Hood confirmed the casualties and the number that had either been taken or were still waiting to go to the hospital

"The trouble is not confined to the factories you know. I have heard there are gangs roaming through the bazaar just looking for a fight and already there are reports of people being stabbed. The police have already called on the army for assistance because they know their mixed force will not be able to handle the situation if it gets any worse. They have also said that Europeans should not go into the town until further notice. Incidentally I was speaking to our office in Madras and they told me there was rioting in some of the factories there."

"Well I suppose this is what we have all been afraid of ever since it was announced there would be separate states for the Muslims and the Hindus" Philip said, "I can only say thank goodness we are not in the North of the country because I don't suppose there will be many trying to move to Pakistan from here so we shouldn't have anywhere near as much trouble as they will up there. But then you can bet there will be trouble here as some people seize the opportunity to settle old scores which have nothing to do with partition." He looked across at the two managers from New Mill.

"What's the damage situation in New Mill" he asked."

"Well obviously there is a lot of clearing up to be done in the blowing room but we can have all but two of the machines back in production straight away and by the weekend the fifth one will be ready but the last one, well that will never work again. All we can do is dismantle what is left of it and put it on the scrap heap" George Smith said. Philip turned to Joe Harvey who was in charge of the spinning department.

"We will have to gather up all the rollers and if they are not damaged put them back on the machines" Joe said. "We will probably be able to refurbish any that are damaged so perhaps some of the frames won't be running to begin with but I suppose everything will be OK before the end of next week."

Philip listened as he was told much the same thing by the staff in Old Mill and for a minute he didn't say anything then he looked up.

"So all that has happened this afternoon, the bomb, the shootings, the killings was really for nothing. All it means is we have lost some production. What a bloody, stupid waste of time and effort." He paused for a moment, "I think the best thing we can do is not let the next shift in. Get the departmental supervisors to go to the gate and between them and the guards and the timekeepers, select enough men from each mill, men they can trust, to come in and start clearing up the mess so that we can be ready to run first thing in the morning." Mark Hood tried to speak but Philip held up his hand.

"I know what you are going to say. You think there could be trouble outside the gate when the next shift can't get in. Maybe, so tell the police what we are planning and ask them to make sure they have enough men at the gate to handle any trouble that may break out. I am also aware that the shift that caused the trouble will be the first back tomorrow morning but when they see that, despite their efforts, both mills are running it might have a better effect on them than anything else we might do and don't forget it was only the lunatic fringe that caused the trouble and most of them would have been forced to join in or risk creating trouble for themselves and their families."

Before the meeting broke up they discussed the matter of pay both for those in the factory when the bomb went off and for the workers who would miss a shift. Finally, Philip emphasised the necessity for increased security and vigilance.

After the others had returned to their departments Philip remained slumped in his chair, his chin almost touching his betel nut stained shirt. Stroking the plaster on his broken arm he thought about the workers who had been killed, his car accident and the events of today wondering if there was any connection. He thought about the effect of the day's events on the company and reflected that never in its history had anything like this happened. Like his father and his father before him he had always worked for the good of the company and its employees but now workers were killing each other and perhaps the lives of the Europeans might be threatened. Suddenly he felt very lonely and he wished that Paul was not on leave so they could discuss what had happened as they discussed so many of the problems of the company.

With his head bowed he sat slumped in his chair churning the events of the day over and over in his mind unaware that the faithful David had peeped over the curtain at the window to see if the Master wanted anything, or that the light was beginning to fade. On top of the events of the day he thought about his family and his wife in particular. Rose had not settled since their return from England and he knew that she also was missing her family and was not happy even though she pretended otherwise and he realised neither was he. Suddenly for the first time in his life he felt lonely. He raised his head, surprised to see the light was beginning to fade and with a glance at his watch he got to his feet. He left the tiffin room and walked through the empty office and out into the yard where the selected workers were clearing up the rollers which had been thrown from the widows. He watched for a second or two and then turned to walk towards the gate where as he approached the tall figure of the Subhadar in charge of the factory guards came out of the gate house to meet him. He was a tall commanding figure, moustached and bearded as all Sikhs are, but with his gleaming boots, stiff pressed khaki uniform and row of medal ribbons all topped off by his khaki turban with its blue flash which was almost like a battle ensign, he was a man both management and workers respected.

He came to a halt in front of Philip, thrust his swagger stick under his left arm and flung his right arm up in a salute. Philip acknowledged the salute and they started to discuss the security of the compound. Suddenly they both jumped at the sound of explosions from the direction of the city. They walked over to the wall dividing the factories from the railway and saw plumes of smoke spiralling into the darkening sky accompanied by the sound of police whistles and the sirens of fire engines as they battled their way through the crowds.

"Probably Moslem owned shops" Philip thought and despite the police activity he knew it was most unlikely that anyone would be caught. He stood for a few more minutes then with a heavy heart turned and walked back through the compound towards where he knew Nathan would be waiting with the car to take him home.

21

March 1947

S.S. Oronsay was one night away from Karachi where it was scheduled to dock just after its passengers had eaten breakfast. In a single first class cabin Sandra Reynolds was getting ready for the gala dance which was always held on the night before the ship arrived in Karachi. In her cabin on 'C' deck Sandra, an attractive, dark haired young lady who was not only sailing for the first time but was also in love for the first time was getting ready for the evening ahead, her eager anticipation only marred by the fact that tomorrow she would have to leave the ship in Karachi while the man of her dreams would be going on to Bombay.

She had met Paul Williams the afternoon after the ship entered the Mediterranean leaving the rough weather of the Atlantic behind. Because of sea sickness it was the first time she had ventured on deck and was playing deck quoits when Paul, who was watching, was invited by some of the other players to join in. From that moment they had been almost inseparable. Paul had escorted her ashore at Port Said where he told her about the canal and which shops to go to for the things she wanted. He had taken her ashore at Port Sudan where they had gone in a glass bottom boat to look at the coral and the multi coloured fish and then again at Aden with its tax free shopping. In the evenings they had danced to the music of the ships orchestra and walked along the dimly lit decks, their arms entwined their kisses becoming more and more passionate culminating in the previous evening when they had made love, she for the first time and she lay back in the bath, her eyes closed, her thighs squeezed together as she relived the events of the night before.

Shortly after, as she dried herself she stood in front of the full length mirror. She didn't look any different from the previous evening but she certainly felt different. Until last night she had been looking forward to her first job abroad as a secretary in the British Embassy in Karachi but now all she wanted was to stay on the ship and go wherever

Paul Williams wanted to take her. Eventually she walked across to the bed where she had laid out her underwear and her best evening dress which she had not worn before. Like all the ladies on the ship Sandra had been saving her best dress for what she knew would be the most special evening of the voyage. She slipped the dress over her head and saw that, just as she expected she would not be able to wear her bra. As she turned to reach for the shoes she was horrified to see in the mirror that the outline of her only underwear showed through the material. She stood for a few moments and then making up her mind stepped out of the offending garment. With her panties in her hand she once more examined her reflection and satisfied with what she saw, threw the offending garment back on the bed. She finished her make up and her hair and after a final look in the mirror stepped out of the cabin and set off to the for'ard bar where she knew Paul would be waiting. As she acknowledged the greetings of other passengers she couldn't help the frisson of excitement as she wondered what they would think if they knew how she was dressed.

Paul was sitting at the corner table where they usually sat and as soon as he saw Sandra he got to his feet at the same time signalling to one of the Goanese stewards.

"You look very attractive this evening" Paul said as they sat down, "that is a lovely dress."

"Thank you" Sandra replied "I've been saving it specially for tonight."

"Well it definitely suits you and you look very beautiful" Paul said as he took her hand in his.

Just then the steward returned with the champagne which Paul had specially ordered earlier in the day and after Paul nodded his approval he undid the wire around the cork and with a loud 'pop' opened the bottle and filled the two glasses.

For the next half hour they sipped their drinks occasionally refilling their glasses from the bottle standing in the ice bucket and talking about quite inconsequential things each with their own thoughts of what might happen later on until eventually they were interrupted by the musical gong summoning passengers to the dining room. Paul helped Sandra from her seat and followed her, watching appreciatively the sway of her hips as she made her way past the other tables well aware that many of the other men were surreptitiously watching her as they and their partners made their way out of the bar.

The dining room was decorated with garlands and balloons and there was a special menu with food that Sandra had mostly never seen in her life and which certainly no one in Britain had seen since the outbreak of war. Paul chose wines which he knew Sandra liked and for the next hour or so they enjoyed their meal and the air of gaiety which pervaded the dining room.

After the meal they went up to the aft lounge where the ships orchestra was already playing. Like the dining room the lounge had been decorated and strings of coloured lights had been strung outside near the pool which against the blackness of the dark sky created a carnival atmosphere. Paul led his partner to a table just inside the lounge and ordered some drinks from one of the stewards before leading her on to the dance floor.

As the evening wore on the music became slower and softer giving Paul the opportunity to hold Sandra closer until she was dancing with her head on his shoulder, her waist encircled by both his arms so that her body was pressed close to his, the parting tomorrow almost forgotten. As they danced past the band the drummer leant across to the pianist,

"There's a lucky chap" he said indicating Paul and Sandra, "I wish I was in his shoes tonight."

The pianist glanced over his shoulder, smiled and nodded.

As they were walking back to their table after yet another dance Paul whispered something to his partner who nodded and taking her hand in his he led her out on to the open deck which was only lit by an occasional light fastened to the roof formed by the deck above. Neither spoke as they walked, their arms round each other, the only sounds being those of their feet on the wooden deck and the soft sighing of the sea many feet below them, the usual heat of the tropics tempered by the soft gentle breeze caused by the forward speed of the ship. They walked, still not speaking, with Sandra's head on Paul's shoulder now very conscious of the fact that she was not wearing any underwear. After almost a full circuit of the deck they stopped and looked over the rail into the velvety blackness in the direction they were headed but apart from the slight phosphorescence of the waves there was no sign of land not even one solitary light. After a few moments Paul gently pulled Sandra away from the rail and lead her towards his cabin where he unlocked the door and stood back to allow her to enter. With only the slightest hesitation Sandra led the way inside where on the dressing table was a silver ice bucket in which stood yet another bottle of champagne. Paul filled the two glasses and carried them across to Sandra and handed one to her before sitting on the edge of the bed and gently pulling her down next to him.

As they drank their champagne they kissed and held each other close Sandra doing nothing to stop him when she felt Paul undoing the buttons at the back of her dress and easing it down allowing her breasts to tumble free. She put both arms around his neck in an attempt to pull him closer wanting his arms around her, needing to feel his body next to hers and was disappointed when he drew away. She held out her hands to him wanting him to take her back in his arms but instead he took hold of her hands and pulled her to her feet. He released her hands and taking hold of her dress slowly pulled it over her curving hips and let it fall to the floor. Then holding her hands once again he took a step backwards, holding her at arms length, so that he could look at her, now totally naked except for the pool of material at her feet. Hurriedly he unbuttoned and removed his shirt followed by the rest of his clothing then both totally naked they clambered onto the bed.

Next morning Paul was awakened by the different rhythm of the ship's engine. He glanced across at the curtained window where the first grey smudges of the dawn were seeping round the edges. It was still too dark to see his watch but he guessed it was about five o'clock and was surprised when he glanced across at his partner to see the pale light of the dawn reflected in her eyes and her outstretched arms in silent invitation.

Three hours later Paul was standing near the top of the gangway looking down as the passengers disembarked and watched Sandra, a lonely figure, as she made her way to the dark, grey cement customs shed. She was carrying a canvas hold all and her handbag the rest of her luggage already having been unloaded and waiting for her in the customs hall. At the door of the building she turned, her eyes searching the ship's rail for the sight of her lover. At last she found him and their eyes met and silently she mouthed the words "Write soon. I love you."

Paul who had promised that he would write, but had no intention of doing so mouthed back silently, "I love you too." From the droop of her shoulders it was fairly obvious that the job at the Embassy in Karachi was no longer as appealing as it was when she left U.K. but then with a last wave she disappeared inside the customs hall.

Next morning the ship docked in Bombay and by ten o'clock Paul was facing Mr. Ghosh across his old desk which miraculously was cleared of all the papers and documents except those that appertained to Paul, himself. In fact he realised, as he glanced around the office, how neat and tidy the office was, not at all like he remembered it.

"Have you been having a clear out?" Paul asked jokingly.

"In a way I suppose I have" replied the lawyer. I have decided to retire so during the past few weeks I have been seeing all my clients to settle all their affairs with new advisors. I didn't write to tell you of my decision because you had already informed me you were going to U.K. and would call on your return. Before Paul could say anything the lawyer swivelled round in his chair and reached for the bulging file lying on a cupboard behind him and placed it on the desk.

"This file is unique because unlike any other clients it started before you were born so I suppose it is almost the story of your life."

"Do you know it never entered my head that you might retire" Paul said, "I never thought of you as being old but as someone I could always depend upon. When will you actually finish?"

"Well I thought Independence Day would be very auspicious" he said with a little smile, "independence for the country and for a tired lawyer as well."

Paul reached out and took the file Mr. Ghosh was holding. The silence in the room was broken only by the regular ticking from the revolving ceiling fan as he slowly turned the pages. Apart from his birth it seemed to be a catalogue of death. First his father killed in France. Then his adoptive parents, first Bert and then Eunice Williams both victims of quite unrelated accident and then his dearest friend Nirmala, who apart from Mr. Ghosh, had been the only link to his real parents

"There is something missing from this file" Paul said, "I haven't been able to tell you yet but when I was in England I discovered my real mother, Margaret Leather, who turned out to be the wife of the owner of the factory where I worked when I was studying in England. If I hadn't gone home when I did it would have been too late because she actually died whilst I was visiting her. In fact I think it was the hope of one day seeing me that had kept her alive."

He reached down and took some papers from the brief case which he had placed on the floor.

"This is a copy of her will which my solicitors in England have but which I want you to see so you have a full record of all my affairs."

Mr. Ghosh adjusted his spectacles, glanced at the opening preamble and then gave the details his full attention. From time to time he glanced up at Paul without speaking and then he put the papers down carefully making sure they were straight and square on the desk in front of him. He removed his glasses, rubbed his eyes then putting back his glasses he looked directly at his client.

"You are now a very rich man Paul, very rich indeed" he said. Paul nodded in agreement. "So why have you come back to India when you have all this money? You could live anywhere, do anything you want." For a moment Paul didn't answer then he sat up straight in his chair and pointed to his file which was still on the desk where he had put it.

"You know very well why. The answer is in there. My father was cheated by his family of what was rightly his so I intend to get it back—for him. I know he is dead but I will get what should have been his. He was never chairman of Ramuda Textiles but I am determined I will be."

As he spoke Mr. Ghosh saw the almost maniacal gleam in the eyes of the man opposite and he realised that only now he was seeing the real Paul Williams. He remembered that even as a young boy how determined he could be but now he realised this man sitting in front of him would be capable of anything to get what he wanted and he wondered what he might have done to get what he already had. For a few moments he toyed with the idea of pointing out to Paul that his father, who he so idolised, was not the man he thought he was but was, in fact, a drunk and a philanderer and that his uncle had been left with no option but to dismiss him and even if he hadn't it was most unlikely he would ever have been made chairman of the company. He could have told him that had he not been killed in the war that, even though he had been dismissed, his father would still be receiving dividends from the company and would have been able to live fairly comfortably, but he didn't. He knew it would be no use. Almost afraid that Paul would somehow know what he was thinking he looked down at the files lying on the desk and for the first time since he had made the decision, he was glad he had decided to retire and that after Independence Day would no longer have to represent Paul Williams.

Later that evening on the overnight train to Madras Paul's thoughts turned to his cousin Philip. Ever since he had left Ramuda he had been waiting for news about him but as he had not heard anything he had to assume his plan had not worked but as an aside it was with a grim smile he determined he would never ride in Philip's car. But what to do about him? That was the question.

Perhaps the revolver he purchased in Port Said and which was now lying at the bottom of one of his suitcases might have to be the way.

22

March 1947

As Independence Day approached India was in turmoil. In the East Hindu's from what was to become East Pakistan were flocking into Calcutta, a city which was already overcrowded whilst in the West millions of people were on the move in both directions between India and what would become West Pakistan, Hindus to the East and Muslims to the West. One problem was that the army, which should have been the main stabilising force, was having to be divided between the two emerging countries with the result that officers and men, often from the same regiments were finding themselves on different sides and were so busy organising themselves that they could not help to quell the civil disorder. The few British troops remaining in India were not enough to make any difference and in any case were preparing for their final departure from the country.

Hordes of refugees swamped the trains, either riding on top or clinging to the sides of the coaches when the compartments were full desperate to move to the country of their religion. When they failed to get on the trains they crowded on to lorries and cars, anything with wheels even wheelbarrows were used to transport their few meagre possessions to their new country. Pillaging and robbing and in some cases, mass murder was rife, old arguments, imaginary or not, were renewed and fought over, frequently to the death.

As well as the deaths there were those, mainly old people and young children who became detached from their family or group with whom they were travelling and were left to wander aimlessly not knowing why they were moving and, unless someone bothered to help them, not knowing where to go. With so many people on the move many were easy prey to the gangs of thieves who raped the women and robbed them and their helpless men folk of their few valuables and then, as often as not murdered them.

In the cities in the South, away from the great migration, the Muslims knew they could not make it to either East or West Pakistan so had to stay where they were and try and evade the marauding gangs who were out to rob or kill them. Many of them in Ramuda owned shops and as the violence increased the owners put up shutters and hoped that would be sufficient to keep their properties safe. Unfortunately not all were lucky and hardly a night passed without another store being torched. As Independence Day drew near more and more shops either didn't open at all or closed early so the European women only went into town early in the day and only then if they were accompanied by one of the European men. This meant whenever Paul went into the bazaar he was usually accompanied by at least one of the European ladies and so it was that one morning he manoeuvred his car round a stationary bullock cart and parked outside Spencer's general store.

P.K. Ramanathan was also in the bazaar buying foodstuffs in readiness for the Independence day celebrations when the driver of a stationary bullock cart raised his arm as P.K. approached that he recognised Ram, a farmer who rented a small patch of land which P.K. owned about twelve miles out of town. P.K. had inherited the land from his grandfather and as he had no interest in farming he rented it out to tenant farmers. Ram had just told P.K. that the boy with him was his youngest son Sunil, when Paul, accompanied by Beth, got out of the parked car and walked into the store. Sunil started to pull at his father's arm, wanting to speak but Ram continued talking to P.K. about crops and prices completely ignoring him. Eventually Ram looked towards his son

"What do you want?" he asked irritably.

"Remember a few years ago when I told you about that man and woman the ones I saw in those trees near the old brick kiln, well that's them going in the shop."

"What's he talking about? P.K. asked.

"Oh it's nothing" Ram replied. "A few years ago, I can't remember just when but he told me he saw a white couple in some trees not far from the farm" P.K. was immediately interested.

"When was it. Can you remember?" he asked the boy.

The youth screwed up his face in an exaggerated attempt to remember until eventually he said, "I'm not sure just when it was. It's a few years ago now but I remember it was near my birthday."

"When was his birthday" P.K. asked. Now it was the turn of the boy's father to screw up his face. He had five sons and had to think just when it was the boy's birthday and which birthday it was.

Father and son then discussed when it was until Ram could only say it was a few years ago and he reached for his cane.

"I'll have to be going" he said "I want to be back before dark" as he cracked the cane on the bullock's rumps leaving P.K. standing deep in thought as he watched the cart find a place in the stream of traffic. Thinking about what Sunil had said P.K. was amused that Paul Williams had probably been seen with Mark Hood's sister-in-law in some trees just off the main road.

Next day P.K. was still thinking about what Ram's son had said he saw before when Mark Hood sent for him. Pushing the thoughts of Paul Williams from his mind he made his way to Mr. Hood's office. Mark Hood was not alone. A woman was looking through the window and, at first, because of the sun streaming through the window, he could only see her in silhouette but his first thought was that it was Mark's wife Vera which he knew was impossible but then his thoughts went back to the evening before and what Ram's son had said and instantly he realised the boy, whoever he had seen, couldn't have seen Beth with Paul because she had never been to Ramuda before so it must have been Vera the boy had seen.

P.K. answered Mark's queries and returned to his desk where he just sat staring at the open ledger in front of him. It now looked as if Paul Williams and Vera Hood had been having an affair. But did it go deeper than that? In the hope that he might discover something that might give him a clue he brought out the desk diaries he assiduously filled in every day. He flipped through the pages until he found the entry concerning the death of Mrs Hood and was surprised to see that she had died shortly after the purchase of B & M Textiles. If anyone had asked him he would have said the purchase had been completed before her death but here it was in his own handwriting, she had died only a day after the purchase was completed then remembered Williams had been asking a lot of questions about the small company so was it possible that he had started his affair with Vera just to find out about the purchase.

If this is what happened the only person who would know, apart from Williams, was Vera and she had been murdered. How convenient. His mind went even further back to the death of Philip's father. He was shot but again who benefited, Paul Williams again. Had anything else happened? He remembered Philip's car accident. Was it an accident? If it wasn't then surely Paul Williams couldn't be involved because he wasn't even in the country when that happened. Then he smiled to himself. What better alibi could someone have than to murder someone and be thousands of miles away?

Next day P.K. walked round to the garage where he chatted to the supervisor a Brahim like himself, and led the conversation round to Philip's accident.

"The car's not been repaired" the supervisor said "come on I'll show you" and led P.K. to the back of the garage.

"Have you any idea what caused the accident?" P.K. asked.

"Well as you can see from the damage it would be almost impossible to say. We asked Nathan, the driver, but he doesn't know why the crash happened. He remembers swerving to avoid a lorry and that's all. In my own mind I think something probably broke when Nathan swerved."

"But didn't you find anything?" P.K. asked putting his hands on the crumpled radiator and looking down into the engine compartment where at the bottom he could see broken parts and the front left wheel twisted and hanging at a crazy angle almost parallel to the ground.

"If something did break and cause the accident what would be the most likely thing?" he asked. The garage supervisor stood looking at the car and after a few moments pointed down.

"Most likely the track rod there" he said. P.K. looked where the man was pointing and saw that the track rod was indeed broken.

"Well it is broken so that caused the accident" he said.

"It's not as easy as that" the supervisor answered "it's impossible to tell whether It broke before the accident or as a result of the accident" P.K. bent down to get a closer look at the broken part and rubbed his thumb along the broken edge. To him it felt partially smooth. Was it possible that it had been partially sawn through before the accident? He was no expert but it seemed a possibility.

"Thanks very much" he said to the garage supervisor as he turned to walk away, "when you see how bad the car is I think the boss and Nathan were very lucky. P.K. went to see the clerk who kept the records of all the company vehicles, how many miles the cars or lorries travelled each day, how much fuel they used and when maintenance was carried out. P.K. asked if he could see the record of the wrecked car and discovered that just before he had gone to U.K. on leave, Paul Williams had been using Philip's car. Why? He looked at the log of Paul's car and was slightly disappointed to discover that he had used Philip's car simply because his own was being serviced. At first he felt somewhat deflated, but then he reasoned, what did it matter why he used Philip's car the fact that he had the use of it would give him the chance to do whatever he wanted.

P.K. sat musing over what he had discovered, cracking the joints of his fingers something he frequently did when he was thinking. He knew that what he had discovered was only circumstantial and proved nothing but he was convinced Paul Williams was responsible for the accident.

He was sure he had tampered with Philip's car. When he did it he could not have known that Nathan would have to swerve to miss a lorry but he did know that at some time the track rod he had tampered with would break and that whoever was in the car when it happened might be killed. He thanked the clerk for letting him look at the car records and back at his desk tried to analyse why he didn't like the man, after all he had never done him any harm so far as he knew but he was a man of mystery who had joined the firm just before the war and in the few years since, had been promoted, twice as a result of someone dying, from being almost the office boy to Managing Director. Vera Hood had been the first, killed in Madras when Williams was in Delhi finalising the purchase of B.& M. Textiles. But was he? Could he have been on his way back to Ramuda and was actually in Madras meeting Vera Hood and was she killed as a result of helping him to organise the purchase of B. & M. He would never know, but as a result of the purchase Paul Williams was promoted to manage the newly acquired factory which P.K. had to admit he did extremely well. The next death was that of George Brent shot by a Japanese agent who had suddenly appeared at the recruiting office where George Brent was working and shot him dead. Paul Williams didn't do that, P.K. reasoned but then suddenly he remembered Paul Williams had been at the recruiting office when it happened so had he seized his chance? Another murder and again Williams in the vicinity and again profiting, this time being promoted to Managing Director. All very tenuous he had to admit but not beyond the realms of possibility.

P.K. was not the only person thinking about Paul Williams that morning. Sitting in his own office Philip was contemplating his own future. Ever since their return from holiday, Rose who had lived nearly all her life in India just as he had, wanted to go and live in England. When she had first mentioned it to him Philip had been horrified. He had never contemplated living anywhere other than India but now with Rose wanting to go home, the bomb and the shootings in the factory, the rioting in the cities about Independence and doubts about what might happen to India afterwards he had decided to do what his wife wanted. He would retain a directorship which meant that he, and Rose if she wanted, could visit perhaps every other year. All that remained was to tell Paul of his decision and ascertain if he was prepared to accept the position of Chairman of the company. He had wondered when to tell Paul of his decision and had decided to tell him on Independence Day. He smiled when he thought of the day he had chosen, Independence Day, a new beginning for India, a new beginning for him and Rose and a new beginning for Ramuda Textiles and Paul.

Just as Philip had decided on his future and picked out the 15th of August to implement it his cousin was also thinking about the future. Even though he was now rich, very rich, he had not yet achieved what he had set out to do. He had come to Ramuda Textiles where eventually he developed just one objective which was to avenge the death of his father by becoming Chairman of the Company a position which he believed his father should have held. Although he was well aware that no-one in the Company had actually killed his father they had effectively signed his death warrant when he was dismissed making him go back to England, joined the army and, like so many others, killed fighting in France.

Amongst his mail this morning there had been a letter from the solicitors in Bolton to inform him that his mother's house and effects had been sold and included the final statement regarding his mother's estate. What he read had only served to confirm what he already knew that financially he could, if he wanted, return to the U.K. and never have to work again if that is what he chose to do. The idea was certainly appealing. Nobody suspected what he had already done so if he stopped nobody would ever know. But he had gone too far to stop. Just for a second he thought about the possibility of being caught but dismissed it from his mind in an instant. He would not be caught, Why should he? He was too clever for everybody. Nobody would suspect Paul Williams. But his revenge was not complete. He still had to remove Philip. Ever since his return from the U.K. when he discovered his car crash plan had failed he had tried, without success, to devise a way to complete what he had started

The last weeks leading up to Independence seemed to pass so slowly as the religious populations tried to guess where the boundaries between East and West Pakistan and India would fall and then to move to Pakistan if they were Muslim and to India if they were Hindus or Sikhs. In an office in Delhi Sir Cyril Radcliffe who had never been to India before had arrived from the U.K. and was drawing on an ordnance survey map where these boundaries should be without ever having been to the areas concerned or consideration for their ethnicity. Day by day there was news of the terrible massacres taking place in the Punjab. It was now estimated that as many as a million people, Hindus, Sikhs and Muslims would be killed and probably twenty million displaced. Only the other day it was reported that a train arrived in Lahore where it was discovered that apart from the two engine crew everyone else was dead. All the passengers, men women and children, had been murdered.

Sometime later and with only a week to go to independence P.K. was sitting on the small verandah of his house with Krishnan a cousin who had arrived by train from Madras on his journey back home but as the train for Trivandrum did not leave until early evening he had taken the opportunity to call and see P.K. They talked about work and what was happening in the country their conversation to family matters when suddenly Krishnan said,

"I almost forgot. Where's my bag?" I have something you might like to see." He picked up his bag and rummaged inside and eventually took out some photographs and handed them one by one to his cousin.

"Uncle Ram in Madras gave them to me and I thought you might like to see them, particularly this one" he said picking out a badly faded picture. "This one is of your father" P.K. reached out for the picture which showed a group of Indian men standing with two Europeans.

P.K. could hardly believe what he was seeing. He instantly picked out his father but surely the European on the right was Paul Williams. For a moment he felt as if he could hardly breathe and he looked away for a moment before turning to see the photo in a better light. He looked at it more closely but apart from the man he thought was Paul Williams and his father he didn't know any of the others.

He turned the picture over and discovered someone had written the names of all the people in the picture. He looked at the names of the two Europeans and saw the name Walter Brent who he knew had been the manager at Melur the man who had hounded his father to his death and was responsible for all the troubles his family had suffered since. He studied the picture again and although he now had to admit the likeness was not as obvious as he had at first thought it was enough to convince him he knew who the mysterious Paul Williams really was.

Paul walked into his bedroom and unlocked the top drawer of a chest of drawers in which he kept important documents and valuables. He lifted the papers and from the bottom of the drawer took out a small locked box and carried it over to the bed. Choosing another key from his key ring he opened the box and took out the only thing it contained. The blue grey steel of the revolver didn't reflect any of the pale light from the curtained window as Paul examined it as he had done so many times before. It was already loaded with the six bullets he had purchased when he had bought the gun in Port Said whilst Sandra had been buying underwear at Simon Arzt. He had not bought it for any specific purpose but now this might be the weapon which would finally avenge his father.

While in the bungalow next door his cousin was sitting with his wife.

"I wish we could leave now" Rose said, "Why do we have to wait any longer before you tell Paul about your future plans?"

"You know why. We have discussed it before. I don't think it would be fair to leave before Independence. I think I ought to be here to make sure the business is secure and surely another six months won't matter and after all you used to like it here so much."

"Normally it wouldn't matter but you know I have been worried for some time. I just have this feeling that something bad is going to happen."

Wednesday the 14th August 1947 was not like any other day in Ramuda. It was hot, as usual, with no sign of rain or even a breeze to temper the heat but the day was different. The city was quiet as if it and everything in it was holding its breath waiting for what was about to happen. The factories of Ramuda Textiles were silent as they had been yesterday and as they would be tomorrow and the day after that. Not only was it unusual for the factories to be stopped for four days but all the workers had been paid for the holidays before they started, a concession never before granted in the history of the company.

The day before Paul and Philip and the other European managers had visited the factories as they did on every stop day to ensure that their departments were as secure as they could be and as usual had found nothing untoward. Eventually just before lunch time the two cousins were the only ones left.

Philip and Paul drove round to the main gate to wait for the police to arrive to see how they were deployed before leaving and had not been at the gate very long when the blue truck arrived carrying a small detachment of police sent to supplement the factory guards.

"Are those the only men you have?" Philip asked as he walked across to the police inspector, "I expected at least three times as many."

"We are totally stretched" the inspector replied "We just don't have sufficient men for all we have to do so I'm afraid these are all we have.'

"I must say I expected more than this" Philip repeated "are you sure you can't get any more?" The inspector shook his head.

"You can ring headquarters if you like but I can assure you there are no more men available. If all the mill guards are working as usual I think we might manage between us."

Paul called for the subhadar in charge of the factory guards and for the next few minutes discussed with him and the police inspector how they thought the guards and police might be deployed to give the best security and then told them that he and Philip would come to the factory each evening for a look round the compound to see if there was anything that might need their attention.

The road back to their bungalows was unusually quiet, hardly any people moving around, no children playing or women chattering at the communal well it was as if the small shacks as well as the people who inhabited them were just resting, waiting for whatever the next twenty four hours would bring. The uncanny silence was broken only by the occasional blaring of a loudspeaker somewhere in the distance as one of the local politicians tried to drum up support for his party in readiness for the elections which would be held after independence.

In his bungalow next day Paul switched on his radio and heard that India was now divided into three separate entities, East and West Pakistan who would be declared independent at noon and India who would be granted their independence at midnight.

At the factory compound the young police inspector checked his meagre force of police and factory guards unaware that there was a gang of men hiding among the cotton bales at the back of Old Mill. Even if he had been told they were there he would never have found them. From their positions they could see anyone approaching and if necessary could move to some other hiding place. Apart from occasionally stretching they only moved as twilight approached when they went to an agreed position at the perimeter wall where friends were waiting to supply them with food lowered in brass tiffin carriers on the end of a rope.

Apart from the guards and police and the concealed gang the only other people in the compound were four boiler room staff in the boiler rooms of each factory to stoke the fires of the boilers to ensure there would be sufficient steam to power the two large engines when the factories restarted.

Paul and Philip, as on the two previous evenings, met at the club and had a drink with the others who were playing snooker. But even here the feeling of unease caused by the uncertainty of the future had created an air of depression which drove these usual habitués of the club home earlier than usual until only Paul and his cousin were left. Paul finished his drink and glanced across at Philip who nodded and without a word finished his drink and followed Paul to his car. As Paul walked out the gun secreted in the waistband of his trousers suddenly felt very heavy and even though it was quite small he was irrationally afraid it would drop out. Killing Vera had been easy but this time it would be different. This time he had to put the gun to his cousin's head and pull the trigger and even though he had been planning Philip's death for a long time, now he was afraid.

For the first part of the journey to the factory Philip hardly spoke but just sat staring through the windscreen as Paul negotiated the way through the unusually sparse traffic. Suddenly Philip cleared his throat and Paul almost lost control when he heard his cousin say,

"Rose and I have decided to go home. I am going to resign."

Paul couldn't take in what he was hearing. What about the company? Did this mean he would now be chairman? He stole a glance at his cousin who was still staring straight ahead through the windscreen.

"Rose doesn't want to live in India any longer. She has not settled since we came back off leave and I am not enjoying it as much either so we talked it over and I have decided to resign and hand the company over to you.

"But where, I mean what are you going to do? I can't believe it" Paul stammered as he steered the car into the compound relief surging through him as he realised he would no longer need the gun he was carrying.

"I have lived here all my life" Philip said "but tomorrow a new country will be born so I thought it would be an auspicious day to bring my family's management of the company to an end. I don't know if the new country will be better than the old but I am sure that with you as chairman of the company it will be in good hands so if you agree I will make the announcement after the holiday.

"Paul could hardly stop himself from laughing out loud. If only Philip knew. He was not ending his family's management of Ramuda Textiles. The Brent's would still be managing the company long after he had gone back to England.

Paul brought the car to a halt in its usual position under the large mango tree in front of the office block. He switched off the engine and almost as if they had rehearsed their actions, they got out of the car, walked through the general office, out through the other side and into the tiffin room where they sat in their usual chairs at the large, oval table surrounded by the empty chairs of all the other Europeans. They discussed at length what Philip had said but throughout the discussion the main thing in Paul's mind was that he no longer had to kill the man sitting opposite. He was now convinced that he could and would have done it but now there was no need. All that he had ever wanted was now going to be his without any more danger to himself. His revenge was complete.

After about half an hour Philip suggested they should check the factories before it got too dark so they left the Tiffin Room and made their way to the dark and silent Old Mill. Philip led the way walking along the narrow alley ways between the machines finding their way by a combination of their knowledge of the layout of the factory and the glimmer of light from the compound lights coming through the windows. They walked through the card room towards the passage which led into the blowing room the furthest part from any light and Paul was feeling for the wall so he wouldn't walk into it when there was a slight noise and he was grabbed by two figures who had been standing silently waiting for the two approaching directors. From the scuffling noises Paul knew that Philip had been grabbed like himself and was just about to call out when a bag was pulled over his head and tightened round his neck followed by a sudden pain crashing through his skull.

Slowly he opened his eyes and tried to get to his feet but he couldn't move. The bag had been removed from his head but now he was bound hand and foot to what felt like two Palmyra wood rafters used for stacking cotton bales. In the darkness he tried to look round but as he moved to try and see what was happening he couldn't suppress a groan from the pain at the back of his head. Immediately one of his attackers put his bare calloused foot across his mouth to silence him. Paul looked up to see if he could recognise the man but the only thing he could see in the almost non existent light was the gleam of his eyes but then from somewhere behind his head he heard a voice that seemed faintly familiar and the foot was removed from across his mouth and placed on his stomach.

"I am going to ask you some questions and you will only have one chance to answer them correctly so I advise you to think very carefully before you reply. What is your name?"

Without hesitation and in as strong a voice as possible Paul replied. "Paul Williams".

Almost immediately the foot on his stomach lifted and then a split second later it crashed down driving all the breath from his body. As he fought for breath but not able to take in the air his body so desperately needed he knew that the blow had at least broken one of his ribs.

There was silence only broken by Paul as he gasped and wheezed trying to draw air into his damaged lungs until his inquisitor spoke again.

"Try again but this time I want your real father's name not your adopted name." Paul hesitated and he felt the foot on his chest lift.

"Paul" and then he said in a whisper "Brent"

He heard a gasp from somewhere in he darkness and then Philip started to speak which ended in a cry of pain as he received attention from the man guarding him.

"You keep quiet and listen" the voice said and then he said to Paul.

"Right then Paul Brent, who was your father?"

"Walter Brent" Paul muttered almost inaudibly. The foot was lifted from his chest and then he was kicked in the ribs, not as hard as before but still with sufficient force to drive the breath from his body.

"I couldn't hear what you said" the voice said and he repeated the question. "Who was your father?"

Still fighting for breath Paul said as loudly as he could, "Walter Brent."

In the silence Paul heard Philip cry out again and start to struggle but he was quickly silenced and his struggles ceased as the voice said,

"Stop struggling Mr. Brent. I want you to hear what your cousin has to say. Just listen."

"Who killed Mrs Hood?" the voice suddenly asked

Paul sucked in his breath. How did they know about this? What could he say? No matter what happened he could not tell anyone what had happened to Sybil. He would be writing his own death warrant and he didn't want to hang in an Indian gaol. He drew in his breath to try and prepare for what he knew would happen.

"I don't know. She was murdered in a hotel in Madras. It had nothing to do with me."

Again the foot lifted off his chest and he tried to screw up his muscles to withstand the blow that he knew would follow but nothing happened except for some whispering somewhere above him. Then one of the men squatted down beside him and started to undo the ropes which held his hands. Surely they couldn't be about to release him. His hopes were soon dashed however when they only released one hand leaving the other securely tied before they retied the hand they had just released to the iron upright of a nearby machine. He was aware of someone crouching by his side and only realised what was going to happen a split second before a hammer came crashing down on his index finger. The scream started in Paul's throat just before the hammer landed and was strangled just as quickly by a hand over his mouth which was only removed when he fainted.

Paul had no idea how long he was unconscious but when he came round he was still tied to the wooden planks with one hand fastened to the machine. He lay for a few seconds his eyes tightly closed against the pain coursing up his arm and exploding in his brain. But even with all the pain he couldn't help a feeling of disgust when he became aware of a wet feeling in his crotch and realised that his bladder had betrayed him. He just wanted to lie in the comparative safety of the darkness and didn't think that he had moved but somehow the men who held him knew he was no longer unconscious and their leader spoke again.

"What happened to Mrs.Hood." he asked again. "We know she was murdered in Madras and her murderer was never found. We also know you had an affair with her taking her out to the old brick kilns on the Coimbatore road because you were seen."

Paul didn't answer as he tried to control the pain in his smashed hand and his chest amazed that despite all their efforts someone had seen him and Vera together. He realised his mistake in not answering when he realised the hammer was about to come down again.

"Wait, wait" he screamed but he was too late and the cry turned into a scream as it smashed into the second finger of his hand. This time he didn't lose consciousness and the flash of almost unbearable pain crashed through his nervous system and for a second almost succeeded in wiping out all the pain he had already suffered. A hand, which even through his pain smelled of curry, smothered the scream almost before it had begun and was only removed once the scream had given way to whimpering.

"Now for the last time. What happened to Mrs. Hood?"

Philip had been shocked when he heard Paul say that his real name was Paul Brent but surely he couldn't have murdered Vera. He tried to appeal to the men who were torturing his cousin and then he heard Paul start to speak.

Yes I murd . . . killed Vera Hood" he whispered.

"Louder" the voice said. I want everyone to hear what you have to say.

Now that he had started to confess there was no use trying to deny what he had done.

"Yes I killed Vera Hood. I killed her in the hotel in Madras."

"Why" the leader of the gang asked.

"I only went with Vera because her husband was working on the purchase of B & M Textiles. I knew that if I could persuade her to let me see what he was proposing I might be able to arrange a better deal which I did. Once the deal was completed I wanted to stop seeing her but she threatened me that if I did she would tell her husband and my career with Ramuda Textiles would be finished. At her request we met in Madras but when I told her that this would be the last time she again threatened me. So there was no other way. I had to kill her."

For a few minutes there was silence and Paul began to think the inquisition was over and not knowing if his assailants were still there he cautiously tried to look around which only brought another kick in the ribs and a foot over his mouth to prevent him screaming out.

"Keep still" the voice said softly, "Your Uncle was the next to die. Why did you kill him?"

Even in the state he was in Paul knew he had heard that voice before but try as he might he could not identify the speaker.

"I didn't kill my uncle. He was killed by some stranger at the recruiting office during the war. I tried to save him."

"That is what you say and what most people think but I don't think that is the truth. I think you shot him."

Paul started to wriggle, trying to free himself from the ropes that held him as someone pulled at his injured hand, placing it against the machine support and stretching out one of his uninjured fingers. Desperately he fought against the man holding his hand and begged to be released promising a thousand rupees, two thousand to any of the men if they would let him go free.

"No, no stop I will tell you please stop" How these men knew he had shot his uncle he didn't know. Perhaps they were only guessing but now it didn't matter. Now it was too late. He sucked in his breath into his protesting lungs. Not any more. He couldn't stand any more.

"When I went to England I discovered my real mother and then who my father was and how he had been dismissed. If he had not been sent back to England he would have been Chairman of the company and wouldn't have been killed. The Brent's were responsible for his death so I decided to take the company back from them and in order to do this it was necessary to kill my uncle"

No one spoke and Philip who had been struggling to get free lay completely still as he tried to take in what he had just heard. Surely nobody could have hated his father that much. Tears rolled down his cheeks. Paul must be lying in order to be set free. He wouldn't kill his uncle. The unseen questioner was speaking again.

"What happened after you had killed Mr. Brent?"

Although no one could see him he nodded in the direction of his cousin,

"He got his father's job and I was promoted to Managing Director."

"But there was still more to do wasn't there?" the voice enquired.

"I don't know what you are talking about" Paul almost whispered "I didn't do anything else." Almost before he had finished speaking there was another crashing pain up his arm and into his brain as the hammer slammed down once more on his damaged hand and he slid into merciful unconsciousness.

Slowly he recovered to the tast of vomit mixed with blood in his mouth and what he thought was the sound of waves beating on a sandy shore but which he eventually realised were really waves of pain pulsing through his body in rhythm with his every heart beat.

He tried not to move and kept his eyes closed in the vein hope of avoiding any further torture or least to delay it, but it was no use. They knew he was conscious again and once more he felt a foot on his chest pressing harder and harder, grinding his broken rib against the others until he could stand the pain no longer and screamed out.

"You tried to kill your cousin next didn't you?" the voice from the darkness said, "tell us about that. Let Mr. Brent hear what you did."

Paul knew it was no use trying to lie, this gang, whoever they were, knew everything and he couldn't stand any more pain so he told them what he had done to Philip's car.

"But that is not all. That is not the end of it." The voice from the darkness said, "We found a revolver in your pocket. You failed to kill him in the car so you decided you would kill him tonight, here in the factory didn't you?"

No, no it wasn't like that. I brought the gun for our protection. I didn't intend to kill my cousin" he lied desperately and he cringed as he waited for another blow but when none came he began to hope that because they had heard his confession there would be no more pain and his assailants would leave him alone.

In the hot silent darkness that surrounded the group Philip lay completely still, silently crying to himself, horrified that this man whom he had liked and trusted and who in fact he had just discovered was his cousin, hated him and his family so much that he had set out to totally destroy it.

The man who had been asking all the questions looked down at the snivelling heap that was Paul Brent then touched the arm of the man wielding the hammer who brought it crashing down for the last time on their prisoner's thumb.

Paul slowly recovered consciousness and tried to move but now he was gagged and bound tighter than ever to the planks of wood and he realised he was being carried somewhere and wondered what was going to happen next. It was much cooler and when he opened his eyes he could see the stars so he knew they were no longer in the factory but where were they taking him and why? He tried to see who was carrying him but could not raise his head sufficiently and all he could see were the back of the heads of the two men in front. Frantically he moved his eyes from side to side but it was not until he was carried past another compound light that he knew in which direction they were heading and then overcome by horror he knew what they intended to do. Despite his injuries he thrashed and struggled against the ropes alternately screaming and pleading with the men who were carrying him but the sounds were totally unintelligible through the tight gag. Then he heard again the voice of the man who had been questioning him earlier and now he knew who he was. Desperately he struggled pleading for his release but despite the sounds coming from behind the gag the portly, bespectacled Brahmin never even looked at him as he marched silently by his side.

Suddenly the small procession halted and without looking at his prisoner the leader started to speak.

"Ever since you came to Ramuda you have been intent on revenge but you are not the only one. When your father worked in Melur he wrongly accused my father of theft and dismissed him. But he was not satisfied with that because when he discovered my father had managed to find a job at another factory in Madras he made sure he was dismissed from that job also, despite the fact that he had a wife and a young baby to support This caused him to be so depressed he lay down on the railway line in front of the Bombay express. My family never thought he committed suicide. To us he was murdered. I was that young baby and like you I swore I would avenge his death but although his murderer is already dead, his son is still alive."

The macabre silent procession turned and Paul felt the incline as he was carried down a ramp and even through the gag he smelt the acridness of burning coal. When they halted he felt the heat of the boilers on his feet and legs and then he heard the clang of the furnace door as it was opened and he saw the red maw of the fire reflected off the whitewashed roof. Behind his gag he was screaming and he lost all control of his bodily functions as slowly he was pushed, feet first, like unwanted rubbish, into the fire of the boiler.

Less than five minutes after leaving him P.K. Ramanathan and the four members of his gang returned to where Philip was lying. With a fairly light blow they knocked him out, untied him and left him to regain consciousness while they climbed over the wall separating the factory from the railway and disappeared in the maze of city streets.

P.K. made his way to a coffee shop which he often frequented because the owner had a radio. Even though it was almost midnight the shop had remained open and many of the regular customers had come to listen to the momentous news which was expected in the next few minutes. He ordered a coffee and after he had exchanged greetings with some of the other customers and sat back to listen. The speaker was talking about what was going to happen the next day the parades in Delhi, for example,

253

but at five minutes to twelve he introduced the new President of India Mr. M.R.Jawaharlal Nehru who began to speak.

At the stroke of midnight while the world sleeps India will awake to light and freedom . . . . he began.

P.K. listened to the speech and though later in life he would only be able to remember an outline of what was said he never forgot those stirring words because to him they meant that not only was his country free but he and his family were free.

He regarded it as hugely symbolic that not only had he avenged his father's death and regained his family's honour on the same day that his country had gained its independence, he was also convinced that the future for his family and the country would be a lot better than in the past.

23

Bolton August 1947

Audrey Hart was returning home from the factory where she was employed as a spinner. Now that she had purchased a house with the money from Paul it meant that she had further to travel and so it was always a rush to get home and prepare tea for her son and her father who still lived with her but it was worth it to live in a house with a garden and not in the dingy back to back houses which surrounded the factory. In her hand she carried a copy of the Bolton Evening News which someone had left on the bus. It was just starting to rain as she closed the garden gate and hurried up the path past her pride and joy, the small garden with its lawn and surrounding flower beds, and opened the front door. As usual her widowed father who suffered from byssinosis, a disease brought on by years of work in the dusty card room of the same mill where Audrey worked, was sitting hunched in his chair in front of the coal fire and this evening, because of the rain, her son, Ian, was sitting at the table reading a comic instead of playing outside as he usually did. Hanging her coat in the hallway she went straight to the kitchen to prepare the meal while Ian continued reading and her father sat staring into the fire silently sucking on his unlit pipe. Apart from their initial greeting neither father nor daughter spoke because over the years everything seemed to have already been said.

The old man had always been a strict husband and father and even though she now provided him with a home, much better than he had ever had, he had never forgiven his daughter for becoming pregnant, in fact he would have thrown Audrey out of the house but for her mother. In view of all that had happened later it was lucky for him that his wife's counsel had prevailed because shortly after his grandson was born his wife had died and then three years later he had been forced to stop work because of his illness which meant that Audrey had become the only wage earner.

After they had eaten Ian helped his mother with the dishes then seeing that the rain had stopped went out to join his mates in a game of football in the street. Audrey watched him through the window for a few minutes then turning from the window she picked up the newspaper and settled into the chair on the opposite side of the fireplace to her father. She smoothed out the the paper and gave the front page a cursory glance. She wasn't interested in the world or political news and was just about to turn the page to look at the local news when a headline near the bottom of the page caught her attention.

LOCAL MAN DISAPPEARS IN INDIA

Philip Brent the Chairman of Ramuda Textiles reported to police that Paul Williams, Managing Director of the Company had disappeared after he and Mr. Williams disturbed a gang of intruders in their factories in Ramuda, S. India.

It is understood that both Mr. Brent and Mr. Williams had gone to the factories on a routine visit during which they discovered the intruders who turned on them. Mr. Brent was rendered unconscious and when he recovered there was no trace of Mr. Williams. A search of both factories was carried out but they could find no trace of the missing man nor any evidence to show that he ever left the factory.

The police believe Mr. Williams may have recognised the intruders, who because of this, probably killed him and then disposed of his body in the fire of the boilers.

Mr. Williams came to Britain from India in the thirties and studied textiles at the Technical College during which time he worked at Oceanic Mill owned by the late Mr. Leather.

The missing man, who was unmarried, is represented by local solicitors, Gray and Booth, Maudesley Street, Bolton. Tel Bolton 8972.

Through her tears Audrey read the report over and over and then sat with the paper on her knee staring into the fire.

"What's do wi' thee?" her father asked. Why art' cryin?"

Without a word she passed the newspaper to him and indicated the article at the bottom of the page. Tommy Hart leant down, picked up his spectacles. Silently he read the account of what had happened and then looked at his daughter.

"That's 'im I'nt it?" he asked "that's Ian's fayther."

Silently Audrey nodded.

"Yes that's him, the man who gave me enough money to buy this house and made sure my son will have a better chance in life than I had."

"Don't be so bloody stupid" her father grumbled his voice rising "if tha'd kept thi legs shut tha coulda bin wed bi' now. Wheer wer 'e when 'e knew that were pregnant? E nar did owt fer thi then did 'e?"

Audrey rubbed at her eyes.

"I've told you before" she said in a quiet voice "he never knew I was pregnant. He had gone back to India by then but when he did know he gave me enough money for this" she said indicating the house, "and more besides and it was damn lucky for you he did because I don't know where we'd a bin if he 'adn't."

Just then Ian came in dirty and dishevelled from the games he'd been playing. Ignoring his protests Audrey took him into her arms and held him close as tears, the only ones shed for Paul Williams coursed down her face.

Next morning during the short morning break at the factory Audrey dashed from the spinning room, down the stairs and out to the telephone box situated just outside the mill gate. She lifted the receiver and when the operator answered gave her the number of Gray and Booth, Solicitors. After a slight pause a voice answered so she pressed button A and asked to speak to Mr. Gray.

She was the only person who ever called about Paul Williams.

Lightning Source UK Ltd.
Milton Keynes UK
UKOW03f2246060314

227704UK00003B/57/P